A Theological Reader on Human Sexuality and Gender Diversities: Envisioning Inclusivity

A Theological Reader on
Human Sexuality and Gender Diversities:
Envisioning Inclusivity

Editors
Roger Gaikwad and Thomas Ninan

National Council of Churches in India (NCCI)
2017

A Theological Reader on Human Sexuality and Gender Diversities: Envisioning Inclusivity — jointly published by the Rev. Dr. Ashish Amos of the Indian Society for Promoting Christian Knowledge (ISPCK), Post Box 1585, 1654, Madarsa Road, Kashmere Gate, Delhi-110006 andNational Council of Churches in India (NCCI), Nagpur – 440 001.

Online order: http://ispck.org.in/book.php

Also available on amazon.in

ISBN: 978-81-8465-622-0

Front Cover Title:	An Inclusive Church
Illustration and Artwork:	Jebasingh Samuvel
About the Artist:	Jebasingh Samuvel is a graduate of Theology from Tamilnadu Theological Seminary, Madurai.
Back Cover Title:	Inclusivity: Sharing the Cross together
Illustration and Artwork:	Rijo Geevarghese
About the Artist:	Rijo is a Seminary student at St. Thomas Orthodox Theological Seminary, Kalmeshwar. Basically an artist, he is these days more a passionate iconographer.

Laser typeset at **ISPCK,** Post Box 1585, 1654, Madarsa Road, Kashmere Gate, Delhi-110006.
Tel: 23866323, Fax: 91-11-23865490
e-mail: ashish@ispck.org.in • ella@ispck.org.in
website: www.ispck.org.in

Contents

Unit - 1
Theological Perspectives: A Critical Evaluation
of Early Teachings on Human Sexuality

Unit - 2

Church and Sexual Morality: A Critical Evaluation

Unit - 3

Legal Perspectives on Human Sexuality and Sexual Morality

Unit - 4

Towards a Liberative Theology of Human Sexuality

Contents

Foreword

Concerns of Justice, Liberation, Rights, Space and Participation in society, and of Fullness of Life and of All Creation are very crucial and urgent in our world today. Among several factors, theology gives shape to our understanding and practice of those concerns. Theologies are derived from the interpretation of scriptures, spiritual experiences of religious founders and the community of disciples, the context in which a religious movement was born and its history, and rational and ideological reflections of people.

To a very large extent, our traditional theologies are formulated by patriarchal heterosexual mindsets. It has been realized that such dominant theologies do not render justice to women and to persons having gender and sexual diversities. Such theologies have for centuries formed our socio-cultural practices, rites and rituals, and ways of life. In our times transgender people as well as those having diverse sexualities are posing questions to such theologies: When we say that all human beings are created in the image of God, are we also not bearing the image of God? When the psalmist says that God has created each individual ("For it was you who formed my inward parts; you knit me together in my mother's womb. Ps. 139:13), then why are we being condemned as being depraved persons or sinners? To persons who were so much obsessed about heterosexual monogamous marriage, did not Jesus Christ say that in the resurrection they neither marry nor are given in marriage, but are like angels in heaven (Matt. 22:30)?

Therefore today there is a call to critically re-examine heteronormativity with its belief that people fall into distinct and complementary genders (male and female) with natural roles in life, and that heterosexuality is the only sexual orientation or only norm. So also there is the need to look at sexual morality afresh as propagated by the Church. Along with theology, legal perspectives on human sexuality and sexual morality require to be addressed. Even the Supreme Court of India on 2nd February 2016 has decided to continue the debate on the legality of Section 377 of the IPC, which criminalises sexual activities "against the order of nature", arguably including homosexual sexual activities. It is in such a context that there is a call to be committed to formulating a liberation theology of human sexuality as well as just and liberative Christian sexual ethics.

We are grateful to the Senate of Serampore College for taking the initiative in encouraging students and faculty to address this important concern in its theological education curriculum. The book in your hands hopes to be a contribution to this on-going theological discourse.

Rev. Dr. Roger Gaikwad
General Secretary,
National Council of Churches in India,
And Project Holder of NCCI's ESHA Program

Preface

It has been a learning process to recognize that human endeavours in understanding the human physiology, whether medically or theologically or in any other ways, has been progressive in nature and never a constant. Holding on to certain age old constants has been found, either irrelevant or misplaced, which goes on to express itself in various forms of abuse, injustice and violation of basic human rights. This theological reader is a sincere effort to arrive at some of the root causes behind the keeping of these age old constants relating to human sexuality and gender diversities, of how it has influenced the human understanding, particularly in the Christian purview and the imminent consequences because of the keeping of these constants. We are confident to present here, a good mixture of theology, history of Christianity, ethics, law and social aspects, in an academic way, which we hope will be essential first steps for any serious academic engagement in this field.

The first unit will engage with theological perspectives whereby a critical evaluation of some of the early teachings about human sexuality has been attempted. Beginning with the Philosophy and Theology of Mind – Body Dualism, Mothy Varkey traces the historical trajectory of mind – body dualism, giving a glimpse of the philosophies of Plato and Descartes and thereafter to the Artificial intelligence thesis of Alan Turing, which he terms as the New Dualism. Varkey thereafter offers a theological critique of Mind – Body Dualism giving an analysis of various theories attempted in this regard. Jogy George offers a brief study on the doctrine of original/ Adamic sin, whereby some pertinent questions like; Has Adamic sin become a part of human nature, What is the consequence of Adamic sin and certain confusion related to this doctrine has been discussed with special references to Augustine of Hippo and his influence on the Western churches as well as the distinct response of the Eastern churches with respect to this doctrine.

Bendanglemla Longkumer offers a hermeneutic of suspicion as a viable process to theologically re-formulate the predominant theological stance on the Creation narrative, which because of its Patriarchal leaning has been one of the root causes behind the dichotomy related to sexuality and gender.

S.D. Deva Jothi Kumar engages with the understanding of sexuality in the early church life when the tradition of monasticism started amidst the influences of the Jewish, Greek and Roman cultures. Jothi Kumar brings out interesting facets of sexuality within the monastic practice.

Bandangtemjen investigates the understanding of homosexuality in the thought and times of John Chrysostom, critically analysing within the Graeco – Roman historiography, some of the methodological issues involved in his understanding of same sex.

Reji Mathew offers the biblical concept of *Imago Dei* while engaging with the understanding of human sexuality of some of the early teachers of the Church, such as Origen, Hilary of Poitiers, Ambrose of Milan, Augustine of Hippo, Thomas Aquinas, Martin Luther and Pope John Paul.

J.M. John Marshal re-visits the teachings of Augustine of Hippo and Thomas Aquinas about human sexuality, probing the value of re-analyzing them in the light of an inclusivistic approach.

Rohan Gideon discusses Martin Luther's views on sexuality, whereby he brings out the contradicting views of Luther, whereby on one hand he breaks his own celibacy vows to marry a nun, while on the other hand, has a conservative view on sexuality and physical pleasure within marriage.

Lalnghakthuami offers a critical analysis of John Calvin's views on human sexuality, as expressed in his writings in Institute of the Christian Religion and a few other sources.

Geevarghese Mor Coorilos offers some random thoughts on the Orthodox concept of God and theological anthropology vis-a-vis human sexuality. Coorilos identifies human sexuality as part of God's image, reflecting the Trinitarian relationality of God, the mode of *perichoresis* (mutual indwelling).

Unit 2 on Church and Sexual morality includes two articles, by Gladson Jathanna and Aruna Gnanadason. Jathanna deals with the Victorian morality of the 19th and the early 20th centuries, analyzing how these ideals influenced the colonized. A critical evaluation of the Western Christian missionary enterprise is attempted from a post colonial view, whereby with a few examples from Indian Christian historiographies, the article demonstrates how Victorian ideals of morality and sexuality influenced the natives. Gnanadason critically analyzes some of the imminent attitudes of the churches in India, which has from time to time moralized on sexuality and gender issues.

Unit 3 deals with legal perspectives on human sexuality and sexual morality, whereby four different areas have been addressed by Pawan Dhall, Debjyoti Ghosh, Gowthaman Ranganathan and Sandhya Raju. While Dhall introduces some key international human rights conventions and resolutions with specific policy and service level commitment of sexual minorities in India, Ghosh analyzes legislations of several countries to see how the LGBTIQ rights have manifested within the realm of law. Ranganathan analyzes the practicality of IPC 377, which specifically has affected the lives of the LGBTIQ persons. Raju introduces the legal issues that the Transgender communities in India face with respect to their rights.

Unit 4 deals with liberative theology on human sexuality, whereby five articles give different perspectives in this regard. Santosh Koshy Joy engages through an interview with a Transgender leader, who shares her struggles from her childhood, from her Christian home, to the seminary and on the streets of Chennai, Mumbai and Delhi. While Jacob Mathew introduces an LGBTIQ friendly anthropology, suggesting the biblical idea of kinship for a meaningful public theology for the church engagement with gender and sexual minorities, Lai-shan YIP proposes a queer affirming sexual ethic and spirituality, in the context of heterosexism and devaluation of sexual pleasure, introducing an ethical model of just good sex which exemplifies a spirituality of sexual justice and sexual integrity. Philip Vinod Peacock looks at how patriarchy intersects and interconnects with other social structures such as race, caste and communalism to both oppress women as a class as well as to construct particular forms of masculinity. L. Jayachitra attempts to offer new insights in the interpretation of the Bible in the context of the diverse queer identities.

Unit 5 engages with a liberative Christian sexual ethics through five articles. Ronald Lalthanmawia gives the medical perspectives on body, gender, sexuality and sexual differences, whereby he brings out some key aspects from medical research, of how this has evolved through the past few decades. Arvind Theodore outlines the need for having a sexual and queer ethics in the context of the various negative attitudes about sex, the human body, women and other marginalized people. Miak Siew looks at finding a new framework of Christian Sexual ethics against the conventional Christian framework of sex within marriage and the secular moral approach of sex acts between consenting adults in private being respected, both of which are inadequate. Phanenmo Kath outlines the traditional views of marriage and family as understood within a Christian or Church context. Miak Siew critiques this approach, bringing out some key inputs that needs consideration.

Unit 6 through four articles engages broadly with a responsible and life – giving ministry in the context of sexual and gender diversities. Rosy Zoramthangi Ralte challenges the prejudiced reding and interpretation of the bible by analysing a prominent homophobic passage of Genesis 19: 1-11. Pauline Ong engages with pastoral ministry among those marginalized, promoting life-giving ministry among gender and sexual minorities. Wati Longchar deals with various moralizing attitudes prevalent in Church and Society towards those who are different in their sexual orientation and gender identity. Both Anshi George Zachariah and K.S. Jacob introduce various advocacy issues related to the LGBTIQ communities in the Indian context.

It is our fervent hope that these articles will inspire the Reader in engaging with serious issues related to gender and sexual minorities, both at an academic level and real life context. We are indeed privileged to have received these well researched and analysed articles from unique authors who have passionately engaged with their respective areas. May I take this opportunity to acknowledge with gratitude, the invaluable contribution of each author of this book. May I specially place on record, the invaluable support offered by Rohan Gideon, Arvind Theodore, Rosy Zoramthangi Ralte, Lalrinawmi Ralte, Akhil Kang and Pawan Dhall who contributed by offering to do the peer review of the articles. I am also grateful to the support offered by Sadhona Ganguli and Susan Justin who helped with the language editing.

I am indebted to Rijo Geevarghese and Jebasingh Samuvel who have designed the cover pages of the book. Last but not the least, may I place on record the invaluable support and inputs of the NCCI – ESHA Team of Roger Gaikwad, Philip Kuruvilla and Vijayan Pillay, without whom, this endeavour would have been incomplete.

Fr Thomas Ninan
General Coordinator, NCCI – ESHA Program
National Council of Churches in India, Nagpur

Definitions – Understanding Gender, Sex and Sexuality

Gopi Shankar

"Gender" is related to the physical and emotional perception of an individual. Restricting gender in the binary categories of female and male is erroneous as we have to be aware of the existence of more than twenty categories of gender. The same is also true for the sexual orientation where the dominant public knowledge is only limited to the heterosexual orientation. Here we do not want to narrow down our emphasis on homosexuality, rather we emphasize the Gender-variants, which transcend the binary categories. Gender and sexuality are the rights of an individual and an interferance would refer to violation of personal freedom.

In India, thanks to the colonial legacy of shallow Victorian values, we have come to see this as a deviant behaviour or violation. The Indian culture is originally abundant with legends and mythologies where heroes and heroines have chosen various genders without guilt and their choices accepted and respected. Ironically, today the western nations are progressive in researching and educating about gender and sexuality expressions, while we, despite our rich cultural heritage lag behind and even lack sensitivity.

While the students of medicine, engineering, law and literature specialize to practice their own functions, we fall short with no studies or synthetic disciplines to probe the biological, bioethical, legal, psychological, social dimensions of the very basic emotions concerning sexuality and gender.

Though the Indian universities can offer worldwide recognized studies, we certainly lack any rudimentary axiomatic framework pertaining to gender and sexuality, while the foreign universities have even started their own departments and research activities. The most painful condition is that psychologists are mostly unaware of Gender-variants and their localized issues related to Indian conditions. India's pre-colonial traditions as well as various localized folk traditions have taken a far healthier attitude in dealing with sex-education (it may surprise many people on both sides of the fence of sex-education) who want to map Indian culture with dominant Victorian male value systems. Various folk deities and traditions emphasize the fluid nature of gender and mythologies have stories that reinforce this idea. So, a child growing up will not have a strong shock value or guilt feeling in relating to one's own sexuality or others as gender- variants. Devi Mahatmya and Mahabharata are two such examples. The temple festival in Tamil Nadu is another example of local folk tradition organically linked to the pan-Indian culture in dealing positively with creating an awareness for and empowering gender-variants. These cultural possibilities need to be taken up and explored to create a democratic social space for gender-minorities.

Generally, the terms gender, sexuality and sex are taken to be the same. But they all are distinct. Gender is self-identity or a socio-cultural and behavioural perception. Sexuality refers to the sexual attraction towards a particular sex whereas sex is a biological definition. Within the mainstream LGBTQIA+ community (Lesbian, Gay, Bisexual, Transgender, Queer, Intersex, Alliance etc)2 in India, the existence of these many genders is largely unknown. Some forms of genders don't have a proper word in the dictionary and we have coined terms both in Tamil and English for a few. There are more than 20 different types of genders other than male, female and transgender.

What is Sex?

The sex of a person is assigned based on biology, which means that if a baby is born with a vagina, that baby is a female and if a baby is born with a scrotum and a penis, then a male. However, there also exist many intermediate sexes. These intermediate sexes could have different reasons, like a difference in sex chromosome configuration (beyond the XX and XY possibilities), difference in responsiveness of the foetus or adolescent to hormones, or a difference in the mode of sexual development. These are collectively referred to as intersex variations and may or may not be accompanied by ambiguous genitalia (which is genitalia which are not strictly male or female) and Intersex is an assigned sex like male and female. For clarity, Intersex does not come under the category of transgender.

What is Gender?

Gender is a social construct. For instance, the perception that girls like to gossip and boys don't like to talk about their feelings is a societal norm, not something that is biologically ingrained. A person is actually conditioned into his / her gender through years of interaction and cultural references associated with that particular sex.

Now that brings us to the relationship between gender and sex, and here's the funny thing, there may be none. The conventional norm as to the sex of the person is assigned based on birth anatomy. However, an individual may choose to identify himself / herself themselves outside one's social and conventional definitions. For instance, I may be a girl but I may choose to assert my gender expression by undertaking a traditionally masculine act of riding a motorcycle. I may also choose to identify as a man regardless of my birth assigned sex and gender expression. Meanwhile, a man may enjoy wearing women's clothing for any reasons suitable to him.

Further, there is a wide spectrum of gender expressions and gender identities which people may associate with, it does not have to be just male and female.

The most salient example here is of transgender persons. For instance, a person who identified as a woman (gender) born into the body marked a male (sex) and may be attracted to activities, features and traits that are considered feminine (socially constructed). Such a person may choose to dress in a saree, grow hair and wear jewellery as these things become a conduit for them to express the gender that they identify with. It can also happen the other way round where a female (sex) may identify more as a man (gender).

Gender Expression

External manifestations of gender expressed through a person's name, pronouns, clothing, haircut, behaviour, voice, and/or body characteristics. Society identifies these cues as masculine and feminine, although what is considered masculine or feminine changes over time and varies by culture. Typically, transgender people seek to align their gender expression with their gender identity, rather than the sex they were assigned at birth.

Gender Dysphoria

In 2013, the American Psychiatric Association released the fifth edition of the Diagnostic and Statistical Manual of Mental Disorders (DSM-V) which replaced the outdated entry "Gender Identity Disorder" with Gender *Dysphoria*, and changed the criteria for diagnosis. The necessity of a psychiatric diagnosis remains controversial, as both psychiatric and medical authorities recommend individualized medical treatment through hormones and/or surgeries to treat gender dysphoria. Some transgender advocates believe the inclusion of Gender Dysphoria in the DSM is necessary in order to advocate for health insurance that covers the medically necessary treatment recommended for transgender people.

Transgender women are not crossdressers or drag queens. Drag queens are men, typically gay men, who dress like women for the purpose of entertainment. Be aware of the differences between transgender women, crossdressers, and drag queens. Use the term preferred by the person. Do not use the word "transvestite" at all, unless someone as such specifically mentions to be identified.

Transgender (adj.)

An umbrella term for people whose gender identity and/or gender expression differs from what is typically associated with the sex they were assigned at birth. People under the transgender umbrella may describe themselves using one or more of a wide variety of terms - including *transgender*. Some of those terms are defined below. Use the appropriate term preferred by the person. Many transgender people are prescribed hormones by their doctors to bring their bodies into alignment with their gender identity. Some undergo surgery as well. But not all transgender people can or will take those steps, and a transgender identity is not alone dependent upon physical appearance or medical procedures.

Transsexual (adj.)

An older term that originated in the medical and psychological communities. Still preferred by some people who have permanently changed or seek to change their bodies through medical interventions, including but not limited to hormones and/or surgeries. Unlike de, *transsexual* is not an umbrella term. Many transgender people do not identify as transsexual and prefer the word *transgender*. It is best to ask which term a person prefers. If preferred, use as an adjective: a transsexual woman or transsexual man.

Transman

Term used to identify a person who was assigned a female gender at birth or is female bodied, and who identifies as a male, lives as a man, or identifies as masculine. This includes a broad range of experiences, from those who identify as men or male to those who identify as transsexual, transmen, female men, new men, or FTM.

Transwoman

A transwoman (sometimes spelt as trans-woman or trans woman) is a male-to-female (MTF) transsexual or transgender person. Many people in this group like the name trans woman over the many medical terms.

Indigenous Gender Minorities of India

Sangam literature uses the word 'Pedi' to refer to people born with the Intersex condition, it also refers to *antharlinga hijras* and various *Hijra*. The Aravan cult in Koovagam village of Tamil Nadu is a folk tradition of the trans women, where the members enact the legend during an annual three-day festival. This is completely different from the sakibeki cult of West Bengal, where trans women don't have to undergo sex change surgery or shave off their facial hair. They dress as women still retaining their masculine features and sing in praise of Lord Krishna. Since the Tamil society is more conservative and heteronormative, trans women completely change themselves as women. In the ancient times, religion had its own way of accepting these fringe communities. The *Bachura* Devi worship in Gujarat and Jogappa cult of Karnataka are the other examples. Various dialects and languages are spoken by these communities in different parts of the country with a socio-cultural impact on the lingo. 'Hijra Farsi' is the transgender dialect, a mix of Urdu, Hindi and Persian spoken in the northern belt of India, Pakistan and Afghanistan; 'Kothi Baashai' is spoken by the transgender community in Karnataka, Andhra, Orissa and parts of Tamil Nadu. "They have sign languages and typical mannerisms to communicate. The peculiar clap is one such sign.

Jamaat System

The '*jamaat*' system, where individuals, upon realizing their transgender or transsexual identities, may escape their unsupportive families and be taken under the wing of a transgender or *hijra 'guru'*. Here, they are often compelled into beggary and sex work. And if the guru approves their sex reassignment surgery, the individual must do the guru's bidding (beggary, mujra, sex work) until he/she repays the debt.

Understanding Sexual Orientation

The scientifically accurate term for an individual's enduring physical, romantic and/ or emotional attraction to members of the same and/or opposite sex, including lesbian, gay, bisexual, and heterosexual (straight) orientations. Avoid the offensive term "sexual preference," which is used to suggest that being gay, lesbian, or bisexual is voluntary and therefore "curable." People need not have had specific sexual experiences to know their own sexual orientation; in fact, they need not have had any sexual experience at all.

Homosexuality

"Many highly respectable individuals of ancient and modern times have been homosexuals, several of the greatest men among them. (Plato, Michelangelo, Leonardo da Vinci, etc). It is a great injustice to persecute homosexuality as a crime —and a cruelty, too." -Sigmund Freud, Psychoanalyst.

Homosexuality is found in nature. Well documented in 500 species and observed in 1500 species apart from human species, exclusive homosexuality occurs in the species Ovis Aries apart from human species. So, now say, which assumption is against nature? Accepting homosexuality as natural or unnatural? Some people who may lack scientific knowledge on this issue may select the second choice.

Gay

The adjective used to describe people whose enduring physical, romantic, and/ or emotional attractions are to people of the same sex (e.g., a gay man, gay people). Sometimes lesbian (n. or adj.) is the preferred term for women. Avoid identifying gay people as "homosexuals" an outdated term considered derogatory and offensive to many lesbian and gay people.

Lesbian

A woman whose enduring physical, romantic, and/or emotional attraction is to other women. Some lesbians may prefer to identify as gay (adj.) or as gay women. Avoid identifying lesbians as "homosexuals," a derogatory term (see Offensive Terms to Avoid).

Conversion Therapy

Anti-LGBTIQ activists have argued for years that sexual orientation is a choice and changeable but only for people attracted to the same sex, not heterosexuals. They often claim "homosexuality" is not real, but rather a form of mental illness or an emotional disorder that can be "cured" through psychological or religious intervention. Anti-LGBTIQ activists claim that being attracted to the same sex is a curable condition, and therefore people attracted to the same sex do not need or deserve equal treatment under the law or protection from discrimination. Such programs have recently come under increased scrutiny. The largest program, Exodus, closed in 2013, apologizing for the harm that was caused by those who participated in its programs. Additionally, lawsuits have been filed against other "exgay" programs, noting that they did not produce the orientation change promised, but instead brought great harm to those who participated. In the past, treatments have included inducing vomiting and using mild electric shock while patients viewed homoerotic images. Since the 1990s, however, the therapy has been denounced by many medical and scientific societies and outlawed in a handful of states. In 2015, the Obama administration expressed disapproval of the practice after Leelah Alcorn, a 17-year-old transgender teen took her life in Ohio after being forced by her parents to undergo conversion counselling.

Experts around the world have condemned conversion therapy as not only lacking empirical validity but as unhealthy, especially for young people, causing depression, anxiety, addiction and even suicide.

The American Psychiatric Association depathologized homosexuality in 1973, when it was removed from the Diagnostic and Statistical Manual of Mental Disorders. Other professional groups quickly followed suit: In 1975, the American Psychological Association urged its members to help remove the stigma of illness from gay people.

In 1981, the World Health Organization removed homosexuality from it's list of mental illnesses.

In 1994, the American Medical Association released a report calling for "nonjudgmental recognition of sexual orientation."

Other Sexual Orientations

Bisexual, Bi

A person who has the capacity to form enduring physical, romantic, and/ or emotional attractions to those of the same gender or to those of another gender. People may experience this attraction in differing ways and degrees over their lifetime. Bisexual people need not have had specific sexual experiences to be bisexual; in fact, they need not have had any sexual experience at all to identify as bisexual. Do not use a hyphen in the word "bisexual," and only capitalize bisexual when used at the beginning of a sentence.

Asexual

An adjective used to describe people who do not experience sexual attraction (e.g., asexual person). A person can also be aromantic, meaning they do not experience romantic attraction.

Heterosexual

An adjective used to describe people whose enduring physical, romantic, and/ or emotional attraction is to people of the opposite sex. The term 'straight' is also used to refer to heterosexual person.

Other important terminologies

Homophobia

Fear of people attracted to the same sex. Intolerance, bias, or prejudice is usually a more accurate description of antipathy toward LGBTQ people.

Biphobia

Fear of bisexuals, often based on stereotypes, including inaccurate associations with infidelity, promiscuity, and transmission of sexually transmitted infections. Intolerance, bias, or prejudice is usually a more accurate description of antipathy toward bisexual people.

Coming Out

A lifelong process of self-acceptance. People forge a LGBTQ identity first to themselves and then they may reveal it to others. Publicly sharing one's identity may or may not be part of such a process.

Out

A person who self-identifies as LGBTQ in their personal, public, and/or professional lives. For example, Karan Johar from Bollywood is gay.

Openly Gay

Describes people who self-identify themselves as gay in their personal, public, and/or professional lives. Also openly lesbian, openly bisexual, openly transgender, openly queer. While accurate and commonly used, the phrase still implies a confessional aspect to publicly acknowledging one's sexual orientation or gender identity.

Closeted

Describes a person who is not open about their sexual orientation. Better to simply refer to someone as "not out" about being LGBTQ. Some individuals may be out to some people in their life, but not out to others due to fear of rejection, harassment, violence, losing one's job, or other concerns.

Queer

An adjective used by some people, particularly younger people, whose sexual orientation is not exclusively heterosexual (e.g. queer person, queer woman). Typically, for those who identify as queer, the terms lesbian, gay, and bisexual are perceived to be too limiting and/or fraught with cultural connotations they feel don't apply to them. Some people may use queer, or more commonly genderqueer, to describe their gender identity and/ or gender expression (see non-binary and/or genderqueer below). Once considered a pejorative term, queer has been reclaimed by some LGBT people to describe themselves; however, it is not a universally accepted term even within the LGBT community.

LGBTQI

Acronym for lesbian, gay, bisexual, transgender, queer and Intersex. Sometimes, when the Q is seen at the end of LGBT, it typically means queer and questioning. LGBTI and/or GLBTI are also often used. The term "gay community" should be avoided, as it does not accurately reflect the diversity of the community. Rather, LGBTQI community is preferred.

Cisgender

A term used by some to describe people who are not transgender. "Cis-" is a Latin prefix meaning "on the same side as," and is, therefore, an antonym of "trans-." A more widely understood way to describe people who are not transgender is simply to say, non-transgender people.

Gender Non-Conforming

A term used to describe some people whose gender expression is different from conventional expectations of masculinity and femininity. Please note that not all gender non-conforming people identify as transgender; nor are all transgender people gender non-conforming. Many people have gender expressions that are not entirely conventional – that fact alone does not make them transgender. Many transgender men and women have gender expressions that are conventionally masculine or feminine. Simply being transgender does not make someone gender non-conforming. The term is not a synonym for transgender or transsexual and should only be used if someone self-identifies as gender non-conforming.

Non-binary and/or genderqueer

Terms used by some people who experience their gender identity and/or gender expression as falling outside the categories of man and woman. They may define their gender as falling somewhere in between man and woman, or they may define it as wholly different from these terms. The term is not a synonym for transgender or transsexual and should only be used if someone self-identifies as non-binary and/or genderqueer.

Trans

Used as shorthand to mean transgender or transsexual - or sometimes to be inclusive of a wide variety of identities under the transgender umbrella. Because its meaning is not precise or widely understood, be careful when using it with audiences who may not understand what it means. Avoid unless used in a direct quote or in cases where you can clearly explain the term's meaning in the context of your story.

Cross-dresser

While anyone may wear clothes associated with a different sex, the term cross-dresser is typically used to refer to men who occasionally wear clothes, makeup, and accessories culturally associated with women. Those men typically identify as heterosexual. This activity is a form of gender expression and not done for entertainment purposes. Cross-dressers do not wish to permanently change their sex or live full-time as women. It replaces the term "transvestite".

Transition

Altering one's birth sex is not a one-step procedure; it is a complex process that occurs over a long period of time. Transition can include some or all of the following personal, medical, and legal steps: telling one's family, friends, and co-workers; using a different name and new pronouns; dressing differently; changing one's name and/or sex on legal documents; hormone therapy; and possibly (though not always) one or more types of surgery. The exact steps involved in transition vary from person to person. Avoid the phrase "sex change".

Sex Reassignment Surgery (SRS)

Also called Gender Confirmation Surgery (GCS). Refers to doctor-supervised surgical interventions, and is only one small part of transition (see transition above). Avoid the phrase "sex change operation." Do not refer to someone as being "pre-op" or "post-op." Not all transgender people choose to or can afford to, undergo medical surgeries.

Sodomy Laws

Historically used to selectively persecute gay people, "Sodomy" should never be used to describe same-sex relationships or sexual orientation.

Terms To Avoid (Deemed Offensive)[1]	Terms To Use (Preferred)
"homosexual"	"gay" (adj.); "gay man" or "lesbian" (n.); "gay person/people"
"homosexual relations/relationship," "homosexual couple," "homosexual sex," etc.	"relationship," "couple" (or, if necessary, "gay couple"), "sex," etc.
"sexual preference"	"sexual orientation" or "orientation"
"special rights"	"equal rights" or "equal protection"
"transgenders," "a transgender"	"transgender people", "a transgender person"
"transgendered"	"transgender"
"sex change," "pre-operative," "post-operative	"transition"

"biologically male," "biologically female," "genetically male," "genetically female," "born a man," "born a woman" Defamatory: "tranny," "she-male," "he/she," "it," "shim"	"assigned male at birth," "assigned female at birth" or "designated male at birth," "designated female at birth"
"transgenderism"	"being transgender"
Referring all Transgender people as Kinnar, Aravani and Hijras etc.	Not All Transgender people are Hijras, Transgender is a gender identity whereas Indigenous Gender Minorities identities refers to the sociocultural communities.
Hermaphrodite people (Highly offensive)	Intersex person or people
Intersex people are transgender people	Intersex people are not transgender people

References

Gopi Shankar Madurai , *Maraikappatta Pakkangal* (Hidden Pages), Illustrator Julian Wrangler, Germany, New Horizon Media., 2014, ISBN 9781500380939.

The Many Genders of Old India- Gopi Shankar. the Harvard Gay & Lesbian Review Worldwide, Boston (*http://www.glreview.org/article/the-many-genders-of-old-india*)

Theological Perspectives:
A Critical Evaluation of
Early Teachings on Human Sexuality

Philosophy and Theology of Mind-Body Dualism

Mothy Varkey

Introduction

The term 'dualism'(from the Latin word *duo* meaning 'two') denotes the state of two parts. It was originally coined to denote co-eternal binary opposition, a meaning that is preserved in metaphysical and philosophical duality discourses but has been more generalised in other usages to indicate a system which contains two fundamental kinds or categories of things or principles.

'Dualism' has a variety of uses in the history of philosophy and theology. Moral dualism is the belief of the great complement of or conflict between the benevolent and the malevolent. It simply implies that there are two moral opposites at work, independent of any interpretation of what might be 'moral' and independent of how these may be represented. In ontological dualism, the world is divided into two overarching categories.[1]In theology, for example a 'dualist' is someone who believes that Good and Evil—or God and the Devil[2]—are independent and more or less equal forces in the world.[3]In the philosophy of mind, dualism is the theory that the mental and the physical—or mind and body or mind and brain—are, in some sense, radically different kinds of things.

In contemporary theology, 'mind-body dualism'is often used to criticise world views which are male chauvinistic (patriarchal), ecologically inimical, and generally disparaging the physical reality/existence. Its historical roots can be traced to both Hebraic and Hellenistic thought forms. Thus the Biblical accent on divine transcendence and sovereignty is perceived to set God above and beyond the world in a way that undermines our need to connect with one another and to foster relationships of equality and mutual self-giving. Similarly, the Platonic division of mind and body is viewed as leading to the devaluing of the physical world in a way that privileges the mind, denigrates the body and promotes the exploitation of nature/matter.

Mind-Body Dualism: A Historical Trajectory

In 'mind-body dualism', 'mind' is contrasted with 'body', but at different times, different aspects of the mind have been the centre of attention. The classical emphasis originates in Plato's *Phaedo*. Plato believed that the true substances are not physical bodies, which are ephemeral, but the eternal forms of which bodies are imperfect copies. As a result, he conceived the material world as evil and "feminine" on the one hand, and the spiritual as good and "masculine". This not only succeeded in creating a negative and static dualism between the material and spiritual worlds, but also had a major impact on Christian anthropology.

The Platonic understanding of the person as a soul imprisoned in a body created a further disabling dualism between males and females. The association of matter with 'feminity' and evil meant that women were associated more strongly with their bodily natures and the life of the flesh in its fallen state. Men, on the other hand, were deemed to be closer to their higher spiritual nature and the life of the spirit in relation to God. This deeply entrenched association of women with the natural world and evil, and men with the world of spirit. Scholars have traced how later Hebraic and Christian thinkers elaborated this Platonic theme in ways which connected it explicitly with the theme of man's rightful domination of both women and nature.[4]

The more modern versions of mind-body dualism have their origin in René Descartes'*Meditations*. Descartes (1596–1650) was a *substance dualist*.[5] Substance dualism is also often dubbed 'Cartesian dualism'.[6]Descartes believed that there were two kinds of substance: 'matter', of which the essential property is that it is spatially extended; and 'mind', of which the essential property is that *it thinks*. Descartes' conception of the relation between 'mind' and 'body' was quite different from that held in the Aristotelian tradition. For Aristotle, there is no exact science of matter. How matter behaves is essentially affected by the form that is in it. You cannot combine just any matter with any form—you cannot make a knife out of butter, nor a human being out of paper—so the nature of the matter is a necessary condition for the nature of the substance. But the nature of the substance does not follow from the nature of its matter alone: there is no 'bottom up' account of substances. Matter is a determinable made determinate by form. This was how Aristotle thought that he was able to explain the connection of soul to body: A particular soul exists as the organising principle in a particular parcel of matter.

The crux of Descartes' method is radical doubt. He doubts everything he can manage to doubt—all traditional knowledge, the impressions of his senses, and even the fact that he has a body—until he reaches one thing he cannot doubt, the existence of himself as thinker. Thus he arrives at his celebrated statement, *Cogito, ergo sum* ("I think, therefore I exist"). From this Descartes deduces that the essence of human nature lies in thought, and that all the things we conceive clearly and distinctly are true.

Descartes' *cogito*, as it has come to be called, made 'mind' more certain for him than 'matter' and led him to the conclusion that the two were separate and fundamentally different. Thus he asserted that there is nothing included in the concept of 'body' that belongs to the 'mind'; and nothing in that of 'mind' that belongs to the 'body'. The Cartesian division between 'mind' and 'matter' has had a profound effect on Western thought. It has taught us to be aware of ourselves as isolated egos existing "inside" our bodies. Descartes based his whole view of nature on this fundamental division between two independent and separate realms; that of mind, or *res cogitans*, the "thinking thing," and that of matter, or *res extensa*, the "extended thing." In other words, 'mind' is a substance completely distinct from the 'body'. Thereafter human reason became the sole key to unlocking the external world, with nature becoming a vast soulless plane of matter to be examined, ordered, and classified by the human mind.

Artificial Intelligence (AI): The New Dualism/Cartesianism?

The computer model of the mind, pioneered by Alan Turing's strong Artificial Intelligence (AI) thesis prophesied the development of software that would enable computers to stimulate human 'intelligence'.[7] The potential that human have to create a machine that may successfully stimulate human capacities is at once attractive and threatening. However, to create a machine in the human image (capacity to reason) is not equivalent to creating a person. There are differences between the way in which the brain and the computer process information although many in the AI community dispute this observation. It is a question of whether a dynamical system such as nervous system can be modelled by a computer, after all the brain is not a computer and consciousness is not the running of a programme.

From a Christian theological perspective the human being is purposefully created in the image of God, which means that the human being is created to know, worship, and glorify God. This implies that apart from the human capacity for rational thought, belief is yet another criterion of what it means to be human.

John Searle has broached this question from two vantage points.[8] Firstly, he argues that since computers are made of silicon chips and not brains and that brains are necessary for belief, this suggests that a computer cannot believe in the same way that a human being can. That a computer can stimulate intelligent behaviour, which is characteristically a feature of brains, suggests that intelligent behaviour can be carried out without a brain. This point has been raised by AI adherents against Searle's "brain chauvinism".

However, Searle relates this first point with his second argument, which is that there is a distinction between genuine belief and stimulated belief. The former has a requisite what Searle refers to as 'intrinsic' intentionality, which is about something or is directed towards something which is in contrast to an 'as-if' intentionality. The belief here is seen to be in the eye of the beholder, therefore it is not genuine belief. In Searle's view, the fact that the computer is run through the manipulation of symbols in accordance with rules is sufficient proof of mere as-in intentionality and as-if belief, as such, this does not mean that it possessess intrinsic intentionality and genuine belief.

Underlying all this is that we may trace a certain reluctance to take our bodiliness seriously. Until such time as computer hardware can resemble the human body it does not make much sense to speak of minds alone. As Fergus Kerr reminds us, "the bodiliness that seems to keep us apart is exactly what makes our being together possible in the first place".[9] It is this "rancour against the physical and historical condition of human life" that creation-centred non-dualist theology makes it most valuable contribution.[10]

Mind-Body Dualism: A Theological critique

As with the scientific revolution of the 17th and 18th centuries, Descartes' radical dissociation of the 'mind' from the 'body' and the subsequent exaltation of 'reason' over 'emotion' further reinforced the view of women and nature as objects for male use and pleasure. Feminists and ecologists, such as Lynn White, have argued that the separation of 'mind' from the 'body' is to seen as directly responsible for the subjugation and oppression of women and for the environmental crisis. This is because, as Marti Kheel rightly contends, dualism has two characteristics in common: the first half of the duality is always valued more than the other; and, the more valued half is always seen as "male" and the less valued half as "female".[11] Christian eco-feminists like Sallie McFague focus more on the inadequacies of Platonic and Enlightenment dualism for rendering a relational theology of nature.[12]

Rosemary Ruether and McFague argue that, due to the way in which dualism has functioned in creating binary oppositions, such as body/mind, male/female, and reason/emotion, it is necessary for the sake of integration and unity that we use relational language in our theological discourse, beginning, of course, with body-mind dualism. Ruether for example, argues that feminism needs to develop an anthropology which rejects traditional male definitions of certain physic attributes as being 'masculine' and 'feminine', referring here to the reason-emotion dichotomy. As she states, "there is no biological connection between male gonads and the capacity to reason", nor there is any "biological connection between female sexual organs and the capacity to be intuitive"; "all humans possess a full and equivalent human nature and personhood, as *male and female*…since obviously males and females possess both sides of the brain" [emphasis original].[13] It shows that there is no biological basis for differentiating males and females into different physic profiles, but rather both sexes have the capacity for physic wholeness.

But the recent studies regarding transvestites and sexual identity call into question Reuther's argument that due to socialisation, males have developed their "left-and right-brain" capacities, while women have developed their right-and left-brain" capacities. The studies point to the fact that those individuals born and socialised as male and female, yet who within their innermost being felt that they were trapped in the wrong body, there was tremendous inner turmoil until such time that they could change their sex/gender role.

Furthermore, in an age when we can transplant blood and organs from one person to another in order to bring life; when people's bodies can be augmented by artificial means; when person sex can be altered; when beings can be cloned; when heterosexual and patriarchal understandings of the body are breaking down, issues of bodily identity worry us and yet in an age when aesthetics appears to have largely replaced metaphysics, the body seems to be all we have.

Maurice Merleau-Ponty and dynamic non-dualism

The writings of the famous phenomenologist Maurice Merleau-Ponty have been recognised by many in the last two decades as providing alternatives to a Cartesian-dualist and Enlightenment-subjectivity world view. Merleau-Ponty's writings illuminate ordinary human experience through an examination of the extraordinary-traumatic experience. According to Merleau-Ponty, human experience is a whole, not dual ('mind' and 'body'). And as a whole, it unites mind–body–world while maintaining singularity and plurality. It unites them in a story that uses the language of 'intention', 'motivation', 'direction', 'desire', 'sexuality', 'expression', and 'thought' to describe and intertwining human behaviours. It dynamically unites—or tries to—traditional dichotomies of 'mind' and 'body', 'interiority' and 'exteriority', and 'subject' and 'object'. What becomes visible is corporeity existing as communication.

In the *Phenomenology of Perception*,[14] Merleau-Ponty appeals to the case studies of brain-injured men, and amputees of World War I—survivors of 'physical' and 'psychological' trauma.[15] By examining the physiological and psychic phenomena that arise in the aftermath of traumatic experience, Merleau- Ponty magnifies human corporeality as a directed self-showing. For Merleau-Ponty, trauma operates like a prism through which the body as it is experienced, lights up. Merleau-Ponty explores three kinds of bodily adaptations: anatomical, technical and verbal—as expressions of preconscious bodily desire and especially of that which is arguably a human being's most intense kind of pre-conscious desire—that generated by traumatic experience.

By *anatomical* adaptation, Merleau-Ponty means the spontaneous mobilising of an organism's body cells, tissue and organs, in response to preconscious felt needs. In the case of paralysis from spinal cord injury, the anatomical body marshals a complex set of internal adjustments to strike an equilibrium with its new circumstances. Skin adaptation is another example of anatomical shifting and a consequence of trauma to the spinal cord. Unremitting pressure on muscle and skin tissue cuts of blood circulation to the tissue and tissue dies. People with healthy spinal cords spontaneously shift their sleeping and sitting positions countless times during a day, in part because their bodies are responding to felt needs of which they are generally unaware.

If anatomical adaptation both shows and participates in life as directed towards such self and other signification, the same might be said of technical adaptation. By *technological* adaptation, Merleau-Ponty means a dually reflective and bodily process. Our body exercises reflection and built-technology in order to accommodate bodily needs that are not or cannot be met by anatomical shifting. Walking sticks, contact lenses, hearing-aids, wheelchairs, and other assistive technologies show themselves likewise of and expressing bodily needs. Important here is the way corporeal responsiveness reveals anatomical and technological adaptations to exist as communication. If the example of anatomical shifting returns communication to physiology, the example of technological adaptation extends bodies beyond physiology and shows how one's self-designating self-showing adapts to include the technologically appended lived body.

Anatomical and technological adaptation show themselves as two of many processes through which human corporeality signifies both itself and a beyond-self; for Merleau-Ponty, a third such process is 'speech' (*verbal* adaptation). By 'speech' Merleau-Ponty means spoken or written languages that accomplish through words and thoughts. The *Phenomenology of perception* makes explicit the body as the basis of speech. Speech, like anatomy and technology, shows itself as signification of and intention towards expressing bodily desire to demarcate and signify self and other. For Merleau-Ponty, speech is not only inseparable from corporeity but emerging from and existing as corporeity, especially of and as desire.

In short, for Merleau-Ponty, trauma operates as a magnifying extreme that makes visible, dynamic adaptations of our verbal, anatomical, and technological bodily processes. These processes show lived body as an intended self-showing rooted in and displaying bodily desire. Finally, that each of the explored bodily processes (speech, anatomy, and assistive technology) participates in a shared aim of self and other designation, also underlines Merleau-Ponty's view of human experience as a dynamic whole, which suggests the experience of self and world as non-dual.

Alternative/Embodied Anthropology

One of the primary aims of a theological/non-dualistic critique of 'mind-body dualism' is to construct an alternative anthropology, a new understanding of human nature, that recognises the centrality of embodiment/body. Dermot Lane identifies the following steps to construct an embodied anthropology:[16]

- We must accept the relational self, "indeed, it must be said that relationality is a primary category, a fundamental characteristic of all beings in the world and not just human beings".[17] It is out of this relationality that individuality emerges and that individuality can only be maintained through continuous relationality.

- We must recognise that "human beings belong to each other in an extraordinary degree of natural solidarity and social togetherness...[which] can be seen not only at the human level but also on a wider cosmic scale in the light of the emerging creation story".[18]

- We must take the cosmic nature of human embodiment on board in our task of constructing a new anthropology. Postmodern science has taught us that all bodies—cosmic, animal and human—have an effect upon another and that effect can reach across space and time.[19]

- We must recognise the social and communal nature of human beings. Lane argues that such an alternative anthropology is fundamentally eschatological.[20]

If we are going to emphasise the relational nature of the human self, the embodied nature of the self and a self that is 'social and cosmic' in origin, then questions about the realisation of the universe, and communal and individual relationships with God are unavoidable. There is a need to move away from purely individual, disembodied anthropology to embodied anthropology.[21]

Conclusions

As the locus of divine revelation, 'body' is established both as a point of contact with God and as a gulf between the divine and the human, even as we touch the divine presence we lose him/her. The human experience of embodiment is complex, ambiguous and diverse. What is remarkable is that both conservatives and feminist/queer theologians are in agreement that "the flesh is the hinge of salvation".[22] This common starting point has the potential to produce the kind of creative dialogue that has recently been lacking in theological conversations. What must be guarded against at all costs is the disappearing of the real, lived, birthing, suffering, dying, and resurrecting body underneath the philosophical and theological discourses it is called to bear.

Endnotes

[1] The opposition and combination of the universe's two basic principles of *yin* and *yang* is a large part of Chinese philosophy, and is an important feature of Taoism, both as a philosophy and as a religion (it is also discussed in Confucianism).

[2] In theology, *dualism* may refer to duotheism, bitheism, or ditheism. Although ditheism/bitheism imply moral dualism, they are not equivalent: ditheism/bitheism implies (at least) two gods, while moral dualism does not imply any *-theism* (*theos*=god) whatsoever. Dualism can also refer to the relationship between God and creation, which exists in some traditions of Christianity (e.g.Paulicianism, Catharism, and Gnosticism). The *Dvaita* Vedanta school of Indian philosophy also espouses a dualism between God and the universe.

[3] Dualism contrasts with monism, which is the theory that there is only one fundamental kind, category of thing or principle; and, rather less commonly, with pluralism, which is the view that there are many kinds or categories.

[4] Genevieve Lloyd, *The Man of Reason: "Male" and "Female" in Western Philosophy* (London: Methuen, 1984), 6. See also Rosemary Radford Ruether, *Sexism and God-Talk: Towards a Feminist Theology* (London: SCM, 1983), 83.

[5] There are two important concepts deployed in this notion. One is that of *substance*, the other is the *dualism* of these substances. A substance is characterized by its properties, but, according to those who believe in substances, it is more than the collection of the properties it possesses, it is *the thing which* possesses them. So the mind is not just a collection of thoughts, but is *that which* thinks, an immaterial substance over and above its immaterial states.

[6] But some substance dualists like Lowe is keen to distinguish their theories from Descartes's. See Edward Jonathan Lowe, "Non-Cartesian substance dualism and the problem of mental causation,"*Erkenntnis*, 65/1 (2006): 5–23.

[7] Fergus Gordon Kerr, *Theology after Wittgenstein* (Oxford: Basil Blackwell, 1986), 185. As Kerr says, "the internal states of information-processing machines have become the paradigm for the psychological states of creatures of our kind" (183).

[8] John Rogers Searle, "Minds, Brains and Programs," in *Artificial Intelligence* (ed. Rainer Born; London: Croom Helm, 1987)

[9] Kerr, *Theology after Wittgenstein*, 188.

[10] Kerr, *Theology after Wittgenstein*, 188.

[11] Marti Kheel, "The Liberation of Nature: A Circular Affair, Environmental Ethics," *Sociological Abstract* 7/2 (1985), 136.

[12] Sallie McFague, *The Body of God: An Ecological Theology* (London: SCM, 1993), 33.

[13] Rosemary Radford Ruether, *Gaia and God: An Ecofeminist Theology of Earth Healing* (London: SCM, 1992), 113.

[14] Maurice Merleau-Ponty, *Phenomenology of Perception* (trans. Colin Smith; London: Routledge & Kegan Paul, 1962 [1945]).

[15] Although Merleau-Ponty indicates the exceptional status of trauma for his project, he does not explicitly explore, specify, or reveal his implied concept of trauma.

[16] Dermot Lane, "Anthropology and Eschatology," *Irish Theological Quarterly* 61 (1995): 14–31.

[17] Lane, "Anthropology and Eschatology,"19.

[18] Lane, "Anthropology and Eschatology," 22.

[19] Brian Swimme and Thomas Berry, *The Universe Story: From the Primordial Flaring Forth to the Ecozoic Era–A Celebration of the Unfolding Universe* (New York:

HarperCollins, 1992); Rupert Sheldrake, *A New science of Life: The Hypothesis of Formative Causation* (Los Angeles: J P Tarcher, 1981)

[20] Lane, "Anthropology and Eschatology," 24, 27.

[21] Lane, "Anthropology and Eschatology," 27.

[22] Tertullian, *De resurrection carnis*, 8.6–12.

Doctrine of Adamic Sin –
A Theological *Crux Interpretum?*

Jogy C. George

Introduction

Original Sin[1] otherwise known as 'Adamic/'ancestral sin'[2] is the sin of Adam and Eve. It is explained differently among the churches. This doctrine has a great impact on the theology of the Church because upon it rests a whole series of interrelated dogmas. The existence of evil and the consequence of the Adamic sin was and is always a problem for the Church. This is a brief study on the doctrine of original/Adamic sin. While discussing this doctrine we will also try to answer some pertinent questions like; Has Adamic sin become a part of human nature? What is the consequence of Adamic sin? etc. The contradiction and confusion in juxtaposing the inherited sin and the salvation in Christ could be unravelled by a proper understanding of this doctrine.

1.   Doctrinal Point of Views

1.1. Roman Catholic Church

The basic understanding of the Roman Catholic Church is based on the teachings of St Augustine of Hippo, who first used the phrase 'Original Sin' to develop it as a Christian doctrine. According to this doctrine, the sin of Adam is transferred to his offspring and therefore, humanity is sinful with no possibility to do good (Augustine's doctrine is further discussed below).

In the twelfth century, Pope Innocent III taught that the sin which is inherited, i.e., the ancestral/Adamic sin (also called 'contracted sin') will be forgiven through Baptism without our will, but the 'committed sin' or personal sin, which is done out of our will, will be forgiven only with our will.

The Council of Trent (1546) made an official declaration on the doctrine of 'Original Sin' and it became a part of the Roman Catholic faith. And this council anathemized all who believe against this teaching.

1.2. Orthodox Churches

Orthodox churches prefer to use the phrase, Adamic Sin rather than Original Sin, to denote the sin of Adam because the later indirectly could convey the message that it is something common to - humanity. The phrase 'original sin' is never mentioned in the liturgy of the Orthodox churches not even used in the Syriac or Greek language. Orthodox (theology) rejects the scholastic dogma of original sin, particularly as it implies the transmission of the sin and guilt of Adam to succeeding generations, like some genetic effect.[3]

The Orthodox churches also teach that while sin is not transmitted from generation to generation, the consequences are transmitted. It is not sin or guilt that is inherited from Adam but what we inherit is the subjugation to death. "The difference between Eastern and Western perspectives on the fall lay first in the determination of how all humanity is connected with the sin of Adam and Eve and the second in the subsequent result of this fall."[4]

For the East sin is alienation from God and thereby a rejection of the life in communion with God. Death is the natural result of the turning away from God. Death and corruption are not originated from God, it is the consequence of the disobedience of Adam.

1.3. Reformation Churches

The doctrine of original sin as interpreted by Augustine was affirmed by the Protestant Reformers Martin Luther and John Calvin. Both Luther and Calvin agreed that humans inherit guilt from the sin of Adam and are in a state of sin from the moment of conception. This inherently sinful nature (the basis for the Calvinist doctrine of "total depravity") results in a complete alienation from God and the total inability of humans to achieve reconciliation with God based on their own abilities. Not only do individuals inherit a sinful nature due to Adam's fall, but since he was the head and representative of the human race, all whom he represents inherit the guilt of his sin by imputation.

Because of this spiritual problem, Protestants believe that God the Father sent Jesus into the world. The personhood, life, ministry, suffering, and death of Jesus, as God incarnate in human flesh, is meant to be the atonement for original sin as well as actual sins committed by humans; this atonement is, according to some Protestants rendered fully effective by the resurrection of Jesus.

2.   Original Sin - Eastern and Western Teachings

The doctrine of Original sin has its beginning in Augustine of Hippo. The Western Church only added or modified this teaching but the East opposed it or explained it differently. Here we have some samples, beginning with Augustine followed by some Eastern Patristic views.

2.1. Augustine of Hippo

As we have mentioned above, original sin was developed into a doctrine in the teachings of Augustine. The biblical basis for the Augustinian teaching on Original Sin and the later official teaching of the Catholic Church was Psalm 51:5 and Romans 5:12.

According to Augustine, human will cannot do good, because a human being is 'one condemned mass of sin' (*massa damnata*). It is a sum of sin, death and moral weakness which it inherited from Adam. Therefore, everybody is born as a sinner and condemned. "The *massa damnata* of the fallen humanity is the object of God's wrath because it is *guilty*. It can be justified by *grace* which alone can *forgive*, then restore man to the natural capability of his soul to contemplate God's essence. The latter can occur only beyond the grave; in the present life, man can never be anything else than a forgiven sinner."[5]

It is through lust that sin spread over humanity. And hence a child born of baptised parents is unholy. Thus they inherit original sin by birth. (Since sexual union is sinful, the product of that union is tainted by sin). Augustinian teaching affirms that children are born sinful, not because they have sinned personally, but because they have sinned 'in Adam'; their baptism is therefore also a baptism 'for the remission of sins.'[6]

Augustine quoted Psalm 51:5, which reads, "Indeed I was born guilty, a sinner when my mother conceived me," to support his thesis (which according to the Orthodox interpretation is the confession of David about his weakness) and also the Latin version of Romans 5:12 with a wrong interpretation of the text[7].

He teaches that original sin is infused or imputed to the soul of Adam and Eve. And this is passed on to the successive generations through their seed. Since the image of God and free will were marred by the fall of Adam there is no possibility that the offspring of Adam could do anything good of themselves.

Many questions arise when we analyse Augustine's teaching on original sin.

1) If everybody inherits Adamic sin, the tendency to sin would be equal in all human beings.

2) If Baptism cleanses us from sin, then how does a child of a baptised parents inherit Adamic sin/original sin.

3) According to St Paul, "For the unbelieving husband is made holy through his wife, and the unbelieving wife is made holy through her believing husband. Otherwise your children would be unclean, but as it is, they are holy" (1 Cor 7:14). And so, when both the husband and wife are believers how come the child is unholy!

4) If all are considered as sinners, Enoch and Elijah, who were taken up to heaven and Judas Iscariot, who betrayed Jesus are on equal footing-.[8]

2.2. Severus of Antioch

Severus, while dealing with this *crux interpretum* says, it is true that Jesus took the fallen nature of Adam which is perishable and mortal, but, since sin is not a part of the human nature when the Son of God became a human being, he took only the perishable and mortal nature of human body. Severus strongly believed that sin is not transferred from generation to generation. He affirms, the teaching that the Adamic sin has been passed down to generations is not Christian.

Severus adds that if sin is transmitted from Adam to his offspring as part of the human nature then each and every sinner is a 'sinner' because of Adam and therefore, his/her sin is not a mistake in itself.

He concludes, we are no partakers in the sin of Adam and are not born as sinners but we are subject to death because we are offspring of Adam, who is a mortal and sinner. Adam and Eve lost the grace of immortality through disobeying the commandment of God and that led to their mortal nature. This we inherit from them but not sin.[9]

2.4.   Paulos Mar Gregorios

A twentieth century theologian and philosopher Paulos Mar Gregorios observes that the consequence of Adamic sin affects the whole humanity but it won't inherit Adamic sin by birth. He strongly opposes the doctrine of Original Sin. With Patristic evidences, Mar Gregorios observes that sin is not a part of the human nature and sexual union in a married life is not evil but holy.

2.5.   Byzantine Teaching

"...the rebellion of Adam and Eve against God could be conceived only as their personal sin; there would be no place, then, in such an anthropology for the concept of inherited guilt or for a 'sin of nature,' although it admits that human nature incurs the consequences of Adam's sin." Mortality or 'corruption' or simply death (understood in a personalized sense), has indeed been viewed, since Christian antiquity, as a cosmic disease which holds humanity under its sway, both spiritually and physically, and is controlled by the one who is 'the murderer from the beginning' (Jn 8:44). It is this death which makes sin inevitable, and in this sense 'corrupts' nature.[10]

3.   Evil: Not Created - Non Existent

Evil[11] has no existence, thus says the Fathers of the Church-He exists in non-existence. It is not created by God because God is good and hence what God created is also good (Gen 1:4). Therefore, the origin of evil is not from God but in the freedom of the created being. Thus it is very clear that sin is not a part of human nature. It has no other source than the freedom of the being who accomplishes it. "Man has thus given a place to evil in his will and introduced it into the world. Certainly man, who was naturally predisposed to know and love God, has chosen evil because it was suggested to him: that is exactly the serpent's role (Gen 3:1)."[12] It is the misuse of this free will of man that led to his fall and the consequent *death*. Adam, who was called to live in union with God, because of his disobedience, reached a state where he could no longer correspond to his vocation.

4.   Sin - Missing the Mark

Man's first sin is disobedience as opposed to the will of God and this resulted in the expulsion from paradise. The image of God in which the Adam was created is obscured through the first sin. Some of the notable consequences of this 'missing the mark' are as follows;

> "Simplicity in the communication with God is substituted by fearful shame. Instead of 'clothes of sanctity,' the 'leaves of fig' are found, a symbol of the fallen state. Human nature is held prisoner by the devil. At the heart of the consequences of the fall is the 'double death': The soul is stripped of divine life, while the body is destined to dissolution."[13] Man by the misuse of his free will, not only lost the possibility to be immortal but also became mortal.

4.1. Sin and Salvation

The doctrine of salvation is based, not on the idea of guilt inherited from Adam and from which man is saved in Christ, but on a more existential understanding of both 'fallen' and 'redeemed' humanity. From 'old Adam,' through his natural birth, man inherits a defective form of life, bound by mortality, lacking fundamental freedom from Satan[14]. The alternative to this 'fallen' state is a 'life in Christ,' for He took upon that fallen nature and redeemed it by His death and resurrection. This life in Christ, the gift of God bestowed in the mystery of the Church, is the going back to the original image of man.

The Son is incarnated to make possible the union of man with God. The obstacles of sin and death were overcome by the incarnation, crucifixion and resurrection of Jesus Christ. "Thus the death of Christ removes, from between man and God, the obstacle of sin; and his resurrection takes from death its 'sting'."[15] The disobedience of the first

Adam resulted in death, while the obedience of the Second resulted in everlasting life and salvation (cf. 1 Cor 15:45-49).

4.2.   Sin and Baptism

Baptism is 'new birth' and is a free gift from God. Through Baptism we are buried with Christ and raised with him (Romans 6:3-4). In Baptism we put off our old self and put on the new (baptised into Christ and we put on Christ, Galatians 3:26-27). In order to regain the obscured image, this is a gift from God. Therefore, it is in no sense dependent upon human choice, consent, or even consciousness. Whether you are grown up or an infant does not create any barrier to this new life in Christ. Hence, infant baptism is legitimate and logical. This is based, "not on the idea of a 'sin' which would make even the infant guilty in the eyes of God and in need of baptism as justification, but on the fact that, at all stages of life, including infancy, man needs to be 'born anew' - i.e., to begin a new and eternal life in Christ. The ultimate eschatological goal of new life cannot be fully comprehended even by the 'conscious adult.'"[16]

According to the Eastern Orthodox understanding, "...the Church baptizes children, not to 'remit' their yet nonexistent sins, but in order to give them a new and immortal life, which their mortal parents are unable to communicate to them. The opposition between the two Adams is seen in terms not of guilt and forgiveness but of death and life (1 Cor 15:47-48)."[17]

Since a person, through baptism becomes a member of the body of Christ, and thereby becomes 'theo-centric', that is, he recovers his original destiny, which is eschatological and mysterious, because it participates in the very mystery of God. Though it is a free gift from God, it is not a suppression of human freedom, but enables to restore the original and natural form.

4.3.   Adamic Sin and Nature

According to the Western understanding of Adamic sin, human nature is sinful after the fall and all human beings are equally sinful and man cannot do anything good but sin. Paulos Gregorios, a great theologian, philosopher and thinker, in his profound work *Cosmic Man* observes thoroughly analyses the thoughts of Gregory of Nyssa. Gregorios finds an enlightening explanation regarding this theme in the teachings of Gregory. Gregory is not denying human sin. He accepts the fact that sin is separation from God, the source of all being, and therefore, death. But Gregory denies some affirmations about the human nature.

Gregory observes that human nature cannot be sinful, for nature is created by God, and therefore, it was not created evil or sinful. The uniqueness of human nature is that it was created in the Image of God, who is the perfection of all goodness. Since freedom is part of the image, the created nature has to be 'worked out' through human freedom. Hence, there are two possibilities for human beings, either to say 'yes' to the existence given to us by affirming that it comes from God or to say 'no' to that existence by refusing to acknowledge that it comes from God, thinking it is one's own. This is alienation from God and hence, death.

Gregory argues that the sin of Eve was that she chose something which seemed good, but was not good for her. The tree of the knowledge of good and evil was good because it was created by God. But it was not good for Eve, that is why God forbid Adam from eating its fruits. She could have obeyed realizing that it was not good for her. But the devil convinced her that it was good for her. Evil is the result of the and possibility in the misuse of the good. It was this misuse of the good that resulted in the first sin. So the fruit of the tree of the knowledge of good and evil, which was good in itself, when misused became the cause of evil. Gregorios quotes the words of Gregory:

> "Since he foresaw this possibility, the Serpent points to this evil fruit of sin, not as having evil as its nature, or manifestly appearing as evil (for then man would not have been deluded into choosing manifest evil), but decking the phenomenon she saw with a glamour and conjuring up in her taste the potential pleasure of sense-experience, he (the serpent) appeared convincing to the woman, for as the Scripture says: 'And the woman saw that the Tree was good for food, pleasing to the eyes, and ripe for knowledge, and she took the fruit thereof and ate.' But this food has become the mother of death to human beings." A sin is an act of the will, not the bodily drives or the surge of the passions. Gregory leaves us in no doubt what the source of evil is—the freedom of Man."[18]

4.4. Sin as Alien to Human Nature

Paulos Gregorios, observes that all sin is against nature. This is a fundamental principle in Eastern patristic thought. Gregorios continues his observations on the thoughts of Nyssa.

> "Gregory opines that Human nature has become enslaved to sin and through sin to evil, but sin is an alien master that now rules man, not something that belongs to his nature. Gregory makes this clear in his commentary *On the Inscriptions of the Psalms*. The source of sin is in Man's changeability which is also the arena of his freedom and self-creation. Human nature, for Gregory, is not sinful in itself, but ever under pressure to change, either for the better or for the worse. The need is to reverse the direction of the change; not to become changeless, which is impossible for any created nature, but to be redeemed from slipping down the path of evil, to be set up again on the upward climb into the infinite good."[19]

Conclusion

Augustine's teaching on 'original sin' ended up in an extreme dogmatic stand point. Further theological discussions and doctrinal point of views of the Western Church were greatly influenced by his teaching. But the East was very cautious in its approach towards this teaching. The very choice of the phrase 'Adamic/Ancestral' sin confined it to Adam and Eve. The freedom and dignity of human nature were maintained and emphasised in their teaching. The sanctity of human sexuality was upheld and the possibility of regaining the obscured image of a human being was highlighted.

Endnotes

[1] This phrase was first used by St Augustine of Hippo in his treaty *De Peccato Originale*

[2] These are the phrases preferred by the Orthodox churches instead of 'original sin.'

[3] J. Breck, *The Sacred Gift of Life. Orthodox Christianity and Bioethics* (New York: St Vladimir's Seminary Press, 1998), 29.

[4] D. Haynes, "The Transgression of Adam and Christ the New Adam: St Augustine and St Maximus the Confessor on the Doctrine of Original Sin," (St Vladimir's Theological Quarterly 55/3, 2011), 294.

[5] J. Meyendorff, *Catholicity and the Church* (New York: St Vladimir's Seminary Press, 1983), 67. Also cf. M. Pomazansky, *Orthodox Dogmatic Theology* (California: Saint Herman of Alaska Brotherhood, 1997), 162.

[6] J. Meyendorff, *Byzantine Theology. Historical Trends and Doctrinal Themes* (New York: Fordham University Press, 1979), 193.

[7] "Western and Orthodox interpretation of 'original sin' are based largely on different interpretation of Romans 5:12, 'As sin came into the world through one man and death through sin, so death spread to all.' The crucial phrase is one that follows: *eph' hô pantes hêmarton*. To what does the relative clause *eph' hô* refer? Western scholastic theology renders it 'in whom,' implying that all are subject to death because all sin *in Adam* (*in quo omnes peccaverunt*, in the Vulgate version). Eastern patristic tradition, followed by most Protestant versions, on the other hand, renders *eph' hô* as 'because': all die *because* all commit sin. According to this interpretation, what is 'inherited' from Adam is not the stain of guilt in consequence of his sin in Paradise. Rather, if we can speak of 'inheritance at all, it must be seen as the inheritance of *mortality*: 'death spread to all *because* all sin.'" J. Breck, *The Sacred Gift of Life* (New York: St Vladimir's Seminary Press, 1998), 30. "Such a translation renders Paul's thought to mean that death, which was the 'wages of sin' (Romans 6:23) for Adam, is also the punishment applied to those who, like him, sin. It presupposes a cosmic significance of the sin of Adam, but does not say that his descendants are guilty as he was, unless they also sin as he sinned." J. Meyendorff, *Byzantine Theology* (New York: Fordham University Press, 1979), 144.

[8] Paulos Gregorios, *Paurasthya Chraisthava Darsanam* (Kottayam: Divyabodhanam Publications, 1996), 158.

[9] Paulos Gregorios, *Paurasthya Chraisthava Darsanam* (Kottayam: Divyabodhanam Publications, 1996), 156-157.

[10] J. Meyendorff, *Byzantine Theology. Historical Trends and Doctrinal Themes* (New York: Fordham University Press, 1979), 143.

[11] V. Lossky gives a profound explanation about evil. "Evil certainly has no place among the essences, but it is not only a lack: there is an activity in it. Evil is not a nature, but a state of nature, as the Fathers would say most profoundly. It thus appears as an illness, as a parasite existing only by virtue of the nature he lives off. More precisely, it is a state of the will of this nature; it is a fallen will with regard to God. Evil is revolt against God, that is to say, a personal attitude. The exact vision of evil is thus not essentialist but personalist." V. Lossky, *Orthodox Theology: Introduction* (New York: St Vladimir's Seminary Press, 1989), 80.

[12] V. Lossky, *Orthodox Theology: Introduction* (New York: St Vladimir's Seminary Press, 1989), 80.

[13] M. Hauke, "Original Sin" in *The Brill Dictionary of Gregory of Nyssa*, eds. L.F. Mateo-Seco, G. Maspero (Leiden: Brill, 2010), 557.

[14] J. Meyendorff, *Byzantine Theology. Historical Trends and Doctrinal Themes* (New York: Fordham University Press, 1979), 193.

[15] V. Lossky, *Orthodox Theology: Introduction* (New York: St Vladimir's Seminary Press, 1989), 92.

[16] J. Meyendorff, *Byzantine Theology. Historical Trends and Doctrinal Themes* (New York: Fordham University Press, 1979), 193.

[17] J. Meyendorff, *Byzantine Theology. Historical Trends and Doctrinal Themes* (New York: Fordham University Press, 1979), 146.

[18] Paulos Gregorios, *Cosmic Man. The Divine Presence* (New Delhi: Sophia Publications, 1980), 156-157.

[19] Paulos Gregorios, *Cosmic Man. The Divine Presence* (New Delhi: Sophia Publications, 1980), 161-162.

Patriarchy vis-à-vis Human Sexuality: Depatriarchalising in the Theology of "Created in the Image of God"

Bendanglemla Longkumer

1.   Introduction

It is now more than –seven decades that India is journeying as a free country. However, there –are a majority of our people who are still not free or independent. There are many reasons to state, one of which could be the s discrimination being meted out based on poverty, caste issues, gender and sexual orientation issues and so on. This paper is a critical survey of some key theological deliberations within this emerging area of scholarship. It will touch on the key features that tickle the scholars' thoughts to address this issue and make attempts to move beyond the constraining gender dichotomy, taking in particular the perspective of the excluded bodies.

The pyramidical structure is still visible/valid in our society. Men are placed at the top of the pyramid of human relationships and are systematically encouraged to view power as dominating and controlling. Besides, the patriarchal religious tradition has long seen God in male terms, legitimizing male dominance. A closer look at the creation account reveals the emphasis laid on God creating humanity as male and female in God's image. However, throughout history, cultural, religious and other social factors have led us to think and act in ways which are inconsistent with the fact that both male and female were created in God's image. Eventually such people began to yield to values that seem to glorify gender injustice.

Such practices are justified either by citing Biblical references or church doctrines.

A re-reading of the Bible, acknowledging that human beings (male and female) are created in the Image of God, demands that we look–at everyone as human/people, fully entitled and responsible citizens in society and religion. If men have been culturally and socially conditioned to having a hegemonic self- understanding, our coming to faith in Christ calls us to begin putting off this "burden" and to begin to learn ways in which God calls men and women to partnership, in living in the community as well as in engagement in God's mission. This calls for appropriating the hermeneutic of suspicion in our theological constructions particularly in the context of understanding human sexuality.

2. Appropriating the Hermeneutic of Suspicion[1] in our Theological Construct

An understanding of human sexuality is intricately related to the understanding of the nature of man. It is significant to note that the Genesis creation account unquestionably affirms human sexuality as good; as God's willful intent for human existence. Hence human sexuality must be seen neither as a mistake by God, nor a sin of man. Rather it should be seen as part of God's intention and therefore a meaningful aspect of human existence. In effect human sexuality participates in his creation, in God's image.

Citing religion as active and influential in defining the meaning of the bonding, which sanctions blessings to a particular group i.e., heterosexual monopoly, Chrisida Nithyakalyani[2] argues that it has also been a place of victimizing the sexual minorities. She further argues that scripture has been used as a weapon toward violence committed against the people who belong to LGBTIQ community and are further discriminated and marginalized in the church. In and through scriptural passages the existence of sexual minorities is condemned labelling them as 'sinful' 'cursed' 'damned'. Several scriptural passages are frequently adduced to buttress the proscription of homosexuality (Lev 18:22; 20:13; Rom1:26f). Thus we must ask, according to Jennings, in each case whether the passage in question brings to expressing a central principle of the faith or is to be understood as accidental, peripheral or time bound. He further comments that sometimes the Old Testament proscribes homosexual acts because they are non procreative, but this connection is never made in Leviticus- or elsewhere in Scripture. Thus we must ask to what extent we consider the proscriptions against homosexual acts in Leviticus generally binding upon the Christian conscience. Unless we understand ourselves bound to all Levitical proscriptions equally, then some reason in principle must be provided for discrimination among them. We have seen that principles normally invoked to make the proscription of homosexual acts binding do not in fact justify such a procedure. We must conclude that the Levitical texts do not provide us with sufficient grounds to enforce such a proscription.[3]

In this context it is to be noted that Christian theological framework, being formulated with the influence of Greek philosophy, tends to develop hierarchical structure. The *kyriachal* model of imperial power was further legitimized by Neo-Aristotelian philosophy which later found its way into the Christian scriptures in the form of patriarchal injunctions to submission.[4] Meanwhile in the Greco-Roman world, there was - less sexual mutuality; thus men took possession of women, taking control of female promiscuity and procreation. Here too one identifies a strong norm of phallocentric hegemony.

Eventually the sexual minority are treated outside the framework having been treated as imperfect, weak, and abnormal. Since they are imperfect beings they are of no value or worth. They are manifestations of sin and hence subjected to pain (Zeph 1:17; John 9; Gen 19; Rom 1:26-27 etc). One can notice here how Scripture which is one of the formative tools for theology is often interpreted from the dominant perspective. It is used as a destructive weapon in the context of the key affected which deny their existence or peaceful living and many times they are push out of the periphery. According to Chrisida, such exclusivist reading of the scriptures, which are made out of the context, turn the minds of the society to be narrow and the church fails in its duty to educate her members.[5] Furthermore the discrimination and marginalization of these people continues which challenges us to look closely to the hermeneutic of suspicion in our theological articulation. The hermeneutic of suspicion reminds us to discover/unravel the hidden reality of the text and also to be aware of the resources we borrow from others.

3.   Need for Re-constructing Theology on Sexuality

3.1.   Influence of Imperialism

With the spread of Christianity the dominant cultures penetrated shaping their cultural reading of Christianity. Indian Christianity too, according to Sandhya Jha, was shaped in many ways by Victorian era Anglicanism. All of us who have been saved through the powerful teachings of missionaries have also unintentionally been misshaped by their cultural reading of Christianity.[6] She continues to argue that we are trained to read scripture through the lens of Empire, and when we believe scripture is sacred word of God, we often do not recognize the ways in which Empire has crept into how we are taught to interpret the text. For instance, when we say the Lord's Prayer it should reflect on the community. But sadly most Christians read it as if it is about me and God. This is so because, in the words of Phil Lawson, we were taught to read that text through the lens of a culture that preferences the individual and does not value community, even though right there in the Bible the words are "our", "us" and "we" and not "me" and "I".[7] In the same manner Christian's way of conceiving the salvific plan of God, relation with Jesus and the like became too personal and hence individualistic spirituality became dominant. It shaped our way of reading the Bible, conceiving/formulating theology gradually resulting –in an exclusivist interpretation.

3.2.   Concept of Perfection in Creation

Meanwhile, the Christian doctrine of creation has to be put under a scanner. Due attention has to be given to the issues such as issues of gender, sexuality in particular. By delving into the diverse interpretations of the ancient creation stories one can expect changes that would help us come to terms with several challenges. It would also transform the traditional understanding of creation story which is often stigmatizing and oppressive. Perhaps the most significant point to be found in the Genesis creation stories, especially in light of traditional Christian interpretations, is the unquestionable affirmation of human sexuality as good, as God's wilful intent for human existence. One sees God the creator who intricately orchestrates every item of this creation is created perfectly.[8] Furthermore, human sexuality is the concrete manifestation of the divine call to completion, a call extended to each individual in the act of creation and it is rooted in the very core of his or her being. Thus human sexuality is a part of our personality, which involves the interrelationship of biological, psychological and socio-cultural dimension.

Hence the term perfect is just a human construct (lubricated by anthropocentric language) which results –in looking at creation within hierarchical terms. The definition of perfection may vary in the sense that each views things from a different perspective and hence our perceptions should not lead us to devalue the persons who have different appearances, or different sexual orientations. On a closer look –at the doctrine of creation, the Genesis account declares that God saw the created order as very good. Being created good does not mean that it is perfect, therefore the purpose and appropriateness of each creation should be seen.

3.3.   Created in the Image of God

Christian understanding of human identity is based -on the Word of God, which is evident in the account of creation. The complementary nature of human sexuality is affirmed and the sexual difference between man and woman are pronounced as good. Therefore we affirm human sexuality to be the gift of God, which enriches and fulfils our personhood. Besides, the diverse sexual orientation is also affirmed, much to the contrariety, to have the divine image within.

In the same manner, the traditional interpretation of being created in the Image of God is also questioned. Genesis 1:27 reads, "So God created humankind in his image, in the Image of God he created them, male and female he created them." What is being indicated here is that to realize the totality of being created in the image cannot be represented by a single human entity, but only to all of them together. Rather it should be looked at collectively which implies that God is best represented by diversity, the whole diversity of the world in terms of different cultures, genders, races, castes, sexual orientation and religious experiences   only can represent who God is. It is indicating that no single unit or entity can claim superiority over the other because both male and female were created simultaneously in the image of God with the blessing of fruitfulness and dominion. The text does not suggest male headship nor female submission, both are charged with responsibility for all of God's creation (Gen 1:26, 28). Hence it is clear that both man and woman are necessary for the completion of God's creation of humankind. Eventually it is in only in the togetherness of the whole entity that the totality of being created in God's image can be realized.

Besides varied explanations on this idea, one can arrive at the fact that human life in itself is the presence of the image of God. Different entities of humankind are God's intention in creation and this challenges the traditional understanding of 'created in the image of God' that sidelines the sexual disorientation from being created 'perfect'. The notion that such people are being cursed, damned to hell has to change. Because people are precious to God, because we reflect something of our Creator, each person is to be valued. None is to be denigrated, belittled of cursed (James 3:9-12). In some special way they reflect God's image.

On the other hand, Johannes de Moore, while defending the androgynous nature of original man in the priestly writer, asserts that the first man was a bisexual human being.[9] Rather than such an extreme assimilation of the priestly code by reworking the ancient traditions one can maintain that, to be the image bearer of God humankind we are set apart from animals. That they are created according to their kind (Gen 1: 21, 24, and 25). Human sexuality, therefore, must be seen as neither a mistake by God nor the consequence of man's sin, but as part of God's intention and therefore a meaningful aspect of human existence.[10] Since it was God's intention in the creation of diverse kinds, that we should not separate the 'others' on the basis of being perfect or having normal sexual orientation and so on. Rather they should be looked at as co-creatures, furthering the scope as co-travellers in life's journey and together confess one Lord, one faith, one baptism, one God and Father of all (Eph 4:5-6). Sexuality is presented as fundamental to what it means to be human and thus must be taken very seriously. [11] Everyone belongs to the one body of Christ, and each of you is a separate and necessary part of it (1 Cor 12:27), must challenge the church's approach to the people with different sexual orientation.

4.   Siding and Standing with the Excluded and Outcast

One of the theological principles which emanate from the Scripture is God's identification with the poor, the outcast and the oppressed. However one can possibly question as to how far this can be applied to the LGBTIQs. Many Christians will still have reservations to come to this conclusion.

But further studies reveals that they fall within this category, on the fact that they are the persons against whom the existing laws are enforced arbitrarily, continuously threatened from every angle of their life aspect, with loss of job, respect, dignity and being ostracized.

Having said this, it is noteworthy that conversations on these key affected people, namely the LGBTIQs are being carried forward worldwide. Deliberations from different perspectives point to the fact that it is not just concerning some particular church or region but it should be the conversation of the life of the Church. The traditional concept of the church as *ekklesia, qahal* which means an assembly of the people is being deviated with the double standard hierarchical system and attitude. Our church is a worshipping community where everyone comes to praise and rejoice in the Lord in worship (Psalm 100). The motive of the church as a worshipping community where everyone can come and be part of the body of church should not be pushed aside with its stereotypical attitude particularly to the term "LGBTIQ" and also to the member of the LGBTIQ community. Created in the Image of God, asserts the accountability of all entities who long for liberation. Perfection or goodness can be complete only when there is no discrimination on the basis of sex, caste, colour, and race. Only when all of God's creation is equally treated in the sense of sameness and enjoy opportunities -that life has to offer, equality can be realized.

Even in the modern society and churches, a mistaken attitude is common and thus it results –in isolation, exclusion, discrimination and stigmatization. As hinted earlier our society and churches are rooted in the traditional understanding of perfection and hierarchy in the creation and therefore people with sexual disorientation are treated poorly, as inferior, cast out sinful and damned beings. Our theology should be articulated to stand with the excluded ones against the social and political structures that deprive them of the law and rights and privileges of full members of - society. This should go together with the concern for justice and compassion for the marginalized. This will help us appreciate anew the paradoxical relation between sin and grace, affirm the transforming power of salvation and give an identity in Jesus Christ for human character and moral choices, in which both love and discipling of one another will be embraced.

Endnotes

[1] Hermeneutics in simple term is the theory of text interpretation. Hermeneutic of Suspicion is the phrase first used by Paul Ricouer who says that all hermeneutics involves suspicion; which means, the text presents us with a challenge to believe that the true meaning of the text emerges only through interpretation. Interpretation is ocassioned by a gap between the real meaning of the text and its apparent meaning, and in the act of interpretation suspicion plays a pivotal role. See for details, David Stewart, "The Hermeneutic of Suspicion," *Journal of Literature and Theology*, 3/3 (November, 1989):296-309.

[2] Chrisida Nithyakalyani, "Affirming Beauty in God's Creation: Probing Biblical Sanctions" in *Disruptive Faith, Inclusive Communities: Church And Homophobia*, edited by George Zachariah &Vincent Rajkumar (Delhi, Bangalore: ISPCK/CISRS), 108-120.

[3] Theodore W. Jennings, "Homosexuality and Christians Faith: A Theological Reflection," *The Christian Century* (February 16, 1977):139.

[4] Elizabeth Schüssler Fiorenza, *Wisdom Ways: Introducing Feminist Biblical Interpretation* (Maryknoll, New York: Orbis Books, 2001), 118.

[5] Chrisida Nithyakalyani, "Affirming Beauty in God's Creation: Probing Biblical Sanctions" in *Disruptive Faith, Inclusive Communities...*, op.cit, 109.

[6] Sandhya Jha, "Creating a Safe Place for God's Children," in *Disruptive Faith, Inclusive Communities...*, ibid, 238.

[7] Cited by ibid, 238-239.

[8] Gordon Cowans, "Towards a Liberatory Theology of Disability: Humanity in Creation and the Image of God" in *Disabled God Amidst Broken People: Doing Theology from Disability Perspective*, edited by Wati Longchar and Gordon Cowans (Manila: ATESEA, 2007), 42.

[9] De Moore understands the *imago dei* in a physical way, this androgynous nature of man can be extended to a duality in God. the fact that "androgynous deities are not only creator-gods who are predominantly depicted as male but also great goddesses like the Babylonian Istar, the Hurrian Sauska, the Ugaritic 'Anatu and the Phoenician Tinnit". He concludes that "apparently bisexuality was seen as a sure sign of exalted divinity, a quality reserved for the highest divine beings who transcended the all too human limitations of split gender". Cited by E Noort, "The Creation of Man and Woman in Biblical and Ancient Near Eastern Traditions", in *The Creation of Man and Woman: Interpretations of the Biblical Narratives in Jewish and Christian Traditions*, edited by Gerard p. Luttikhuizen (Leiden, Boston: BRILL, 2000), 1-18.

[10] Stephen Sapp, Biblical Perspectives on Human Sexuality, ebsco.pdf

[11] Stephen Sapp, *Biblical Perspectives on Human Sexuality.*

Monasticism and Sexuality

S. D. Deva Jothi Kumar

Introduction

Every religious institution has its own hang-ups about sex – but most of them don't want sex to be a topic of conversation. The church at large feels the same and tear themselves apart arguing about the role of women, contraception, abortion, homosexuality and how to deal with revelations about gay marriages. And our modern Christian pride in our openness about talking and laughing about sex in almost any situation is simply a reversal of two millennia of largely negative Christian chatter on that same subject. This negative attitude is caused due to complex and perplexed ideas developed over sexuality. Monasticism which sneaked in to the church and became a source of its development, by the way of setting the fashion of its growth and the norms related to its institutional structures were set to have insisted and legitimized patriarchal and heterosexual orientations.

Origin and development of Christian culture over gender and sexuality

Christianity was never conceived by Jesus however when it took a form of a movement it had forcibly and hastily adopted traditions, practices and moral standards available closer to its birth place. Jesus being the central figure in this religion had very little to say about sex. True, he insisted on monogamy in marriage, and on no divorce (both insistences being new to his own Jewish culture, and rather shocking) – but beyond that, virtually nothing.

So how did our Christian churches turn Jesus' few quiet words about sex into an ill-tempered centuries-long argument? Probing in to Christianity's origins, we can find that it springs out of two cultures, one Jewish, the other Greek. Judaism had a very positive attitude to sex, as long as it was concerned with procreation, building up families: God's Chosen People, after all, were constantly threatened with annihilation at the hands of great empires around them, and needed to 'increase and multiply'. Any sexual alternative, such as celibacy or homosexuality, was liable to get categorized as 'an abomination'. And Judaism was very male-centred – there really is an ancient Jewish prayer which runs: "Blessed be thou O Lord God, who has not made me a Gentile, a woman, or an ignoramus."[1]

But when the first Christians thought about sex, they heard other, more powerful voices, from completely outside the Jewish world. The prestige culture was that of the ancient Greeks: there was a Greek-style town (called Sepphoris) just down the road from Jesus' Galilean home in Nazareth. The Roman imperial power that ran Jesus' homeland deeply admired the Greeks, and between them, they created the classical civilization which, as we know from many an epic movie or any visit to museums full of Greek and Roman sculpture, celebrated physical beauty, especially male beauty.[2] So it's easy to tell a simple story: Christianity poised between Jewish family life and Greek easygoing acceptance of male homosexuality, with Roman culture a den of decadence and orgies. That contrast became a disapproving Christian cliché: Christians loudly condemned Greek and Roman immorality.

Monasticism

The word monasticism is derived from the Greek word "monochos" (living alone).Monasticism is the devotional practice of individuals who live ascetic and typically cloistered lives that are dedicated to Christian worship. It as a reaction against worldliness in the church.[3] It began to develop early in the history of the Christian church, modelled upon Scriptural examples and ideals, including those in the Old Testament, but not mandated as an institution in Scriptures. It has come to be regulated by religious rules (e.g., the rule of St. Basil, the rule of St. Benedict, the rule of St. Augustine) and, in modern times, the canon law of the respective Christian denominations that have forms of monastic living. Those living the monastic life is known by the generic term, monk) and nun (women). In modern English, they are also known by the gender-neutral term "monastics". Monastic life plays important role in Christian church especially in in Catholic and Orthodox traditions.

If we read the New Testament with a fresh eye, we will notice something missing: no mention of monasteries, monks or nuns, anywhere. Yet the monastic life has been crucial for later Christian history. The fact that it can be first traced to Syria in Christianity makes it most plausible that Syrians, the ancient east's great traders, brought back the idea from India, where for centuries there had been exactly that sort of institution in Hinduism and Buddhism. Syrian merchants introduced it into Christianity as an invisible import, along with all the Indian and Chinese luxuries which they sold around the Mediterranean.

The approach to monasticism is only the approach to Christianity through the narrow door. It is simply the man in the monastery is trying to ensure a more single minded attention to the work.[4] Monasticism is not an ideal only; it is a way. Neither aesthetic nor abstract beauty is the object of monk's search. The monk in looking for beauty which is moral and supernatural which can be discovered on earth and perfectly posed only in heaven.[5] So there was a background noise in the Mediterranean culture that increasingly celebrated austerity and elevated the soul above the flesh. It chimed with a new movement, which first appeared in the Christian world in the second century AD.

Monks on Gender and Sexuality

Church fathers who were trained in monasticism praised and blamed, honoured and disparaged women as the perpendicular example for ambivalence. One undoubted manifestation of this ambivalence lies in the fathers' selective appeal to the bible. Their interpretation of the scriptures tailored their views on women subordination. They quoted and used the bible to serve to bolster and justify traditional attitudes toward women, attitudes derived from the Old Testament's adulation of the busy house wife and warnings against "loose women," pagan antiquity's ideal of the chaste and retiring matron, and the unfavourable representation of women in some classical literature, especially satire.[6] Women were viewed as almost solely in their sexual roles as allayers of male lust and as bearers of male's children were now to raise to personhood through renunciation of sexual function. Just as the fathers wariness about marriage stemmed first and foremost from their ambiguity.

The seed of misogyny that was implanted in the Christian psyche by the bible was brought to its fullness by the fathers of the church. The hatred of women is found almost without exception in all the major Christian theologians throughout Christianity's early formative centuries. Clement of Alexandria[7] in his book *PEDAGOGUES* writes about women that "the consciousness of their own nature must evoke feelings of shame".[8] According to him, women are the weaker sex. "Nor are women to be deprived of bodily exercise. They are not to be encouraged to engage in wrestling or running, but are to exercise them in spinning, weaving and superintending in cooking if necessary… And it is no disgrace for them to apply themselves to the mill. Nor is it a reproach to a wife-housekeeper and helpmeet-to occupy her in cooking, so that it may be palatable to her husband. And if she shake up the couch, reach a drink to her husband when thirsty, set food on the table as neatly as possible, and so give herself exercise tending to sound health, the instructor will approve of a woman like this, who stretches forth her arms for a useful task, resets her hands on the distaff opens her hand to the poor, and extends her wrists to the beggar".[9] Tertullian[10] opined women neither were to teach or to baptize nor were they to engage in any kind of public discussion, either debating a theological question or asking questions for their own instruction.[11]

Origen[12] an influential theologian is well known for his hatred of sex and women. According to him, women are worse than animals because they are continuously full of lust. Origen does not approve of the sexual act even in marriage.[13] He further said women are the devil's gate way and deserter of the divine law … women destroyed so easily God's image in man. On account of their desertion – that is, death- even the Son of God had to die.[14] St. Gregory[15] the Bishop of Constantinople had this to say about women, "Fierce is the dragon and cunning the asp, But women have the malice of both."[16] St Ambrose[17] says the way women were created tells her second class status " remember that God took the rib out of Adam's body, not a part of his soul, to make her. She was not made in the image of God like the man.[18] "The whole of her bodily beauty is nothing less than phlegm, blood, bile, rheum, and the fluid of digested food… if you considered what is stored up behind those lovely eyes, the angle of the nose, the mouth and cheeks you will agree that the well-proportioned body is merely a whitened sepulchre."[19]

Austerity and celibacy mandate for monastery

One of the most interesting facets of human sexuality to come to the fore in the recent years has been the concern over the psychosexual growth and development of celibates. As we have become more conscious of the fact that sexuality touches people on every level of their existence, it has become clear that sexuality pertains not only to married persons, but to all humans. For celibates as for everyone else, sexuality is a great and good gift of God. Celibates are called to serve God and their fellow human beings as sexed persons, not as people whose sexuality has somehow been neutralized or taken away. The love celibates bring to the world is profoundly qualified by sexuality.[20]

Asceticism has provided greater freedom to Christian women. Most of the fathers believed that women who renounced the sexual life were elevated above their natural abject condition to the degree that they almost constituted a "third sex," so much did they change from females still in the thrall of Eve's birth Pains and submission to husbands. Marriage by definition placed women in an inferior role; sexual functioning in itself made women subordinate. Thus it can be argued that in one way in which the father effectively encouraged greater freedom for women was in their championing of asceticism.[21] This is a hyphenated interpretation of the fathers who justified woman subjective role.

St. Augustine of Hippo (c354- c450 AD)

Augustine gave his negative opinions on sex a biblical twist: he turned to the story of Adam and Eve in the Garden of Eden, and decided that God's punishment for their plucking the apple from the Tree of Knowledge was to curse Adam and his wife with a new sensation – sexual lust. He suggested that before they ate the apple, Adam and Eve had enjoyed full control of their genitals. Their sexual intercourse had been calm, rational and dispassionate. After the fall came loss of control, the violent passions released in orgasm. Holiness demanded control.All ancient societies had regarded women as inferior; now Augustine taught that Eve had lured Adam into sexual passion. It's led to some extraordinary Christian misogyny, which has an extra depth to the West because Popes in the western (Latin or Catholic) church decided in the 11th and 12th centuries to take a remarkable step, which no other Christian church has imitated. The papacy made all its clergy behave like monks: from now on, all of them, not just those living the monastic life, would be celibate.[22]

St. Jerome (c 347- c420 AD)

Monastic chastity may have been introduced originally to curb- wrongful desire, it does not expect this alone. The mistake is to think of chastity as a holy discipline and not as a holy state. In fourth-century Rome, a highly influential Christian spokesman, Jerome, who fancied himself as a moral arbiter for the fabulously wealthy Roman families who were flocking in to the newly powerful church, had some extraordinary things to say about marriage. He perverted a parable of Jesus, and told his adoring pious ladies that wives would reap a 30-fold harvest of heavenly reward, but widows who did not remarry would get a 60-fold harvest. Top of the score came virgins, with a 100-fold prize. Jerome was so disgusted by sex and marriage that he advised a young and childless widow not to re-marry. Why he asked her, would she wish to imitate the dog in the Book of Proverbs, and "return to her own vomit"? To him, a woman is the root of all evil.[23]

Monasticism and homosexuality

Boswell observes that the relationship between religious life and rich history, which has been complicated by shifting majority attitudes toward same sex desire. He maintains that monastic life has been one of the most consistent and widespread institutionalized forms of homoerotic desire within Christian society, and he traces the encouragement of homoerotic romantic bonds among both male and female monasteries.[24]

Christian monastic communities have been a homosocial, mono-gendered environment, which has provided Christians with an opportunity to establish a religious existence outside of married life. In such homosocial environments, a fair number of people have been attracted to the same sex and have discovered meaningful relationships to the members of their own sex. Without such attraction, there would be no need for prohibitions against same sex contact, attachments, or sexuality in monasteries and convents.[25] He further documents how monastic communities were never free of homoerotic desire or secret love affairs. He demonstrates that many monastics developed strong feelings of intimacy and love with fellow monks.[26]

Brundage argues where there are prohibitions against homoerotic behaviours by monasteries, there is same sex activity. The texts explain that St. Augustine cautioned a group of monastic women to love one another, but not in a carnal fashion. Similarly St. Basil warns fellow monks of the dangers of a handsome, young monk. He understood well that attraction to the same sex can be a natural inclination, and he encouraged physically attractive young monks to hide their beauty. The second council of tours in 567 prohibited monks and priest from sleeping more than one to a bed. The Benedictine rule, along with most monastic rules and charters, instituted regulations to prevent sexual relations between monks. For example, St. Benedict mandated that a light be kept burning at night in the dormitory and that monks sleep with their clothes.[27]

A Cistercian abbot Aelred of Rievaulx (1109- 1166) gave homoerotic love a central place in his instruction to fellow monks. Earlier in his life Aelred was involved in an intimate relationship with a man, but he fell in his love for God and his love for another female. He abandoned his lover to devote himself more completely to God, and he then began to reconcile his passionate love for God with his passionate love for men. He wrote candidly about his passionate attachments with a monk called Simon and with other monks. Russell is willing to label the Cistercian abbot's homoeroticism as gay.[28]

Conclusion

Christian understanding of sexuality from its very beginning adopted negative approach towards sex woman and sexuality. While poised between Jewish family life and Greek easygoing acceptance of male homosexuality, with the Roman culture, it loudly condemned Greek and Roman immorality. And to make Christian movement unique and dissimilar from other existing religions of his time Paul set being heterosexual as a moral standard for this budding movement. Monks continue to ride on this patriarchal wheel and maintained hatred against sex and hence demoralized woman. Celibacy was made compulsory in a way to prevent priests from being nepotistic and to fully concentrate on their religious service. However in the monasteries, the impulse to homosexuality as an instinct in human sexual appeal continued to dominate, hence rigid rules for austerity and celibacy were imposed. In the recent past, the church had realized its mistake for being heavy on woman homo sex and other sexual orientations. It began to understand their sexual orientations as God's design plan. Celebration of marriage as a holy sacrament, Pope Francis' speech on people who have same sex orientation, that they cannot be stopped from worshipping Jesus and lesser arrogance shown towards austerity, woman, sex and sexuality, all invite us to understand that the church started correcting the aberrations committed in the past.

Endnotes

[1] Kathey Rudy,*Sex and the church: Gender Homosexuality, and the transformation of the church (Michigan: Beacon Press, 1997)* 27.

[2] Early E. Cairns, *Christianity Through Centuries* (Michigan: Grand Rapids, 1996) 42.

[3] William G Young, *Handbook of Source materials for students of church history* (Delhi: ISPCK, 1999), 306.

[4] Dom Hubert Van Zeller, *Approach to Monasticism* (USA: Sherd & Ward, INC, 1960), 8.

[5] Dom Hubert Van Zeller, *Approach to Monasticism*, 173,174.

[6] Elizabeth A Clark, *women in the Early Church* (Wilmington: Michael Glazier, INC. 1983) 15-16. Hereafter quoted as Elizabeth Clark.

[7] Greek theologian, head of the catechetical school at Alexandria and known as father of Greek Church Lived Between c150-215.

[8] Ranke Heinemann, *Eunuchs for the kingdom of heaven: Women, Sexuality and the Catholic* (Doubleday: 1990), 186.

[9] Karen Jo Torjesen, *when women were priests:* (Newyork: 1995) 84.

[10] Quintus Septimius Florens Tertullian From Cartage in the Roman Province of Africa Lived Between (c160-c225 AD).

[11] Karan Jo, 161.

[12] Theologian From West (c185-c254AD).

[13] Ranke Heinemann, *Eunuchus for the kingdom of heaven: 52.*

[14] Karen jo, 36.

[15] Gregory of Nazianus, a theologian lived between (329-390AD).

[16] Karen Jo 36.

[17] Archbishop of milanmost influential ecclesiastical figure in 4th century. 19 PheliesVivian, *The Church and Modern Thought: an influence in to the ground of unbelief and an appeal for candour,* (Harvard, 1906), 145.

[18] Warner marina, *Alone of all her sex: the myth and the cult of Virgin Mary* (Oxford; 1990) 77.

[19] Felix Podimattam, *Celibacy and sexual integration* (Delhi: Media House, 1997) 7-8.

[20] Elizabeth Clark, 17.

[21] PheliesVivian, *The Church and Modern Thought: an influence in to* 32.

[22] Ranke Heinemann, *Enuchus for the Kingdom of Heaven, 132.*

[23] Boswell, John, "Homosexuality and religious life: A Historical Approach, "*In Homosexuality in the priesthood and the religious life,* edited by Jeannine Gramick, (New York: Crossroad, 1989).125.

[24] Robert E. Goss, Timothy Murphy (ed), Christianity: Monastic Traditions, *Reader's Guide to Lesbian and Gay Studies*(Routledge) 136.

[25] Boswell, John, *Christianity, Social Tolerance, and Homosexuality: Gay People in Western Europe from the beginning of the Christian era to the Fourteenth century,*(Chicago: university of Chicago press, 1980) 57.

[26] James Brundage A, *Law, Sex, and Christian Society in Medieval Europe,* (Chicago: University of Chicago Press, 1987) 45.

[27] Russell, Kenneth C., "Aelred, the gay abbot of Rievaulx" *Studia Mystica,* 5(4), 1982. 125.

Historiography of John Chrysostom's Concept on Homosexuality: Mapping the Partnership Trajectories[1]

Bandangtemjen

1.   Introduction

Saint John Chrysostom[2] was a courageous man whose outspoken criticism of the Empress eventually led to his exile and death in the desert. This paper is to investigate John Chrysostom concept of Homosexuality and how he structured his attack against it. Chrysostom's construction of Homosexuality is a conglomeration of numerous discourses of abnormality and criminality. This paper -firstly, deals with the classification of Historiography and brief sketches of Chrysostom's life and the methodological issues related to his understanding towards same-sex.[3] However, more efforts will be given to how Chrysostom understood the discourse of nature in relation to Homosexuality and specifically its effect on his understanding of gender inversion and ambiguity, as well as passion, pleasure, and the affluent life. Finally, the paper examines Chrysostom's understanding of Homosexuality in the light of which reconstructing the image of the Homosexual-as partners in Gods Mission.

2.   Historiography

2.1. General Historiography

Historio-mology[4] of Historiography literally means the art of writing history,[5] especially the writing of history based on the critical analysis, evaluation and an examination of sources, the selection of particulars from the authentic materials in those sources, and the synthesis of those particulars into a narrative that will stand the test of critical methods. One of the eminent historians, E.H Carr, defined history as a continuous process of interaction between the historian and his facts, an unending dialogue between the present and the past. [6] The study of historiography demands a critical approach that goes beyond the mere examination of historical fact. Keith Jenkins used this term to refer to the particular angle or take of the historian. This approach enables us to view the study of history (the past) necessarily a study of - (historians), historiography therefore being considered not as an extra to the study of history but as actually constituting it.[7] Hence a survey of-this different genre of historiography is needed to identify the growth of historical social consciousness.

Earlier, known as Philosophy of History, it was first used by Voltaire in the eighteenth century to denote 'critical or scientific history which was free from medieval Christian history and its perspective.'[8] Hegel used it in a different sense, to indicate a universal or world history which is ontological history of the progress of mankind that is of Europe.[9] Now the term historiography is applied to designate the epistemological study of- history writing. However - the discourse of history of historiography reveals, how differently homosexuality has been perceived and judged at different times in different cultures.

2.2. Classical Historiography

The classical historiography refers to the Ancient Greek and Roman historiographies. The classical scholar's approach was more speculative towards the past and the course of events. M.C. Lemon identifies three important characteristics of the classical Graeco-Roman historiography.[10]

1. The notion that time, and the events it contains, go round in a huge circle. They follow the example from nature. The seasons repeat. If the 'nature' goes round in a circle, so does man and society. It gave the idea that history repeats itself. Not only that it gave rise to essentialism which means that the things and events are essentially same, and therefore no change is affected or possible.

2. Another idea related to the idea of history of the classical period was the belief in fate and fortune. It means that the things and

events are simply as they are and there is no explanation for them. And indeed, in both Greek and Roman mythology, so widely exploited and much beloved in classical literature, 'fate' was a god-namely' the Fates which determined one's character, destiny and time of death.

3. The third idea is the principle of growth. Everything has come to being, they grow to fulfil their end and then decay. This is the foundation of the theological principle. The classical Graeco-Roman historians followed these principles in their historical formulations. Graeco- Roman historiography does not cover the entire ancient world of history writing. Ancient India, China, and the Hebrew world has produced histories of different worldviews. But they do not come under the scope of this essay because of time and space limitations.[11]

2.3. Newer Historicism

The term New Historicism was coined by an American critique Stephan Greenblat.[12] It is a method based on the parallel reading of literary and non-literary texts, usually of the same historical period. New historicism refuses to 'privilege' the literary text: instead of a literary foreground and a historical background it envisages and practices a mode of study in which literary and non-literary texts are given equal weight and constantly inform or interrogate each other.[13]

So the newer historicism is a form of literary theory which aims at understanding intellectual history through literature and literature through its cultural milieu. This approach' understands past literature or text, as available to historians only through languages and texts. Henceforth, sub-literary texts and uninspired non-literary texts all came to be read as documents of historical discourse, side by side with the larger emphasis on literature. The ontological fact is that the past no longer exists only the textual remains. Therefore both literary and non-literary texts circulate inseparably. Thus, the Newer Historicism acknowledge both the literary theory not merely as a work of literature that is influenced by its author's times and circumstances, but that the critic's response to that work is also affected by his/her environments and beliefs. The only access to any past event is through reading and interpreting its textual content as it reveals more about the text and its history.

3.   Terminology of Homosexuality

Historically, the ancient Greeks had no word that corresponded to the modern usage of the word "homosexual." *Paiderastia,*[14] as the closest they came to it, that meant literally "boy love," that is, a relation between an older male and someone younger, usually a youth between the ages of fourteen and twenty. The older man was called *erastes* or lover.

The word "homosexual" comes from the Greek root "homo," meaning "same,"[15] although the word itself was not coined until the late nineteenth century. It can be used either as an adjective (as in a homosexual act, a homosexual bar) or as a noun that describes men or women who have a preferential sexual attraction to people of their same sex over a significant period of time. Members of the same sex and generally do not find themselves particularly attracted sexually to people of the opposite sex, neither of these two conditions are required to fit the definition we have offered.[16] Homosexuality refers to sexual attraction involving thoughts, feelings, and actions toward a person of the same sex. These thoughts, feelings, and actions may be covert or overt, that is, they may take place only in the person's inner mental life or they may be expressed either directly or indirectly in words and actions.

4.   Typology of Homosexuality

It is possible to construct a typology of homosexual relationships. In some societies, the most common type of same-sex relationship is highly structured and institutionalized. The typology of homosexuality can be further divided into various norms. They are:

4.1. Close-Couple homosexuals living in a one-to-one same-sex relationship. They have few sexual problems, few sexual partners, and infrequently engage in cruising (searching for a sexual partner).

4.2. Open-Couple homosexuals living in a one-to-one same-sex relationship but typically have many outside sexual partners and spent a relatively large amount of time cruising.

4.3. Functional homosexuals are those who are not 'coupled', who have a high number of sexual partners and few sexual problems.

4.4. Dysfunctional homosexuals are not 'coupled' and while scoring a high number of partners or the amount of sexual activity have a substantial number of sexual problems.

4.5. Asexual homosexuals are low in sexual interest and activity and are not 'coupled'. They tend to be less exclusively homosexual and more secretive about their homosexuality than others.[17]

5.   Biographical Sketch of John Chrysostom: A Brief Introduction

St. John Chrysostom (347-407) Patriarch of Constantinople, who was born in Antioch, son of a general in the imperial army, and a Christian mother Anthusa.[18] Best known for his liturgies, homilies and writings in defence of the Christian faith, was an ardent missionary advocate. He was baptized (c.370) became a hermit (c.381) and was ordained a priest in Syrian Antioch from 386-397.[19] After which he became a bishop of Constantinople on 15 December 397.[20] He studied the law under The great pagan orator Libanius. At Antioch, he studied theology under Diodore of Tarsus, the leader of the Antiochene School.[21] Early in life he felt a call to the monastic life. As the care of his widowed mother (Anthusa) prevented the immediate fulfilment of his desire, he lived some time under the rule of this zeal and later became a hermit.[22] As the ablest Greek preacher of the fourth-century, he came to be called Chrysostom, "golden-mouthed (Chrysostom, meant "golden-mouthed)."[23]

He was consecrated bishop of Constantinople in 398 and sent monks from Constantinople to evangelize pagan peoples including Goths.[24] Refusing to depend on imperial decrees or the use of force to win converts, he insisted that the example of Christian living is the most effective way to evangelize non-Christians. As a patriarch of Constantinople, he spoke with such fire and eloquence that the congregation frequently interrupted with applause. As late as the eighteenth century, Peter the Great, no model of piety himself, ordered that all Orthodox priests must possess and read his works. He ranks as the most influential of the Greek Fathers, second only to Augustine in his influence on Christendom as a whole.[25]

Chrysostom who was an extremely able orator and fearless preacher and set about correcting abuses was exiled in 403, he continued to encourage missions to Cilicia and Phoenicia. He was recalled to his Episcopal office after one year but was again exiled to Cucusus in Armenia. In he was summoned to a more remote exile in Iberia, but he died en-route on 14th September 407 CE.[26] Over the centuries, both East and West came to recognize his sanctity and greatness. As a modern writer put it, 'he whose life was embittered and destroyed by the enemies, now has no enemies at all.'

6.   Methodological Issues

St. John Chrysostom has compiled his methodological issues towards homosexuality basesd on socio-cultural settings of that contexts. So he began his methodological historiography based on the very cultural context of Greco-Romans and Jews as well. It came as a surprise to find how much literature on homosexuality had survived in the form of Greek poetry, biography, history, literature, arts and philosophical ways.[27]

6.1. Jewish Cultural Influence

Since the Torah[28] is fundamental to the Judaic tradition, that text's denunciations of same-sex sexuality carried over into rabbinical commentary and religious practice. Early Judaic scholars accepted the prohibition on male same-sex relations in Leviticus.[29] Homosexuality was clearly condemned in the earliest Jewish tradition. In the Bible, we are told, "And if a man lay with mankind, as with womankind both of them have committed abomination; they shall surely be put to death, their blood shall be upon them."[30] Christianity was the child of Judaism and inherited much from the earlier faith. Historically, Jews have often been subjected to persecution by the same persons and governments that persecuted those who engaged in same-sex relations.

6.2. Greek Cultural Influence

In ancient Greece, homosexuality in certain forms was widely accepted as natural in all segments of society. Plato's Symposium[31] praised the virtues of male homosexuality and suggests that pairs of homosexual lovers would make the best soldiers. Many of the Greek mythological gods and heroes such as Zebus, Hercules, Poseidon and Achilles were linked with homosexual behaviour.[32] The ancient Greeks wrote openly about sexual matters, as well as provided frank depictions of sexuality in their artwork. Consequently, there is a wealth of material to draw on in discussions of ancient Greek sexuality, although almost all of it was written or made by men.[33] The fact is that in all history, no society has aroused the same enthusiasm as ancient Greece. Greek achievements in literature, art, and architecture[34] set norms for the Western world as well. When we think, we still employ the intellectual categories its philosophers and scientists devised. The Greeks charm many by their sociability, their lively openness to ideas, and their liberality of spirit. Its peculiar note of exaltation echoes repeatedly through all levels of Greek society. Like the rest of humanity, the ancient Greek was susceptible to various erotic moods heroic, tender, frivolous, ribald, even, on occasion, brutal.[35] In ancient Greece, there was tolerance and even enthusiasm regarding male homosexuality in certain forms.[36] However, the exclusive homosexuality and homosexual contact between adults were frowned upon and homosexual contact between adults and boys under the age of puberty was illegal.

6.3. Roman Cultural Influence

In the early days of the Roman Empire, homosexuality was apparently unregulated by law and homosexual behaviour was common. When the Roman Empire became Christian in the fourth century, the Old Testament death penalty for male homosexual behaviour was incorporated into Roman law.

6.4. Early Christianity

As Christianity was born when Rome stood at the peak of its power and Greek culture still dominated the Mediterranean world. Although, most historians who have written on the subject suggest that Christianity more or less from the beginnings strongly condemned and persecuted homosexuality. The primary ammunition for the church's position against homosexuality came from the writings of St Augustine[37] and Thomas Aquinas,[38] who both suggested that any sexual acts that could not lead to conception were unnatural and therefore sinful.[39] Using this line of reasoning, the church became a potent force- in the regulation of sexual behaviour. John Chrysostom was the contemporary of St Augustine who harshly denounced same-sex relations.

6.5. Patristic Tradition

Early Christian theologians, collectively known as the Patristic writers, harshly denounced same-sex relations and looked upon any type of sex as immoral. Their role in shaping early Christian doctrine, including attitudes toward sexuality, helps explain ancient Rome's increased hostility to same-sex relations after Christianity became the Roman Empire's dominant religion subsequent to the rule of Emperor Constantine. The early church also held that several writings against homosexual lust. John Chrysostom was an early proponent of that Christian reinterpretation. His works and sermons are notable in part for being an early example of the melding of anti-Semitism[40] with a loathing of same-sex love.

7.   Mapping John Chrysostom's Concept of Homosexuality

In mapping Chrysostom's concept of homosexuality, one has to illustrate how much Chrysostom despised homosexuality. Surely, these aspects will reveal themselves rather, it is to enquire about those pervaded and integrated discursive frameworks, strategies, and apparatuses operating within Chrysostom's rhetoric against homosexuality. Thus, the aim is to critically investigate how John Chrysostom understood homosexuality and how he structured his invective against it.

In Chrysostom's thought, many concepts may be grouped under homosexuality, especially pederasty, male courtesanship and prostitution, and quite often males who simply act or appear effeminate. The problem we face is that Chrysostom rarely discerns between persons engaged in pederasty, same-sex prostitution, or same-sex relations. Despite their considerable differences, these are all part of the same transgression to Chrysostom. Chrysostom's invective against homosexuality is based exclusively on paradoxes and opposites. This paradoxical rhetoric facilitates the bifurcation of sexual morality, setting up normal sexual intercourse against the abnormal, godly lust against excessive and unnatural lust, true pleasure against the false, moderation and self-sufficiency against affluence. Homosexuality is seen as an inversion of nature (Ref. Romans 1:25-32).[41] The cultural roles of men and women are inverted, while lust and pleasure, originally meant to stimulate sexual intercourse for the purpose of conception, and are twisted into something unnatural and excessive. The initiator of this inversion is the devil, and it is especially evident in the way heretics invert orthodox doctrines.[42]

Persons who participated in homosexual relations were especially maleficent to Chrysostom. In fact, all of the invective discourses

Chrysostom used against the Jews were also used against persons "guilty" of same-sex passion. Furthermore, as we saw above, Chrysostom used the stereotype of the effeminate male to denigrate the masculinity of Jewish men. Because of the highly androcentric nature of the Roman world, an assault against one's masculinity was an assault against the very core of one's identity. Even in the case of women, masculinity was often used as a tool of invective: a woman who was too masculine, whether in behaviour or appearance, was commonly antagonized.[43]

In an early essay, against the opponents of the monastic life, Chrysostom had urged parents to immure their sons in monasteries to preserve them from this evil. Chrysostom made homosexuality as its unique sin. "If any one disbelieves hell, let him consider Sodom, let him reflect upon Gomorrah, the vengeance that has been inflicted . . . Would you wish also to know the cause for which these things were then done? It was one sin, a grievous one, yet but one. The men of that time had a passion for boys, and on that account they suffered this punishment."[44]

During his tenure in Antioch, Chrysostom preached a series of sermons.[45] Those sermons were, consequently, the fullest and most detailed ecclesiastical pronouncement on homosexuality. Liberal in his use of epithets, Chrysostom denounces male love as "monstrous," "Satanical," "detestable," "execrable," and "pitiable." Those who speak in defence of Greek love he calls "even worse than murderers . . . For there is not, there surely is not, a more grievous sin than this insolent dealing."[46]

Chrysostom also addresses the question of punishment. He follows Roman law in denouncing homosexuality chiefly as a contravention of ordained sex roles but prescribes the Jewish option of death by stoning: "For I should say not only that you have become a woman, but that you have lost your manhood, and have neither changed into that nature nor kept that which you had. You have been a traitor to both of them at once, deserving . . . to be driven out and stoned, as having wronged either sex."[47] Above all, in his homily homosexuality is no longer merely a detail in the story of the Cities of the Plain (Sodom and Gomorrah) but the prime cause of their destruction. Their men exchanged natural relations for the unnatural, and similarly the women gave up natural relations with men and were inflamed with passion for one another, men conducting shameless acts with men and receiving in themselves the due penalty for their error.[48]

8.   Reflection on John Chrysostom's Concept of Homosexuality

The concept of nature has always been inextricably linked with discussions of homosexuality. The same is true when it comes to Chrysostom's views on the topic. Therefore, the first steps in understanding Chrysostom's views on homosexuality would be to inquire what for him the function of nature is.

8.1. The Discourse of Nature

Chrysostom realized that nature is a very potent power discourse, the operation of naturalization, as a discursive strategy in Chrysostom. Chrysostom added authority to the argument. Nature in this instance is seen as a stable norm, and its authority derives from its divine origin. Thus, being in violation of nature is tantamount to insulting God. What is natural is good and normal, yet the unnatural is bad and abnormal. Along with the written and oral Torah, nature was the primary source from which the ancient Jewish sages deduced their wisdom. Most likely, this profound position of nature in Judaistic wisdom literature shaped Paul's argument of nature and homosexuality, thereby indirectly influencing Chrysostom.

Nature was the religio-ethical framework for early Judaism and Christianity; it also influenced Rabbinic formulations of purity and impurity well into late antiquity. Moreover, as Williams[49] has shown, nature, and especially the language of nature in terms of sexuality, was a common feature of Roman rhetoric.[50] Hence, when Chrysostom utilizes the discourse of nature he does so in a very Roman way. Appeals to the violation of nature and the unnatural were useful to Chrysostom, especially when the meaning of biblical terms related to homosexuality was ambiguous and the terms themselves unfamiliar and alien.

Chrysostom refers how the divine nature shines out of the very manner of creation, how he executes his creation in a way contrary to human procedures. Unlike many modern views on the topic, for Chrysostom there is no distinction between nature in "science" and religion, they are equivalent, nature proceeds from God.[51] Because of its authority, goodness, and structural fidelity, nature is something that should be imitated.

According to Chrysostom, one of the main activities of the devil is that he imitates nature in a contrary way. Natural imitation is another assumption behind arguments against homosexuality. Thus, what is important to see here is that homosexuality becomes taboo even at the level of speech and discourse, and Chrysostom believes that even speaking about homosexuality can cause shame.

8.2.   Gender inversion and gender ambiguity

The discourse of nature and naturalness was especially applied to ancient conceptualizations of gender difference and gender relations. When Chrysostom speaks of male and female "natures," they are not simply referring to the biological features of sex. Yet, male and female nature was more related to the cultural and societal expectations of men and women. Social status, for instance, also influenced formulations of gender roles and gender difference. We will see then that Chrysostom defames same-sex passion as a sin that disrupts the natural and conjugal roles of men and women.[52] Not so much in terms of sexual activity and passivity, but because of the apparent gender inversion which results in division and enmity between male and female, in the first instance, and secondly, because of the gender ambiguity it causes.

Chrysostom believed that homosexual behaviour caused a gender inversion, which replaced natural relations with the unnatural, and caused enmity between the sexes which made marriage obsolete. Chrysostom continues, "For this is the work of the devil, to subvert and overturn everything, to cross the boundaries that have been set from the beginning, and remove that which God has set in nature."[53] To delineate the unnaturalness and abnormality of homosexuality, Chrysostom presents an interesting yet dynamic diabology. The inversion of gender roles is caused by the devil, thereby rendering homosexuals demonic. This is the same reason why Chrysostom relates homosexuality with heresy from the very beginning.

8.3.   Homosexuality and Luxury

Chrysostom understands homosexuality as a consequence of the affluence and decadence of the wealthy. "From where are these evils brought forth?" Chrysostom asks, "from luxury, from not knowing God."[54] Affluence causes the "soul to get soft in all of this." Homosexuality should not simply be seen as a concept restricted to the sphere of sex and sexuality in Chrysostom's thought it is an entire habitus, a whole corporeal vernacular of which the most extreme expression is sexual, but it also exhibits numerous other social traits.

This demonstrates the dynamic interplays between wealth/poverty and sexuality. Chrysostom's negative attitude toward wealth includes the idea that it makes its keeper soft, wealth renunciation is seen as a defining characteristic of masculinity in Chrysostom,[55] the monks of course being most adept in this case. But by increasing one's wealth and luxury, one's manliness is also decreased. This was, according to Chrysostom, the great sin of Sodom that led to their demise.

8.4. Nature and Pleasure

There has been some confusion about Chrysostom's views on pleasure. Boswell[56] for instance, writes that "Chrysostom was influenced both by Manichean opposition to pleasure and Stoic reverence for nature, and this led him into the paradoxical position of condemning sexual pleasure."[57] Such a statement does not account for the complexity of Chrysostom's thought regarding the nature of pleasure, and Chrysostom was certainly not influenced by Manichean opposition to pleasure.[58] True, Chrysostom was skeptical of lust and pleasure, but he was not opposed to it in a Manichaean anti-somatic sense.

Chrysostom rather naturalizes pleasure in order to normalize and abnormalize various sexualities. Pleasure is confined to the marital relationship alone this is natural and true pleasure while all other forms of pleasure are in fact unnatural, false, and destructive. Nature reveals the will of God, which in turn has brought judgment on those engaging in same-sex passion. Nature shows the true purpose of lust and pleasure, and these passions may only be present within the context of marriage.

9. Reconstructing Chrysostom's Concept of Homosexuality for Inclusivity in Understanding Partnership in God's Mission

1.1. Gender Equality

Chrysostom's history speaks of male and female "natures," they are not simply referring to the biological natures of sex. Yet, male and female nature was more related to the cultural and societal expectations of men and women. When Chrysostom speaks of homosexuality he features the nature and role of male and female values. Social status, for instance, also influenced formulations of gender roles and gender difference. Slave women were treated very differently from freeborn women. [59]   Even one's religious affiliation played a role: the above discussion shows that Chrysostom labelled Jews and heretics as effeminate.[60] Nature in this instance is seen as a stable norm and its authority derives from its divine origin, to both the genders. Thus being in violation of nature is the same as to be insulting God. Perhaps, Chrysostom speaks of all who destroy - natural identity and its value,-and calls them even worse than murderers.

Every human being, created in the image of God, has the right to live as a full human being with dignity and honour. Therefore if the Churches believe that the life of any man or woman is sacred as that of a fully human person, then the Christian community must assume the responsibility of working towards the liberation of humanity in our society. Moreover, it is time to reconsider the traditional attitude towards homosexuality; for all humans are equal in the sight of God and they are to complement each other. Our society should annihilate the old patriarchal structures, which upholds gender discrimination in order to provide meaningful participation in God's mission.

9.2. Materialism and Spirituality

Homosexuality should not simply be seen as a concept restricted to the sphere of sex and sexuality. In Chrysostom's thought, it is a consequence of the affluence and decadence of the wealthy. This demonstrates the dynamic interplay- between the nature of materialism and spirituality as it plays in nature and sexuality.[61]. Chrysostom's negative attitude towards increasing one's wealth and luxury leads to the decrease in many areas of an individual life and community as well.

With the increasing influence and impact of materialism and luxury in post-modern era, many countries especially in Asia continue to experience challenges and stagnation in spirituality. These include loss of focus in discipleship and spiritual formation, loss of indigenous wisdom, character and values and infiltration of western culture and ideology through the various movements.

9.3. Identity Struggles

To Chrysostom, gender identity or the gender ambiguity supposedly caused by homosexuality was a major source of anxiety. Because of homosexual behaviour, men are no longer men. Whereas men had to be in relation with women, men now have relationships with other men as if they are women, yet they are something else.[62] The inversion of gender is therefore not absolute. Chrysostom explains how serious this gender ambiguity is:

> "For I do not only say that you have become a woman, but that you have also lost your masculinity, and have neither changed into that nature, nor kept that which you had, but you have become a traitor to both of them at once, and deserving to be driven out and stoned by both men and women, since you have betrayed the entire race."[63]

Male homosexual renders the male useless because he has lost his identity of masculinity. The loss of masculinity or the loss of manhood, implies that this man can no longer be identified as a man, the role that God destined for him. Most communities have experiences of identity crisis through history. In the process of post-colonial impact, some experienced a 'hybrid identity.'[64] Similarly to this is the question of what kind of world order is churches partnering in mission to project that is consistent with its hope for the kingdom of God, as the people of minority communities' rise to claim and identify their basic rights and rightful place in the world.

9.4. Mobilizing Ecumenism

According to Chrysostom, one of the main activities of the devil is that he imitates nature in a contrary way. Natural imitation is another assumption behind arguments against homosexuality, which caused to the partition in God's natural creation. Nature, as a discursive strategy, had various channels through which the flow of power was regulated. But nature in itself was also a modality for speech, dialogue and apparatus for speaking about things that are difficult and dangerous to express. It exhibited a very specific type of the pure and chaste. Thus, what is important to see here is that nature of language becomes unthinkable even at the level of speech and discourse of unity.

Enhancing Christian unity and cooperation is a vital nature of language to challenges with the Christian minority and multi-denominational context. In seeking to fulfil the great commission the present-day churches need not only a spiritual unity but now they need an effective church unity to witness the one Lord among the people. According to Pauline Webb,[65] one of the glorious values of interreligious unity is that it has to be a conversation of love rather than of logic. The language of spiritual experience is the language of the heart rather than of the head. This does not mean that it is mindless, but it does mean that we have to learn to listen and understand each others' languages. Language gives the partners a greater knowledge of each other and of each others' religious/church traditions, and thus helps people to overcome prejudices, misinformation and negative attitudes. Learning from the past history of ecumenism must not just be seen in functional terms but as a dynamic unity. Ecumenism is about a vision of God's household where the members seek to listen to a variety of voices, and to practice intra faith dialogue in order to promote peace, healing and reconciliation as partners in God's mission. A mission is God's mandate to God's people to participate in unity towards the continuing saving work. It belongs to the very nature of the church and her unity.

10. Conclusion

In order to understand Chrysostom's view on homosexuality, one needs to place it in his/her broader framework of historicity. Historians of homosexuality need to exercise caution when using sources like those of Chrysostom to reconstruct a form of "ancient homosexuality." The discourse on homosexuality, especially in the late Roman world, and was shaped by several other very complex discourses. It is made even more complex by the presence of the tautological intelligibility and gender complexity we see in the late ancient rhetoric of same-sex passion. The diverse changes in Roman homosexuality discourse, like the absence of an active/passive scheme of sexuality in late antiquity, also contribute to the problem. The point is that late ancient homosexuality cannot be read in isolation from these other discourses. Late ancient homosexuality was not what we would call a "sexual orientation" today.

The methodology of partnering historiography on John Chrysostom concept of homosexuality causes his outlook to be nature-centric, oppressive and paradoxical. New study should focus on the social formation of John Chrysostom concept of homosexuality and different possibilities of its origin. Instead of treating him (Chrysostom) as a monolithic identity, different historicity within the Chrysostom's concept must be traced and studied. Apart from theological significance, how far socio-cultural settings and Greco-Roman play important role in shaping his discourse on homosexuality is an important area of research. A post enlightenment historiography includes the study of traditions, memories, social settings, speeches, homily and records. to understand the socio-cultural and theological praxis of Chrysostom's views on homosexuality. So on mapping, John Chrysostom Trajectories is not a final answer to the historical problems of homosexuality. Instead, a critique of this historical methodology opens up a vast area of issues and debate on historical research.

Endnotes

1 Bandangtemjen, "Historiography of John Chrysostom's concept on homosexuality: Mapping the partnership trajectories," in *Samskriti*, School of Research, Leonard Theological College, Jabalpur, 2017, Vol 17 (1 & 2), 68-91.

2 St. John Chrysostom was one of the fourth century Church Father, who was known for his excellent homily and orator, as a result the name Chrysostom or 'Golden-Mouthed,' was attributed to him.

3 In this paper I will be using simultaneously the both term 'homosexuality' and 'same-sex.' The reasons is that as the survey shows there was no concrete terminology to coined until the late nineteenth century to correspond the words same-sex.

4 Historio-mology here I mean 'study of the origin and the discourses of the word,' especially the writing of historicity.

5 E. Sreedharan, *A Textbook of Historiography: 500 BC to AD 2000* (Delhi: Orient BlackSwan, 2009), 2.

6 E.H. Carr, *What is History?* (London: Macmillan, 1961; Harrondsworth: Penguin Book, 1988), 30.

7 Keith Jenkins, *Re-thinking History* (London: Routledge Classics, 1991; Chennai: Routledge, 2006), 14.

8 R.G. Collingwood, *The Idea of History* (London: Oxford University Press, 2004), 1.

9 Collingwood,. *The Idea of History* ..., 1

10 M. C. Lemon, *Philosophy of History* (London: Routedge Classics, 2008), 31-44, cited by Eappen Varghese, New Historicism and Michelle Foucault: Historiographical Missionary Account of Indian Christianity, *Mar Thoma Journal of Theology*, 1/1 (June 2012): 103-115.

[11] Lemon, *Philosophy of History...*, 31-34.

[12] Stephan Greenblat, *Renaissance- Self fashioning from more to Shakespeare* (London: Guilford Press, 1980).

[13] Peter Barry, *Beginning Theory* (New Delhi: Viva, 2008), 172, cited by Eappen Varghese, New Historicism and Michelle Foucault ..., 107.

[14] Pederasty- A term derived from the ancient Greek words for "boy"(*paida*) and "to desire" (*eran*, the verb form of eros), pederasty in ancient Greece was the socially idealized practice of men engaging in relationships with boys. The relationships were not necessarily consummated or even sexual in nature, although many were, and were ideally to be directed at the improvement of the boy's character. There is some debate over the age range that "boy" referred to, although from mid-teens to perhaps early 20s is a reasonable estimate. Pederasty is distinct from pedophilia (also from the ancient Greek, meaning the love of boys), in that the latter is thoroughly sexual in nature and directed at children. While many ancient Greeks praised pederasty, pedophilia was unacceptable and those caught were punished. The first extant use of the word *paiderastia* is in Plato's *Symposium*. (Ref. Brent L. Pickett, *Historical Dictionary of Homosexuality* (Lanham, Maryland: The Scarecrow Press. Inc., 2009), 153.

[15] Gilbert Herdt, "Homosexuality," *The Encyclopedia of Religion*, edited by Mircea Eliade, vol. 6 (New York: Macmillan Pub. Co.; London: Collier Macmillan Publishers, 1987): 445-452.

[16] Williams H Masters, Virginia E. Johnson and Robert C. Kolodny. *Sex and Human Loving* (Mumbai: Jaico Publishing House, 2006), 345.

[17] Masters, *Sex and Human Loving...*, 364-365.

[18] Norman A. Hurner, "Chrysostom, John." *Biographical Dictionary of Christian Mission*, edited by Gerald H. Anderson (Grand Rapids, Michigan: William B. Eerdmans Pub. Co. UK, 1998). 134-135.

[19] J.N.D. Kelly, *Golden Mouth: The Story of John Chrysostom Ascetic, Preacher and Bishop* (New York: Cornell University Press, 1995), 3.

[20] Hurner. "Chrysostom, John ..., 135.

[21] Tony Lane, *The Lion Book of Christian Thought* (Oxford: A Lion Paperback, 1984), 38.

[22] F. L. Cross, ed. *The Oxford Dictionary of the Christian Church* (London: Oxford University Press, 1874), 285.

[23] Hurner, "Chrysostom, John..., 135..

[24] Lane, *The Lion Book of Christian Thought* ..., 38.

[25] Crompton Louis, *Homosexuality and Civilization*. 3rd ed. (London: The Belkenap Press of Harvard University Press, [2003] 2004), 139.

[26] Hurner, "Chrysostom, John…, 135.

[27] Boswell. J., *Christianity, Social Tolerance, and Homosexuality: Gay People in Western Europe from the Beginning of the Christian Era to the Fourteenth Century* (Chicago: University of Chicago Press, 2009), 56-57.

[28] Torah; The five books that constitute the Torah are central to Judaism; the tradition's adherents consider them the most sacred of all religious texts. Although the Torah, or Law, is supposed to have been handed down by Moses, contemporary scholars agree that it is largely a compilation from centuries after Moses lived. The Torah most likely dates from the sixth century B.C.E. One of the books, Leviticus, contains a harsh denunciation of same-sex sexuality along with a prescribed penalty of death. Since the five books (Genesis, Exodus, Leviticus, Numbers, and Deuteronomy) were later incorporated into the Bible, the Torah's hostility to same-sex relations has also been central to the history of Christianity. Some have interpreted the proscription of same-sex relations as a primitive pro-natal policy, but the language and the context of the passage suggest concerns for ritual purity and avoidance of defilement, perhaps arising from suspicions of rival tribes that practiced same-sex cult prostitution. (Ref. E.E. Urbach, Torah, *The Encyclopedia of Religion*, edited by Mircea Eliade, vol.14 (New York: Macmillan Pub. Co.; London: Collier Macmillan Publishers, 1987):556-565.

[29] Pickett, *Historical Dictionary of Homosexuality* …, 111.

[30] Leviticus 20:13. *Revised Standard Version* of the Bible.

[31] Plato, an Athenian philosopher, friend and pupil of Socrates, whose ethical teachings are preserved in his early dialogues. In 387 BCE he founded the Academy, which was to remain a center of philosophical activity until 592 CE. His philosophies were to be particularly influential for the development of Christian thought, and Symposium is one of his philosophical teachings on the immorality of the soul or the concept of Eros. (Ref. Pickett, *Historical Dictionary of Homosexuality…*, 153.

[32] Masters, *Sex and Human Loving* …, 346.

[33] For example, in parts of Ionia there were structures against same-sex Eros, while the people of Elis and Boiotia approved of and even celebrated it.

[34] In Greek history and literature, on the other hand, the abundance of accounts of homosexual love overwhelms the investigator. Homer's intentions in the *Iliad* (c. 800 bce) have been the subject of much debate. There is ample evidence, however, that by the beginning of the classical era (480 bce) his archaic heroes Achilles and Patroclus had become exemplars of male love. Greek lyric poets sing of male love from almost the earliest fragments down to the end of classical times. Five brilliant philosophical dialogues debate its ethics with a wealth of illustrations, from Plato and Xenophon to Plutarch and the pseudo-Lucian of the third century ce. In the public arena of the theater we know that tragedies on this

theme were popular, and Aristophanes' bawdy humor is quite as likely to be inspired by sex between males as by intercourse between men and women. Vase-painters portray scores of homoerotic scenes, hundreds of inscriptions celebrate the love of boys, and such affairs enter into the lives of a long catalogue of famous Greek statesmen, warriors, artists, and authors. Though it has often been assumed that the love of males was a fashion confined to a small intellectual elite during the age of Plato, in fact it was pervasive throughout all levels of Greek society and held a honored place in Greek culture for more than a thousand years, that is, from before 600 BCE to about 400 CE. Greek religion, too, testifies to the hold pederasty had upon the Greek imagination. Mythology provides more than fifty examples of youths beloved of deities.

[35] Pickett, *Historical Dictionary of History...*, 133.

[36] Homosexual relations between an adult man and adolescent boy past the age of puberty were commonplace, usually occurring in an educational relationship where the man was responsible for the boy's moral and intellectual development. Cf. Masters, *Sex and Human Loving..*, 12.

[37] Augustine (354-430) was raised in Roman North Africa, educated in Carthage and employed as a professor of rhetoric in Milan by 383. Born in North Africa on the outskirts of the Roman Empire, Augustine eventually became one of the most important theologians in Christianity. While his mother was a devout Christian, Augustine was a pagan in his youth, devoted to Manicheanism, which was then an important dualistic faith. In his autobiography, *The Confessions*, Augustine wrote about a male friend he had in his youth. The friend died and Augustine suffered profound grief. Many have interpreted the relationship as homosexual, due to the manner in which he wrote about the friendship and his mourning. Certainly Augustine had extensive sexual experiences, with his wife and mistress, and wrote frankly about his struggle with lust. Against the early Patristic writers, Augustine argued that lifelong celibacy was unnecessary. Instead, sexual expression governed by reason is moral while that dictated by the appetites is not. Augustine's account emphasized procreation as the natural outcome of the proper use of genitalia, and other uses as unnatural. From this, he argued that marital heterosexual sex out of a desire to have children is acceptable, as long as it is done without lust. This theological view placed an emphasis on the gender of one's partner, in contrast to previous understandings in ancient Rome, and ruled out the possibility of moral same-sex sexuality. Augustine was also one of the first to argue that the story of Lot, from the Old Testament, was a denunciation of homosexuality. Cf. Pickett, *Historical Dictionary of Homosexuality...*, 26.

[38] Thomas Aquinas (1225–1274). Thomas Aquinas set out the most influential statement of natural law theory, which today stands as the most common defense for the unequal legal (and social) treatment of gays and lesbians. Integrating Aristotle's philosophy with the theology of Christianity, Aquinas emphasized the

centrality of certain human goods, including marriage, procreation, and the raising of children. While Aquinas did not write much about same-sex sexual relations, he did write at length about various sex acts as sins. For Aquinas, sexuality was only permissible and good if it was within the bonds of marriage and helped to further what he saw as the distinctive goods of marriage, mainly love, companionship, and legitimate offspring. Aquinas did not argue that procreation was a necessary part of moral sex; married couples could enjoy sex without the motive of having children. Sex in marriages where one partner is or both partners are sterile is also potentially just, given a motive of expression and cultivation of love. It is worth noting that Aquinas' view at this point need not rule out homosexual sex. For example, a Thomist could embrace same-sex marriage, and then apply the same reasoning, simply seeing the couple as a reproductively sterile, yet still fully loving and companionate union. Andrew Sullivan sympathetically explores a natural law position from this type of perspective. Aquinas, however, added the requirement that for any given sex act to be moral it must be of a "generative" kind. Since only the emission of semen in a vagina is potentially reproductive, only sex acts of that kind are generative, even if a given sex act does not lead to procreation. The consequence of this addition, of course, is to rule out the possibility that homosexual sex could ever be moral, even if done within a loving marriage. Aquinas did not spell out a justification for this generative requirement, and many contemporary natural law theorists continue to struggle with this area of Thomist thought. (Cf. Pickett, *Historical Dictionary of Homosexuality…*, 19.)

[39] Masters, *Sex and Human Loving..*, 346-347.

[40] Anti-Semitism-the belief or behaviour hostile towards Jews just because they are Jewish. It may take the form of religious teachings that proclaim the inferiority of Jews, for instance on political efforts to isolate, oppress or otherwise injure them. It may also include prejudiced or stereotyped views about Jews. For John Chrysostom statements against Jews and Christians who partook in Jewish religious and cultural observances. In a series of homilies "against Jews," Chrysostom calls them murderers, diseased, and, ironically, dogs, and associates them with heretical groups like the Anomoeans. and the Manichaeans. Jewish men he labelled as "softies" or even "fags" and the women he branded as whores these Jews are gathering choruses of 'soft' men," Chrysostom bemoans, "and a great hash heap of prostituting women" In these homilies Chrysostom "revealed a nagging sense of inferiority in relation to the historical claims and current attractiveness of Judaism, dread feelings he compensated for with a violent and extravagant rhetoric". Yet, there is one other group that matches, or even surpasses, the great revulsion Chrysostom harboured for Jews, namely persons in homoerotic relationships. Boswell (2009, 347) notes that "John Chrysostom probably wrote more about the subject of same-sex sexuality than any other pre- Freudian writer except Peter Damian." (CF. Chris L. *John Chrysostom homoeroticism…*)

[41] De Wet, C. L. *John Chrysostom homoeroticism….* Romans 1:25-26)

[42] De Wet, C. L. "Paul, Identity-Formation and the Problem of Alterity in John Chrysostom's Homilies," *In epistulam ad Calatas commentarius. Acta Theologica Supplementum* 19 (2014):18-41.

[43] Louis, *Homosexuality and Civilization …,* 139.

[44] Louis, *Homosexuality and Civilization …,* 141.

[45] Indeed, his sermons mark an epoch in the history of anti-Semitism. In the eight sermons against Judaizing Christians which he delivered in Antioch in 387, Chrysostom denounced the Jews as "sensual, slippery, voluptuous, avaricious, possessed by demons, drunkards, harlots, and breakers of the Law" and condemned them as murderers of "the prophets, Christ, and God." "Saint John Chrysostom," writes a modern commentator, "up to his time stands without peer or parallel in the entire literature *Adversus Judaeos.* The virulence of his attack is surprising even in an age in which rhetorical denunciation was often indulged with complete abandon." The effects of his preaching, we are told, "wielded a baleful influence not only on the clergy and populace of his time but on those of centuries thereafter." Another Catholic scholar, looking at Chrysostom's discourses from the point of view of the modern Church, has concluded that they could not have been delivered after Vatican II's "Declaration on the Church's Attitude toward Non- Christian Religions." "For these objectively unchristian acts he cannot be excused, even if he is the product of his times." The main text in Chrysostom's writings corpus that addresses the question of homosexuality is his fourth homily on Romans, a homily that expounds Rom 1:26-27. The provenance of this homily is somewhat difficult to determine, as there are no direct clues in the texts as to its origin or context. It seems plausible that the homily, along with much of the series on Romans, may have been preached at Antioch. There is also a shorter section specifically against pederasty in his treatise, of which there is more certainty about an Antiochene provenance. The similarities between these two texts, however, do not necessarily account for a shared provenance. Neither is it particularly helpful to ask whether homosexual behaviour was more prevalent in Antioch than in Constantinople, especially since the face of homoeroticism may not have differed much between these two cities. (CF. Chris L. *John Chrysostom homoeroticism…*)

[46] Louis, *Homosexuality and Civilization …,* 142.

[47] Louis, *Homosexuality and Civilization …,* 143.

[48] Louis, *Homosexuality and Civilization …,* 191.

[49] C. A. Williams, *Roman Homosexuality* (New York: Oxford University Press, 2009), 44-45.

[50] Williams, *Roman Homosexuality …,* 45.

[51] M. Balberg, *Purity, Body, and Self In Early Rabbinic Literature*. (Berkeley: University of California Press, 2014), 56.

[52] Shore, S., (trans). 1983. *John Chrysostom, On Virginity, Against Remarriage*. (Lewiston: Edwin Mellen,1983), 67.

[53] R. J. Wright, "Boswell on Homosexuality: A Case Undemonstrated." *Anglican Theological Review* 66/1 (1984):79-94.

[54] A. M. Hartney, 2004. *John Chrysostom and the Transformation of the City* (London: Duckworth, 2004), 45.

[55] Chris L. DeWet, *John Chrysostom homoeroticism*, (Paper) Department of Biblical and Ancient Studies, P. o. Box 392, Unisa 0003, South Africa

[56] J. Boswell, *Christianity, Social Tolerance, and Homosexuality: Gay People in Western Europe from the Beginning of the Christian Era to the Fourteenth Century*. Chicago: University of Chicago Press, 2009, 156.

[57] Boswell. *Christianity, Social Tolerance, and Homosexuality:...*, 156.

[58] De Wet, C. L. "Paul, Identity-Formation and the Problem of Alterity in John Chrysostom's Homilies, 18-41.

[59] Monique.Wittig, "The Point of View: Universal or Particular," *Feminist Issues* 3(1983): 63-69.

[60] W. Mayer, and P. Allen. *John Chrysostom* (London: Routledge, 1999), 46.

[61] E. A. Clark, Sexual Politics in the Writings of John Chrysostom, *Anglican Theological Review 59*/1 (1977): 3-19.

[62] R. Hill, (Trans). *St. John Chrysostom: Homilies on Genesis 1-17*, (Washington, D.C.: Catholic University of America Press, 1999), 35.

[63] M. Kuefler. *The Manly Eunuch: Masculinity, Gender Ambiguity, and Christian Ideology in Late Antiquity* (Chicago: University of Chicago Press, 1991), 47.

[64] Simon S.M. Kwan, *Reflection on the Critical Asian Principle, CAP Continual Discussion Group Report*, 2006.

[65] Pauline Webb, "The Risks of Inter-Faith Dialogue," *Christian Witness and Society*, edited by K. C. Abraham (Bangalore: BTE/SSC, 1998), 179.

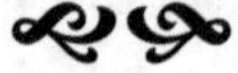

A Biblical and a Theological Critique of Select Ecclesial Leaders

Reji Mathew

Abstract

This article highlights the Patristic view on Human Sexuality and a few teachers of Christianity are selected from the ancient and medieval periods. To make some conclusions about their ideas of Human Sexuality their writings in theological topics like Incarnation, anthropology, asceticism are discussed. As a background the Biblical concept of the Image of God is presented. However, the main focus of the article is on developing a theology of people with different sexual orientations. It will help us to consider their identity as a child of God and to deal with them without theological prejudices.

There is a necessity for making a methodological statement at the beginning of this article: The Christian teachers of the Middle Ages as well as that of the Antiquity had an inhibition to talk about "human sexuality". Even today it is difficult for many theologians to make an open discussion about human sexuality and those who involve in such endeavours may limit their studies only to "men" and "women". All the modern day talks on "gender issues" highlight marginalization of women only. Then what about those who are "neither men nor women"? To find something in favour for these people in the patristic writings is very difficult. Direct references to the social, political and religious issues faced by those who were "neither men nor women" are apparently absent in such writings.

Therefore we have to glean scanty information from these writings in the discussions on the theology of Incarnation, on anthropology, on asceticism, on marriage etc. Exhortations to Christian values like ritual purity, chastity and morality may also deal with the said people.

The Image of God and Human Sexuality

A joint statement of the Anglican Church and the Roman Catholic Church highlights the anthropology on the basis of the declaration of the Council of Chalcedon: "Our churches together affirm the Christology of the Chalcedonian definition: at once complete in Godhead and complete in manhood, truly God and truly man (the word used here was *anthropos* - human, not *aner* - male), …begotten, for us men and for our salvation, of Mary the Virgin, the God-bearer (*theotokos*); one and the same Christ, Son, Lord, only-begotten, recognized in two natures without confusion, without change, without division, without separation."[1] Thus Jesus Christ is simultaneously one in being with the Father as regards his Godhead, and one in being with us as regards his humanity. He is, therefore, described, as we have seen, as the image of the invisible God".

Most of the Christian thinkers of antiquity and medieval ages anchor their anthropological ideas on the theology of Image of God (*Imago Dei*).[2] They take us back to the Book of Genesis for a description about the Image of God. The English word "image" translates the Hebrew word *selem* and the English "likeness" translates the Hebrew *d'mût* (except in Genesis 5:1, where "likeness" translates *selem*). In the Old Testament, *selem* is used, but for the two exceptions, to refer to the physical likeness of a person or thing, and almost uniformly these images are abominable. The two exceptions of this usage, however, broaden the possibilities of the meaning of this important word. In Psalm 39:5, 6a we read: "Behold, thou hast made my days a few handbreadths, and my lifetime is as nothing in thy sight. Surely every man stands as a mere breath! Surely man goes about as a *selem*!" The RSV renders *selem* "shadow," which points to its meaning as a resemblance or reflection of something greater. It certainly is not a material idol or the like. Thus we have some evidence the *selem* is not bound to denote a physical image. Similarly, in Psalm 73:20 Asaph, speaking of the rich heathen, says; "They are like a dream when one awakes, on waking you despise *salmam*." Here the RSV renders *salmam* "their phantoms." Thus we are not dealing with a concrete, tangible image, but again, a more abstract likeness. Gerhard von Rad, the renowned Old Testament scholar *selem* "means predominantly an actual plastic work, a duplicate, sometimes an idol...; only on occasion does it mean a duplicate in the diminished sense of a semblance when compared with the original...."[3]

The second important word, *d'mût,* outside the Genesis texts, has a greater flexibility than *selem*. It is used in a concrete sense almost synonymously with *selem*, and in the abstract sense of resemblance. Although the abstract quality is there, *d'mût* is used uniformly in connection with a tangible or visual reproduction of something else. So again, as with *selem*, the usage of *d'mût* urges us very strongly in the direction of a physical likeness. Now we have to ask whether or not a substantial distinction is meant between these two words when the writer says, "Let us make man in our image, after our likeness" (Genesis 1:26)? If the author conceived of an important distinction between *selem* and *d'mût* in Gen 1:26, which is God's resolution to create, then why did he omit *d'mût* in verse 27, the record of the very act of creation? For von Rad the most obvious explanation for the oversight, either by God to create man in his likeness, or by the author to record it, is that there really was no oversight by either and that nothing is lost either from man or from the meaning of the text by the omission of *d'mût*. Another bit of evidence which points to the interchangeability of these two words is that in Genesis 5:1 and 9:6, only one word is used to denote the image, *d'mût,* in 5:1 and *selem* in 9:6. The Septuagint translators used both *d'mût* and *selem* in the texts by the one word *eikôn*. Karl Barth says that man is not created to be the image of God but - as is said in Gen 1:26 and 27, but also Gen 5:1 and Gen 9:6 - he is created in correspondence with the image of God.[4]

Since human beings are made in the image of God, and are sexual, the question presents itself: Is God imaged forth more adequately in one sex rather than the other? Of course there is a preponderance of masculine over feminine imagery for God in the Bible. In the Old Testament, God is depicted, for example, as shepherd, king, father and husband: as shepherd, true guardian of Israel (Gn. 49:24), gatherer of stray sheep, who leads them to their own pasture, binds up their wounds, watches over and feeds them as he guides them toward messianic restoration (Ez. 34:11-

12); as king, ruler of Israel (Nm. 23:21), leader of all nations (Ps. 22:29), creator (Ps. 74:12) and savior of Israel (Is. 33:22); as a father who loves his child, Israel (Hos. 11:1), provides for him (Ex. 4: 22f; Dt. 1:31), has compassion on him and forgives him (Is. 64:8; Jer. 31:20; Ps . 103:13f); as a husband who rejoices in his bride (Is. 62:5) and longs for the affection of his wayward wife (Is. 54:5-8). Some understand this imagery to depend in large part upon the patriarchal structure of the social order in ancient Israel.

However, there are also passages in the Old Testament where God's actions and attitudes in relation to Israel are depicted in feminine images. The Wisdom texts of the Old Testament are brought forward and interpreted as describing an eternal aspect of God in feminine terms; these are at times associated with the Word and at times with the Holy Spirit. God's mother-love for his child is faithful and unconditional: God knows what it is to carry a child in the womb, to cry out in labour, to give birth (Is. 46:3-4; Dt. 32:18; Is. 42:13-14); God's attachment to his child is just as strong as any nursing mother's (Is. 49:14-15); her tender compassion (Jer. 31:20) moves her to carry her child at her breast and comfort him (Is. 66:12-13), and to stand by her child all the days of its life. The psalmist envisions God as a mother (Ps. 131:1-2), as mid-wife (Ps. 22:9f) and as mistress of a household (Ps. 123:2), an image echoed in the Wisdom literature (Prov. 9:1-6). God's Wisdom, personified, is feminine (Wis. 7:25-8:1). Wisdom shares in the divine attributes, and appeals to the faithful disciple to embrace her as bride and mother (Prov. 4:6-8, Sir. 15:2; Wis. 8:2) ; she can satisfy the heart's desire.

The above line of thought is pursued by the Eastern theologians. The Holy Spirit is hymned as "mother" by Ephrem the Syrian, and Christ is praised as "mother" by Clement of Alexandria and later by St. Anselm and Dame Julian of Norwich. In the medieval West, mystics and theologians exhibit great freedom in applying masculine and feminine names to God. The maternal imagery of bearing, birthing, nursing, nurturing, comforting etc. carries forward a rich expression of divine-human intimacy. Christ himself was sometimes depicted as feminine and motherly (often drawing on the mother-hen passage): giving us birth from his pierced side, feeding us on his own flesh and blood, embracing us tenderly as his beloved children. Christian religious experience and theological reflection, then, have discovered a full range of human characteristics, male and female, in the sacred humanity of Jesus.

In the New Testament, the reference to God as Father predominates. God is uniquely the Father of Jesus Christ (Mt. 11:27 and par.). This name, "Father," becomes synonymous with God in the fourth Gospel. Jesus teaches his disciples to address God as Father in prayer (Mt. 6:9-13, Lk. 11:2-4), following his own example (Mt. 11:25f; Mk. 14:36; Jn. 11:41f, 12:27f, and ch. 17). In and through Christ we become God's adopted children, able in the power of the Spirit to share in his relationship with the Father (Gal. 4:6; Rom. 8:15f). Jesus, the incarnate Word of God, is a male. The maternal love of God for Israel, however, is recalled in Jesus' lament over Jerusalem: He longs to gather her children as a hen gathers her chicks under her wings (Mt. 23:27).

The female imagery of God, Christ and the Holy Spirit appears in certain strands of patristic and medieval theological reflection and piety. The Wisdom texts of the Old Testament are brought forward and interpreted as describing an eternal aspect of God in feminine terms; these are at times associated with the Word and at times with the Holy Spirit. Greek theology in Byzantium pursued this line of thought and dedicated many churches to the divine Sophia. The Holy Spirit is hymned as "mother" by Ephrem the Syrian and Christ is praised as "mother" by Clement of Alexandria and later by Anselm and Dame Julian of Norwich. In the medieval West, mystics and theologians exhibit great freedom in applying masculine and feminine names to God. The maternal imagery of bearing, birthing, nursing, nurturing, comforting and so on, carries forward in the spiritual writings of this period a rich expression of divine-human intimacy. Christ himself was sometimes depicted as feminine and motherly (often drawing on the mother-hen passage): giving us birth from his pierced side, feeding us on his own flesh and blood, embracing us tenderly as his beloved children. Christian religious experience and theological reflection, then, have discovered a full range of human characteristics, male and female, in the sacred humanity of Jesus.

"Human Sexuality" in the Writings of Ancient Christian Teachers

However, the thinking of the teachers of Christian antiquity was much influenced by Plato and Aristotle.[5] Plato's basic anthropology was adapted first into Christian theology by the Alexandrian theologians of the third century, especially **Clement of Alexandria** (ca. 150-216 CE), **Origen** (ca. 185-254 CE), and **Athanasius** (ca. 293-373 CE). However, it was the fourth century anti-Arian works of **Hilary of Poitiers** (ca. 300-368 CE) that translated Platonic ideas regarding the body into the Latin language of the emerging western church. In his major treatise *De Trinitate*, Hilary's defence of Christ's divinity utilized Clement of Alexandria's view regarding the body of Christ by stipulating that, although the human body of Christ was a real body, it was a - celestial body (*corpus caeleste*).[6] As such, Christ's body did not share in the same weakness or present the same hindrances as the bodies of humanity descended from Adam and Eve. In Book X of *De Trinitate*, Hilary put forward the idea that the body of Christ receives the force of pain…but without feeling pain. It was transformed into heavenly glory on the Mount, it put fevers to flight by its touch, it gave new eyesight by its spittle.

Ambrose of Milan (ca. 339-397 CE), was much influenced by the Platonism embedded in the works of Philo and Origen, although the former's moral works seem to be influenced by Stoicism. However, Ambrose avoided Hilary's platonically-driven, quasi-docetic view of the body of Christ and was generally very careful to correct the more dangerous aspects Platonism suggested about Christ. In his In *Hexaemeron* and *De Paradiso*, Ambrose relied especially on the platonic thought of Basil of Caesarea [329-379] for his presentation on the opening chapters of Genesis.[7] For Ambrose, the soul constituted the person; the body was at best only an outward instrument. Human beings were created in the image of Christ; Christ, in turn, is the - Image of God by virtue of the union of Christ's mind by grace to the Holy Spirit. Christ's body the outer man -was in harmony with his mind in one spirit. Adam's voluntary fall resulted in the alienation from God of the human person both soul and body, inner and outer man so that humanity no longer possessed God's image. Rather, the human person was now flesh which manifested itself in the inherent weakness of the body. The image is restored by grace, but warfare continues between the inner and outer man, between spirit/soul and flesh/ body until – 'paradisal' peace is restored in the resurrection of the *eschaton*.[8]

The modification and synthesis of the Platonic body with the anthropology of Scripture in western Christian theology reached its zenith in the thought and writing of **Augustine of Hippo** (ca. 354-430 CE) who fixed this tradition for much of the subsequent history of the Latin Church. Augustine was the earliest Christian theologian who saw the necessity of understanding the body as an integral part of the human person, interdependent with the soul. In Augustine, the antipathy toward the body inherent in Platonic thought (as so strongly expressed in Porphyry, Augustine's erstwhile philosophic mentor) was suppressed. In contrast to Porphyry the mature Augustine came to affirm the body positively such as when he said in a 417 sermon: "Take away death, the last enemy, and my own flesh will be my dear friend throughout eternity".[9] Upon his conversion in 386, Augustine found that he had to let go of his pre-Christian denigration of the body in the face of the creation story (Gen. 1:31). The body also was "good" and an integral component of the human person despite the younger Augustine's reflexive stress on the soul as the better or higher part. The human body is both *corpus* and *caro* in Augustine's early parlance, but these terms are not necessarily equivalent: *omnis enim caro etiam corpus est, non autem omne corpus etiam caro est.*[10] The *corpus* tended to emphasize the human body's congruence with bodies in general, that is, material beings possessing *mensura, numera, et pondus.*[11] Caro too was a body, but it often highlighted the flesh, i.e. that which is sin in humanity. Thus, these body terms for Augustine could refer to the sinful inclinations due to the fall, to the *habitus* of sin in fallen humanity, or they could refer simply to the physical human body. However, T. J. van Bavel suggests that even when speaking about the body as code for what is sinful in humanity, Augustine's repeated use in his earlier works of terms such as withdraw, leave behind, and renounce in connection with the body reflected in congruence with Scripture on his part rather than simply a reflexive denigration of the body qua body. Indeed, early on Augustine saw that the good of the body was integral to the good of the soul. Indeed, in combination with the senses, the body is a kind of image of the truth. Augustine was further informed in his understanding of the physical body by his thinking about the Incarnation. In the early writing *Contra Academicos* (386 CE) he stated that the authority of the Divine intellect (*divini intellectus auctoritatem*) –Christ - was placed into a body - so that souls would be aroused not only by divine precepts but also by divine acts to yearn for their fatherland. Similarly, the early Augustine affirmed the certainty of the resurrection of the body because of the resurrected body of Christ, even if he vacillated for a time in his understanding of the continuity of the temporal body in the body resurrected to eternal life.[12]

One who wrote something important for our present discussion is **Thomas Aquinas** (1225-1274 CE), the star of the Middle Ages. In his dialogues with Bonaventure Aquinas held that the whole "creation is hierarchical in its design and that no two different natural beings can be on the same level". [13] For him and other Christian thinkers of antiquity a woman is necessary "for the generation of species" and nothing else. Aquinas quotes Aristotle on issues like this and the latter's characterization of the female body as "misbegotten male" opens a Pandora's box of medieval thought and culture.[14] It saw the body of a female as "weak and inferior" to that of men and all discussions about women are male bound and there is no discussion about the people who are neither men nor women.[15] But unlike Augustine the gender difference is not interpreted by Aquinas as an outcome of sin; both men and women – their body and soul - are created for the ultimate beatitude. Human sexuality shares the debilitation brought about by the fall of Adam. The union of both soul and body is underlined by Aquinas and for him, it is natural for the soul to be with the body. Even though the soul departs from the body by death it there will be a reunion with the body in the resurrection. The immortality of the soul demands a future resurrection of the body. Humanity is one and it is sexless; only the temporal nature of the body has a male or female identity. Human being returns to God as a spiritualized human person.

Himself being a master theorist of a morality of natural law Thomas Aquinas points out that we all have "a natural inclination to follow our bodily feelings and desires even against the good of being reasonable." This is one of many "natural" i.e. innate, deep-seated, typical inclinations which should not simply be followed: some people are more inclined to anger, including immoral anger, than others; some are more inclined to greed, some to crippling fear, and so forth. Aquinas, following a lead from Aristotle's research and reflections, calls inclinations such as the desire of some men to have bodily fellowship with other men as "bad habits" or "inclinations of people with defective psycho-physical constitution,"[16] i.e. from inclinations incipiently present even from conception.[17]

Martin Luther (1483- 1546 CE) addresses the issue of sexuality in human being. For him "sexuality can be integral to the desire to commit oneself to life with another, to touch and be touched, and to love and be loved. Such powers are complex and ambiguous. They can be used well or badly. They can bring astonishing joy and delight. Such powers can serve God and serve the neighbour. They also can hurt self or hurt the neighbour."[18] Following this Lutheran understanding sees sexuality as "a rich and diverse combination of relational, emotional, and physical interactions and possibilities. It surely does not consist solely of erotic desire. Erotic desire, in the narrow sense, is only one component of the relational bonds that humans crave as sexual beings. Although not all relationships are sexual, at some level most sexual relationships are about companionship. Although some people may remain single, either intentionally or unintentionally, all people need and delight in companionship, and all are vulnerable to loneliness".[19] Though sexual love remains God's good gift, sin permeates human sexuality as it does all of life; when expressed immaturely, irresponsibly, or with hurtful intent, then love or its counterfeit, coercive power, can end in harmful doings and even in death.[20]

Pope John Paul's study on human body emphasized the historical theology of human being as it was practised in the past. This document is widely discussed now.[21] Pope John Paul relies on both accounts of creation in the book of Genesis as his starting point. For him the first account, Gn 1:1-4, simply gives the objective facts about the creation of humanity: created male and female; created in the image of God; created to be fruitful and multiply (and fill, subdue, and have dominion over the earth); and seen by God as good. But the second account, Gn 2:5-25, has a subjective character and is concerned with humanity's self-knowledge. John Paul II maintains that the subjectivity of this second account corresponds to the objective reality of the first account. Both are significant for his theology of the body and his gender theory but he focuses much more on the second account.[22]

Neither Male and nor Female

Why should we blame the ancient writers for excluding the "third gender" etc.? Even today, the gender based theology is limited to issues regarding the female. It is a fascinating experience to read the description of philosopher Judith Butler on the theology of sex/ gender.[23] But are we not still on the path to search something for the people who are neither male nor female. Even though in ancient days human sexuality was not so open as of today we find some references to the eunuchs; the term covered all people who were neither male nor female. Bible passages like Dtn 23;1, Is 56:3-4, Act 8:26-39 were interpreted by the ancient Christian teachers. The most interesting thing for us is the fact that they were neither branded nor "spiritually" segregated in such writings. "Eunuchs" were members of the Kingdom of God as well as the Church just like the "men" and "women" and there was no "spiritual apartheid" for them in the discussions about the eternal life. See for example an exegesis of Is 56:3-4: "God by the prophet Isaiah, unto whom He saith that He will give in His house and in His wall a place by name, much better than of sons and daughters, save concerning these, who make themselves eunuchs for the sake of the kingdom of heaven? ...For, when He saith, "I will give unto them a place much better;" He shows that one is also given unto the married, but much inferior. Therefore, to allow that in the house of God there will be the eunuchs after the flesh spoken of above, who were not in the People of Israel: because we see that these also themselves, whereas they become not Jews, yet become Christians... For, although at times the Church, even that which is at this time, is called the kingdom of heaven. Certainly, it is so called for this end, because it is being gathered together for a future and eternal life. Although, therefore, it has the promise of the present, and of a future life, yet in all its good works it looks not to "the things that are seen, but to what are not seen. For what are seen are temporal; but what is not seen, are eternal".[24] Another interesting passage is the following:[25] "For the Lord Himself, being asked by one when His kingdom would come, replied, "When two shall be one, that which is without as that which is within, and the male and female, neither male nor female. Now, two are one when we speak the truth one to another, and there is unfeignedly one soul in two bodies. And "that which is without as" that which is within meaneth this: He calls the soul "that which is within," and the body "that which is without." As, then, thy body is visible to sight, so also let thy soul be manifest by good works. And "the male, with the female, neither male nor female," this He saith, that brother seeing sister may have no thought concerning her as female, and that she may have no thought concerning him as male. "If ye do these things," saith He, "the kingdom of my Father shall come." Adam Bede caricatures the positives of the Ethiopian eunuch in his commentary on Acts 8:26-39: "He is called a man because of his virtue and integrity of mind, and not undeservedly, for he devoted his study solely to the Scriptures, and he did not stop reading them even when he was on the road. Also he showed so much love in religion that, leaving behind a queen's court, he came from the farthest regions of the world to the Lord's Temple. Hence as a *just steward* 'while he sought the interpretation of something that he was reading', he found Christ whom he was seeking."[26] This invites our attention to the fact that neither Jesus nor the Kingdom of God are exclusively meant for "men' and "women" only. In his Commentary on Acts of the Apostles Jerome said about the Ethiopian eunuch as one who "found Church's font there in the desert rather than in the golden Temple of the synagogue".[27] Indicating to the Ethiopian who changed his skin in Jeremiah 13:23 Jerome said: "with the stain of his (of the Ethiopian Eunuch) sins washed away by the waters (of Baptism) he went up shining white to Jesus.[28]

Conclusion

The historical teaching of the Church on human being tells us the following:

1. It is an accepted fact that human sexuality was not openly discussed in the medieval as well as ancient Church.

2. What is available are often discussions about the male female differences.

3. However, there is not an essential difference between male and female in Christian anthropology as far as spirituality is discussed. Both male and female are same at the spiritual level; their difference is only at the level of the body.

4. In the patristic writings the only word used for people who are neither "men" nor "women" is "eunuch".

5. The "eunuchs" were not socially marginalized for their sexual nature; some of them like the Ethiopian Eunuch of Acts 8 were placed in a high rank and they possessed important social and political assignments.

6. The Fathers teach us that human beings who are "neither men nor women" are within the Kingdom of God and they are able to receive the love and grace of God; they also are endowed with the promise of eternal life.

7. Just like the "men" and "women" they can meet Jesus and enter in the Kingdom God by putting their faith in Jesus and by living according to the Scripture.

What we have to do is to accept people as the Image of God and not on the basis of their sexual orientation or bodily appearance. Churches which oppose all forms of verbal or physical harassment and assault based on sexual orientation have to move further. The support for legislation and policies to protect civil rights and to prohibit discrimination in housing, employment, and public services are good.[29] But we have to look back to Jesus who loved the people who were neglected or branded on the basis of their sexual identity and to accept the fact that it is not a charity to accept and respect gender differences.

Endnotes

[1] *http://www.usccb.org/beliefs-and-teachings/ecumenical-and-interreligious/ecumenical/anglican/images-of-god-anthropology.cfm* accessed on July 2017.

[2] John Piper, "The Image of God: An Approach from Biblical and Systematic Theology,"*Studia Biblica et Theologica*, March 1971.

[3] Gerhard von Rad, *Genesis: A Commentary*, translated by John H. Marks, The Old Testament Library (Philadelphia: The Westminster Press, 1961), 56.

[4] Karl Barth, "The Doctrine of Creation," *Church Dogmatics*, III/I, ed. G. Bromiley and T.F. Torrance (Edinburgh: T. & T. Clark, 1958), 197.

[5] Peter Brown, *The Body and Society: Men, Women, and Sexual Renunciation in Early Christianity*, (New York: Columbia University Press, 1988), 17.

[6] Aloys Grillmeier, *Christ in Christian Tradition*, 2nd ed., trans. John Bowden (Atlanta: John Knox Press, 1975), Vol. 1, 135-137. See also Johannes Quasten, *Patrology*, vol. 1, ed. Angelo di Berardino, trans. Rev. Placid Solari, OSB (Notre Dame, IN: Christian Classics, 1986), 57.

[7] Johannes Quasten, *Patrology*, 154.

[8] Johannes Quasten, *Patrology*, 154-5.

[9] Augustine, Sermo CLV (CCSL 41), 15. detrahatur mors novissima inimica, et erit mihi in aeternum caro mea amica (emphasis added); Mary T. Clark, Augustine

of Hippo (Georgetown University Press, 1994), 32. See also Margaret R. Miles, Corpus, Augustinus Lexicon, vol. 2, ed. Cornelius Mayer (Basel: Schwabe & Co. AG, 1996), 6.

[10] Augustine, *De Fide et Symbolo,* (CSEL, 41), X, 24.

[11] For a fuller discussion of the significance of these terms for Augustine, see Lewis Ayres, "Measure, number, and weight," in *Augustine Through the Ages*, ed. A. D. Fitzgerald, OSA (Grand Rapids, MI: William. B. Eerdmans, 1999), 550-552.

[12] Margaret R. Miles, *Augustine on the Body* (Missoula, MT: Scholar's Press, 1979), 108. See more by Johannes van Bavel, OSA,"The Anthropology of Augustine," *Louvain Studies* 5, no. 1 (1974-75): 46-47.

[13] See more on this in Étienne Gilson, *The Philosophy of St. Bonaventure*, (Paterson, NJ: Saint Anthony Guild Press, 1965), 402-416. M. Evangeline Anderson, OSB, *The Human Body in the Philosophy of St. Thomas Aquinas* (Washington, D.C.: Catholic University of America Press, 1953).

[14] Caroline Walker Bynum, *Fragmentation and Redemption* (New York: Zone Books, 1992), 218, 220.

[15] See more on this in Bynum, *Fragmentation and Redemption*; Alexandra Cuffel, *Gendering Disgust in Medieval Religious Polemic,* (Notre Dame, Indiana: University of Notre Dame Press, 2007)and Peter Biller and A. J. Minnis (eds), *Medieval Theology and the Natural Body*, (New York, York Medieval Press, 1997).

[16] John Finnis. "Reason, Faith and Homosexual Acts", *The Catholic Social Science Review*, Vol. VI (2001), 64.

[17] John Finnis. "Reason, Faith and Homosexual Acts", pp. 61-70 .

[18] A Social Statement on Human Sexuality: Gift and Trust This social teaching statement was amended and adopted by a two-thirds vote (676-338) by the eleventh biennial Churchwide Assembly on August 19, 2009, at Minneapolis, Minnesota, 11.

[19] A Social Statement on Human Sexuality, 11.

[20] Charles Lloyd Cortright , "Poor Maggot-Sack that I Am": The Human Body in the Theology of Martin Luther, Dissertation, Milwaukee, Wisconsin May 2011 in Marquette University e-Publications@Marquette, 2011.

[21] Christopher West, Theology of the Body Explained: A Commentary on John Paul II's "Gospel of the Body" (Boston: Pauline Books and Media, 2003).

[22] Michael Waldstein, trans., Man and Woman He Created Them: A Theology of the Body, by John Paul II (Boston: Pauline Books and Media, 2006), 18-23; and William S. Kurz, "The Scriptural Foundations of The Theology of the Body," in Pope John Paul II on the Body: Human, Eucharistic, Ecclesial: Festschrift Avery

Cardinal Dulles, ed. John M. McDermott and John Gavin (Philadelphia: Saint Joseph's University Press, 2007), 27-46.

[23] Judith Butler, *Gender Trouble: Feminism and the Subversion of Identity* (New York: Routledge, 1990).

[24] *On the Holy Trinity; Doctrinal Treatises; Moral Treatises*, NPNF 1-03; s. *http://www.ccel.org/ccel/ schaff/npnf103.v.iii.xxv.html* accessed on July 13, 2005.

[25] Philip Schaff, ANF09: Chapter XII.—We are Constantly to Look for the Kingdom of God.

[26] Francis Martin, Acts, Ancient Christian Commentary on Scripture, New Testament V (Illinois: Inter Varsity Press, 2006) 97.

[27] Francis Martin, Acts, Ancient Christian Commentary on Scripture, 97.

[28] Francis Martin, Acts, Ancient Christian Commentary on Scripture, 97.

[29] See ELCA, Social Statement on Human Sexuality: Gift and Trust, Minneapolis, 2009.

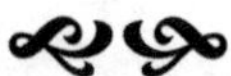

Critiquing Augustine and Thomas Aquinas on Sexuality

J.M. John Marshal

Introduction

Sexuality is God's gift to Human beings. However there are many ways in which this sexuality itself, tainted with the effects of the Sin has become a source of serious disorders in many ways. Though there is a greater advancement in the sciences, what the humans have understood about the mysteries of Sexuality is very –little indeed. A proper understanding of sexuality involves listening to the voice of the Holy Spirit, who is the author of all life. There is also a possibility of understanding the nature of sexuality from a theological perspective by paying heed to the teachings of the great Fathers of the Faith such as St. Augustine and St. Thomas Aquinas, both Doctors of the Church. Their writings provide us with a moral understanding of the acts associated with sexuality and how to orient it towards God.

St Augustine's View on Sexuality

Past Life of St Augustine

In His own words, St Augustine lived a sinful life.

> For my will had been perverted and had manufactured lust; the more I gave in to lust, the more it developed into a habit and when I failed to check the habit it became a necessity. These were all the links in the chain that had me enslaved.[1]

As a young man he was sexually very active and lived openly with a concubine who bore him a son. He abandoned the Catholic Faith and became a hearer of the sect of Manicheans. However when he heard the sermon of St. Ambrose in Milan he got converted and once again reconciled to the Catholic Church.[2]

Many authors propose that the Manichaeism had great effects on St. Augustine's understanding of sexuality. But some authors also suggest that St. Augustine had to strike a balance between the Manichaeism and Pelagianism in his views.[3] But we should understand that being a man of God, St. Augustine's views were shaped by the work of the Holy Spirit and it was not a mere outcome of a philosophical enquiry. It is never to be misunderstood that his works were revealed by Spirit, but rather shaped by the presence of the Spirit.

Disobedience and its consequence on Sexuality

Man disobeyed the Will of God by eating the fruit from the tree that was forbidden to be eaten as per the command of the Lord.[4] St. Augustine sees the imperfections of man in the light of the Original perfection desired by God.[5] Concupiscence or the tendency to be inclined towards evil is the result of the fall according to the Catholic doctrine. St Augustine hypothesizes that this disobedience of man merited him the just punishment by God. His genitals which were under the control of will before fall, started to disobey the will after the fall. St Augustine cites the Covering of their genitals by fig leaves as the evidence for this.[6] He interprets that these organs once treated without shame in innocence became an object of shame because of the consequence of the disobedience of man. For he quotes as follows:

> For it was not fit that his creature should blush at the work of his Creator. But by a just punishment the disobedience of their genitals was the retribution to the disobedience of the first man, for which disobedience they blushed when they covered with fig- leaves those shameful parts which previously were not shameful…..They were suddenly so ashamed of their nakedness, which they were daily in the habit of looking upon without embarrassment, that they could now no longer bear those sexual members naked, but immediately took care to cover them! Did they not thereby perceive those members to be disobedient to the choice of their will, which certainly they ought to have ruled like the rest (of their body) by their Voluntary Command?[7]

Sexuality Marked by Passion, not by Reason:

In the Original state it is reason that controls the sexuality. Reason, the Power of Will might have properly used the sexual organs at the disposition of God's Will. Since man disobeyed God, the Sexuality came to be under the control of Sexual Passion which St Augustine describes as "tumultuous". This passion runs contrary to the Peace and Tranquility of - Married Life.[8]

The shameful motion of the organs of generation", writes St Augustine is the consequence of the Original sin. In absence of Original Sin, with greater ease and quietness that the generative organs of our body might have - involved in intercourse.[9]

The Carnal sexual desire is considered by St. Augustine as the daughter of sin and that whenever it yields to assent to the commission of shameful deeds, it becomes also the mother of many sins.[10]

St Augustine's Conception of Sexuality without Intercourse:

According to St Augustine, in the absence of the Control of human sexuality by tumultuous passion (which itself is a consequence of Original Sin according to St Augustine) there must have been a method of begetting children without intercourse. He states that as God was able to create the First Parents without parents and formed the flesh of Jesus Christ in a Virgin womb without the Process of Intercourse, the proposed form of begetting children without intercourse have been possible.[11] In other words according to St Augustine, the original sexuality must be a sexuality in which the seed of man was dispatched into the womb without the loss of Virginity.[12]

Original Sin and Sexuality marked by Sexual Passion:

St Augustine states that even in the lawful union of a male and a female in the bond of marriage the intercourse involves sexual passion. The sexual passion which itself according to St Augustine is a consequence of Original Sin thus affects the Purity to intercourse. The sexual intercourse is the way by which the children are born and this sexual intercourse is marked by the presence of the influence of sexual passion (a product of Original sin) and hence it follows that the "infants although incapable of sinning, yet not born without the contagion of sin, -not, indeed, because of what is the lawful, but on account- of that which is unseemly; for from what is lawful nature is born; from what is unseemly Sin".[13]

According to St. Augustine whatever that comes into being by from the carnal sexual desire is bound by the original sin.[14]

Position on the Conception of Lord Jesus Christ

The Catholic Doctrine holds that Jesus was born in a supernatural way in the womb of Mary without the natural intercourse between Joseph and Mary. As the Apostles Creed echoes "He was conceived by the Holy Spirit in the womb of Virgin Mary". St Augustine says that as Jesus was not born of the intercourse that is marked by the sexual passion or sexual desire, he was not born of the sinful flesh.[15]

He also says that the conception of our Lord Jesus Christ is an exception to the conception by the sexual desire. We should be born again in Jesus Christ, who himself was born untainted from the Original Sin.

> ..Now from this sexual desire whatever comes into being by natural birth is bound by Original Sin, unless, indeed, it be born again in him whom the Virgin conceived without this sexual desire. Wherefore, when he vouchsafed to be born in the flesh, he alone was born without sin.[16]

Purpose of Sex

According to St Augustine the only purpose of sexual intercourse is to beget a new life. Anything contrary to that purpose comes under the dominion of sin.[17]

Sexual Intercourse in Marriage according to St Augustine

Sexual intercourse, according to Augustine, is for procreation and therefore it is not faulty. But for the purpose of satisfying the sexual passion is a venial sin.[18] Even in a marital relationship the intercourse should have the purpose of begetting new life. But a proper reading of *De bono Coniugali* shows that sexual pleasure when sought temperately and rationally is not termed concupiscence.[19]

St Augustine on Marriage

St. Augustine praises Marriage, unlike Manichaeism which denounces marriage. For instance, *"Marriage is itself honourable in all the goods which properly appertain to it"*[20].There are three ways a Christian may live with his wife according to St Augustine: a) Either with her fulfilling the Carnal sexual passions a thing which St Paul the Apostle speaks by permission; b) Providing for the Procreation of Children, which is praiseworthy to a certain degree; and c) Living in a brotherly-sisterly friendship without any sexual intercourse having his wife as though he had her not is the most excellent.[21]

St Augustine takes the words of Jesus about the condition of men and women after final resurrection like Angels of Heaven who don't give themselves in marriage to others. St Augustine exhorts to live in view of that. He advises to focus on those eternal things but not on the passing things such as intercourse and begetting children. St Augustine's heavy insistence on such a life promised by Christ that he even marks "to hate these things".[22]

Sins associated with Sexuality

As the only purpose of the sex is the procreation, therefore all other forms of sexual expressions such as Adultery, Fornication etc. are considered by Him as mortal sins.[23] He also objected -to homosexuality, since it is contrary to the God's plan for procreation. He even advocated punishment for such sins.

Sexuality according to St Thomas Aquinas

According to St Thomas Aquinas sexuality must be governed by the right reason, which in turn is derived and illumined by the Divine Law. When the gifts given by God are used by man according to the will of God for the very purpose for which they were created they are satisfying the natural order/natural law which governs them.[24] (*Note: All the references to Sexuality according to St. Thomas Aquinas section of this article are taken from this single reference no. 18. Hence the points in the article are mentioned here for reference. Eg. article 1, art. 1)*

Sins of Lust

Following Decretas, St Thomas classifies Simple fornication, incest, adultery, incest, seduction, rape and the unnatural vice under the category of sins. (article 1). He defines lust as seeking sexual pleasure not in accordance for the right reason. He measured the gravity of sin with regard to the sin in itself and/or some accident. The nature of the sin is determined by the good that which is opposed to it. (article 3). Moreover he agrees with St Gregory the Great that the sins of the flesh are less grievous in comparison with spiritual sins. St Thomas says that every sin depends on the judgement of reason. Thus in the absence of reason's judgement there is no sin in an act. (article 5).

Classification of Sexual Sins

1. Sexual Sins contrary to right reason

2. Sexual sins contrary to the natural order.

Sins Contrary to Right reason

Here the sin committed is against the right reason in using the gift of sexuality. They are enumerated as follows:

a) **Simple Fornication**: Fornication and intercourse with other than one's wife is a mortal sin citing Tobit 4: 13 and Deuteronomy 23: 17. Fornication is a mortal sin because it is incompatible with matrimony and opposed to the good of the child's upbringing.

b) **Touches and Kisses**: Following Scripture St Thomas Aquinas concludes that the touches and kisses done with the intention of lust is a Mortal sin. (Matthew 5: 28).

c) **Nocturnal Pollution**: Nocturnal Pollution in itself has not the character of sin. In cases such as an excess of seminal fluids they naturally discharge during sleep. But if the excess of seminal fluid itself is caused by a sinful cause (e.g. Excessive eating or drinking), neglect to guard against the sins of devil is considered sinful.

d) **Seduction:** Unlawful violation of a virgin while still under the guardianship of her parents is a mortal sin. St Thomas cites Deuteronomy 22: 28-29, Numbers 5:13 and Sirach 42: 11 to prove his claim.

f) **Rape:** Rape is an unlawful sexual intercourse where violence is employed. It is a mortal sin. However according to St Thomas the Judgment on the sin of rape varies based on the contexts. When a woman who is betrothed to someone is raped, this act of rape doesn't dissolve the contract of marriage, but it is an obstacle to marriage. Thus once the obstacle is cleared they can marry as betrothed. However St Thomas says that rape done by a husband on wife, he isn't guilty of rape because he has certain right in her (Article 7)

g) **Adultery:** According to Thomism adultery is a mortal sin because it is against human chastity and the good of human procreation.

h) **Incest:** Incest involves the unlawful intercourse with a woman related within the immediate family. It is a mortal sin because it is contrary to the natural honour that we owe to parents, against friendship and that could act as a way of encouraging the expression of lust in a greater magnitude.

i) **Sacrilege:** Sacrilege is a sin that is committed directly against God. When a person under the vow of chastity goes against their vow, it is an act of sacrilege since sexuality in these cases has a religious nature too. Violation of a consecrated virgin is also therefore a serious crime because it is committed against God directly.

Sins contrary to Natural Order

These unnatural sins corrupt the very principles of Natural Law. All unnatural sins are mortal by nature. They are also not for the right reason. Following St Augustine, Thomas calls for punishment of all unnatural offences.

a) **Pollution/Masturbation:**It is a sin that is purely committed for the sake of sexual pleasure without any copulation.

b) **Vice of Sodomy**: Copulation with an undue sex, male with a male, or female with female is called the Vice of sodomy as per St Thomas Aquinas. In modern terms it is understood as homosexuality. It is a mortal sin. He cites Romans 1:27 in support of his view.

c) **Bestiality**: Copulation with an undue species ie. an animal is called - bestiality. It is a mortal sin. St Thomas Aquinas cites Genesis 37: 2 as scriptural evidence.

d) **Unnatural means of Copulation**: Copulation done by not observing the natural manner. It is a mortal sin. A modern example is the usage of condoms in having sex, not observing the natural means of sex.

Gravity of Sins

1. According to St Thomas, among the sins that are committed contrary to right reason Sacrilege is the worst followed by rape, adultery, seduction and simple fornication respectively.

2. Among the sins that are contrary to natural order (i.e. unnatural vice) the most grievous one is bestiality followed by the vice of sodomy and the sin of pollution/uncleanliness respectively.

Factors Considered by St Thomas Aquinas in Classifying the Sins of Lust

I.   Divine Law

a.   Precedence of the Will of God

According to St Thomas Aquinas the reason of man should be guided by the Natural Order of laws given by God. (Art.12). In Thomism the natural order ordained by God with respect to sexuality is the proper disposition of sexuality towards procreation. Hence anything that runs contrary to procreation is considered as sin. Along with the natural order, the right reason should be the criteria to judge the morality of a sexual act. However the Will of God should be given precedence over the others citing the example of Prophet Hosea marrying an adulterous according to the Will of God, which by right reason is certainly invalid but as it was from the Will of God it isn't considered a sin (article 2).

b.   Authority of Bible

St Thomas Aquinas frequently comments from the citations from both the Old and New Testament. For example in arguing against the sin of fornication he cites 1 Corinthians 6: 17, *"He who is joined to the Lord is one spirit"* (Article 3).

c.   Teachings of the Church

St Thomas Aquinas' writings were guided by the teachings of the Catholic Church in classifying the species of the sin of lust. For example he cites the teachings of Pope Symmachus on the violation of widows and virgins. (Article 7). Moreover the division of lust as simple fornication, adultery, incest, seduction, rape and the unnatural vice was taken by St Thomas

Aquinas from Decretals. (Article 1).Decretals, are the letters of a Pope that formulate decisions in ecclesiastical law of the Catholic Church.

d.   Religious Vows

A person who takes the vow of chastity consecrates himself to God and His service. Hence the observance of chastity is here directed to the worship of God, thus an act of religion. If the sin of lust runs contrary to the observance of the vow of chastity then following St Augustine, Thomism declares that it is a sin of Sacrilege committed against God. (Article 10).

e.   Sacramental Nature

Marriage is a sacrament according to the Catholic Church. Marriage cannot be dissolved when the partners are alive. The same sacramental nature of marriage was the criteria used by St Thomas Aquinas in treating the questions of rape, adultery etc. In the case of rape of a maiden who is promised to marriage, the promise must be restored since rape does not dissolve the contract of marriage. (Article 7).

f.   Reason and Free will

The Catholic Theology teaches that God gifted human beings with a free will. An act could be considered as a mortal sin if it is committed with the free will. Thus a sinful act done under the absence of reason's judgment is imputed as a sin. St Thomas argues in this line to reason out that nocturnal pollution isn't a sin. (Article 5).

II.   Social Factors

a.   Social Authority

According to Thomism the social structure of relationships between Father-Mother-Son-Daughter is an important factor. Anything that runs contrary is considered a sin. For example St Thomas Aquinas rules out against Incest by arguing that it deprives the natural honour that we owe to our Parents. (Article 9). Another important factor is also the social authority of religion. In article 10 following St Augustine, St Thomas Aquinas affirms that although the close relationships between brothers and sisters were allowed in olden times, it should be condemned since

Religion condemns it. Moreover the authority of the male figure is emphasized.

b. Control of Lust

Controlling of lust has both spiritual as well as a moral nature. In arguing against incest, St Thomas Aquinas says that the sin of incest runs contrary to the controlling of lust since as the members of the same family need to live closer together, it'd give a frequent opportunity to participate in sex. (Article 10)

c. Good of the Child

St Thomas Aquinas considers the wellness and proper upbringing of a child as a criterion for judging the nature of sins associated with lust. Any sexual act that directly or indirectly affects the healthy upbringing of a child is considered under the criteria of Sin. St Thomas Aquinas argues that adultery is a sin based on these arguments, since adultery is contrary to the good of the upbringing of their own children. (Article 8).

d. Friendship

Quoting St Augustine St Thomas Aquinas says that the law of love is satisfied more perfectly in a marriage when with distant ones (not close relatives) the relations are united by special bonds of friendship. Anything that runs contrary is considered in the line of sin. Hence, incest in which people within a family are in physical intimacy is a hindrance to the social friendship and enlargement of social relationships. (Article 10).

III. Sexual Behaviour of Animals

The Angelic doctor had also drawn conclusions from the sexual behaviour of animals in judging the nature of the sin of lust. In arguing against incest he cites that even some animals owe their natural respect for their parents. (Article 10). Moreover in discussing the upbringing of Children, Aquinas cites the behaviour of many animals which require both parents to take care of their offspring. (Article 2).

Influences on St Thomas Aquinas' view of Sexuality

Indeed St. Augustine has a great influence in shaping the view of St Thomas Aquinas on Sexuality. He cites

St Augustine in discussing fornication (art. 2,3), Nocturnal Pollution (art. 5), Seduction (art.7), adultery (art. 8), Incest (art. 9), Sacrilege (art 10) and Unnatural vice (art. 12).

St Jerome (art. 7)

St Ambrose (Fornication – art. 2)

St Gregory the Great (Fornication – art. 3)

St Cyprian(On touches and kisses – art. 4)

Historian Valerius Maximus (art. 9-incest)

Aristotle (art. 9- incest)

Emperor Justinian (art. 10- Sacrilage) etc are also quoted.

Discussion

Both St. Augustine and St. Thomas Aquinas show their dependence on the Catholic Doctrine, Scripture, and Social Customs on the understanding of the Sexuality. St. Augustine has an enormous influence on St. Thomas Aquinas' view of sexuality. Both of them agree with the Concupiscence, the Goodness of Sexuality within the context of Marriage and the Natural Law concept of the Church. St. Augustine's view is also influenced by his past sinful sexual life. But St. Thomas Aquinas and St. Augustine accepts the Goodness of God who has provided us with the gift of Sexuality. It is a modern trend to equate that St Augustine and St Thomas Aquinas were responsible for introducing anti-sexual views in the Church, but we should understand that what these Doctors emphasize is to use the gift of sexuality only according to the Will of God which undoubtedly brings freedom to the human heart.

We should also understand that the laws of God are eternal and everlasting and cannot be changed. Hence the sins contrary to the Will of God as clearly mentioned and derived from the Scripture and Christian Tradition should be preserved and encouraged as these two Great Fathers of the Church Propose.

However we should also emphasize here the need for the Room for Mercy of God is not much emphasized in their writings. The scripture clearly connects the mercy of God and His Omnipotence.[25] They approach the sexuality in a legalistic manner of defining Sin, Categorization of Sin, and it's Punishment etc. but history has seen a countless number of people touched by the mercy of Christ and their lives transformed. From the Gospel the best example we could cite is the woman caught in adultery.[26]

Today's Psychology has revealed to us that Human Sexuality is a very complex system to understand. This Psychological view of Sexuality is missing from the views of these Doctors of the Church since in those early ages the field of Psychology was unchartered. Especially the Role of Unconsciousness in Sexuality isn't dealt by these Doctors of the Church. Psychoanalysis explains the role of social influences in sexuality through the complex concepts such as Oedipus complex, Transference, sublimation.[27] The reasons behind the sexual behaviours weren't studied by these Doctors, but a moral judgment of their actions were expressed.

The next criticism is that these Doctors provide us with a moral analysis of Sexuality, but not a theory to explain the complexity of sexuality. St. Augustine, however proposes us to view sexuality from a view of the Original perfection of Man and the effect of Original sin and its consequences.

Conclusion

St Augustine and St Thomas Aquinas has provided us with a view of sexuality from a Christian theological Perspective. A blind application and reading of their views to today's understanding of sexuality could lead to a number of misunderstandings. They should be approached with the modern understandings of Sexuality from a Scientific as well as a Sound Christian theological discourse. A sound knowledge of Scripture and reading in the light of the third person of the Trinity provide a valuable understanding of their works.

Endnotes

[1] *Augustine and Sexual sin https://pastordougroman.* Wordpress.com/ 2008/05/15/ Augustine-and-sexual-sin/ accessed 13-06-2017.

[2] F. Cayre A.A *Manual of Patrology* Society of St. John the Evangelist 616-617.

[3] *Saint Augustine and Conjugal sexuality http://www.churchinhistory.org/pages/booklets/ augustine.pdf* accessed 13-06-2017.

[4] Genesis 3:1-24 [NRSV].

5 *Augustine and Sex-The body is Sacred*, On Sexual Desire, Book II Chap 53, *http://www.thebodyissacred.org/origin/augustine.asp* accessed 13-06-2017.

6 *Augustine and Sex-The body is Sacred* ,Against Two letters of the Pelagians 1.31-32, *http://www.thebodyissacred.org/origin/augustine.asp* accessed 13-06-2017.

7 *Augustine and Sex-The body is Sacred* , On the Grace of Christ, Book II, 42, *http://www.thebodyissacred.org/origin/augustine.asp* accessed 13-06-2017.

8 *Augustine and Sex-The body is Sacred*, City of God, Book 14, Chapter 26.

9 *Augustine and Sex-The body is Sacred*, On Sexual Desire, Book II Chap 53.

10 *Augustine and and Sex-The body is Sacred*, On Sexual Desire, Book I, Chap. 27, *http://www.thebodyissacred.org/origin/augustine.asp* accessed 13-06-2017.

11 *Augustine and Sex-The body is Sacred*, On Marriage, p. 2, *http://www.thebodyissacred.org/origin/augustine.asp* accessed 13-06-2017.

12 *Augustine and Sex-The body is Sacred*, City of God, Book 14, Chapter 26.

13 *Augustine and Sex-The body is Sacred* , On the Grace of Christ, Book II, 42.

14 *Augustine and Sex-The body is Sacred*, On Sexual Desire, Book I, Chap. 27.

15 *Augustine and Sex-The body is Sacred*, On Sexual Desire, Book I, Chap. 13, *http://www.thebodyissacred.org/origin/augustine.asp*   accessed 13-06-2017.

16 *Augustine and Sex-The body is Sacred*, On Sexual Desire, Book II Chap 53.

17 *Augustine and Sex-The body is Sacred*, On Marriage, p 1, *http://www.thebodyissacred.org/origin/augustine.asp*   accessed 13-06-2017.

18 *Augustine and Sex-The body is Sacred*, On Marriage, p 6, *http://www.thebodyissacred.org/origin/augustine.asp*   accessed 13-06-2017.

19 *Augustine and Sex-The body is Sacred*, De bono con., c. 16, n. 18, *http://www.thebodyissacred.org/origin/augustine.asp*   accessed 13-06-2017.

20 *Augustine and Sex-The body is Sacred*, On Sexual Desire, Book II Chap 53.

21 *Augustine and Sex-The body is Sacred*, Sermon on the Mount, Book I, p 42, *http://www.thebodyissacred.org/origin/augustine.asp*   accessed 13-06-2017.

22 *Augustine and Sex-The body is Sacred* , Sermon of the Mount, Book I, P. 41 , *http://www.thebodyissacred.org/origin/augustine.asp*   accessed 13-06-2017.

23 *Augustine and Sex-The body is Sacred*, On Marriage, p 6, *http://www.thebodyissacred.org/origin/augustine.asp*   accessed 13-06-2017.

24 *Summa Theologiae (SecundaSecundaepartis, q. 153). www.newadvent.org* › Summa Theologiae › second Part of the Second Part. accessed 13-06 2017

25 Wisdom of Solomon 11:23 [NRSV]

[26] John 8: 1-11 [NRSV]

[27] Oedipus Complex- Wikipedia 2017, *https://en.wikipedia.org/wiki/Oedipus_complex* accessed 11-06-2017.

Martin Luther on
Gender and Sexual Diversities

Rohan Gideon

Introduction

This paper is an appraisal of Martin Luther's theological and biblical expositions on sexuality. It presents a mixed bag of interpretations that Luther exhibits in his teachings on human sexuality. Luther and sexuality is a less explored area of interest and research as ecumenical movements, especially as they celebrate the grand anniversary of Reformation focus on the much glorified and discussed themes such as interrogating ecclesiastical structures, contextual forms of Reformation, the unity of the church as so on. Sexuality studies in Christian theology is gaining prominence by the day and a study of Luther's notions of sexuality richly adds to the burgeoning discourse and helps us move beyond the conventional tenets.

On one hand, Luther shows the ability to challenge and transcend the conservative notions of sexuality attached to celibacy by breaking the celibacy vow and marrying a nun. But his notions of sexuality and physical pleasure within marriage to some extent contradict his contentions about celibacy vows. On the other, he makes incendiary remarks about homosexuality as a "monstrous depravity" which is "contrary to nature" and coming "undoubtedly from Satan." Therefore, one can notice Luther's varying degrees of acceptance or rejection of different sexual orientations. It is significant that we revisit Luther's theology of sexuality especially as we observe 500 years of the Reformation and review Luther's homopressive[1] as well as radical theological notions.

Luther's Conflicting Reading Postures on Sexuality

a.   Problematizing Luther's basis for his Understanding of Sexualities

Many of Luther's audacious statements on sexuality, especially his antagonistic comments on homosexuality, are biblical commentaries that exhibit either subtle or clear allegiance to cultural arguments of his times. Therefore, one can safely say that Luther was a child of his time who struggled in his interpretation of gender diversities. To present a feeler to initiate this discussion, this is how Luther creates binaries about mind and body about a human's exploration of one's sexuality:

> The uncleanness, or effeminacy, is every [sic] intentional and individual pollution that can be brought aboutin various ways: through excessive passion from shameful thoughts, through rubbing with hands, through fondling of another's bodies, especially a woman's, through indecent movements, etc. I have called it 'intentional' in order to differentiate it from the pollution that takes place during the night and sometimes during the day and the waking hours, but which happens to many people involuntarily. Such things are not intended.[2]

Significantly, Luther's negative approach to homosexuality starkly contradicts his radical questioning of the traditional notions of sexuality attributed to a celibate body and his breaking away from the institutional norms regarding marriage, sex and bodily pleasures. For Luther, marriage stops or reduces fornication and therefore marriage has to be looked at as a binary opposite to singlehood or celibacy. His commentary on 1 Corinthians 7 is one of the classic cases.[3] Therefore, Luther's theological understanding of homosexuality needs a probing of his scripture-reading posture.

Luther's contradictory positions on different types of sexuality raise a few questions: Why did Luther, who boldly questioned and violated the norms of celibacy and went on to marry a nun, not question the negative theological notions of homosexuality but only got harsher about it? What does that suggest about his scripture reading posture and what authority does Luther attribute to the Scripture while making theological judgments on sexualities? It is appropriate to start answering these questions through Luther's own question on the purpose of reading the scripture: "What is Scripture-good for?"[4] In other words, what is the significant role of the Scripture in times of controversies? Luther used verbs like "preach," "teach," and "inculcate" because they naturally carry oral, spoken connotations. Luther employed the same notion of testing and judging that he had used just a little more than a year earlier. Here he provides the theological depth to his earlier formulation. Precisely because Christ is the test and judge of the Holy Scriptures are the Scriptures qualified to test and judge all other writings.

Perhaps a classic nomenclature for Luther's reading posture is offered by Richard Neibuhr in his debate on *Christ and Culture*. Neibuhr calls Luther's theological style a 'paradox'. In Luther's writings, one predominantly finds conflicting ideas that sit alongside a lesser sense of continuity of traditions and ethical notions. This is clearly recognizable in his debates on law and grace, wrath and mercy, revelation and reason, time and eternity where the latter in these dualisms are viewed as positive outcomes and the former as conflicting with his new found scriptural understandings on the issues. [5] In other words, in spite of the presence of homosexuality as a negative presence within German culture, Christians may need to believe in and revitalize higher ethics of eternal life. Extending this argument, the understanding of sexuality in marriage and celibacy are less contradictory to scriptural values compared to sex within marriage, despite the belief that at a certain level sex in marriage is sinful but still could be practiced as sacred between husband and wife to sustain the cultural practice of heterosexual marriage. So there is a clearly drawn line between sex as acceptable in a marriage and sex among homosexual as Satanic and contrary to nature. For Luther, it is in this agonizing paradox that God's grace becomes more than sufficient in ways mysterious to human thought. This for Luther is necessary as it corresponds to every experience.[6]

b.   Luther and Body: Sex in Marriage and Celibacy

Luther's understanding of sexuality is based on a theological exposition of a judgmental God. The notion of the judgmental God is justified by the notions of the authority of the Scriptures to teach and judge. This is a dominant mode comes to him not just through reading of the Scripture but also with the church structure he grew up in. For Luther, the judgmental God manifested himself in Jesus Christ as revealed in the scripture. However, the act of judgment is secondary in relation the one who judges and where we find those judgments. Summarily, it is Jesus who is the resource for discerning the right decision as explained in the scripture. This can be well argued by Luther's own scripture-reading style. A significant biblical basis for his argument is from John 5:39: *You search the scriptures because you think that in them you have eternal life; and it is they that testify on my behalf.*[7]

Luther's understanding of love and sin needs some brief background explanation here. Since his childhood, Luther was surrounded by theologies that focused on purgatory, hell, angels, demons, sin, judgment and the saints. Jesus was depicted as an unapproachable, terrifying judge, but believers knew they could call upon the Blessed Virgin and other saints to intercede on their behalf. Therefore Luther was groomed into pondering upon the destiny of the soul and give scant regard to an elevated understanding of the body. This argument has a strong basis in the Augustinian theology and so Luther was greatly influenced..

A brief biographical note about Luther allows us an insight to his theological growth and mind. Influencing Luther's decisions on sexuality is his understanding of the role of God in a human's life. Luther was enmeshed in the theology of a strong judgmental or vengeful God who would not spare a sinner. It was not until Luther's superior, Johann von Staupitz, tried to counsel Luther to stop worrying about the judgmental attitude of God and simply start reading the scripture from the perspective of the love God showed that Luther realized the loving and welcoming nature of God. The turnaround from fear of judgment to a hospitable God was not an easy transition for Luther. Luther later recalled his true feelings: "Love God? I hated him!" This, of course, only added to his spiritual fear and turmoil. Finally, the annoyed Staupitz strongly suggested that Luther pursued a doctoral research at the local University of Wittenburg, hoping the rigours of academia and involvement in hard physical work would force Luther to focus on the issues of the body than just the state of his soul. This is because, for Luther, the body was the site of sin which needed justification. He stretched the idea of sexual sin even to the sexual union in a marriage. For instance, Luther thought that even the purest of marital sexual union or intimacy had sin lurking around it when he says:

> The temptation of the flesh has become so strong and consuming that marriage may be likened to a hospital for incurables which prevents inmates from falling into graver sin.[8]

Luther's theology of Incarnation has specific ramifications for his views concerning the body, sensuality, desire, and sexuality. From Luther's reading of Scripture alongside the knowledge of his pastoral and familial work, he came to expound that humans are bodily creatures with physical needs, driven to provide for these needs by desire. The human need for a relationship is also driven by desire. As Christ befriended, healed, fed, and washed the bodies of those he met, so too the Christian is called to human relationship with others and the bodily service of the neighbour. This is also true in a romantic relationship, which has a bodily element for Luther. Based on this argument he casts off sexual abstinence as a human virtue.[9] However, at an intensive theological argument, we can understand from his hospital analogy that all sexual intimacy even within the marriage has only a temporary significance. The need to spiritually transport the soul to the divine is the highest priority compared to sexual pleasure even within a marriage.

Luther's advocacy for leniency on the connection between celibacy and sexual relationship can best be explained through debunking of his own celibacy. He said that the monks might have resisted the temptation, but "the rest of these celibates can only desire that kind of will; they cannot produce it".[10] Here Luther was seeing in the sexual desire of a celibate only a natural desire that cannot be suppressed through religious and institutional censures.

Luther married Katherine von Bora, a former nun. According to Ozment, Luther actually encouraged fathers to remove their daughters from convents. In 1523, he praised Leonhard Koppe for engineering the escape of his daughter and 11 other nuns, among them was Katherine von Bora (Luther's future wife). Luther would compare Koppe's freeing the sisters to Moses' deliverance of Israel from Egyptian bondage.[11] Luther explains his struggle to settle between the ideas of celibacy and marriage because of their strong links with the theology of body and sin. He says

> When I was a boy, marriage was considered so infamous on account of
> impious and impure celibacy that I thought I could not think about married
> life without sin. For all were convinced that if anyone wished to live a life
> holy and acceptable to God, he must never become a spouse but must live
> a celibate and take the vow of celibacy. This was why many men who had
> married became monks or contemptible priests (sacrificuli) after the death
> of their wives.[12]

Luther advocated divorce according to biblical principles at a time when
divorce was almost impossible; he encouraged priests to marry by showing
that there was no conflict between their calling and marriage; he denounced
celibacy, blaming it for encouraging lust rather than aiding chastity; he
restored marriage and family life back to the arena of spirituality and
respectability in society. Luther lived out his own advice by getting married
and living an exemplary married life. What made Luther so effective was
the passionate intensity with which he advocated these reforms. He wrote
and spoke with such power and backed up his words with such a bold and
courageous life, although living in the shadow of constant threats, that
centuries after his death, the power and conviction of his ideas still
resonate.[13]

c.   On Women Priesthood, Body and Subjugation

Luther says no to women pastors based on the argument of competence.
Firstly, we see that Luther maintains male-female dichotomy. He further
complicates it by strongly suggesting that only an abled-bodied male is
chosen for the priesthood. His mentioning of women and children clearly
keeps away people from any other sexual-orientations and therefore shuts
them off from taking up the priesthood. Luther explains:

> It is, however, true that the Holy Spirit has accepted women, children, and
> incompetent people from this function, but chooses (except in emergencies)
> only competent males to fill this office, as one reads here and there in the
> epistles of St. Paul that a bishop must be pious, able to teach, and the
> husband of one wife – and in I Corinthians 14 he says, 'The women should
> keep silence in the churches.[14]

In summary, it must be a competent and chosen man. Children, women,
and other persons are not qualified for this office. Moses says in Genesis
3, 'You shall be subject to man.' The Gospel, however, does not abrogate
this natural law but confirms it as the ordinance and creation of God.[15]

Preaching is entrusted to the man and not to the woman, as Paul also teaches, insofar as this has to do with Christian matters. Otherwise, it can occasionally happen that a woman gives better advice, as one reads in Scripture. But apart from that, the offices of leading, preaching, and teaching God's word are commanded to the man.

d.   Homosexuality and Cultural Biases in Luther's Biblical Interpretation

Luther attributes his hatred of homosexuality to his upbringing and cultural influence alongside his literal reading of specific verses from the Bible on homosexuality. On the argument why he is homophobic, he explains that homosexuality infiltrated into Germany through licentious Italians and that the Germany of his time was unaware of such a *"monstrous depravity"*. *This argument of Luther leads us to ask why he had to bring in the nationalism-arguments into his scriptural interpretations.* There seems to be deep cultural and nationalist biases in Luther's interpretations. We see that Luther grew up with the notion especially about Italians and other European countries as being licentious and polluting Germany with homosexual practices.

Initially Luther legitimizes his cultural argument with a strong biblical prelude referring to the sin of Sodom. Giving his thoughts on Genesis 19:4-5, Luther wrote:

> the heinous conduct of the people of Sodom extraordinary, inasmuch as they departed from the natural passion and longing of the male for the female, which is implanted into nature by God, and desired what is altogether contrary to nature. Whence comes this perversity? Undoubtedly from Satan, who after people have once turned away from the fear of God, so powerfully suppresses nature that he blots out the natural desire and stirs up a desire that is contrary to nature.[16]

Luther's argument about natural passion is part of his unabashed priority to heterosexual relationships based on his understanding of the God's intended natural order. All sexual relationships should be restricted between man and woman and they should be kept within marriage. As could be notice in the following statement, which is a part of his biblical exposition on the issues, Luther projects his cultural hatred for homosexuality and resorts to blaming strategy on nationalistic lines in which he places Germany on high moral grounds:

> I for my part do not enjoy dealing with this passage because so far the ears of the Germans are innocent of and uncontaminated by this monstrous depravity; for even though disgrace, like other sins, has crept in through an ungodly soldier and a lewd merchant, still the rest of the people are unaware of what is being done in secret.[17]

Also built into Luther's biblical interpretation of homosexuality is the German nationalistic spirit that prevailed during his time. Luther blames the practice of homosexuality in Germany on Carthusian monks of Italy by overlooking the fact that homosexuality was no alien a practice in his Germany. As a continuation of the previous quote, Luther claims: The Carthusian monks deserve to be hated because they were the first to bring this terrible pollution into Germany from the monasteries of Italy.[18]

His comparison of homosexuality with idolatry and Italian monks refers back to the art of Italian Renaissance that reintroduced sensuality. Luther believed that this reintroduction made homosexuality and pederasty rampant among the Italians. Even the Roman Catholic religion became lenient with different sexual orientations.[19]

Conclusion

From the above arguments of Luther about various sexual orientations, we notice that Luther carries a deep cultural bias that he grew up with and attempts to justify those biased arguments through scriptural expositions. Luther's rejection of homosexual activity is a theological judgment rooted in the reality of the way the wrath of God is revealed against all ungodliness that will not acknowledge God to be the Creator and Lord that He is. For Luther, homosexuality is a form of idolatry. When he senses that the scriptural arguments are inadequate to support his arguments, as in the case of his disregard for homosexuality, he resorts to an extra-scriptural resource such as a nationalistic argument. It confirms that while Luther on one hand is pragmatic about his resistance to forms of sexuality that constricts his freedom as in celibacy, he resorts to despicable extremes in suppressing the forms of sexuality, as in homosexuality, that he does not follow or disagrees with.

While it can be argued that Martin Luther was a child of his time and therefore raised discomforting questions on sexuality, especially homosexuality, it is clear that Luther himself has raised questions on issues like homosexuality and has made absolute statements in the light of the Scriptures. Therefore, it becomes important that we discuss his reading postures more than ever in the light of increasing issues on sexual identity and the role of scriptures.

Endnotes

[1] The term 'homopression' is intended to highlight the oppressive effects on gay/lesbian persons of homophobic behaviour, attitudes, fears be they on the part of others or the gay or lesbian persons own internalized homophobia. Rick Reinkraut, "Moral Awareness and Therapist use of Self", *The Journal of Pedagogy, Pluralism and Practice,* (Summer, 2008) IV/1.

[2] Martin Luther, "Lectures on Romans," *Luther's Works,* v. 25, 166.

[3] Martin Luther, "Commentary on 1 Corinthians 7 (1523), in *Luther Works 28:III*

[4] Martin Luther, "Defense and Explanation of All the Articles" (1521), in *Luther Works* 32: II, 1.

[5] Richard Neibuhr, *Christ and Culture,* 151.

[6] Neibuhr, 187.

[7] Martin Luther, "Preface to the Epistles of St. James and St. Jude" (1546; 1522) in *Luther's Works* ed. Jaroslav Pelikan and Helmut Lehmann, 55 vols. (Philadelphia and St. Louis: Fortress and Concordia, 1955-1986) 35, 96.

[8] Luther, *A Sermon on the Estate of Marriage,* LW 44, ed., James Atkinson, Fortress Press, Philadelphia, 1966), 9.

[9] Jennifer Hockenbery Dragseth, Martin Luther's Views on Bodies, Desire, and Sexuality, Oxford Research Encyclopedia of Religion, Online Publication, Oct 2016

[10] Martin Luther, *Works,* vol. 44, ed., James Atkinson (Philadelphia: Fortress Press, 1966), 341.

[11] Steven Ozment, *When Fathers Ruled: Family Life in Reformation Europe (Harvard, 1983),* 17.

[12] LW, 1: 135.

[13] Trevor O. Reggio, "Martin Luther on Marriage and Family", *History Research,* March 2012, Vol. 2, No. 3, 195-218.

[14] Luther on Women: A Sourcebook edited by Susan C. Karant-Nunn, Merry E. Wiesner-Hanks, (Cambridge: Cambridge University Press, 2003), 75

[15] Martin Luther's Basic Theological Writings, Third Edition, eds., Timothy F Lull and William R. Russell (Minneapolis: Fortress Press, 2012).

[16] *Luther's Works*, Vol. 3, 255 ("Lectures in Genesis: Chapters 15-20"), ed: Jaroslav Pelikan. (Saint Louis: Concordia Publishing House, 1961).

[17] *Luther's Works*, Vol. 3, 251-252

[18] Kirk Rodby, *The Dark Heart of Utopia: Sexuality, Ideology, and the Totalitarian Movement* (Universe, 2009), 132.

[19] Kirk Rodby, *The Dark Heart of Utopia*, 132-133.

A Critical Evaluation of John Calvin's Teachings on Human Sexuality

Lalnghakthuami

Introduction

John Calvin, the sixteenth century Geneva reformer led a sweeping reformation of Genevan religious, political and legal institutions in 1536 to 1538 and 1541 until his death in 1564. He introduced fundamental changes in Church-State relations, moral and sumptuary laws, criminal laws and procedures, education and poor relief, marriage and family laws and many others. His influence was so profound on Western legal tradition that even after two centuries a religious skeptic such as Jean-Jacques Rousseau had only praise for his compatriot: "Those who consider Calvin only as a theologian fail to recognize the breath of his genius. The editing of our wise laws, in which he had a large share, does him as much credit as his *Institute of the Christian Religion*…So long as the love of the country and liberty is not extinct among us, the memory of this great man will be held in reverence."[1] His ecclesial and theological legacy remains even now in the Reformed Presbyterian Churches all over the world.

Calvin's thought on human sexuality can be traced through the *Institute of the Christian Religion*, 2.8. 41–44, where he had given theological exposition on the seventh commandment of "Thou Shalt Not Commit Adultery". Apart from this his thought can also be traced through his series of letters, sermons and biblical commentaries. The following thoughts would be helpful while evaluating Calvin's teaching on human sexuality:

Sexuality – original sin?

Like Augustine of Hippo (354 – 430 CE), Calvin believed that sexuality or sexual intercourse was created good and as a natural part of God's order. It belonged to the creation ordinance. However, this vision of sexuality did not exist due to the fallen nature of human being. As sexual concupiscence became the perfect illustration of original sin for Augustine, Calvin also said that sexual intercourse was sinful. It was because sex after the fall became the lust of the flesh and the procreative sexuality became questionable. In this regard Calvin was influenced by Augustine on the matter of sexual intercourse.

Calvin's teaching on sexuality may be understood through his formulation of marriage theology of covenant. He developed marriage theology in the context of his attack on the prevailing Catholic theology of marriage. Like the Lutheran reformers, he grounded his attack in the "theory of the two kingdoms".[2] According to him, marriage, family and sexuality are matters of the earthly kingdom alone. For him "Marriage is a good and holy ordinance of God".[3] It is designed to procreate children to remedy incontinence as it belongs to the earthly kingdom and to promote "love between husband and wife".[4] As John Witte Jr. observes, the morals and mores of marriage, for Calvin, are subject to the laws of God that are written on the tablets of conscience, rewritten in the pages of Scripture, and distilled in the Ten Commandments.[5]

In counteracting Roman Catholic views of marriage as sacrament, Calvin argues that marriage, however, is not a sacrament of the heavenly kingdom. As divine promise is not confirmed and sanctifying grace is not conferred upon the marriage like the sacraments of baptism and Eucharist, it should not be regarded as sacrament. Moreover, Calvin states it clearly that marriage has no bearing on one's salvation or eternal life rather it symbolizes the bond between Christ and his Church.[6] Calvin as a person of his time views that marriage is instituted by God but "sexual intercourse is essentially sinful".[7] However, if it occurs within matrimony, then it ceases to be sin.[8]

Calvin views marriage as "the provision for the weakened human condition. And that the conjugal relation was ordained as a necessary means of preventing us from giving way to unbridled lust. The truth is that natural feeling and the passions inflamed by the fall make the marriage tie doubly necessary, save in the case of those whom God has by special grace exempted. Because complete, permanent self-control is rare, marriage is the remedy."[9]

In his mature theology of marriage he used the doctrine of the covenant to describe the vertical relationship between God and human being and the horizontal relationship between husband and wife. In his commentary on Eph.5:22, he concludes that God expects constant faith and good works in our relationship with him. So God expects faithfulness and sacrificial works in our relationships with our spouses. He believes that God is the founder of marriage: "Now marriage was not instituted by men, we know that God is the author of it…it is a sacred covenant and calls it divine for that reason."[10] He wrote: "When a marriage takes place between a man and a woman, God presides and requires a mutual pledge from both." (cf. Mal. 2:14; Eph.5:22-26; Deut. 5:18). God participates in the formation of the covenant of marriage through his chosen agents or parties on earth such as parents, peers, ministers and magistrates. To omit any such party in the formation of the marriage was, in effect, to omit God from the marriage covenant.[11]

Purpose of Sexuality

According to him the covenant of marriage is grounded "in the creation and commandments of God," and "in the order of law and nature" (cf. Gen. 2:18, Deut. 24:1-4; Mal. 2:15). At creation, God ordained the structure of marriage to be a life-long heterosexual union between a fit man and a fit woman of the age of a mature consent.[12] God assigned to this marriage three interlocking purposes:[13]

i.   The mutual love and support of husband and wife
ii. The mutual procreation and nurture of children and
iii. The mutual protection of both parties from sexual sin

Sexual dysfunction, he insisted, was an absolute barrier to marriage, for it vitiated all three purposes of marriage. Marriages of "the frigid and eunuchs" were likewise null, for such union 'completely obviate the nature and purpose of marriage'.[14] He called for an automatic annulment of any marriage of a permanently dysfunctional party. He grounded several biblical norms for married parties in the created purposes of marriage. Most importantly, he urged that married couples retain a healthy sex life, even after their childbearing years.[15] Husband and wife should not, therefore, withhold sex from the other nor should they neglect or reject one another after intimacy or intercourse (cf. Deut. 22: 5:18 Comm. 1 Cor. 7:6). Procreation was only one created purpose of marriage where it could not be achieved, a couple had to double their efforts to achieve the other purpose of mutual love and mutual protection from lust – "treating each other with chaste tenderness" even where God would not bless them with children (cf. Gen 16: 1-6).He also believed that sexual activity within marriage should be done with the intention of honouring God. Sex is a gift of God to the married couple and they should take care of the gift meaningfully.

In his exposition of the Genesis account of woman's creation, he concludes that in nature, man and woman enjoy a "common dignity before God" and a common function of "completing" the life and love of the other (cf. Gen. 1:27) In marriage, husband and wife are "joined together in one body and one soul," but then assigned "distinct duties" and "different authorities" (cf. Gen. 2:18, 22). "The divine mandate was that the husband would look up in reverence to God, the woman would be a faithful assistant to him, and both with one consent would cultivate a holy, friendly and peaceful intercourse" (cf.Gen. 2:18). According to him the created subordination of the wife to the husband was exacerbated by the fall into sin (cf. Gen. 2: 22, 25; I Cor 11:4-10, Eph 5:22-26) At the same time, he called marital couples repeatedly to the mutual love and nurture that God had prescribed for marriage (cf. Gen. 2:18; Gen. 29:18, I Cor. 7:3; 9:11)[16] Here we see Calvin taking a traditional and conservative stance in supporting the secondary role of women which needs to be reviewed and re-examined.

Sexual Sins

He grounded various biblical rules against illicit sexual unions in the created structure of marriage – a lifelong heterosexual union of a fit man and a fit woman.[17] He condemned as 'monstrous vices' sodomy, buggery, bestiality, homosexuality and other 'unnatural' acts and alliances- arguing cryptically that to 'lust for our own kind' or 'for brutes' was 'repugnant to the modesty of nature itself' (cf. Lev.18:22; Deut. 22:13-24). He condemned as 'incestuous' marriages contracted between the blood and family relatives identified in Leviticus – arguing that God had prohibited such unions to avoid discord, abuse, rivalry and exploitation among these relatives. He also condemned the traditional Hebrew practice of polygamy.[18] His arguments were based on the teaching of Christ and his apostles that 'the two shall become one flesh' (cf. Mt.19: 3-9; Mk10:2-12). [19] Witte Jr. observes that in his created structure of the marriage covenant, Calvin was thus able to integrate various biblical and natural norms against bestiality, homosexuality, polygamy, adultery, desertion, and fornication and to smuggle in a tepid endorsement of divorce and firmer prohibition against separation. [20]

Adultery

Calvin regarded adultery as 'the worse abomination' for in one act the adulterer violates the covenant bonds with his/her spouse, God and the broader community.[21] He considered various other acts within the marital estate – besides sexual intercourse with a third party – to be tantamount to adultery. On one extreme, he regarded sexual perversity with one's own spouse as a violation of the spirit of the seventh commandment. "If married couples recognize that their association is blessed by the Lord, they are thereby admonished not to pollute it with uncontrolled and dissolute lust… For it is fitting that a marriage, once covenanted in the Lord, be called to moderation and modesty."[22]

As Witte Jr. writes, for Calvin, the commandment against adultery was equally binding on the unmarried, and equally applicable to both illicit sexual activities *per se* and various acts leading to the same. He condemned with particular vehemence the sin of fornication – sexual intercourse or other illicit acts of sexual touching by a non-married party (cf. Lev. 20:10; 22: 22-27). He decried at length the widespread practice of casual sex, prostitution, concubinage, premarital sex, non-marital cohabitation, and other forms of bed-hopping that he encountered in modern-day Geneva as well as in ancient Bible stories.[23] All these actions, Calvin believed, openly defied God's commandment against adultery and God's commendation of chaste and holy marriage.[24] He also urged a comparable extension of the civil law of adultery. In his more exuberant moments, he tended to treat all manner of mildly sexual activities – lewdness, dancing, bawdy gaming, sexual innuendo, coarse humour, provocative primping, suggestive plays and literature, and much more – as forms of adultery, punishable by the state (cf. Deut. 22: 5-8, 25-30; Eph. 5: 3-5; I Pet. 3:3; Tit. 2:3-5).[25]

Extra-marital Sex

He viewed extra-marital sex as unpardonable sin in the eyes of God. Those who are involved in it would be accused and guilty before God. He said:

> "Any mode of cohabitation different from marriage is cursed in his sight…Let us be aware, therefore, of yielding to indulgence, seeing we re-assured that the curse of God lies on every man and woman cohabiting without marriage"[26]

Calvin did not approve sexual intercourse outside marriage. He encouraged the engaged couple not to have sex before their marriage. Pre-marital sex was forbidden in his parish where he was a pastor.

Conclusion

In general Calvin's teaching on the theology of the marriage covenant in particular and human sexuality, is based on the Biblical teaching of sexuality. He does not distance himself from the patristic theology that eventually led him take the traditional and orthodox stance on sexuality. He sets the agenda for understanding and practising human sexuality for the people of the 16th century. He values human sexuality and preaches against sex outside of marriage. His understanding of sexuality as God's intention within the lifelong relationship between a husband and a wife may be a legacy that we have inherited from Calvin.

However, Calvin's teaching on human sexuality seems to be inadequate as he did not outline the theological foundation of a Christian understanding of human sexuality. As our theological reflections remind us that God is the author of human sexuality, it is a gift of God, therefore, we need to affirm, celebrate and experience it. Since Calvin did not further elaborate of his theological exposition on human sexuality it is impossible to get a new idea for today's understanding of human sexuality. As his contributions are remarkable it is essential that we read his teachings and theology in his own context.

Endnotes

[1] John Witte Jr. "Between Sacrament and Contract: Marriage as Covenant in John Calvin's Geneva" in *Calvin Theological Journal* 33/1 (April, 1998): 12.

[2] John Witte Jr. "Between Sacrament and Contract, 17.

[3] John Calvin, *Institute of the Christian Religion*,Translated by Henry Beveridge (Grand Rapids, Michigan: Wm. B. Eerdmans Publishing Company, 1989), 4.19.34 (Hereafter cited as John Calvin, *Institute of the Christian Religion*).

[4] John Calvin, *Institute of the Christian Religion*, 4.19.34

[5] John Witte Jr., "Between Sacrament and Contract:..." in *Calvin Theological Journal*,18.

[6] John Calvin, *Institute of the Christian Religion*,4.19.39

[7] David K. Semenya, "Pastoral Evaluation on the Basotho's view of sexuality. Revisiting the views of sexuality of Augustine, Thomas Aquinas, Martin Luther and John Calvin" in *Theological Studies* 71/2 (2015). See DK Semenya-HTS TheologicalStudies, 2015-scielo.org.za (accessed on July 14,2017).

[8] DK Semenya-HTS TheologicalStudies, 2015-scielo.org.za (accessed on July 14, 2017).

[9] John Calvin, *Institute of the Christian Religion*, 2.8.42 . See also DK Semenya-HTS TheologicalStudies, 2015-scielo.org.za (accessed on July 14, 2017).

[10] Calude-Marie Baldwin, "Marriage in Calvin's Sermon," in *Calviniana: Ideas and Influence of Jean Calvin*, edited by Robert V. Schnucker (Missouri: Sixteenth Century Journal Publishers,Inc., 1988),122.

[11] Cited by John Witte Jr. "Between Sacrament and Contract: Marriage as Covenant in John Calvin's Geneva" in *Calvin Theological Journal*, 37. See also his Commentaries on Lev.19:29; Serm. 5:16; Comm. I Cor. 7:36,38, Eph.6:1-3).

[12] John Witte Jr. "Between Sacrament and Contract:...", 38.

[13] See also his Commentaries on (Comm.Gen. 1:27; 28; 2:21, 22; Comm.Mt. 19: 3-9; Mk. 10:2-12).

[14] John Witte Jr., "Between the Sacrament and Contract:...", 49.

[15] J ohn Witte Jr., "Between the Sacrament and Contract:...,"52.

[16] See Willis P. DeBoer, "Calvin on the Role of Women" in *Exploring the Heritage of John Calvin: Essays in Honor of John Bratt*, edited by David E. Holwerda (Grand Rapids, Michigan: Baker Book House, 1976), 236 – 272.

[17] John Witte Jr., "Between Sacrament and Contract:...", 41.

[18] John Witte Jr., "Between Sacrament and Contract:...", 42.

[19] See John Calvin, *Institute of the Christian Religion* 4.19.36.

[20] John Witte Jr., "Between the Sacrament and Contract:...," 49.

[21] John Calvin, *Institute of the Christian Religion*, 2.8.41.

[22] John Calvin, *Institute of the Christian Religion*, 2.8.41.

[23] John Witte Jr., "Between the Sacrament and Contract:...," 48.

[24] John Witte Jr., "Between the Sacrament and Contract:...," 48.

[25] John Calvin., *Institute of the Christian Religion*, 2.8.44.

[26] John Calvin, *Institute of the Christian Religion*, 2.8.44.

Orthodoxy and Sexuality: Reflections on the Doctrine of God and Anthropology

Geevarghese Mor Coorilos

Introduction

It was Carl Jung who said: "When people brought sexual questions to me, they invariably turned out to be religious questions and when they brought religious questions to me, they always turned out to be sexual ones."[1] Of all the issues that confront the Church today, that of sexuality, perhaps, is the most sensitive and complex one. It continues to be a divisive issue in several church families. How does Orthodox theology address the concern of sexuality? How does Orthodoxy approach the issue from an ethical perspective? What follows here are some random thoughts on Orthodox concept of God and theological anthropology vis-a-vis human sexuality.

God in Orthodoxy: A Trinitarian Perspective on Sexuality

One of the fundamental tenets of Orthodox theology is its apophatic nature. It affirms that God is essentially ineffable and beyond full human comprehension. The totality of the mystery of God is beyond human reasoning and categories. According to Gregory of Nyssa, God's "*ousia*" or God's "is-ness" remains inaccessible to our concepts and words.[2] This implies that none can make exclusive claims about God, about God's nature, about God's truth and about God's saving power. A theology which is fundamentally apophatic, therefore, cannot be compatible with an ethic that is prescriptive and exclusive. This is particularly pertinent in theological discourses around moral issues such as sexuality. Contextuality and provisionality of ethics are therefore intrinsic to an apophatic theological discourse. Every generation, as Gregory maintains, will have to create its own visions of reality and shape its life in tune with them.[3] Trinity, perhaps, is the best available language to talk about God and the doctrine of the Holy Trinity is foundational to Orthodox theology. What characterizes the Holy Trinity, amongst other things, is love. As Fr. George Morelli explains, "the persons of the Holy Trinity commune among themselves in love".[4] Creation came into being out of this Trinitarian love. In this sense, as Brian Edgar puts it, human sexual relations, in their wider sense, mirror the intra- Trinitarian love of God.[5] This love of God reaches out, in particular, to "the other" rather than to the Self. What is of significance here is that "the other" can be any one-the scope of "the other" is not confined to any particular gender, race, creed, caste etc. This means that God is beyond sex and gender, although the divine does include these dimensions. Whilst God is both male and female, God is also beyond gender and sex. To use a category that is in currency today, God is "trans-gender" as well. Whereas the Hebrew word for Spirit (*ruah*) is feminine, the Greek term for Spirit (*pneuma*) is neuter in gender. As James Nelson argues, Israel's rejection of Canaanite fertility cults and religion was in fact an affirmation that the God of Israel, Yahweh, was neither male nor female. The creator God who is also the creator of sexuality is at the same time the one who transcends human sexuality. There is a "both him and her " in that God is both male and female and trans-gender as well. To put it in the words of James Nelson again: "in the "divine androgyny", personhood transcends gender."

The Pauline affirmation that there is neither male nor female...in Christ (Gal.3:28) can therefore be understood as an avowal not simply of gender parity or equality of sexes but also of the "trans-gender" aspect of the divine. The "third gender" as the transgender people are categorized today in certain contexts is therefore inclusive of the Trinitarian divine being. God is both male and female. Yet God is beyond male and female categories. God is trans-gender: God is love. The Trinitarian love overflows and reaches out to the world and to humanity who in turn is called to do likewise by loving others rather than the self. As has already been made clear, "the other" is anyone except oneself. What Trinity forbids is the love of the Self (Narcissism) not diversity in sexuality. The "other" needs to be understood as a category that denotes those who are being discriminated against and whose identity and being are being marginalized. From this liberationist perspective, sexual minorities such as people with homosexual or bi-sexual orientation and trans-gender people belong to those communities that are being "othered" and discriminated against. Holy Trinity signals a theological and ethical caution against such thinking and praxis that are oppressive and demeaning. What is being argued here, therefore, is that the Triune God represents a Godhead that allows diversity of expression, love included. Integrity and respect for "the other" are the conditions for diversity in a Trinitarian setting. Yet another key feature of the Holy Trinity is that it affirms particularities of persons within the community. The individuality and distinct identity of each person within the Triune Godhead is affirmed and valued. In fact, the theological struggle against the Filioque clause being inserted into the Nicene Creed, for the Oriental theological stream, in particular, was a struggle essentially against the tendency to subordinate the personhood of the Holy Spirit within the Holy Trinity. Thus, social Trinity offers us a collegial vision of social engineering over against a pyramidal pattern. In the context where certain sections of people such as homosexuals and trans-gender people are being denied their right to their identity and individuality, Holy Trinity is a powerful theological guard against such discriminatory systems. As no "*ousia*" in the Trinity is superior or inferior to the others, co-equality and collegiality characterize the Trinitarian community of God. The logic of Trinity is that it is the celebration of diversity and distinct identities in a society that actually leads to harmony, not the suppression of marginal identities. What characterizes the divine community of love, the Holy Trinity, then, is not specifically the gender of Godhead but the "persons" ("is-ness") of the Holy Trinity. What should, therefore, govern genuine sexual relationships, according to Trinitarian ethics, are integrity and commitment of the persons involved in relationships. The Trinitarian God of love casts out all kinds of fear. Phobia and agape do not and cannot co-exist. The latter takes away the former through its persuasive power. The present generation has constructed a culture of phobia through which certain sections of people are being deliberately demonized, dehumanized and discriminated against. Under racism, Blacks have undergone this process of "otherization". Nazi fascism ill treated Jewish people using the same logic. Under castesim, Dalits in India are being treated as subhuman beings. The neo-imperial project of cultural globalization has been involved in a project of villainizing Islam, leading to the creation of an Islamophobic culture worldwide. Fundamentalists among various faith communities have created a similar culture of homophobia where people with different sexual orientations and gender backgrounds are being considered and treated like criminals and condemned as sinners. Trinity has the potential- to address these vital issues. It is a perfect antidote to all kinds of phobias. In the words of Metropolitan John Zizioulas, as quoted by Eric Hyde, "the essence of sin is the fear of the other...".[6] Sin, therefore, is committed when the Self is asserted by hating and rejecting "the other". Somehow, this fear of "the other" is pathologically inherent in our existence. Hence, there is a potential danger of the fear of "the other extending its canvas to the fear of every otherness. Holy Trinity corrects this aberration by affirming that "the other" is an integral part of one's existence because "the other" is affirmed in the Trinitarian community. Fr. Kishkovsky brings out the Trinitarian ethos of hospitality over against the ethos of phobia and hate in his reflections on Genesis 17, the first ever, or perhaps the second, albeit indirect, reference to the Holy Trinity in the whole Bible. According to him, Genesis 17 is an account of Abraham and Sarah offering hospitality to the three strangers-the other(s)-the Holy Trinity itself. The Greek word for hospitality is philoxenia which means "love for the other" and its antonym is xenophobia which actually is the fear of the other/ stranger. Our vision of the image of God is therefore an open invitation to love, respect, welcome, hope and healing. The "content" of Imago Dei is love. Perfect love-Trinitarian love-can be expressed only when there is no discrimination of "the other" and where there is no phobia. In sum, a theology which is essentially apophatic and which is rooted in the Holy Trinity that affirms plurality, equality, egalitarianism, democracy, and interdependence is incompatible with an ethic that promotes discrimination and exclusion. This leads me to my second and final point, that of theological anthropology in Orthodoxy and it's Implications for moral decision making, especially on complex ethical issues such as human sexuality.

Image of God: Orthodox theological anthropology and sexuality

One of the salient features of Orthodox anthropology is that it is in tune with the Orthodox Trinitarian theology. Reflecting on the creation narrative in Gen.1:26-27, Fr. Kishkovsky argues that the account unequivocally asserts that every human being without any exception bears the imprint of God which in turn implies that no one can be discriminated against. "Let us make human beings in our image and likeness". The plural "us" and "our" in this account is perhaps the first reference to the Holy Trinity in the Bible. The image of God that humanity is endowed with in creation is the image of the Triune God, the defining features of which are relationality, equality, collegiality, mutual love, sharing, justice and interdependence. Any practice and action that devalues the identity and individuality of any human being amount to destroying and disrespecting the Triune image of God that every human being possesses intrinsically. As in the case of the doctrine of God, Orthodox theological anthropology also offers a dynamic perspective on moral issues. In other words, Orthodox anthropology is not static. According to Stavros Vangazogolou, "Man (sic) is not merely a biological or spiritual existence, but a being in relation and enroute" It is in the Holy Trinity, once again, that humanity attains the ethos of the person as Trinity affirms the identity of each person. This non-static orientation of the person in the Trinitarian community provides room for integrating the many in the one community of love-the Holy Trinity. The apophatic nature of theological discourse is also applied in Orthodox theological anthropology. As Gregory of Nyssa has it: "the incomprehensibility of the human indeed is an image of God's incomprehensibility" (Cambridge Companion) As there is always more to God than human reason can grasp, there is always more to God's self-revelation within humanity that is yet to be discovered. One could say then that anthropology in the Orthodox theological tradition is evolutionary-it keeps evolving: the human is en-route. As humanity mirrors the Holy Trinity which is still being revealed to us, we cannot pronounce conclusive judgements on human behaviour. If we do, we actually go against the very principle of Orthodox theological system which is the apophatic orientation of theology in Orthodoxy. St. Gregory's emphasis on the Transfiguration and the actual vision of divine light inspire continuing exploration of the height to which human nature is called. This is what Orthodox theology calls an eschatological anthropology: the conviction that the full vision of humanity is only realized and actualized in the eschaton, in the reign of God where moral values reach a completely different stage. In a certain sense, it is a reign where gender and sexual differentiations are transcended. According to Spyridoula Athanasopoulu Kyriou, Gregory of Nyssa outlines such an eschatological vision of the human. Sexuality, per se, holds Gregory, does not have any ontological significance. As Spyridoula succinctly sums it up: "to discover one's ending in one's beginning with Gregory is to go before and beyond sexual differences, to a creation and an eschaton in which humankind is sexless", Spyridoula further argues that an eschatological oriented gender construct, as in Gregory of Nyssa, will not be subservient to a sexual ideology. There is a profound apophatic sensibility about the divine in Gregory's notion of the soul as the bride. Although humanity is created as male and female, the male female differentiation is not absolute because in the eschaton gender differentiation is transcended. It is, therefore, an eschatological statement to say that there is neither male nor female in Christ. However, as a people of God's reign, as the kin(g)dom people, we are called to live out the eschaton in the here and now, by already transcending the gender constructs and stereotypes. An eschatological perspective on anthropology would therefore consider God (creator) rather than creation as normative for humanity. Since the Triune God, as we have already seen, transcends gender absolutes and affirms pluriform ways in which love is expressed, in Orthodoxy, there cannot be a strong case that can be made for any kind of "human-ordained" normativity, Spyridoula concludes beautifully: "The eschatological oriented gender theory of Eastern Christianity subverts gender essentialism and the culturally repressive web of sexual stereotypes". Gregory of Nyssa and Maximus, the Confessor pronounce this conviction thus: "if there were any ontological significance to sexual differentiation then it necessarily would limit how we act and exist and in so doing would interfere with our freedom to act ultimately and fundamentally as human beings". This is the depth in which a dynamic anthropology is delineated by Church Fathers in Orthodoxy. As they seem to suggest, it would be sensible to make sense of sexual differentiation as human characteristics outside the framework of *Imago Dei*.

Conclusion

Whilst it is true that sexual differentiation isn't an integral component of Imago Dei, human sexuality is. Human sexuality, as part of God's image obviously reflects the Trinitarian relation of God, the mode of *perichoresis* (mutual indwelling). In this sense, human sexuality assumes ontological significance. As Brian Edgar argues, *Imago Dei* as such is related to Christology within the overarching framework of the Holy Trinity. Sexuality becomes an element of creation that is reflective of the *ontos* of God. From this Trinito-Christological viewpoint, concerns such as "abnormality" and "deviance", as Norman Pittenger argues, need to be looked at in relation to the norm of full humanity that is expressed in Jesus Christ who transcends the male-female binary and gender absolutism and the limitations these have imposed on humanity through "moral teachings".[7] From this eschatological/non-static anthropological vantage point, one should be asking these questions today as we struggle with issues around human sexuality both within and without Church: What sexual behaviour will enhance human relationships? What sexual behaviour will damage and destroy the fuller realization of our divinely ordained humanity?

Endnotes

[1] James B. Nelson, *Embodiment: An approach to sexuality and Christian theology*, (Augsbug: Minnesota, 1978), 14.

[2] Paulos Gregorios, *Human Presence: An Orthodox view of Nature*, (Geneva: World Council of Churches, 1978), 59

[3] Paulos Gregorios, *Human Presence: An Orthodox view of Nature*, 59.

[4] George Morelli, "Sex is holy: Psychospiritual considerations," *http://ocampr.org/wp-content/uploads/2011/03/sex-is-holy-psychospiritual-considerations-fr-george-morelli-2005.pdf* accessed on August 02, 2017.

[5] Brian Edgar, "Sexuality, the image of God and the doctrine of the Trinity," *http://brian-edgar.com/wp-content/uploads/downloads/2010/05/Trinity-and-sexuality.pdf*, accessed on August 02, 2017.

[6] Eric Hyde, The individual and the Church: John Zizioulas and the Eastern Orthodox perspective, *https://ehyde.wordpress.com/2011/12/27/the-individual-and-the-church-john-zizioulas-and-the-eastern-orthodox-perspective/*, accessed on August 02, 2017.

[7] Norman Pittenger, *Time for Consent*, (London: SCM Press, 1970).

Church and Sexual Morality: A Critical Evaluation

Victorian Morality and Colonization of the Body in Missionary Discourse

Gladson Jathanna

Abstract

This paper deals with the Victorian morality of the 19th and early 20th centuries and briefly analyzes the ways in which those ideals were transported to and transplanted on the colonized bodies. The Christian missionary enterprise of the West is critically evaluated, mainly from a postcolonial standpoint. The questions of gender and sexuality within western missionary and colonial discourse are at the heart of this paper. With a few examples from Indian Christian historiographies, this paper tries to demonstrate how Victorian ideals of morality and sexuality are re-enforced on the 'docile' and 'fragile' bodies of native women.

Victorian Age and its Moral Ideals

The Victorian Age is both historically as well as ideologically identified with the sovereign regime of Queen Victoria (1819-1901) in England. As Anne Shepherd remarks Victoria was "the first English monarch to see her name given to the period of her reign whilst still living."[1] During this time the British Empire grew and expanded around the world, making a massive economic growth. However, it was an important period not only for the British Empire but also for the entire Western Colonial enterprise. It was during the Victorian Age that a number of important developments happened in different spheres such as industrial work, technology and science which formed the foundational rationales to Colonialism.

Victorian age is also important from the point of gender constructions. The society and culture during the Victorian age were characterized by a sharp distinction between men and women. Whereas men were located in a public sphere, women were placed within a private sphere. Their sexuality was also categorized with a strong binary of men as sexually active beings and women as sexually passive and inactive. Though sexual restraint was considered as morally superior, such ideals were very much ambivalent. As Walter Houghton wrote in his book *The Victorian Frame of Mind*:

> In the Victorian home swarming with children sex was a secret. It was the skeleton in the parental chamber. No one mentioned it. This conspiracy of silence….sprang from a personal feeling of revulsion. For the sexual act was associated by many wives only with a duty and by most husbands with a necessity if pleasurable yielding to one's baser nature. The silence which first aroused in the child a vague sense of shame was, in fact, a reflection of parental shame, and one suspects that some women, at any rate, would have been happy if the stork had been a reality.[2]

As Dominik Wohlfarth says, the Victorian era was full of "prudery, puritanism, sexual repression and moral strictness… [where] cleanliness, health, sincerity, earnestness, morality and manliness were virtues, expected of good British citizens."[3] He further argues that the influence of Christianity intensified the moral expectation of the Victorian society. The Bible and the Prayer Book were used "not just for guidance, they were for obedience and Victorian Society accepted and strictly followed them."[4] That means, a strict moralism, also in relation to sexuality, was vehemently advocated having the endorsement of Christianity. Hence the whole Christian missionary enterprise during the colonial time carried such Victorian moralist ideals and transplanted them in the colonies. The following examples are a few selective references to such ideals.

Colonial Construction of the Victorian Sexual Imperialism

Michael Foucault's concept of the relatedness of language and power[5] helps us to see that the portrayal of the sexuality of the colonized in the writings of colonizers was central to the power and knowledge at work in the Victorian colonial (which includes missionary) enterprise. The production of knowledge on the subjectivity of the indigenous men and women, particularly on their sexualities, served to defend the superiority of the White Western Male birth. Their understanding of Christian mission as transplanting of the Victorian Christianity in colonies reinforced the subjugation of the colonized. It reduced the Christian mission to the changing of religious identities. It also divested the colonized bodies of the natives of their personhood by treating them as either 'stumbling-blocks' or 'stepping-stones' in missionaries' expansionist enterprise.[6] The conversion of "heathen" bodies and minds to Christianity and the spread of Victorian values have been considered 'the white man's burden' in colonial discourse. Gayatri Chakravarthy Spivak points out that such a burden has a gender dimension. She formulates the masculine-imperialist ideological formation as "white men saving brown women from brown men."[7] She argues further that the colonial discourse has legitimized the violent subjugation of the body of the other as if such action was called for and demanded by brown women's situation. Under the pretext of saving brown women, colonial desire and imperialistic advances have been masked and collectively reconstituted in a blatant reversal as 'social mission.'[8]

The western missionary believed in the superiority not only of 'his' religion, race, economy and culture but also of 'his' sex. This superiority called upon 'him' to bear the vocation of converting and ordering the world toward 'his' own identity. Such an ideology was grounded in the beliefs of Victorian morality. And in this discourse native bodies were forced to act as objects of Western imperialism.

Western Women's Agency and the Enforcement of Victorian Sexuality

It is an indisputable fact that the Victorian ideals of womanhood and sexuality was transplanted in colonial context mainly through Christian missionaries, especially in their "conversion space, which had the institutions of church, public administration, school education, language, and trade and its service."[9] Among all these conversion space, Christian schools were of greater importance, as it was in the schools of the missionaries that the Victorian models of sexuality were reproduced.[10] Such schools were mainly supervised by Western women missionaries. Hence the place and position of western women missionaries need a critical examination.

The Victorian novelist Charlotte Bronte, in her novel *Jane Eyre* gives us a glimpse of female mission agency in the Victorian era: "…Jane, come with me to India; come as my helpmeet and fellow-labourer." – the English clergyman St. John River pleads with Jane Eyre in the novel.[11] Jane agrees to accompany him on the condition that she may 'go free,' taking part in missionary ventures not as his wife but as his 'adopted sister.' "God and nature intended you for a missionary's wife. It is not personal but mental endowments they have given you; you are formed for labour, not for love. A missionary's wife you must–shall be. You shall be mine; I claim you – not for my pleasure, but for my Sovereign's service," insists River.[12]

Clarey Midgley, while reading this fictional representation argues that such representation "of the limits of an independent female missionary agency in the early nineteenth century was reaffirmed in pioneering historical and literary scholarship."[13] According to Valentine Cunningham, Jane, through her desire to go out to India as a 'fellow missionary,' "projects an impossibility" because at this period "missionary was a male noun; it denoted a male actor, male action, male spheres of service."[14] In her foundational text of feminist postcolonial critics, Gayatri Spivak argues that the use of the "allegorical language of Christian psychobiography" in this fictional representation genders the missionary as male and "marks the inaccessibility of the imperialist project as such to the nascent 'feminist' scenario."[15] Both the fictional representation of dispute and the above discussed scholarly readings of that representation affirm that there were no possibilities for envisaging independent female missionary agency in the early nineteenth century British India.[16]

But the late nineteenth century and the early twentieth century witnessed an excessive shift in this scenario. By 1899 it was estimated that women missionaries outnumbered men in the 'foreign field' by over a thousand.[17] Eliza F. Kent's recent scholarship on 'gender and Protestant Christianity in colonial South India' argues that the height of British colonialism in India, the Victorian years (from roughly 1870 to 1910), saw a number of independent female missionary agencies (or at least a female wing of the mission activities) coming to India from the colonial West.[18] In the past decades, a great deal of scholarship has uncovered, explored, and analysed the involvement of colonial women during the zenith of colonial rule.[19]

Christian Missionaries, Womanhood and Sexuality: An Indian Example

Missionary women had to have dual identities. On the one hand they were Christian women being the wives of Christian Missionaries and on the other, they were White Western women living in the colonial communities. The contradictory positions of white women in colonial communities need to be given special emphasis in order to understand their position and place better. As Ann Laura Stoler has said, "White women (in colonized land) needed to be maintained at elevated standards of living, in insulated social spaces cushioned with the cultural artefacts of 'being European.'"[20] They were charged to reproduce Victorian domesticity in a strange land and to be guardians of the Victorian morality, especially sexual purity, and to pass these on to the young. Being missionary wives their influence on the missionaries in re-enforcing the Victorian morality cannot be denied.

The missionary wives did make use of their 'vocation' of being teachers and superintendents of girl schools to impart Victorian morality to the native children. The times that they spent with the native girl children in reading, working and singing were the times of introducing the Victorian virtues and values. The missionaries saw 'heathen' children as morally bad and perverted and thus they expected their women to 'free' those children from that 'wretched' condition and train them to be 'good' wives for their converts and mothers for their families.[21] This was one of the channels through which missionaries were able to 'transform' an Indian home into the Victorian ideal. In this process of 'transformation' the native bodies had to undergo techniques of discipline and punishment.

'Disciplining' is a predominant concept in colonial discourse. The docile and fragile body of the colonized needed to be disciplined by the colonizer in order to 'upright' the natives. Michel Foucault identified the body as central to the systems of organisation, and 'discipline', employed in modern societies whereby docile and productive citizens were fashioned from otherwise impulsive and unruly individuals.[22] As the bodies were cleaned up and prepared by the technologies of modern education, and taught the 'correct way' to function in schools, the bodies and sexualities of the students in the schools were also subjected to the institutional process of cleaning the dirt, lighting the dark hearts and making them upright.

Edward Said's work had the representation of the body as its focus and more specifically the representation of the non-Western body.[23] His argument was that the body was a central trope of colonial discourses that constructed difference between the west and the rest.[24] This binary was very much at work in Victorian schools and their representation. Victorian schools, in fact, were seen as the place of binaries and differences. It was the production place of mimics of the West.[25] The missionaries represented schools as the 'converting zones' that hoped to transform darkness into light and dirt into clean, by defining the sexualities of the pupils in Victorian terms and vocabularies.

The missionary accounts are a monolithic and biased construction of native sexuality. As one of the missionary report illustrates, "The women of this country are under the threat of their men. But unfortunately, they do not apprehend that. The men treat their daughters like mere flesh, because they sell them in marriage for a few rupees."[26] These expressions intend to and do portray native women as victims of sexual oppression by their men and objects of compassion by Westerners. As Kwok Pui-lan, a post-colonial theologian has observed, such construction homogenizes women and their sexuality in the Third World, suppressing their differences according to family background, region, ethnicity, class and religion.[27] Stereotypical images of native women as being ignorant of sexual exploitation by their men flooded missionary writings. Such representations entranced the readers of those narratives in the homeland, who contributed generously to support women's mission in India. On the other hand, it was an important way to legitimize women's mission in India and to get it financially supported. It is true that the missionary women preached not only the gospel to the native women but also the Victorian ideals of womanhood. Through such ideals and preaching they re-enforced the imperialist, colonial, and thus sexually strong 'man power' on the docile and fragile bodies of native women.

Endnotes

[1] Anne Shepherd, "Overview of the Victorian Era," *History in Focus*, Issue 1 (Spring, 2001), downloaded from *http://www.history.ac.uk/ihr/Focus/Victorians/article.html#one* accessed on 12 June 2017.

[2] Walter Houghton, *The Victorian Frame of Mind: 1830-1870* (New Haven: Yale University Press, 1985), 353, as cited by Richard J. Evans in his lecture *The Victorians: Gender and Sexuality* delivered on 14 February 2011 at the Museum of London.

[3] Dominik Wohlfarth, *The Initial Perception of the novel "The Picture of Dorian Gray" through the Victorian Public* (Munich: GRIN Verlag, 2003), 4.

[4] Dominik Wohlfarth, *The Initial Perception of the novel "The Picture of Dorian Gray,"* 4.

[5] Michel Foucault, *The History of Sexuality*, vol. 1 (Harmondsworth: Pelican, 1981).

[6] James Taneti, "Empowering Mission or Enslaving Enterprise? Women Missionaries' Attitudes to Telugu

Women," *Bangalore Theological Forum*, 39/1 (June, 2007): 161.

[7] Gayatri Chakravarthy Spivak, "Can the Subaltern Speak?" in *Postcolonialism: Critical Concepts,* edited by Diana Brydon, Vol. IV (London and New York: Routledge, 2000), 1427-1477.

[8] Gayatri Chakravarthy Spivak, "Can the Subaltern Speak?" 1439.

[9] Musa W. Dube, "Postcoloniality, Feminist Spaces and Religion," in *Postcolonialism, Feminism and Religious Discourse,* edited by Laura E. Donaldson and Kwok Pui-lan (London and New York: Routledge, 2002), 101.

[10] Janes Haggis, "'Good Wives and Mothers' or 'Dedicated Workers?'" in *Maternities Madoernities: Colonial and Postcolonial Experiences in Asia and Pacific*, edited by Kalpana Ram and Margaret Jolly (Cambridge: Cambridge University Press, 1998), 90f.

[11] C. Bronte, *Jane Eyre* (New York: Carleton, 1864), 428.

[12] C. Bronte, *Jane Eyre,* 428.

[13] C. Midgley, "Can Women Be Missionaries? Envisioning Female Agency in the Early Nineteenth-Century British Empire," *Journal of British Studies,* 45/2 (2006), 335–358, here 335.

[14] V. Cunningham, "'God and Nature Intended You For a Missionary Wife'. Mary Hill, Jane Eyre, and Other Missionary Women in the 1840s," in F. Bowie, D. Kirkwood, and S. Ardener (eds.), *Women and Missions, Past and Present: Anthropological and Historical Perceptions* (Oxford: Berg Publishers, 1993), 85–108, quotes on 89 and 97.

[15] G. C. Spivak, "Three Women's Texts and a Critique of Imperialism," in R. Lewis and S. Mills (eds.), *Feminist Postcolonial Theory: A Reader* (Edinburgh: Edinburgh University Press, 2003), 306–23, quote on 311.

[16] However, one must note that these arguments do not intend to downplay the European women's early engagements with missionary activities in India.

[17] J. S. Dennis, *Christian Missions and Social Progress: A Sociological Study of Foreign Missions,* Vol.2 (Edinburgh and London: Oliphant, Anderson & Ferrier, 1899), 46.

[18] E. F. Kent, *Converting Women: Gender and Protestant Christianity in Colonial South India* (New York: Oxford University Press, 2004), 83.

[19] E. F. Kent, *Converting Women,* 83; See also A. Burton, *Burdens of History: British Feminists, Indian Women, and Imperial Culture, 1865–1915* (Chapel Hill: University of North Carolina Press, 1994); B. Ramusack, "Cultural Missionaries, Maternal Imperialists, Feminist Allies: British Women Activities in India, 1865–1945," in M. Strobel and N. Chaudhuri (eds.), *Western Women and Imperialism: Complicity and Resistance* (Bloomington: Indiana University Press, 1992); K. Jayawardena, *The White Woman's Other Burden: Western Women and South Asia During British Rule* (New York: Routledge, 1995); I. Grewal, *Home and Harem: Nation, Gender, Empire and the Cultures of Travel* (Durham, NC: Duke University Press, 1996); M. Strobel, *European Women and the Second British Empire* (Bloomington: Indiana University Press, 1991); A. L. Stoler, "Carnal Knowledge and Imperial Power: Gender, Race and Morality in Colonial Asia," in Miceala Di Leonardo (ed.), *Gender at the Crossroads of Knowledge: Feminist Anthropology in the Postmodern Era* (Berkeley: University of California Press, 1991), 51–101; G. H. Forbes, "In Search of the 'Pure Heathen': Missionary Women in Nineteenth Century India," *Economic and Political Weekly,* 21/17 (1986), WS2–WS8; J. Haggis, "'Good Wives and Mothers' or 'Dedicated Workers?'" in Kalpana Ram and Margaret Jolly (eds.), *Maternities and Modernities: Colonial and Postcolonial Experiences in Asia and Pacific* (Cambridge: Cambridge University Press, 1998). M. C. Singh, *Gender, Religion, and "Heathen Lands." American Missionary Women in South Asia (1860s-1940s)* (New York, London: Garland, 2000). E. Cleall, *Missionary Discourse of Difference. Negotiating Otherness in the British Empire, 1840–1900* (New York: Palgrave Macmillan, 2012).

[20] Ann Laura Stoler, "Carnal Knowledge and Imperial Power: Gender, Race, and Morality in Colonial Asia," in *Gender at the Crossroads of Knowledge: Anthropology in the Postmodern Era,* edited by Micaela di Leonardo (Berkeley: University of California Press, 1991), 65.

[21] Janes Haggis, "'Good Wives and Mothers' or 'Dedicated Workers?'" 91.

[22] M. Foucault, *History of Sexuality, vol. 3, The Care of the Self* (New York: Vintage, 1988), 36.

[23] E. W. Said, *Orientalism,* 57–73.

[24] E. W. Said, *Orientalism,* 57–73.

[25] I borrow the term and idea from Homi Bhabha, a postcolonial theorist. See Homi K Bhabha, "Of Mimicry and Man: The Ambivalence in Colonial Discourse"

in Frederick Cooper and Ann Laura Stoler (eds), *Tensions of Empire: Colonial Cultures in a Bourgeois World*, Berkley: University of California Press, 1997, 152-163.

[26] BHFM 1904 (Hermannsburg: Verlag der Missionshandlung, 1905), 7.

[27] Kwok Pui-lan, "Unbinding our Feet: Saving Brown Women and Feminist Religious Discourse," in L. E. Donaldson and K. Pui-lan (ed.), *Postcolonialism, Feminism and Religious Discourse*, 67.

Church and Sexual Morality

Aruna Gnanadason

Reflections on Human sexuality – taboo topic in the Indian church
For the Church in India, issues relating to human sexuality are still, by and large, a taboo topic. The churches have been reluctant to address the manifold ethical challenges as well as the potentials and gifts offered by the human body. The churches rarely affirm the beauty of the female and male human body and the God-given gift of pleasure that it offers. Additionally, we do not acknowledge or condemn gross levels of the use and abuse of the human body and our sexuality. Dealing with human sexuality has been largely relegated to the entertainment industry and media, to the scientific community, to powerful patriarchal forces in the family and in the social structure of Indian society such as the caste hierarchy with its underlying principles of pollution and purity associated with the body. The distorted attitudes to human sexuality have given rise to multifarious cultural practices of discrimination and even violence against women, children, sexual minorities and other oppressed groups such as the Dalits in India.

The churches and women's sexuality
"Made in the image of God", has been the Biblical promise that, has given women the strength to survive in a patriarchal and violence ridden society. Women are made to feel a sense of shame about their bodies and their abilities. This adds to a diminished self-esteem women live with and increases feelings of inferiority, incompetence and weakness. The shame

of being female is projected in the body language of women – many young women crouch into themselves rather than walk with head held high and shoulders held back with pride of their God given sexuality and the beauty of their bodies!

To this has to be added the shame that is attributed to women's bodily functions of menstruation and childbirth. These normal processes have become one of the ways in which women are made to feel unclean and inadequate. Till today there are many women in India who will not partake in the Holy Communion when menstruating – some would even stay away from church! There have been marginal changes: generally the concept of a woman staying away from the church for the first 40 days after childbirth as she is considered unclean; and being "cleansed" on the day she returns to the church; is no longer the required norm in many churches. But, it is regretfully carried out implicitly in many places and is euphemistically called a blessing for a safe childbirth. The Levitical law (Lev. 11-15, 20) that treats women as unclean and defiling restricts the full participation of many women in the public sphere till today. Bleeding symbolized death for a woman in Biblical times because it identified her as a taboo to her society.[1] Jesus broke this taboo in the episode with the woman with the flow of blood. (Mark 5:25-34). However, in India we seem more influenced by the prevailing Indian culture than by Jesus' liberating actions - this attitude to menstruating women can be observed till today in India in subtle ways, restricting the full participation of women. The skewed understanding of women's sexuality and their bodily functions as polluted and polluting has unfortunately been one of the key issues on whether women should be ordained into priestly orders (in those denominations where it is being debated).

Tragically, the church has consigned to others its moral authority and opportunity to deal holistically with female sexuality to teach congregations and the world that the female body is God's temple and ought to be respected and women given the right to control their sexuality. Media and the tourism industry have taken over and have found profitable ways to exploit female sexuality the state "legalises" the sale of the sexuality of women. In India and in many parts of the world, prostitution is seen as "an industry and a legitimate option for work" often ignoring that poor women, particularly. are forced into what is euphemistically termed "the sex industry". We can go on recording just how much the female body has been abused in society and alas even in the church.

The churches on the issue of homosexuality

While discussions on human sexuality *per se* are not easy, the Indian church has had even bigger difficulties in dealing with issues related to homosexuality. The organised presence of the gay and lesbian community in India has been attempting to conscientise the society for some decades now. Additionally, in the recent past, significant attempts have been made by the National Council of Churches in India (NCCI) who began some years ago to organise a series of seminars to open up the discussion. The official journal of the NCCI the *National Council of Churches Review* has devoted attention to the discussion so as to encourage the churches to address the issue.[2] This was followed up with two Study Institutes on Human Sexuality initiated by NCCI for church leaders. The institutes included as speakers, representatives of the gay and lesbian community, transvestites and carriers of the HIV/AIDS virus who personally testified to their struggles and to challenge the church to respond pastorally.

The church has for so long tended to ignore the gay and lesbian community, including gays and lesbians in its own body. The challenge for the churches in India to respond came from LGBTIQ (Lesbian, Gay, Bi-sexual, Transgender, Intersex, Queer) communities in Indian society but also from churches outside India. As the II Study Institute of the NCCI described it:

> We also meet at a significant moment in time when the global churches are not only struggling with these issues but are also expressing them differently. For example, the issues surrounding the Consecration of a gay Bishop, the ordination of gay/Lesbian priests and pastors, and the solemnizing of same-sex marriages. The rapid development of information technology has also enabled openness and offered a new space in relation to human sexuality discourses. This has led to the breaking of the 'culture of silence' with regarding human sexuality.[3]

To take the example of how a church addressed the issue of sexuality we see in a message to the members of the Anglican Church in Canada from the House of Bishops in 1983. They wrote:

> Holy Scripture affirms that God is the Creator of all human beings, both male and female and that all persons male and female have a particular

affinity to the Creator. The Bible states that both men and women are created "in the image of God". They added, "This truth is the ground of our conviction that men and women sharing this "image" share also a common responsibility to each other in their sexuality. Because both maleness and femaleness are part of God's gift in creation, we are able to claim a wholesomeness in sexuality. The relationship between man and woman is God given: beneficial to both and mutually enriching – a gift to be celebrated and enjoyed.[4]

Their statement touches the specific ways in which the church could make real our understanding of human sexuality:

Although this positive biblical attitude to human sexuality is clear in our marriage services, (in India too, if I may add here) we are aware that the church has sometimes failed both in its attitude and its teaching to help its members to understand and express these biblical truths. We recognise that this failure has contributed to some of the negative attitudes to human sexuality which exist today. We recognise that many people both men and women need help in learning to accept their sexuality as a gift from a loving Creator, given to enable us to enter into mutually enriching relationships which affirm the intrinsic value of each person involved. Our sexuality permeates every aspect of our being. Its reality is far wider and deeper than physical contact......value of human beings as persons to be related to and not things to be manipulated or exploited. – perversions to be abhorred.[5]

The above quote, though long, speaks strongly to the churches in India too.

Have we kept God at the centre of our faith?

This becomes a challenge when we as churches discuss the complex questions around questions related to the morality of sexuality - do we not too often keep at the centre of our exploration the institutional life of our churches and our ecclesial interests rather than turning to God who gives us direction and protects us? One of the ways the Indian church has failed its followers is by sustaining an image of God of Father, as a patriarchal, distant figure, who sits in judgement over us, rather than as a compassionate loving God who lives with us and accompanies us – who is immanent in our world and even in our family life, in our relationships with each other, and yes even in our bodies as God created us with our gender identities, with our sexualities in all its diversity. Exploring the many images of God in the Bible will give us some hope.

Brazilian theologian, Ivone Gebara for instance expresses concern that we have placed God outside the world and have attributed total perfection to God and imperfection to the world. She writes, "Our mindset was formed in a patriarchal tradition that caused a break or discontinuity between a Supreme Creator and all of creation."[6] In her understanding, we have set up this dualistic antithesis so as to avoid dealing with our own experiences of impurity and imperfection, our own fragility and weakness. We set up this perfect, all-powerful image of God, so as to avoid our own relative and contingent natures. In fact, we cannot imagine what this perfect being far above us could be.[7] Some of the most relevant metaphors for us here are those which image God as a compassionate, feminine, mothering God who fills the earth with grace and creative power. Such metaphors include God as the shepherd (Ps. 23:1, Matt. 18: 10-14); as potter (Jer.18: 1-6); as a mother (Isa. 42:14 and 66:13, Luke 15:8-10). The image of a child in its mother's womb or at her breast conveys a unique sense of closeness with God.

God, in India, from a liberation perspective is in fact shaped by Indian cosmology, which affirms the interdependence of all forms of life, the dialectical harmony between humanity and the divine; between human beings and the earth and between the male and female principles.

We often claim that much we do, even if it is hurtful or excluding, "in God's name" – even the way we speak of and deal with those who do not in our understanding fall into the "normal" sexual identities. In other words, the way we have interpreted texts leads to an understanding that "heteronormativity" is the norml. This seems to legitimize the right to ridicule, abuse and even hurt, why even kill persons from the LBGTQ community.

The question of sexual morality and the church

Too often moral issues identified in society, in the Church itself, or even at the level of personal lifestyle, and the Church's efforts to deal with them, "have led to painful and often costly divisions within and between churches that are inconsistent with the Lord's own prayer for the Church that "they all may be one" (John 17:21). In the search for visible unity in the Church, the role of moral issues as a church- and community-dividing factor should not be underestimated. Addressing questions of how moral issues become church-dividing can contribute to increased unity as well as help to avoid the pain and human suffering that often results from such division."[8]

There is of course now in the churches in India and in churches globally, as described above, a growing concern that moral questions and issues of moral discernment are addressed systematically. The inclusion of a chapter on this topic in this collection of essays is a sign of hope – the churches recognise the urgency to address the complex moral issues that need to be addressed when discussing sexuality.

The World Council of Churches (Faith and Order Paper) quoted above describes how "developments in the wider society challenge the Church to reflect anew on some of the moral stances it holds".[9] The paper continues, "The interests of individuals and of communities – both internal and external to the church – will always exert an influence on how moral debates and decisions are made in and between churches. On the other hand Christians believe that the Holy Spirit works through the community to guide and assist moral discernment.".[10]

The context, the church, the circumstances within which a church operates all influence the way we interpret and understand sexual morality and these are potentially church-divisive. The challenge, therefore, is on how we can stay in communion in our own churches and between churches even when we do not agree with each other on certain moral questions. The time is come for the churches in India to address these issues squarely – and not shy away from their responsibility to help communities, congregations to develop alternative ways of respecting each other and living as a God empowered community.

Endnotes

[1] See Hisako Kinukawa, Purity-Impurity, Dictionary of Feminist Theologies, Russell Letty M., and J. Shannon Clarkson. eds. *Dictionary of Feminist Theologies*, Louisville, Kentucky: Westminster John Knox Press, 1996, p.232.

[2] NCC Review, Vol. CXXI, No 4, May 2001.

[3] "An Epistle on Human Sexuality to the Churches in India", from the Second Study Institute on Human Sexuality jointly organised by the National Council of Churches in India, with the Student Christian Movement in India, the Indian Society for Promoting Christian Knowledge, the United Evangelical Lutheran

Church in India -HIV/AIDS Desk and the Church's Auxiliary for Social Action
with the assistance of International Services Association (INSA), in Bangalore,
India from 24th to 26th of September 2003.

[4] A Study Resource on Human Sexuality, Approaches to sexuality and Christian
theology. The Committee on HS, the National Exec Council of the Anglican
Church of Canada Ed. James Reed, Anglican Book Centre, Canada, 1986 pp 23-
24.

[5] A Study Resource on Human Sexuality, 24.

[6] IvoneGebara, *Longing for Running Water: Ecofeminism and Liberation* (Minneapolis:
Fortress Press, 1999), 110.

[7] *Op cit.,* 111.

[8] Moral Discernment in the Churches: A Study Document Faith and Order
Paper, No. 215, (World Council of Churches, Geneva, 2013).

[9] Moral Discernment in the Churches, 14.

[10] Moral Discernment in the Churches, 15.

The Church, Sexuality and Phobia

Philip Kuruvilla

Introduction

Never before have the sexual ethics of our culture been faced with such a confusing array of material. Divorce is increasing; live-in-relationships instead of a marriage is fast becoming the norm in Indian metros; new technologies have made pornography immediately accessible to young adolescents through the ubiquitous cell phone and the internet; consensual sex between two heterosexual adults is common, while consensual sex between two homosexuals was [temporarily] decriminalized. The once inconceivable notion of same-sex "marriage" is now recognized by law in a growing number of [albeit, western] countries. What should be our response to the LGBTIQ Communities and the issues that trouble them? The need for a clear voice from the 'Mother' Church in the areas of human sexuality and gender diversity is critical, both for the health of our own faith communities and for our faithful witness to the world. This voice must not be homophobic or transphobic, but rather must use Jesus' responses to the 'sinners' of his day as its touchstone.

In India, the National Council of Churches in India (NCCI) has been in the vanguard of the Church's response to critical issues. NCCI took up the mantle of guiding the Churches through the HIV-AIDS pandemic, making Member Churches aware of the issues involved, as far back as 2003. Today the NCCI's ESHA program is exclusively meant for bringing Member Churches to a better understanding of a topic they have stayed clear from so far, viz., human sexuality and gender diversity. This article attempts to document the history of both the World Council of Churches (WCC) and the NCCI's contributions to assist churches to focus on these issues, in the hope that they will go beyond the traditional ideas of mission to a place where the well-being of *all* humans on this earth become important enough; where the issues around human sexuality and the LGBTI are re-examined in the light of the latest scientific, medical and empirical discoveries in the field. To ask whether, instead of homophobic or transphobic responses, we could deal with them with understanding, with tolerance? Could we give them 'space' to be part of God's community - without judgment, without stigma, without discrimination? Could we remove them from the 'other' category, and instead realize 'they' are part of 'us'?

A. The International Christian Community's Response to the issues of the LGBTI

The World Council of Churches' [WCC] response- a chronological journey

It would be correct to start with the 'fountainhead' - the WCC- and its thrust on this area. **From New Delhi to Canberra**: The survey carried out by Birgitta Larsson[1] best explains how the WCC dealt with issues of human sexuality in the period between the New Delhi Assembly (1961) and the Canberra Assembly (1991). The New Delhi Assembly stated:

> The churches have to discover what positions and actions to take in regard to sexual relations before and after marriage; illegitimacy; in some cultures polygamy or concubinage as a social system sanctioned by law and customs. All this, and much else force the churches to re-examine their teaching, preaching and pastoral care and their witness and service to society.

From Canberra to Harare,[2] (1991-1998), the issue of homosexuality progressively took centre stage. A small consultation in 1997 in Geneva underlined that issues of human sexuality were already on the agenda of many of the member churches and that the different approaches and positions taken posed serious new challenges to the quest for the visible unity of the church. At the Harare Assembly, the Programme Guidelines Committee recommended to the Assembly a shift of focus- from sexual orientation to human sexuality - that would address issues of personal and interpersonal ethics. The Assembly further urged the WCC *"to engage* *in a study of human sexuality in all of its diversity, to be made available for member churches"*. The mandate of the Assembly was not to start a programme, but to "provide space" through which the member churches were enabled to discuss the difficult issues related to human sexuality.

The **Assembly in Porto Alegre[3] [2006]** was devoid of direct references to the issues of sexuality – though the issues of HIV and AIDS and Gender did make their mark. **Busan[4] [2013]** also held much promise but did not take any bold decisions or steps. Even now WCC keeps the issue on a low-key as it has proved to be an emotional and divisive subject. However, a more recent publication from them is a book titled: *"Created in God's Image: From Hegemony to Partnership"*[5]. It is a church manual on Men as Partners, and has a creative 'Module' on Sexuality, that 'invites participants to consciously examine the processes of socialization' of males.

The Churches' Response to Human Sexuality

Within Christianity there are a variety of views on the issues around human sexuality, ranging from outright condemnation, labelling people as 'sinful', to simply being morally unacceptable. However, within any particular denomination, it will be seen that individuals and groups hold differing views, and not all members of that denomination necessarily support their church's stand. To get a better picture, we can examine the responses of some churches on this issue, while accepting that they may not be truly representative. Following are some of the responses from churches from different parts of the world:

I.   Anglican

The second official response to this issue was from the **Lambeth Conference in 1988**, where they resolved this Conference:

> 1. Reaffirms the statement of the Lambeth Conference of 1978 on homosexuality, recognising the continuing need in the next decade for "deep and dispassionate study of the question of homosexuality, which would take seriously both the teaching of Scripture and the results of scientific and medical research."

> 2. Urges such study and reflection to take account of biological, genetic and psychological research being undertaken by other agencies, and the socio-cultural factors that lead to the different attitudes in the provinces of our Communion.

3. Calls each province to reassess, in the light of such study and because of our concern for human rights, its care for and attitude towards persons of homosexual orientation.[6]

In a 1998 Synod, they also stated that this Conference:

- recognizes that there are among us persons who experience themselves as having a homosexual orientation. Many of these are members of the Church and are seeking the pastoral care, moral direction of the Church, and God's transforming power for the living of their lives and the ordering of relationships. We commit ourselves to listen to the experience of homosexual persons and we wish to assure them that they are loved by God and that all baptized, believing and faithful persons, regardless of sexual orientation, are full members of the Body of Christ;

- while rejecting homosexual practice as incompatible with Scripture, calls on all our people to minister pastorally and sensitively to all irrespective of sexual orientation and to condemn irrational fear of homosexuals, violence within marriage and any trivialization and commercialization of sex;

- can not advise the legitimizing or blessing of same-sex unions nor ordain those involved in same gender unions; [7]

In February 2007 a change is noted- the Anglican General Synod debated on Lesbian and Gay Christians and amended the motion, and carried in the last part, *(d)* that this Synod:

affirms that homosexual orientation in itself is no bar to a faithful Christian life or to full participation in lay and ordained ministry in the Church and acknowledge the importance of lesbian and gay members of the Church of England participating in the listening process as full members of the Church.'[8]

In July 2017, the Church of England's ruling body voted overwhelmingly in favour of welcoming transgender people in parish churches. The vote came after bishops overwhelmingly backed a motion calling for a ban on unethical 'conversion therapy' for gays.[9]

II.   Evangelical Christians

Although traditionally Evangelical Christians have been very clear in their non-acceptance of the LGTB community, more recently there are some signs of a softer stance. [See the study, "How the Messy Middle Finds a

Voice: Evangelicals and Structured Ambivalence towards Gays and Lesbians," [10] which analyzed national data from the 2010 Baylor Religion Survey, conducted by Gallup.]. In 2015, *Time* published a piece entitled, "How Evangelicals Are Changing Their Minds on Gay Marriage."[11] The article alleges:

> 'In public, so many churches and pastors are afraid to talk about the generational and societal shifts happening. But behind the scenes, it's a whole different game. Support for gay marriage across all age groups of white evangelicals has increased by double digits over the past decade, according to the Public Religion Research Institute, and the fastest change can be found among younger evangelicals — their support for gay marriage jumped from 20% in 2003 to 42% in 2014'.

On August 30, 2017, 150 prominent evangelical figures joined together to sign a document taking direct aim at the lesbian, gay, bisexual, transgender and queer (LGBTQ) communities. They affirmed what signatories saw as traditional, "biblical" marriage and sexual ethics: between one married man and one married woman. The 14-article document, dubbed the "Nashville Statement,"[12] was released by the Council on Biblical Manhood and Womanhood (CBMW), focusing primarily on issues of gender and same-sex marriage. The document followed the Southern Baptist Conference's Ethics and Religious Liberty Commission's (ERLC) Annual Conference in Nashville.

A theologically liberal coalition quickly issued a counter-statement to the Nashville document. Going under the name "Christians United," [13] the leftist response reverses the historic Christian understanding of homosexuality as a sin and replaces it with the "sin of exclusion," of which it calls on the Church of Jesus Christ" to repent. The leftist "Christians United" statement is being promoted by a host of pro-LGBT groups, including the well-funded LGBTQ lobby Human Rights Campaign, which slammed the evangelical Nashville Statement as a "vicious attack on LGBTQ people." Evidently, there is more to come.

III.   The Roman Catholic

One sees fluctuations in the Roman Catholic Church position. Gossip was swirling around the Vatican at the time of Pope Benedict's abdication[14] that he was resigning because a "gay scandal" was about to break which would implicate high-ranking members of the curia. The present Pope

Francis had spoken openly about a "gay lobby." *The Huffington Post*[15] reports his comments in a meeting with members of the Latin American Caribbean Confederation of Religious Men and Women: *"Yes, it is difficult. In the Curia there are holy people, truly holy people. But there is also a current of corruption, also there is they speak of a 'Gay Lobby' and that is true, it is there... we will have to see what we can do."*. However, in October 2014 the Vatican Synod of Bishops approved a final document *'Relatio Synodi'*[16] which gives greater acceptance to gays: *'men and women with homosexual tendencies must be accepted with respect and delicacy'*. A recent statement by Pope Francis[17], in July 2014 in which he said: *"If someone is gay and seeks the Lord and has good will, who am I to judge?"* is widely discussed and even appreciated.

IV.   NCCI's Intervention in India in the field of Human Sexuality and Gender Identity

When looking at the Indian Church's response in these fields, it would be necessary to look at NCCI's involvement and interventions. NCCI has been working in the field of human sexuality since the early 2000's. After the first intervention came the Statement of the 1st Study Institute on human sexuality in June 2001 in Ooty, TN.   Here the small gathering made some affirmations and a Statement was published. The second intervention was at the 2nd Study Institute on human sexuality, which took place in September 2003, co-organized by Student Christian Movement of India (SCMI), in Bangalore. Here the delegates brought forth *'An Epistle on Human Sexuality to the Churches in India.'*[18]

On 18th July 2009, NCCI organized an interfaith response to the Delhi High Court Judgment of 2nd July 2009, by which Article 377 was struck down and consensual homosexual activities were decriminalized. The Indian Express[19] report, 'Indian Faith-Based Organisation's Response to Human Sexuality' on 18th July 2009 in New Delhi said, *'Among those who spoke on the issue were Mujtaba Farooq, secretary of the Jamaat-e-Islami Hind, Very Rev M.S. Skaria, Orthodox Church, Sd Bhupinder Singh, Delhi Sikh Gurudwara Prabhandak Committee, and Anuradha Mukherji of NAZ India, [the petitioners who fought against the almost 150-year-old Article 377 in the Delhi High Court]. Although the participants showed more of an accommodative attitude, the discussion brought to the fore, friction between the ideologies of the panellists as far as homosexuality was concerned'.*

Then NCCI organized a Study and Public Debate: *'Indian Church and Repealing of Art 377 of IPC'* on 28th July 2009. This was held at ICSA, Chennai. 110 participants from several member churches, related agencies, theological seminaries and the LGBT community came together for a one-day study and reflection. Although there was no uniform consensus, it was the first time all spectrums of the church came together to have an open discussion on this topic.

The fifth meeting – the third to be held in the same year- was the *'Theological Roundtable on the Churches' Response to Human Sexuality'* in Kolkata, on 5th and 6th December 2009. Here, the National Council of Churches in India, in collaboration with the Presbyterian Church of India, the Student Christian Movement of India and the Senate Centre for Extension for Pastoral Theological Research (SCEPTRE) organized in Kolkata a Theological Roundtable on the theme *'Churches' Response to Human Sexuality'.* In their *"Message to the Indian Christian Communities"*[20], they boldly called on the NCCI member churches to initiate an in-depth study of human sexuality, and on theological colleges to integrate issues of human sexuality into the theological and ministerial formation. They affirmed:

- *We recognize that there are people with different sexual orientations….We consider the Delhi High Court verdict to "decriminalize consensual sexual acts between adults in private" upholding the fundamental constitutional and human rights to privacy and the life of dignity and non-discrimination of all citizens as a positive step.*

- *We believe that the Church as 'Just and Inclusive Community' is called to become a community without walls to reach out to people who are stigmatized and demonized, be a listening community to understand their pains, desires, and hopes.*

- *We envision Church as a sanctuary to the ostracized who thirst for understanding, friendship, love, compassion and solidarity, and to join in their struggles to live out their God-given lives. So we appeal to the Christian communities to sojourn with sexual minorities and their families without prejudice and discrimination, to provide them ministries of love, compassionate care, and justice.*

The *Commission on Justice, Peace and Creation* of NCCI was mandated in September 2009 to study the issues related to Human Sexuality in the light of Delhi High Court's verdict to repeal the IPC Sec.377. It came up with "*An Ecumenical Document on Human Sexuality*"[21] which passed through many turbulent stages – including where member churches threatened to withdraw their membership if NCCI pursued this course - and was finally adopted by the General Assembly of the NCCI on 16th September 2011, as a 'Document', and not a `Policy` on Human Sexuality as was originally intended. This was followed by a NCCI Bible Study Workshop in 2011, themed "*Daring to study scriptures publically and sensually*", and attended by about 40 young men and women, some were theological students. The result was a publication by NCCI, "*Public and Sensual: Exploring Solution: Bible Studies on Human Sexuality*" [22]. Subsequently, during the Centenary celebrations of the NCCI in Nagpur, in 2014, a National Ecumenical Forum of Gender and Sexual Minorities was created by NCCI to voice the pains and needs of the LGBTI communities in India.

NCCI's ESHA Program

NCCI started its work among People Living with HIV and AIDS [PLWA's] from 2003, when the India Watch Desk began its journey, with this writer as its Executive Secretary. However the '*Ecumenical Solidarity on HIV and AIDS*' [**ESHA**] program of NCCI, only began among NCCI's member churches in 2009 and went on till 2015. In the process it brought out several supportive publications, including a 'HIV/AIDS: a *Handbook for the Church in India*' *[2004]*, a '*Policy on HIV/AIDS: a Guide to the Churches in India*' [2010], and "*Positive Readings: Biblical Reflections*" [2011]. In 2015, '**ESHA**' – now a name and not an acronym - having come face to face with the issues of human sexuality and gender diversity, decided to focus on sexual minorities, and the Indian Churches and Theological Colleges were brought into the ambit of the Programs of ESHA. This perfectly coincided with the Government of India's focus on justice issues faced by the LGBTI community, and the Transgender Persons (Protection of Rights) Bill 2016, which gave ESHA a chance to enter even the recalcitrant churches with the new message of acceptance.

The Indian Churches' Response

To understand the response of the Indian Churches, it would be useful to see the background. The Indian churches awakened to the issue of homosexuality when a Bench of Delhi High Court struck down the provision of Section 377 of the IPC which criminalized consensual sexual acts between adults in private. It declared in a 105-page judgment on July 2, 2009: *"In our view, Indian constitutional law does not permit the statutory criminal law to be held captive by the popular misconception of who LGBTs are. It cannot be forgotten that discrimination is the antithesis of equality and that it is the recognition of equality which will foster dignity of every individual"*[23]. With this declaration, a 148-year old law that inclined many people in the country to regard same-sex relationships as illegitimate came to an end - under the old law homosexual acts were punishable by a 10-year prison sentence. This judgment had a wide range of responses, for and against, and the majority of those who opposed it were faith leaders. On 11 December 2013, however, the Supreme Court of India set aside the 2009 judgment given by the Delhi High Court, thus ruling homosexuality once again to be a criminal offence.

Traditionally, Indian culture does not exude homo or trans-phobia. Roots of sexuality issues go back to ancient Hindu scriptural writings and can be seen in the carvings of some ancient temples. However, from the modern faith leader's 'non-response' in India, it would seem that the issue was a 'western' one- and not affecting the Indian faith communities. However NGO's and Gay Rights activists in this country have made it evident that the issue can't be glossed over- it is touching our homes and communities, with no barrier of faith. Earlier, after an initial hesitation, the Indian Churches, spearheaded by NCCI, stepped in to deal boldly with HIV and AIDS, and since 2004, they gave leadership even to other faiths on how to remove stigma and discrimination towards PLHIV through their Faith Communities. This work among 'high- risk' communities and Key Affected Populations [KAP]'s automatically led them face to face with the LGBTIQ and the issues that divided *them* from the faith communities. Some Churches had already started working on these issues, but ESHA's support over the last 2 years has given them a deeper level of engagement in this field. A fuller report on the Indian Churches and Theological Colleges could be found in *'Christian Responses to the Issues of Human Sexuality and Gender Diversity: A Guide to the Churches in India*[24].

I.   The Church of North India

A 2004 Consultation[25] on homosexuality at CNI Bhavan in New Delhi brought together nearly 40 persons, including bishops, physicians, pastors, social activists, women's leaders, youth leaders and children's coordinators. The group concluded that homosexuality as an orientation is not a sin and one cannot be blamed for it. Among other things, the consultation recommended that scriptures historically related to the sexuality issue should be re-examined with regard to their socio-cultural context. There was little follow-up on the 2004 report. However, the Moderator of CNI, Rt. Rev. Samanthroy, and the Deputy Moderator, Rt. Rev. PC Singh, [who was also the President of NCCI], were both present at NCCI's Consultation with Key Affected People and the LGBT community in Delhi in August 2015. They subsequently encouraged NCCI-ESHA to empower their Dioceses through joint programs in Amritsar, Shimla, Delhi and Bhopal.

II.   The Roman Catholic

Cardinal Gracias, who is also the Catholic Archbishop of Bombay, gave a statement in response to a letter from Queer Azaadi Mumbai (QAM), an LGBT group, about a sermon at St Thomas Church, Goregaon, where the priest allegedly described homosexuality as "a great sin" and opposed gay marriage. The Hindustan Times[26] reported Cardinal Gracias, in his letter dated August 31, 2014, said "Going by the data in the letter, some of what the priest said is alright and some part is inappropriate. *The Church does not accept gay marriage because the Bible teaches us that God willed marriage to be between man and woman.*" On the other hand, to say that those with other sexual orientations are sinners is wrong. *"I do think we must be sensitive in our homilies [sermons] and how we speak in public and I will so advise our priests."* He added that the Church loved everybody, including those with different sexual orientations. In June 2017, in Aluva, Kerala, Catholic nuns [27] offered to house the transpersons who were given jobs in the Kochi Metro Rail Project. The Catholic Bishops Conference of India [CBCI] does not seem to have shown many initiatives among their member churches in this field.

III.   The Indian Orthodox

Immediately after the Delhi High Court Judgment of 2009, the late Metropolitan of Delhi, Dr Job Mar Philoxenos, sent out an open e-mail stating"*Homosexuality is a criminal offence*"- although it was his personal view. This view was echoed by Ramban Skariah a few weeks later in the interfaith meeting in Delhi[28]. However, in a more recent joint article[29], Metropolitan of Gujarat, Dr Mar Yulios, advocates for a softer stand and more inclusive language towards the gay community. This is also the stand taken in the Indian Orthodox e-group called ICON in a letter by Dr Mar Nicholavos, Indian Orthodox Metropolitan NE America, and member of the WCC. The Metropolitan of Niranam, and the President of the Mission Board, HG Mar Chrysostomos, presented a report at the *"Church Leaders and KAP?"* dialogue in New Delhi on August 27th 2015. He spoke about his experience at a similar dialogue in Tiruvalla in June, organized by the KCC, where he heard the voices of gays and transgender's crying out against homophobia, and where he had recommended a more sensitive approach. *'We must love TG's and those with alternative sexualities, are they not human?'*[30] he asks. In 2016, the Orthodox Seminary organized a one-day Seminar in Kottayam – where the Mar Thoma and CSI seminary students were invited.

IV.   The Lutherans

The United Evangelical Lutheran Churches in India, [UELCI], which represents the Lutheran Churches in India, held a meeting of doctors, theologians, laity etc., in September 2009, where it sympathetically discussed the issue of TGs in relation to the Delhi High Court Judgment. Detailed modules, brochures, pamphlets, posters and study materials were developed and distributed to the participants. Training of Trainers (ToT) programs on prevention, care and support among transgenders has subsequently taken place in Salem, Tricoillur [sic], Tiruvanamallai, Ulundurpet and in Ambur districts[31]. The Gurukul Lutheran Theological College has held several Seminars on the issues of sexual minorities, same-sex marriage. It is the Arcot Lutheran Church under Bishop Socrates, which partnered with the ESHA programs. They have held several awareness sessions for their pastors, and have now set up a *'Department of Transgenders'* in Cuddalore District.

V.   The Mar Thoma Syrian Church

The Diocese of Mumbai began its *Navjeevan Project* working among the CSW's. Subsequently, the *Navodaya Project* has been doing commendable work among Transgender Community - in pockets of Mumbai [Malad & Kalyan] they are working with Transgender CBO's [community-based organisations] assisting them in health and documentation. They also run a 24-hour helpline exclusively for transgenders and their issues. Under His Grace The Most Rev. Dr. Joseph Mar Thoma Metropolitan's leadership, they are now taking the issues of transgenders directly to the Marthoma churches in Kerala to enhance their involvement.

VI. The Church of South India

The Diocese of Madras has had a ministry among transgenders for over 25 years, and since then a pastor has been dedicated to working among them. The Church has extended the celebration of Christmas in sharing with the Transgendered people in different dioceses – Thoothukudi-Nazareth, Madras, Vellore, Madurai and Coimbatore. The Madras diocese has also accepted a transwoman, Noori, into the full membership of the CSI Wesley Church, Perambur, Chennai. She also attended the Diocesan Council as a voting delegate nominated by the Chairperson of the Diocesan Council the Bishop in Madras[32]. With the approval of the CSI Synod, the Bishop of the Diocese of Coimbatore has held several awareness sessions for his pastors and laity in partnership with ESHA, and has appointed a clergyman to a TG ministry. Reportedly he is also in discussion about ordaining a transwoman as the pastor.

VII. The position of the Senate of Serampore:

The Senate has been extremely positive - it began by including HIV and AIDS in the curriculum for BD students in 2012. A Reader, *HIV/AIDS: Towards Inclusive Communities*, edited by Dr Wati Longchar was released on February 4th 2014, which encouraged greater inclusivity of the LGTB or Rainbow" community. In 2014 they also included an optional paper on 'Human Sexuality' in the curriculum for BD students, and through the BTESSC, have been holding Awareness Programs in some Theological Colleges.

Conclusion

The Churches –both internationally and in India - are still not clear on their stand, and diverse voices are being heard, some more shrill and homophobic than others. However, an emerging trend sees more inclusive language and a greater acceptance of the LGTBI community, and a more humane response. In India, starting with the Theological Colleges, it is finding its echo in the Churches, and the NCCI's ESHA program has played a stellar role in bringing this about. It is more and more evident that this issue is not a 'western' or 'foreign' malaise - one that will go away if we ignore it -but one very deeply embedded within the Indian ethos, and therefore in the Indian Church's psyche as well, which is probably why there are such emotional responses. We have come a long way from 2001, and it is evident that the time is right for Christians to bring this issue 'out of the closet' and look for Christ-like responses. Those with diverse sexual orientations [PDSO's] are human beings who also need some 'sacred space' and a greater degree of pastoral understanding. In the midst of all the phobia and confusion, Christians and Churches need to listen to the voices of pain and anguish, understand the issues, and respond, while Church Leaders need to speak out. The need of the hour is for a loving, more inclusive response. Christ would expect no less.

Endnotes

[1] Birgitta Larsson, "A Quest for Clarity," *The Ecumenical Review*, Vol. 50/1, (WCC Publications: Geneva. 1998).

[2] WCC Archives: GEN 14: Aide Memoire, World Council of Churches and Human Sexuality

[3] WCC Archives

[4] Ibid

[5] Philip Peacock and Patricia Sheerattan-Bisnauth (eds.), *Created in God's Image: From Hegemony to Partnership,* [WCRC and WCC: 2010:Geneva]

[6] Lambeth Conference Resolutions Archive: Index of Resolutions from 1988: Resolution 64- Human Rights for Those of Homosexual Orientation

[7] Lambeth Conference Resolutions Archive: Index of Resolutions from 1998: Section I.10 - Human Sexuality

[8] *https://www.churchofengland.org/our-views/marriage,-family-and-sexuality-issues/human-sexuality/lesbian-and-gay-christians,-general-synod-debate-2007*.asp accessed on 10th August, 2017.

[9] *http://www.independent.co.uk/news/uk/home-news/church-of-england-bishops-ban-gay-conversion-therapy-pride-2016-lgbt-ri* accessed on 10th August, 2017.

[10] *https://www.baylor.edu/mediacommunications/news.php?action=story&story=131931* accessed on 10th August, 2017.

[11] *http://time.com/3669024/evangelicals-gay-marriage/* accessed on 10th August, 2017.

[12] *https://www.vox.com/identities/2017/8/31/16226088/evangelical-leaders-signed-sexuality-church-nashville-statement* accessed on 10th August, 2017.

13 *https://www.lifesitenews.com/news/pro-gay-religious-left-condemns-toxic-evangelical-nashville-statement-defen* accessed on 10th August, 2017.

14 *https://www.theguardian.com/world/2013/feb/21/pope-retired-amid-gay-bishop-blackmail-inquiry* accessed on 10th August, 2017.

15 *http://www.huffingtonpost.com/2013/06/11/pope-francis-gay-lobby_n_3420244.html* accessed on 10th August, 2017.

16 *http://www.sify.com/news/vatican-approves-document-accepting-gays-divorced-news-others-oktfueggidjja.html* accessed on 10th August, 2017.

17 *http://www.catholicherald.co.uk/news/2013/07/29/if-a-gay-person-seeks-god-who-am-i-to-judge-him-says-pope/* accessed on 10th August, 2017.

18 The only extant copy of the 'Epistle' remains available with NCCI only in a draft form. It is reprinted in NCCI Review, June, 2015

19 Sukalp Sharma, 'Church Panel organises discussion on Sec 377,' *Indian Express*, New Delhi: July 19th, 2009

20 *'An Ecumenical Document on Human Sexuality,* NCCI: Nagpur: 2012, 6-8

21 *An Ecumenical Document on Human Sexuality,* NCCI: Nagpur: 2012, 1-4

22 Christopher Rajkumar (ed.) *Public and Sensual: Exploring Solution: Bible Studies on Human Sexuality,* [NCCI: Nagpur: 2012].

23 *http://www.infochangeindia.org/environment/37-human-rights/news/7817-gay-sex-not-criminal-delhi-high-court* accessed on 10th August, 2017.

24 Philip Kuruvilla (ed), *Christian Responses to the Issues of Human Sexuality and Gender Diversity: A Guide to the Churches in India,* [NCCI/ISPCK: 2017]

25 'Pratap C. Gine, *Homosexuality: An Indian Issue in Church and State, https://continuingindaba.org/2013/09/18/homosexuality-an-indian-issue-in-church-and-state/* accessed on 10th August, 2017.

26 *https://silentmaj.wordpress.com/2013/09/10/priests-should-be-sensitive-on-issues-of-homosexuality-cardinal-oswald-gracias/* accessed on 10th August, 2017.

27 *http://www.ucanews.com/news/indian-carmelite-nuns-offer-sanctuary-to-trans-people/79625* accessed on 10th August, 2017.

28 Sukalp Sharma, 'Church Panel organises discussion on Sec 377,' *Indian Express*, New Delhi: July 19th, 2009 accessed on 10th August, 2017.

29 Mathai Mampalli and Mar Yulios, *An Aid to Christian Marriage'* [Ahmedabad:2013].

30 *Malayala Manoroma* : June 3, 2015.

31 UELCI Report on work done among the LGBT by the Lutheran Churches, presented to NCCI

32 Asir Ebenezer, "Trans-accompaniment: A trans-experience of the Church of South India," Report of the CSI Synod.

Critical Analysis of Churches Stand on Human Sexuality and a Way Forward

Manoj Kurian

Human Sexuality, a holistic approach

Human sexuality is how people experience and express themselves as sexual beings. Biologically, sexuality can encompass sexual intercourse and sexual contact in all its forms, as well as the physiological and psychological aspects of sexual behaviour. Sociologically, it can cover the cultural, political, and legal aspects; and philosophically, it can span the moral, ethical, theological, spiritual or religious aspects. Sexuality is much more than sexual feelings or sexual intercourse. It is an important part of who every person is. It includes all the feelings, thoughts, and behaviours of being female, male, or transgender, being attracted and attractive to others, and being in love, as well as being in relationships that include sexual intimacy and physical sexual activity. Hence human sexuality and how it is perceived and dealt with in society has profound implications on, ones identity, relationships and ones vulnerability to be marginalised; to be able to live fulfilling lives; to be taken advantage of; and to be succumbed to ill-health and disease in relation to sexual and reproductive health.

As Christians, we believe that all human beings are created in the image of God (Genesis Chapter 1) and we affirm "Jesus Christ is the one in whom true humanity is perfectly realized" (WCC, Jan.2005). Sexuality is recognised as part of the image of God in humanity, and therefore integral to human identity and integrity. Sexuality is considered as a divine gift, intrinsically good, intended by God for humanity to celebrate this divine gift in life giving, consensual, faithful and loving relationships. In dealing with our sexuality with such an approach, we can grow into the fullness of our humanity and divinity.

Churches divided and limited in the ability to address this crucial issue

But unfortunately, human sexuality is one of the most divisive issues that confront the churches today. The inability or the limited capacity of church and society to address this issue, promotes sweeping under the carpet, one of the most critical aspects of human identity and relationships. This lacuna also weakens the ability of faith communities to counter the impact of economic globalization, inequity and the continuing perpetuation of injustices with the changing perspectives on sex and sexuality. This includes the trivializing and commercializing influence of sexuality, fuelled by the fast progress achieved by communications and the internet, that is impacting the lives of all people, especially those who are marginalised and have less power, such as underprivileged sections of the population, women, children and those living with disability.

There is a continuing need to strengthen the capacity of churches and communities to address the issue of human sexuality in its entirety, in a holistic manner, addressing concerns of social, economic and gender justice that influences and is influenced by human sexuality. It is also urgently required for churches and communities, to go beyond being limited to dealing with same sex relationships, when they deal with human sexuality. The discourse and discussion on Human Sexuality also serves to:-

- Give attention to adolescent and young people's sexual and reproductive health and rights. This includes comprehensive sex education to acquire accurate information about human sexuality, explore and nurture positive values and attitudes towards their sexual and reproductive health in the context of their faith, develop self-esteem, respect for human rights and gender justice and to develop life skills (UNFPA 2014).

- Address maternal mortality, reproductive health including unsafe abortion and unmet family planning needs for young women; female genital mutilation, and the prevalence of HIV and sexually transmitted diseases.

- Challenge patriarchy, address gender relations, sexual and gender based violence against women and children.

- Listen to the life, stories, and witness of the faithful, who are of diverse sexual orientations, gender identities and expressions, and sex characteristics as members of our communities and congregations, and to accompany them.

- Countering abuses and human rights violations directed at individuals of diverse sexual orientations, gender identities and expressions, and sex characteristics, occurring across the world, entailing varying levels of severity and suffering for the victims; concomitantly, with varying levels of impunity experienced by the perpetrators.

Reflections on Church Statements on Human Sexuality

It was in this context that following the Harare Assembly of the World Council of Churches (WCC) in 1998 that a Reference Group on Human Sexuality was appointed by the WCC. This mandate was renewed in 2013 at the Assembly in Busan. Based on the request of the then General Secretary Dr. Konrad Raiser, seeking the member churches' to send all available statements produced by churches on the issue of human sexuality, the WCC received over 80 documents from member churches. The Reference Group summarized and reviewed these statements (WCC, Feb. 2005). The number of statements received form Churches in the Global South was much less compared to those from the Global North. This corresponds to the general tendency particularly in Asia and Africa to avoid addressing sexuality related issues. But since the study was conducted, in Asia, there have been very bold and inclusive statements from the Churches in India and the Philippines (NCCI 2010, NCCI 2017, UCCP 2014). There is a conspicuous dearth of statements from the Orthodox Churches. This could be due to the reluctance of both Eastern and Oriental Orthodox churches to address moral issues such as sexuality from a purely civil right (often understood in an individualistic sense) perspective, itself quite characteristic of much of the Western discourse on the issue. The statements from the Orthodox Churches, although few in number, reflected different perspectives from that of the Protestant Churches, reflecting a methodology of theological anthropology, which can be less threatening in spirit in a process of dialogue(Nalunnakkal. G,M, 2005).

Diverse church perspectives of human sexuality and theological considerations

Almost all statements acknowledged the disassociation between traditional church positions on human sexuality and the reality that societies experience. Majority of the Church documents tended to adopt a humble approach by recognizing the need for further study and reflection on this highly sensitive issue of human sexuality. Most statements consider the Holy Bible, as the main foundation for ethical decision-making, albeit in different ways and with varied emphases. The diversity of the stands taken by churches is very significant. One of the reasons for these conflicting positions on human sexuality is the diversity in the way Scripture is understood and interpreted by churches in their respective realities.

Although all major Churches give a central place to Scripture, there exist a variety of approaches in relation to the authority of the Holy Bible in making moral decisions. The nuances of decision-making when dealing with contentious issues such as human sexuality are dealt extensively in the Study Document, - Faith and Order Paper No. 215- Moral Discernment in the Churches (WCC, 2013). Apart from the Scripture (Holy Bible), other faith sources for moral discernment are - guidance of the Holy Spirit, spirituality, Church teaching and traditions.

Apart from faith sources for moral discernment, human reasoning, natural, social, and human sciences also could contribute to decision-making and recommendations regarding normative policies and practises regarding issues related to human sexuality.

The diversity of approaches is directly dependent of the influence of the three streams of influences:-

1.   Scripture and hermeneutical interpretation.

2.   Church teachings, traditions and culture.

3.   Human reasoning, natural, social, and human sciences.

Whether the Holy Bible alone determines our ethical reflections and moral discernment; or whether Church teachings, traditions and culture contribute; andif human reasoning, natural, social, and human sciences have a complementary role to play in moral discourse; all reflect on the stand churches take on Human Sexuality. When Scripture dominates the discussion, with the possibility of various interpretations of the same texts in different cultural contexts and with the question whether the New Testament holds greater authority than the Old Testament – all can contribute to varying outcomes, which are evident in the Church statements.

When the churches follow the Holy Bible literally, combined with an approach to natural law in relation to an archaic understanding of human anthropology, it tends to result in positions that are not inclusive and could promote an inability to deal with issues related to human sexuality in a current and constructive manner.

There were a few documents that reflected such a position, whereas most of the other documents tended to regard the three streams with equal importance. Another positive aspect about these documents was that most of these statements engaged a critical hermeneutical approach to the Holy Bible, whereby hermeneutical tools are applied for contextual interpretation of certain key and controversial passages on human sexuality. The use of the Holy Bible, therefore, holds an important key in addressing the issue in a contextually pertinent manner. All statements tend to affirm sexuality as intrinsically good and as a gift to be celebrated. This is clearly a departure from the classical Augustinian view. But the influence of the teaching and tradition continues to hold sway over Christian societies. The puritanical ideology contributing to repressed sexuality dates back to the fifth century church father and theologian Saint Augustine of Hippo, whose concept of 'Original Sin' became dogma: *sexual desire is sinful; infants are infected from the moment of conception with the disease of original sin; and Adam and Eve's sin corrupted the whole of nature itself.* The popular concepts of the 'original sin' in Christianity further contributes to the negative viewing of human sexuality, reinforcing boundaries, which go against the spirit of Jesus' revolutionary and liberative teachings.

One of the common doctrines addressed by most documents is the 'image of God'. Sexuality is affirmed as part of the image of God in humanity, and therefore integral to human identity and integrity. There are statements that focus on the incarnational integration of body, mind and spirit. The Word becoming body (flesh) is basic to a theological understanding of personhood and therefore of human sexuality as well. The Orthodox statements, by and large, affirm the human person (body included) positively. Spirituality is not opposed to sexuality and salvation even entails the process of recovering sexual wholeness. Some statements from Protestant traditions also synchronize with Orthodox, specifically Patristic strands on human sexuality. However, there are also statements from other traditions that articulate a rather negative anthropology. An overemphasis on humanity as fundamentally and essentially 'fallen creatures' in such statements is also noticed. They also tend to view sin as primarily sexual sin. The understanding of the human person shapes and informs our theological as well as ethical reflections on human sexuality. There are statements that try to argue theologically untenable positions on human sexuality when they follow a dichotomized understanding of the human person. For example, what a person does (becoming) has integral bearing on what a person is (being). This has implications for our understanding of sexuality issues, for instance, as the relationship between sexual orientation and sexual behaviour of persons (WCC, Feb. 2005).

In the 4th century, St. Gregory of Nyssa's liberative Christocentric perspective affirmed that humanity along with the rest of the world is the visible image of the invisible God. According to this view, the glory of God has to be expressed in the world, especially in humanity. This understanding is contradictory to the limited view that humanity's glory is opposed to the Glory of God. In St. Gregory's view, humanity is created in the image of God, beyond ones gender identity. With our union in Christ, we go through a Christological transformation. Some early theologians interpreted the 'garment of skin', in Genesis 3:21, as a metaphorical reference to aspects of human existence which they ascribed a lower status- including physical, bodily, sexual and procreative functions. But St Gregory maintained the 'garment of skin' as an embodiment of humanity's original creation. When used rightly, it serves as a means through which God redirects fallen humanity, with all its brokenness, back to God. (Nyssa St: G, 4th Century CE), (Cortez. M, 2016). St Gregory, also reaffirmed the totality of the mystery of God, beyond human reasoning and categories. No one can make exclusive claims about God, God's truth and God's saving power. A theology that is neither prescriptive or exclusive.

Each generation will have to create its own vision of reality and shape its life according to their context. (Gregorios 1978),(Cherniak. M, et al, 2016)

There are biblical texts that look at sexuality and sexual relationships in a holistic manner, as a gift of God to be cherished, as evidenced in the 'Songs of Songs' (the last section of the Tanakh/Hebrew bible and the fifth book of Wisdom, of the Old Testament in the Christian Bible). Unfortunately too often, the interpretation of these texts has been overtly spiritualized and the overall dominant discourse and the lack of discussion on human Sexuality has tended to promote, sexual repression, ignorance, patriarchy, gender based and sexual violence.

The doctrinal discussions on the doctrine of Trinity, in relation to Human Sexuality, except in the few Orthodox literature, are limited. The doctrine of Holy Trinity has the potential to creatively respond to addressing human sexuality in all its' entirety, with its emphases on justice, community, plurality and identity. Another theological theme that is markedly absent in the discussion and the statements is 'eschatology'. It is essential that Theology is open to the possibility of encountering God's revelation of the Truth in new and novel ways and not to be judgmental about sexuality related issues. In the eschatological community, what determines our identity will not be our sexuality (Lk.20), but our response to the loving and caring initiatives of God in whom sexuality is transcended (Nalunnakkal. G,M, 2005).

Identity, Relationships, vulnerability

The churches stand regarding human sexuality and how it is perceived and dealt with in society has profound implications on one's identity, one's relationships and one's vulnerability to be marginalised or to be able to live fulfilling lives.

Identity

Human sexuality has been addressed traditionally from a morally idealised perspective, with clear dual sexual normative interpretation of relationships. It is also based literally on biblical texts written in an era, with the understanding of human anthropology, two millennia ago. This was long before science was able to better understand that the diversity of sexual orientation and gender identity amongst human beings is not an aberration or a life style choice, but rather, the way some people are created, with genuine affinity, finding love and fulfilment in same sex relationships. In the last two decades evidence from biological research are showing increasing evidence of biological explanations for sexual orientation and gender identity (Bailey J. M., Zucker K. J. 1995, LeVay S, 1991, Witelson SF, et al, 2008, Savic . I, Lindström .P,2008). This overrides the older and traditional view that it is social construction and a choice or a disease- and rejected 'pathologizing' homosexuality or gender non-conformity as an illness, to evoke a world of rigid gender roles.

The traditional perspective does not recognise 'Intersex'-even though eunuchs were recognised- as an identity- and valued by God (Isaiah 56: 4,5). But this acceptance is not reflected in the Judeo Christian tradition, in the context of their sexual identity, needs or relationships.

Globally, majority of churches, from all Christian traditions are only influenced by two of the three streams of influences on how human sexuality is addressed, (*Scripture and hermeneutical interpretation; and Church teachings, traditions and culture*) and the third- (*Human reasoning, natural, social, and human sciences*)- which informs current knowledge on human anthropology, is often rejected or avoided. Churches, predominantly in Western Europe, North America, Australia and a significant minority of churches in Asia, Latin America and in Southern Africa have more inclusive perspectives on human sexuality.

If more churches take a hermeneutical approach, applying contextual interpretation of key and controversial passages on human sexuality and churches and communities are informed and transformed by the current knowledge on Human Anthropology, the difference between churches can be reconciled and human sexuality may no longer divide churches.

Unfortunately, majority of Christian denominations, present serious opposition to a wider acceptance of the rights of people with diverse sexual orientations, gender identities and gender expressions. Christian leaders in Africa and Asia generally oppose any liberalization of laws or social attitudes. Anglicanism suffered a serious divide on the issue of homosexuality (the ordination of gay bishops) in the early 2000s, with almost all African and Asian churches taking the conservative side against liberal North American and to some extent British, Australian and New

Zealand churches. Many senior church leaders support continued criminalization of same-sex conduct, and some have led the way in advocating even stricter laws. The Lutheran and Reformed churches have also experienced major schisms in their communions, based on diverse perspectives on Human Sexuality among their member churches. Catholicism, based on a more centralized hierarchy and doctrine, shows fewer signs of open disagreement on the issue. But the official position of the Catholic Church, voiced on several occasions by the Holy See, expressed that criminal penalties are not an appropriate way of dealing with homosexual conduct. In Uganda, the Catholic Archbishop of Kampala in a 2009 statement was almost alone among major national Christian leaders in opposing the Anti-Homosexuality Bill. Catholic leaders in other countries do not always respect this position (Kerrigan. F, 2013).

The Ecumenical movement's "campaign of love" (as captured in the letter of the WCC general secretary to Ugandan president Yoweri Kaguta Museveni "raising concerns regarding The Anti-homosexuality Bill, 2009") (WCC, 2009) that the WCC had engaged to challenge homophobia and unjust laws targeting homosexuals is a good example of the result of a conviction and is in keeping with the principle of "one people" that defines the ecumenical movement. "One people" does not mean heterosexual people but, rather, an inclusive community that respects sexual diversity. People of different sexual orientations are part of the living community, contributing to the richness and diversity of society.

But discrimination and criminalizing homosexual orientation and consensual relationships infringes on the ability of individuals and groups to live dignified, safe, creative, and fulfilling lives. Whoever stands in the way of the love of God and people does this against the will of God (Rom. 8:35). Keeping silent in the face of injustice and cruelty and compartmentalizing our spirituality and praxis is not an option for people of faith within the ecumenical movement (Kurian.M, 2012).

Relationships

The traditional guidelines for sexual ethics from the Judeo- Christian tradition and teachings, which are two-fold, have a profound impact on human relationships. Relationships and hierarchy in the Judeo-Christian tradition was influenced by the 'property ethic'- where one's spouse is categorized along with other property and the sin of violation is greed, leading one to trespass on one's neighbour's property (refer the 10 commandments: *Exodus 20:2-17, Deuteronomy 5:6.21*). The nature and quality of the relationship have been governed by the 'purity ethic'. Purity indicates avoidance of that would blemish/sully or that which is not proper or that which is disorderly. This avoidance has had a deep influence on popular morality across cultures. The elaborate rules that were evolved are given in the books of *Deuteronomy and Leviticus,* give the boundaries of human behaviour- be it dietary, marital or sexual, so as to ensure purity of the individual and the community, as a people who are set apart by God (Countryman. L. W, 2001)

These traditions have a deep influence on relations between men and women, young and the aged, and between spouses, by introducing hierarchy and power equations that have been used to control and predict societal behaviour. The power gradient and the lopsided relationships also have a strong impact on masculinity and gender-based violence. There are many positive examples of theological approaches to gender relations and of how the traditions and ethics of each of the three major Abrahamic religions can meet the challenge of addressing issues of masculinity, gender-based violence and HIV and AIDS (Chitando. E & Chirongoma. S, 2012)

The political and cultural goals of the theocratic movements have been to de-legitimize and censor all forms of human sexuality that do not fit into the accepted mould: sex between a man and woman who are married- in the strict patriarchal format that was approved by the church. Other expressions of sexuality are deemed sinful and must be repressed or even punished. To that end the theocratic movements seek to see sexuality exclusively as a means for procreation, criminalize homosexuality, promote abstinence-only sex education, and advocate censorship. In light of the taboo nature of discussions of sexuality within many church settings, those who self-identify as "holy", people are prevented from developing new and creative ways of talking about sex (Haddad B, 2006).

If churches and communities are unable to address human sexuality openly and in a forthright manner, respecting the inherent human dignity of each person, society will continue to experience the distortion of human relationships caused by the flawed interpretation and lived experiences of human sexuality.

Vulnerability

Churches and communities need to understand and deal with human sexuality in a holistic manner. It is clear that Human sexuality is dealt with very inadequately by a fragmented world and a broken society. Addressing human sexuality also gives us the opportunity to address many issues that we have generally avoided, to our long-term detriment. It is important to identify the various forms of vulnerability that have put us at risk when we are unable to address human sexuality ineffectively, individual and community experiences of vulnerability including situations of powerlessness. Vulnerability indicates a situation in which something or someone can be hurt or wounded; exposed to danger or attack; or is unprotected. To be vulnerable in the context of human sexuality implies that one has limited or no control over one's risk of suffering from the consequences of the inability of society to address human sexuality and to protect the marginalised from exploitation and have little or no access to appropriate redress, care and support. Vulnerability is the net result of the interplay of many factors, both personal (including biological) and societal. In the theological understanding, it is Jesus Christ who exemplarily shows us at the cross the utmost vulnerability we face in our faith: the moment of feeling abandoned even by God (Matt. 27:46). Yet God does not let God's servants down. In the suffering, death, and resurrection of Jesus, we find our mission for Christian mandate to address human sexuality adequately.

Young girls, widows, transgender people, people living with disability, homosexuals, prisoners, are all, vulnerable in varying degrees, to physical and sexual violence, sexual coercion and exploitation.

Creating safe spaces of grace: Transforming faith communities

As human sexuality is seldom discussed openly, it is vital that there is openness and a non-prescriptive approach, which promote open discussions to prepare the ground for positive transformation. The Ecumenical movement has strived to secure 'Safe Spaces of Grace', in faith communities to address critical issues. To deal with in any degree of helpfulness, churches and communities need safe, trustworthy and non-judgmental spaces. The safe spaces also needs to be consistent, inclusive and dependable to discuss and act on the key issues. We have to aspire that every congregation is transformed as a part of God's household, where the lonely are welcome; where the trampled find dignity and solace and where the excluded discover a sacred and safe family and community full of God's Grace.

Perhaps the most famous promise in the Judeo-Christian Bible is found in Psalms 23, where the psalmist expresses confidence in God's protection, saying, "Even though I walk through the darkest valley, I fear no evil; for you are with me," and concludes with "and I shall dwell in the house of God forever."

Faith communities and churches are mandated to be sacred sanctuaries of trust and confidentiality. They are to be:

- Spaces of grace that promote physical, psychological, and spiritual safety.

- Where one is without fear, shame, and intimidation.

- A place where one does not need to be guarded and intimidated.

- Where one can step outside one's own comfort zone.

- Where the integrity and dignity of each person are respected.

- A non-judgmental space where one is accepted as one is.

- Where a person is seen beyond one's actions.

- Where one can be honest and the truth is spoken with love.

- A space for restoration and positive transformation.

(Developed based on concept suggested by Campbell. C, et al., 2011)

An exemplary example of a "safe space of grace" in action is the Contextual Bible Study movement, which gave birth to the Tamar Campaign. The Contextual Bible Study (CBS) of Tamar's rape (2 Sam. 13:12-18) disrupts our collective silence on violence against women and brings about transformation and effective solutions. This study eventually developed into a campaign against gender and sexual violence. The Tamar Campaign helps churches to address sexual violence and violent models of masculinity. This grassroots initiative has been very effective in South Africa and has spread to other countries within Africa and to other continents (West. G, & Zondi-Mabezela. P, 2004). The WCC Ecumenical Theological Education programme has embraced the methodology since 2004. WCC-Ecumenical HIV/AIDS Initiative &Advocacy- has extensively used CBS to great impact and, because of the strong interconnectedness of sexual and gender-based violence (SGBV) with the HIV pandemic, since 2007 it has become widely popular.

Recognize that the source of grace is God

The safe space of grace is where one receives the other unconditionally, in the presence of God, with all their differences, deficiencies, and strengths as a fellow sojourner in this life. We acknowledge that all fall short of the perfection of God, and we do not merit God's grace. Hence, each of us, as a child of God, is loved by God and sit around the same table, relating with each other with humility and respect, recognizing our mutual vulnerabilities and flaws. "But God proves his love for us in that while we still were sinners, Christ died for us" (Rom. 5:8).

In various Christian traditions, "grace" can be described as the love and mercy that is given to us by God because God desires us to have it, not because of anything we have done to earn it. In the Orthodox Christian tradition, grace is also identified with the uncreated energies of God. These point to the great potential for positive societal transformation, provided we are open to and do not reject the grace of God. The safe spaces of grace require the creation of a space for reflection, for listening, for relational conversations, providing space for God's grace to bring about transformation. This also provides the milieu for serving, empowering, and loving others; building relationships of trust; and facilitating change from within. This space recognizes God's love for the creation and God's will to reconcile and heal the broken relationships with the world. This perspective begins with the understanding that it is God, not human beings, who has taken the initiative to show God's love to the creation. We respectfully provide the space. (Kurian. M, 2016)

Features of Safe Spaces of Grace

•   The presence of knowledge and skills regarding Human Sexuality related issues.

•   Opportunities for critical dialogue and debate about Human Sexuality and related issues.

- Possibility to renegotiate understanding and theology with flexibility to interrogate dogma and moral norms with the view of encouraging social action to deal with the concerned issues.

- Possibility to renegotiate behaviour and identities facilitated in a non-judgmental environment where there is a building up of self esteem and self-worth.

- A sense of individual and collective ownership of the challenges and responsibility for contributing to its solution.

- Confidence in the existence of individual, group and community strengths, which could be mobilized to overcome barriers and challenges.

- A sense of solidarity amongst group members around dealing with human sexuality and related issues. The solidarity is qualified with some key qualities such as

  - space is trustworthy and one that keeps confidentiality

  - members feel they are listened to, accompanied, supported and mentored

  - does not make one more vulnerable

- Strong links with potential support agencies in the public and private sector outside of the community (bridging or linking social capital).

- Inclusivity and the ability to bridge across power gradients.

  - Creating the space for all to participate and contribute irrespective of all potential markers of difference.

  - To link and connect between groups within the faith community with a possibility to influence transformation regarding the issue at hand across the community.

  - To be aware of power dynamics and differentials that could make smother the safe space. For example women-men, minority-majority, resident-migrant etc. (Kurian. M, 2016)

Conclusion

The ecumenical space has the potential for each narrative of each child of God to be valued deeply and acknowledged respectfully. The diversity of opinions and realities of the fellowship and the provision of safe spaces for dialogue and respectful listening gives rise to fresh ideas and perspectives. This contributes to the responsive development of creative initiatives at different levels that have a positive impact on people's lives. Unfortunately, this unity has not been fully and meaningfully realized and experienced in a number of areas, human sexuality being one of the most significant.

The churches acknowledge the fact that issues of human sexuality are among the most contested and potentially divisive issues that the churches confront today. It is also clear that divergences exist not just on perceptions on certain issues, but more significantly, on the way the Scripture is understood and interpreted, the way theology and ethics are done and the way spirituality is perceived and practiced by Christians in various ecclesial and cultural locations. Our prayer and hope is that as we move forward in our pilgrimage of Justice and Peace, struggling with the issues, we would be guided by God's abundant Grace, which would help us forbear one another in love.

Bibliography

Bailey J. M., Zucker K. J. (1995). "Childhood sex-typed behavior and sexual orientation: A conceptual analysis and quantitative review". Developmental Psychology 31: 43–55, 1995.

Campbell. C, Skovdal. M, Gibbs. A, Safe Spaces of Grace was developed from 'Six features of supportive social spaces' suggested in - *Creating Social Spaces to Tackle AIDS-Related Stigma:* Reviewing the Role of Church Groups in Sub-Saharan Africa, AIDS & BEHAVIOUR , 2011 *http://uib.academia.edu/ MortenSkovdal/Papers/199897/Creating_social_spaces_to_tackle_AIDS-related_stigma_Reviewing_the_role_of_Church_groups_in_sub-Saharan_Africa.*

Cherniak M, Gerassimenko O, Brinkchröder M (eds.), "For I am Wonderfully Made": Texts on Eastern Orthodoxy and LGBT Inclusion, European Forum of Lesbian, Gay, Bisexual and Transgender Christian Groups, 2016.

Chitando. E and Chirongoma. S, (eds.) Redemptive Masculinity: Men, HIV, and Religion, WCC, 2012.

Cortez. M, Christological Anthropology, Historical Perspective: Ancient and contemporary approaches to theological anthropology, 2016, Zondervan, Michigan.

Countryman. L. W, 'Dirt, Greed and Sex : Sexual Ethics in the New Testament and their Implications for today', SCM Press, London 2001.

Gregorios, Paulos Mar, The Human Presence: An Orthodox view of Nature, Geneva, WCC, 1978.

Haddad B. "We pray but we cannot heal": theological challenges posed by the HIV/AIDS crisis. J Theol South Afr. 2006;125: 80–90.

Kerrigan. F, Getting To Rights: The Human Rights of Lesbian, Gay, Bisexual, Transgender and Intersex Persons in Africa, The Danish Institute for Human Rights, 2013.

Kurian.M, "An Ecumenical Framework for a Liberative Human Sexuality: Toward a Culture of Justice and Peace," Ecumenical Review 64, no. 3 (October 2012): 338–45.

Kurian. M, 2016, "Passion and Compassion: The Ecumenical Journey with HIV", Geneva, World Council of Churches, 162 p, 2016.

LeVay S, A difference in hypothalamic structure between heterosexual and homosexual men, Science. 1991, Aug 30;253(5023):1034-7.

Nalunnakkal G M, Reflections on Church Statements on Human Sexuality-presentation at the WCC Central Committee Hearing on Human Sexuality, February, 2005, Geneva.

National Council of Churches in India, An Ecumenical Document on Human Sexuality, Adopted by Resolution EC:2010.28(9) of the Executive Committee of the NCCI, 16.09.2010, *http://ncci1914.com/wp-content/uploads/2017/06/Ecumenical-Document-on-Human-Sexuality.pdf.*

National Council of Churches in India,Asian Consultation on Church Responses to Human Sexuality and Gender Minorities Bengaluru, 2017, (*http://queerala.org/asian-consultation-on-church-responses-to-human-sexuality-and-gender-minorities/*).

Nyssa, St: Gregory of, On the Making of Man, Aeterna Press. Kindle Edition.

Okondo H, Racherla SJ, Lukale NH, (2013) RECLAIMING & REDEFINING RIGHTS ICPD +20: STATUS OF SEXUAL AND REPRO*DUCTIVE HEALTH AND RIGHTS IN AFRICA , World YWCA, 2013http://arrow.org.my/wp-content/uploads/2015/04/ICPD-20-Africa_Monitoring-Report_2013.pdf.*

West. G, Zondi-Mabezela. P, The bible story that became a Campaign: Tamar Campaign in South Africa (and Beyond), Ministerial Formation, 103 July 2004, WCC*http://ujamaa.ukzn.ac.za/Files/the bible story.pdf.*

Witelson SF, et al, (2008), Corpus callosum anatomy in right-handed homosexual and heterosexual men, Arch Sex Behav. 2008 Dec;37(6):857-63.

Savic. I, Lindström .P,(2008), PET and MRI show differences in cerebral asymmetry and functional connectivity between homo- and heterosexual subjects, Proc Natl Acad Sci U S A. Jul 8;2008, 105(27):9403-8.

United Church of Christ in the Philippines 2014, 'Let Grace be Total. UCCP Statement on Lesbian, Gay, Bisexual, Transgender (LGBT) Concerns, 2014, *http://www.peaceucc.org/let-grace-be-total-the-ucc-philippiness-initial-statement-on-lgbt-concerns/*.

UNFPA 2014, Operational Guidance for Comprehensive Sexuality Education: A Focus on Human Rights and Gender, 2014.

http://www.unfpa.org/publications/unfpa-operational-guidance-comprehensive-sexuality-education

WCC, Christian Perspectives on Theological Anthropology, Faith and Order Paper 199, January 2005, WCC, Geneva. *https://www.oikoumene.org/en/resources/documents/commissions/faith-and-order/v-theological-anthropology/christian-perspectives-on-theological-anthropology*.

WCC, AIDE MEMOIRE: WORLD COUNCIL OF CHURCHES AND HUMAN SEXUALITY, World Council of Churches, CENTRAL COMMITTEE Document No. GEN 14, Geneva, Switzerland, February 2005 *https://www.oikoumene.org/en/resources/documents/central-committee/2005/reports-and-documents/gen-14-aide-memoire-world-council-of-churches-and-human-sexuality*.

WCC , Letter of the WCC General Secretary to the Uganda President Yoweri Kaguta Museveni, "Raising concerns regarding The Anti Homosexuality Bill, 2009"; *http://www.oikoumene.org/en/resources/documents/general-secretary/messages-and-letters/letter-to-the-uganda-president.html*.

WCC, MORAL DISCERNMENT IN THE CHURCHES: A Study Document, Faith and Order Paper No. 215, WCC, Geneva, 2013 *https://www.oikoumene.org/en/resources/documents/commissions/faith-and-order/i-unity-the-church-and-its-mission/moral-discernment-in-the-churches-a-study-document*.

Legal Perspectives on Human Sexuality and Sexual Morality

Critical Evaluation of Religious, Juridical, and Human Rights Perspectives on Human Sexuality and Morality

Pawan Dhall

Abstract

This article looks at key international human rights conventions, commitments and resolutions, many of which India has signed on and/ or ratified by the Parliament. The article analyses what the human rights situation is at the policy, programmatic and service provision levels with regard to these conventions and commitments in the context of sexual minorities in India. In effect, the article looks at how sexual minorities have been included or excluded from India's democratic structure.

In terms of human rights perspectives on human sexuality and morality, we need to look at key global human rights commitments (especially those which India has signed on and/or ratified) and juxtapose them with ground level realities. We need to examine what has been done in terms of laws, policies and programmes by government and non-government players, as well as the prevailing social attitudes and practices, which have a circular relationship with laws, policies and programmes.

Broadly, the global human rights commitments that have dealt with or have implications for sexual orientation and gender identity issues can be classified as: (a) Formative international covenants like the Universal Declaration of Human Rights (UDHR); (b) United Nations Human Rights Council resolutions; (c) Global development commitments – Millennium Development Goals and the Sustainable Development Goals; (d) Application of human rights laws in relation to sexual orientation and gender identity as in the Yogyakarta Principles; and (e) International donor pledges to committing resources to work with communities marginalized on grounds of sexual orientation and gender identity.

It should be noted here that when the earliest of the human rights commitments mentioned above were drafted, sexual orientation and gender identity diversities were not part of the human rights discourse. Indeed a person's (biological) sex itself was seen as no different from their gender or internal sense of gender, and inconceivable as something indeterminate or in-between, assigned as it were at birth by doctors and parents within the confines of a man-woman or male-female binary. It was mainly key juridical responses to sexuality-based discrimination in later years that read sexual orientation and gender identity into provisions that prescribed discrimination on grounds of sex or gender (this will be discussed further more than once in this chapter).

The **preamble to the UDHR,** drafted in 1948 after the end of World War II, begins as follows: *"Whereas recognition of the inherent dignity and of the equal and inalienable rights of all members of the human family is the foundation of freedom, justice and peace in the world ..."* and further says

> the [United Nations] General Assembly proclaims this Universal Declaration of Human Rights as a common standard of achievement for all peoples and all nations, to the end, that every individual and every organ of society, keeping this Declaration constantly in mind shall strive by teaching and education to promote respect for these rights and freedoms and by progressive measures, national and international, to secure their universal and effective recognition and observance, both among the peoples of Member States themselves and among the peoples of territories under their jurisdiction.[1] All articles in the Declaration are relevant, but the following seems particularly relevant, especially when we assess the ground realities in India. Article 1 states: "All human beings are born free and equal in dignity and rights. They are endowed with reason and conscience and should act towards one another in a spirit of brotherhood".

Sexual orientation or gender identity is not specifically mentioned, but one may argue that the mention of "progressive measures, *national and international, to secure their* universal and effective *recognition and observance*" (authors emphases) in the preamble should allow us today to read these issues into the mention of 'sex'. How else will 'recognition' be 'universal' or 'effective' on grounds of sex if individuals are not allowed the liberty to express the being of their sex in terms of its adjuncts – an internal sense of gender (gender identity) that may not 'match' what is physiologically visible; gender expression; a sense of sexual attraction (or orientation); sexual desires or behaviours; and sexual/romantic relationships? Denial of such expression may well amount to denial of their very existence.

Even the Supreme Court of India could not have made its judgment on transgender identities and rights (*henceforth NALSA judgment*)[2], as can be seen in the analysis of juridical responses, had it not read 'gender' into the mention of sex in the Indian Constitution,[3] itself a supreme statement of commitment to human rights at the national level.

Articles 7 and 9 of the Declaration state: *"All are equal before the law and are entitled without any discrimination to equal protection of the law. All are entitled to equal protection against any discrimination in violation of this Declaration and against any incitement to such discrimination"*; and *"no one shall be subjected to arbitrary arrest, detention or exile"*. In the Indian context, laws like Section 377 of the Indian Penal Code perpetuate inequality as they criminalize specific sexual behaviours and their practitioners without any scientifically sound rationale. Ostensibly they apply to everyone irrespective of sexual orientation and gender identity, but given the deep-seated socio-medical stigma against people with non-normative genders and sexualities and the general assumption that only these sections of society practice *"carnal intercourse against the order of nature"*, they add to the discrimination experienced by LGBTIQ and other queer people in every social sphere, so much so that such individuals are unable to complain about gender or sexuality-based violence like blackmail and sexual assault for fear of they being charged with criminal conduct.

Article 21, among other things, says that *"Everyone has the right to take part in the government of his country, directly or through freely chosen representatives"* and *"The will of the people shall be the basis of the authority of government; this will shall be expressed in periodic and genuine elections, which shall be by universal and equal suffrage and shall be held by secret vote or by equivalent free voting procedures"*. Unfortunately, till recently transgender individuals in India, particularly the *hijras*, did not have voter identity cards, and especially so in their *desired gender identities*. The number of transgender and other queer people visible in the legislatures tells the same story of stigma, discrimination and exclusion. The limits of democracy based on majority rule, which can easily slip into majoritarianism (systemic lack of protection of minority rights), are clearly to be seen in the context of queer people, whose concerns are often not reflected in the *"will of the people"* because they are minorities. But isn't the true spirit of democracy one of taking everyone along together and respecting the right to free expression of even dissenting opinions?

Article 25 states that *"Everyone has the right to a standard of living adequate for the health and well-being of himself and of his family, including food, clothing, housing and medical care and necessary social services, and the right to security in the event of unemployment, sickness, disability, widowhood, old age or other lack of livelihood in circumstances beyond his control..."* Till the NALSA judgment came about, transgender people in India, and in particular *hijras*, were denied these rights even at the policy level. They still are at the service provision level, because the 'spirit' of the judgment, and the understanding of gender and sexuality it pre-supposes, is yet to percolate to the level of the last-mile service provider – that is, officials and staff in both government and private sector organizations.[4] Concepts like 'marriage', 'family' and 'household' continue to be defined in terms of the gender binary and compulsory heterosexuality, which denies legal recognition to same-sex relationships or *hijra* households (*dera, daiyar* or *hamamghar* – as they are known in different parts of India).

Looking at the **International Covenant on Economic, Social and Cultural Rights,** 1966, Article 12 states: *"The States Parties to the present Covenant recognize the right of everyone to the enjoyment of the highest attainable standard of physical and mental health."* In terms of concrete steps that governments must take to achieve the full realization of this right, the article talks about: *"The prevention, treatment and control of epidemic, endemic, occupational and other diseases"* and *"the creation of conditions which would assure to all medical service and medical attention in the event of sickness"*.

Barring a national and state-level response to the HIV epidemic among men who have sex with men (MSM) and transgender women (through the National AIDS Control Programme),[5] the Indian government has not paid adequate attention to both general and specific health concerns of LGBTIQ people. Transgender women across India still report facing discrimination in accessing health services in government hospitals, with reports of barriers at the level of both out-patient and in-patient departments. MSM often report that doctors and counsellors judge them for their sexual behaviours during sexual history taking or during STI and HIV counselling and testing. The impact is on the health-seeking behaviour of individuals, many of whom drop out of treatment and resort to self-medication or accessing unqualified medical practitioners. Those who can afford it, prefer private sector services, where they may be treated better but are charged for services that are meant to be available free of cost in government facilities.[6] As a result, HIV prevalence continues to be 17 and 28 times higher among MSM and transgender women, respectively, than among the overall population in India (this trend, by and large, happens to be a global phenomenon as well).[7]

If we look at the specific health concerns of LGBTIQ people, other than small-scale community and NGO-lead efforts, little attention has been paid by the government and donor agencies to their sexual health needs beyond STIs and HIV, impact of stigma, discrimination and violence on their mental health, and disability related challenges. For most transsexual people, inexpensive, safe and quality sexual reassignment surgery services provided by trained health care providers remain out of reach. Both within the national HIV response and beyond, attention has been paid only to persons assigned male gender at birth, with lesbians, bisexual women and transgender men largely remaining invisible at both policy and programme levels.[8]

Article 26 of **International Covenant on Civil and Political Rights** (ICCPR, 1966) states: *"All persons are equal before the law and are entitled without any discrimination to the equal protection of the law. In this respect, the law shall prohibit any discrimination and guarantee to all persons equal and effective protection against discrimination on any ground such as race, colour, sex, language, religion, political or other opinion, national or social origin, property, birth or other status."* This article proved crucial in one of the most celebrated victories of the human rights of LGBTIQ people internationally. In 1994, in *Toonen versus Australia,* the United Nations Human Rights Committee held that 'sexual orientation' was a status protected from discrimination under the ICCPR equality clauses. The Committee maintained that the reference to *"equal and effective protection against discrimination on any ground"* included discrimination on grounds of sexual orientation.[9] This was reaffirmed by more than one United Nations Human Rights Council (UNHRC) resolution in later years.

This brings us to taking a look at the role played by the **UNHRC** (a subsidiary body of the United Nations General Assembly) in upholding and reaffirming the human rights around gender and sexuality diversity. In 2002, the UNHRC passed a resolution on combating and eliminating extrajudicial, summary or arbitrary executions, including on grounds of sexual orientation (in a continuing series of resolutions in this matter, gender identity was added as a ground in 2012).[10]

In 2011, the UNHRC resolved to commission a study to document discriminatory laws and practices and acts of violence in relation to sexual orientation and gender identity, in all regions of the world, and how international human rights law can be used to end violence and related human rights violations based on sexual orientation and gender identity. This was the first resolution ever to bring specific focus to human rights violations faced by LGBTIQ people, and the study it led to, documented a wide range of discriminatory practices and laws being used against LGBTIQ people around the world. It showed that violence, including sexual violence, perpetrated by law enforcement authorities and society at large, was a pervasive problem in many countries.[11]

Most recently, in 2016, the UNHRC passed a resolution to establish an Independent Expert to document and facilitate protection against human rights violations in relation to sexual orientation and gender identity.[12] This resolution was passed against stiff opposition by several countries from South Asia, West Asia and Africa, and has also survived subsequent efforts at being weakened and even dismantled altogether.

A mention also needs to be made of the 2010 annual report submitted to the UNHRC by the Special Rapporteur on the Right of Everyone to the Enjoyment of the Highest Attainable Standard of Physical and Mental Health, Anand Grover. The main focus of this report was the right to health, need to decriminalize same-sex conduct, sexual orientation and sex work, and impact of criminalization on HIV transmission. The report recommended that, in order to protect the right to health, decriminalization was necessary, alongside other measures necessary for a comprehensive right-to-health approach. Such measures include human rights education, participation and inclusion of vulnerable groups, and efforts to reduce stigma and discrimination in respect of these groups.[13]

Issues specific to lesbians, bisexual women and transgender men have also found space in the United Nations agenda through the world conferences on women organized by UN Women and other United Nations agencies.[14] Notably, the 4th World Conference on Women in Beijing, 1995, saw a significant participation of lesbians and bisexual women, and human rights violations faced by women on grounds of sexual orientation and gender identity were acknowledged possibly for the first time in the agenda of this global event. Fortunately, this early acknowledgement was also followed by legislative changes over the years in a number of countries to protect women from discrimination on grounds of sexual orientation and gender identity. This was evident from the proceedings of the 15-year review of the Platform for Action drafted at the Beijing conference (the review meeting was held in 2010 in New York).[15] However, these positive developments were mainly outside the Global South.

Other key developments at the United Nations level in relation to protecting the human rights of LGBTIQ people include the United Nations Economic and Social Council taking an important step forward in 2013 to make it easier for LGBTIQ NGOs to gain consultative status[16], and the United Nations Secretary-General Ban Ki-Moon's move to extend the marriage benefits to LGBTIQ or same-sex couples in March 2015.[17]

India's record of voting in many of the United Nations resolutions has been a mixed one.[18] While India voted in favour of many resolutions in the period 2010-14, in the last few years there has been a pronounced trend towards abstaining or voting against resolutions favouring LGBTIQ rights. For instance, in 2015, India voted in favour of a resolution moved by Russia that opposed an extension of marriage benefits to LGBTIQ or same-sex couples (the resolution was ultimately defeated); and last year sided (unsuccessfully again) with many traditional opponents of LGBTIQ rights from Asia and Africa to vote in favour of many amendments to dilute the proposed resolution on the establishment of an Independent Expert on monitoring rights violations against LGBTIQ people.

The official justifications for such votes have been 'legal realities' around Section 377 or society's 'unpreparedness' to accept LGBTIQ people. But should specific sexual behaviours (irrespective of sexual orientation or gender identity) being criminalized under Section 377 in any way undermine the imperative to prevent violence against LGBTIQ people *just because they are LGBTIQ*? What harm would result, say, if the United Nations Independent Expert was to document an instance of forced aversion therapy to 'cure' a gay or lesbian person when global mental health bodies have clearly delisted homosexuality and gender variance as illnesses?[19] More fundamentally, was society 'ready' when the practice of *Sati* was abolished or widow remarriage legalized?

In contrast with the proactive stand taken by UNHRC, **global development commitments** like the Millennium Development Goals (MDGs), 2000 and the Sustainable Development Goals (SDGs), 2015 fell far short in acknowledging the health and development concerns of LGBTIQ people. In September 2000, the United Nations member-states gathered to reaffirm their commitment to the United Nations. At this meeting, the General Assembly adopted the United Nations Millennium Declaration which led to the development of the MDGs, a series of eight time-bound goals with sub-goals. The goals "outlined commitments to values and principles; peace, security and disarmament; development and poverty eradication; protecting common environment; human rights; democracy and good governance; protecting the vulnerable; meeting the special needs of Africa; and, strengthening the United Nations".[20] In spite of the concept of human rights being central to the idea, the MDGs did not once make mention of sexual orientation and gender identity[21]. The MDG goal on gender equality was interpreted strictly in the context of women and girls.

The only goal that came close to the concerns of LGBTIQ people was the one on combating HIV/AIDS (and malaria and other diseases). But this was yet another instance of prioritizing only MSM and transgender women, leaving out the psycho-social health, sexual and reproductive health, and sexual reassignment surgery concerns specific to people assigned gender female at birth. In the context of MSM and transgender women too, in India and many other countries of the Global South, the focus was on a narrow medical response to HIV. Not surprisingly, even after the MDGs ran their course of 15 years, HIV prevalence rates among MSM and transgender women remained among the highest in any vulnerable social group.

In 2015, the MDGs were succeeded by the SDGs, another 15-year old framework of 17 global goals and 169 targets between them. The goals were adopted at the UN Sustainable Development Summit held September 25-27, 2015 in New York. Setting the post-2015 development agenda, these goals aimed to address a wide variety of issues of including ending poverty and hunger, improving gender equity, health and education, making cities more sustainable, combatting climate change, and protecting oceans and forests.[22] But once again under pressure from many governments, there was no explicit acknowledgement of the relationship between sexual orientation, gender identity and development.

It was only after strong advocacy by global civil society actors that these issues received some attention in the SDGs. Eventually, paragraph 19 of the *SDG Outcome Document 2015* stated that the language of non-discrimination should be applicable to persons of 'other status', which, based on resolutions passed by the UNHRC in 2009, is implied to include persons with diverse sexual orientations and gender identities. This addition meant that several SDGs became applicable to LGBTIQ people.[23] It remains to be seen how this development pans out at the ground level – not just in India, but globally.

Next, we look at the **application of human rights laws in relation to sexual orientation and gender identity**, and an apt example is that of the Yogyakarta Principles (2006). The introduction on the Yogyakarta Principles website says:

> "The international system has seen great strides toward gender equality and protections against violence in society, community and in the family. In addition, key human rights mechanisms of the United Nations have affirmed States' obligation to ensure effective protection of all persons from discrimination based on sexual orientation or gender identity. However, the international response to human rights violations based on sexual orientation and gender identity have been fragmented and inconsistent . ..

The International Commission of Jurists and the International Service for Human Rights, on behalf of a coalition of human rights organisations, have undertaken a project to develop a set of international legal principles on the application of international law to human rights violations based on sexual orientation and gender identity to bring greater clarity and coherence to States' human rights obligations.

"A distinguished group of human rights experts has drafted, developed, discussed and refined these principles. Following an experts' meeting held at Gadjah Mada University in Yogyakarta, Indonesia from 6 to 9 November 2006, 29 distinguished experts from 25 countries with diverse backgrounds and expertise relevant to issues of human rights law unanimously adopted the Yogyakarta Principles on the Application of International Human Rights Law in relation to Sexual Orientation and Gender Identity."[24]

Once again, ground-level contradictions abound in the Indian context. For example, Principle 1 of the right to universal enjoyment of human rights requires governments to *"embody the principles of the universality, interrelatedness, interdependence and indivisibility of all human rights in their national constitutions or other appropriate legislation and ensure the practical realization of the universal enjoyment of all human rights."* It further says governments must *"integrate within State policy and decision-making a pluralistic approach that recognizes and affirms the interrelatedness and indivisibility of all aspects of human identity including sexual orientation and gender identity."* When we look at the verdict of the Supreme Court of India on Section 377 in December 2013 and the NALSA judgement in April 2014, the two verdicts of the Supreme Court have led to an unparalleled contradiction where an Indian citizen may now self-determine the gender identity, but will attract punishment if they choose to have non-penile-vaginal sexual relations. So, say, for a transgender woman who is not post operative transsexual, her choice of gender identity as a woman will be respected, but her sexual relations with a man will perforce fall foul of Section 377. Some people have argued that this amounts to *"taking the sex out of sexuality!"*[25]

Principle 19 says: *"[States shall] take all necessary legislative, administrative and other measures to ensure the full enjoyment of the right to express identity or personhood, including through speech, deportment, dress, bodily characteristics, choice of name or any other means."* And yet, gender queer and transgender persons still, face entry barriers into health facilities or bullying and other violence in educational institutions. An analysis of all 29 Yogyakarta Principles will reveal much more such systemic human rights violations around sexual orientation and gender identity in India.

The global human rights commitments described so far have also informed a number of other **multilateral agreements and donor pledges**. Significantly, a majority of these are in the context of HIV and focussed on the concerns of MSM and transgender women. A short list follows:

- The Global Fund Strategy in Relation to Working with Sexual Orientations and Gender Identities, 2009 – a strategy document of the Global Fund to Fight AIDS, Tuberculosis and Malaria, one of the largest donors to fund HIV and other public health interventions across the world.

- UNAIDS Action Framework: Universal Access for Men Who Have Sex with Men and Transgender People, 2009 – a framework to push for universal access to HIV prevention, care, support and treatment for MSM and transgender women globally.

- Asia Pacific Forum of National Human Rights Institutions workshop of member commissions (which includes the National Human Rights Commission of India) to discuss their role in promoting the implementation of the Yogyakarta Principles, 2009 – the workshop resulted in the Advisory Council of Jurists of the Asia Pacific Forum issuing a comprehensive set of recommendations in line with the mandate of National Human Rights Institutions, which protect and promote human rights of all persons.[26]

- South Asian Roundtable Dialogue: Legal and Policy Barriers to the HIV Response, 2011: Organized by the International Law Development Organization, United Nations Development Programme, SAARCLAW, World Bank and UNAIDS – the roundtable brought together community leaders and advocates, representatives of the judiciary, human rights institutions, parliamentarians, government officials, lawyers and law students dealing with HIV, and key affected populations to strategize on strengthening the rights-based response (as against a narrow medical response) to the HIV epidemic in their countries.[27]

- Global Commission on HIV and the Law – Risks, Rights and Health, 2012 – an 18-month review process of the legal environments prevailing in different countries in relation to LGBTIQ issues and HIV vulnerability. This was an initiative of the United Nations Development Programme and resulted in a comprehensive set of recommendations on legal reforms for governments and international bodies.[28]

In winding up this chapter, a brief mention of the National Human Rights Commission of India (NHRC). This is an autonomous public body constituted in 1993 under the Protection of Human Rights Ordinance of the same year and in relation to India's ratification of the ICCPR. It was given a statutory basis by the Protection of Human Rights Act, 1993. Considered to have had a mixed record in terms of its goal of protecting and promoting human rights, including against violence committed by both State and non-State actors, the NHRC has taken up LGBTIQ issues occasionally. It has engaged with LGBTIQ communities mainly in the perspective of the HIV epidemic, and recommended a reformulation of Section 377 as long back as 2000 when it organized a national conference on human rights.[29]

However, in 2001, it resorted to a rather narrow outlook on the scope of its own powers when it refused to entertain a complaint filed by a queer activist on behalf of a boy who had been administered aversion therapy to 'cure' him of his homosexual orientation. The reasoning provided was that the case involved the Indian Psychiatric Society, a private body, but not any omission or commission by a public servant.[30] The NHRC's state level counterparts have intervened in matters of the right to vote, discrimination in employment, and illegal detention and police abuse faced by transgender women.[31] Clearly, there seems to be scope for a much more proactive involvement of the NHRC in protecting the human rights of LGBTIQ people.

Endnotes

[1] Pawan Dhall, and Paul Boyce. *Livelihood, Exclusion and Opportunity: Socioeconomic Welfare among Gender and Sexuality Non-normative People in India.* Report. Institute of Development Studies. Brighton: Institute of Development Studies, 2015.

2 India. Ministry of Health & Family Welfare, Government of India. Department of AIDS Control. *National AIDS Control Programme Phase-IV (2012-17) Strategy Document.* Delhi: National AIDS Control Organisation, 2012.

3 *Health Policies and Sexual and Reproductive Health Needs of People Living with HIV and Sexual Minorities in Orissa and West Bengal.* Issue brief. Kolkata: SAATHII, 2011.

4 *National Integrated Biological and Behavioural Surveillance (IBBS) 2014-15 - High Risk Groups.* Report. National AIDS Control Organisation. Delhi: Ministry of Health & Family Welfare, Government of India, 2015.

5 *National Integrated Biological and Behavioural Surveillance.*

6 Nicholas Toonen versus Australia, Human Rights Committee, 50th Session, Case No. 488/1992, UN Doc. CCPR/c/50/D/488/1992. **Note:** This was a landmark *human rights* complaint brought before the *United Nations Human Rights Committee* by *Tasmanian* resident Nicholas Toonen in 1994. The case resulted in the repeal of *Australia's* last *sodomy laws* when the Committee held that sexual orientation was included in the anti-discrimination provisions as a protected status under the ICCPR (*https://en.wikipedia.org/wiki/Toonen_v._Australia* - last accessed February 2, 2017).

7 United Nations General Assembly. Human Rights Council. *Resolution adopted by the General Assembly: 57/214. Extrajudicial, Summary or Arbitrary Executions.* United Nations General Assembly, 2003.

8 *Discrimination and Violence against Individuals Based on their Sexual Orientation and Gender Identity.* Report. UNHCHR. Office of the United Nations High Commissioner for Human Rights, 2015.

9 Morello, Carol. "U.N. Council Creates Watchdog for LGBT Rights." *The Washington Post,* June 30, 2016. *https://www.washingtonpost.com/world/national-security/un-council-creates-watchdog-for-lgbt-rights/2016/06/30/54976de6-3eee-11e6-80bc-d06711fd2125_story.html?utm_ term=.5f5303063d37* accessed February 2, 2017.

10 Anand Grover, *Report of the Special Rapporteur on the Right of Everyone to the Enjoyment of the Highest Attainable Standard of Physical and Mental Health.* Report. United Nations General Assembly. UNHRC, 2010.

11 UN Women. *http://www.un.org/womenwatch/daw/daw/index.html* accessed February 21, 2017.

12 United Nations. ECOSOC. "UN Committee Recommends LGBT Organizations for ECOSOC Consultative Status." News release, June 01, 2013.OutRight Action International. *https://www.outrightinternational.org/content/un-committee-recommends-lgbt-organizations-ecosoc-consultative-status* Accessed February 17, 2017.

                    Pawan Dhall

[13] Suhasini Haidar, "India Vote at UN Not Anti-gay, Explains Government." *The Hindu*, March 26, 2015. *http://www.thehindu.com/news/national/india-vote-at-un-not-antigay- explains-government/article7032970.ece* accessed February 17, 2017.

[14] Avinaba Dutta, "India's Abdication in UN Queer Vote."*Varta* August 21, 2016. *http://www.vartagensex.org/details.php?p=57b941b5e0ad1* accessed February 17, 2017.

[15] Dinesh Bhugra, , Kristen Eckstrand, Petros Levounis, Anindya Kar, and Kenneth R. Javate. *World Psychiatric Association Position Statement on Gender Identity and Same-Sex Orientation, Attraction, and Behaviours.* March 2016.

[16] Bhugra et. al., *World Psychiatric Association Position Statement on Gender Identity.*

[17] Samy Nemir Olivares,. "Sexual Orientation and Gender Identity at the United Nations." Youth Coalition. June 29, 2015. *http://www.youthcoalition.org/sexual-orientation-gender-identity/sexual-orientation-and-gender-identity-at-the-united-nation/* accessed February 17, 2017.

[18] Sustainable Development Goals. *http://www.un.or g/sustainabledevelopment/sustainable-development-goals/* accessed February 20, 2017.

[19] Elizabeth Mills,. "Gender, Sexuality and the SDGs: An Evidence-base for Action," Institute of Development Studies. October 20, 2015. *http://www.ids.ac.uk/opinion/gender-sexuality-and-the-sdgs-an-evidence-base-for-action* accessed February 20, 2017.

[20] " Introduction to the Yogyakarta Principles," The Yogyakarta Principles. *http://www.yogyakartaprinciples.or g/*, Accessed February 20, 2017

[21] "Introduction to the Yogyakarta Principles"

[22] The Capacity of National Human Rights Institutions to Address Human Rights in Relation to Sexual Orientation, Gender Identity and HIV, Report. Bangkok: United Nations Development Prog ramme and Inter national Law Development Organization, 2013.

[23] South Asia Roundtable Dialogue: Legal and Policy Barriers to the HIV Response, Report. Kathmandu: International Law Development Organization, 2011.

[24] *South Asia Roundtable Dialogue: Legal and Policy Barriers to the HIV Response.*

[25] Bina Fernandez, *Humjinsi: A Resource Book on Lesbian, Gay and Bisexual Rights in India.* Mumbai: Combat Law Publications, 2002.

[26] Sherry Joseph, *Social Work Practice and Men Who Have Sex with Men.* Delhi: Sage Publications, 2005.

[27] Sherry Joseph, *Social Work Practice and Men Who Have Sex with Men.*

Mapping queer margins

A sampling of the situation around LGBTQI rights in different corners of the world

Debjyoti Ghosh

Abstract

This article goes through the legislations of several countries to see how LGBTIQ rights have manifested within the realm of law. It considers the treatment of the colonial anti-sodomy laws of the former British Empire and investigates the differing treatments of the rights of LGBTIQ populations in various countries of Europe and the Global South. It also examines the United States of America. It aims to show that while there has been a growing trend of LGBTIQ acceptance in law, even where rights have been achieved, the path to claiming them is fraught with difficulties and obstacles.

Introduction

LGBTIQ[1] populations around the world have often been forced to survive on the margins. Gender and sexuality are relevant factors in virtually all socio-economic and socio-cultural contexts. Many a time, members of the LGBTIQ community are doubly marginalised due to the intersectionality of identities such as race, gender, class, colour, religion, and in the case of the Indian sub-continent, caste,[2] among others.

Leaving aside the intersectional aspects, the legal situation regarding rights of LGBTIQ people are anything but a positive global consensus at the current moment. From the West to the East, from the North to the South, there is a growing trend of becoming more tolerant and legally accepting towards sexual and gender minorities through decriminalisation and in some cases embracing marriage equality, but when powerhouses like Russia, China and India hold out against equal rights, it brings about a critical discord within the rights dialogue.[3]

Constitutional morality, in modern usage, has come to mean the substantive values of a constitution, such as non-discrimination. Populist morality entails popular movements, mass demonstrations, etc., but are often representative of a particular group, generally, the majority While both can be the backbone of social change, many a time populist morality can endanger the rights of minorities. In order to protect minorities against majoritarian tyranny, constitutional morality (i.e. the morality of the constitution) has to be upheld. Constitutional morality exists in abstraction, and is thus supposed to distance itself from a person or a group of persons, who might insist on representing the values of all people.[4] However, it is up to us how we interpret the constitutional values to meet circumstances.

This notion of not following populist morality has been seen in various socially conservative countries when it has come to empowering minorities and criminalising discriminatory behaviour. However, at the same time, populist sentiments have been at the heart of demonstrations across the world against legislations and adjudications by courts for ending racial discrimination, anti-miscegenation laws, and in turn, against decriminalising homosexual behaviour and legalising same-sex marriage.

The main aim of this article shall be to provide a comprehensive comparative picture across several countries. It will traverse several constitutions and legal systems to show that many a time constitutional morality has gone against contemporary populist morality in order to ensure LGBTQI rights. The article will glance at the legal journeys in various countries across the world with special focus on India and other countries of the former British Empire which had or still have the burden of the colonial anti-sodomy legislation. It will also glance at legislations and movements of some of the members of the European Union, the relatively new BRICS[5] bloc, as well as the United States of America.

Queer-mapping – a sampling of the legal status of LGBTIQ people across the world

India

In India, the overall debate about legally legitimising queer presence and rights is highly contested. The Indian queer rights movement is relatively new.[6] Currently, a colonial law, Section 377[7] of the Indian Penal Code, promulgated in 1860, is still in force in the country, criminalising any type of sexual behaviour by "whoever", "against the order of nature." This includes non-procreative, hence same-sex, sexual behaviour. While this law obviously applies for heterosexual people who are indulging in non-procreative sexual acts as well, it has seldom been used beyond homosexual acts. For this reason, it is often referred to as the "anti-sodomy" law.[8]

In Indian law,[9] marriage has never been described strictly as a union between a man and a woman. However, such an inevitable assumption has been generally drawn from customary traditions and from various religions existing within the sub-continent, as well as from different personal religious laws, thus leading to the conclusion that marriage necessarily presupposes the sexual difference of the parties. Moreover, the various legislations, read as a whole, refer to the husband and the wife, the bride and the bridegroom, and thus indirectly assuming opposite-sex couples. However, till now, there has been no legal situation whereby a same-sex couple or a couple where at least one partner is transgender has tried to register their marriage in India, and have been refused. Given that customary traditions also allow for marriages to take place outside and ungoverned by state law, there are no legal mechanisms to stop same-sex couples from performing such rites,[10] but there is no legal validity of these ceremonies.

In 2009, after many years of activism and a lot of judicial back-and-forth, the Delhi High Court passed a ruling in favour of decriminalising same-sex sexual activity under Section 377 of the Indian Penal Code.[11] However, this victory was short-lived. In 2013, the Supreme Court of India heard the case on appeal, and concluded, among other things, that the issue could not be settled by the Supreme Court but had to be referred to the Parliament of India.[12]

However, beyond Section 377 of the Indian Penal Code, other laws are relevant in issues of sexual minority rights. The Immoral Traffic (Prevention) Act of 1956,[13] for instance, prescribes against aiding and abetting prostitution and forbids solicitation in public spaces. This law has often been used to harass, among others, transvestites, transgender people and *Hijras* in cruising spots and in generally occupying public spaces. These legal instruments, when abused, often allow sexual and gender minorities to be bullied and blackmailed, and sometimes even physically and sexually abused, and leave little room for legal recourse for the victims.

The Former British Empire and allies – a few members of the Commonwealth and beyond

The anti-sodomy law was not only promulgated in India but also across 42 other former British colonies during the days of the Empire at different times during the 19th century. Ironically, Great Britain itself has moved ahead from criminalising same-sex sexual behaviour to legitimising same-sex relationships through marriage.[14] Several former colonies have already repealed the law, such as Hong Kong (1991), Australia (1997),[15] New Zealand (1986) and Fiji (1997).[16] Yet, many others still carry it forward, either in the form that was first drafted by the British colonial government or in a slightly varied format.

For instance, in Singapore, Section 377A[17] of the Penal Code, which was brought into force in 1938, is still in place. Covering so-called "Outrages on decency," the Section specifically focuses on male-on-male sexual acts, and states that "[a]any male person who, in public or private, commits, or abets the commission of, or procures or attempts to procure the commission by any male person of, any act of gross indecency with another male person, shall be punished with imprisonment for a term which may extend to 2 years." In 2014, the Singapore Supreme Court upheld the ban on same-sex sexual relations, stating further that the matter was for the Parliament to decide, which much resembles the situation in India.[18]

Australia is an interesting case study. Being federal in nature (like the USA), each territory separately allowed a male same-sex conduct. South Australia was the first jurisdiction to decriminalise homosexual activity in 1975, followed by the Australian Capital Territory in 1976,[19] and the rest of the states (barring Tasmania)proceeding in the same direction at different points in time between 1980 and 1990. However, Tasmania held out in repealing its sodomy law, which led to the case of *Toonen v. Australia*[20] at the United Nations Human Rights Committee. The Committee decided that such laws were not only already defunct in the other states of Australia but were also in contravention to the right to privacy under the International Covenant of Civil and Political Rights. When Tasmania refused to comply with the order, the Federal Government took action and passed the Human Rights (Sexual Conduct) Act of 1994 for all of Australia. This Act legalised all sexual activity between consenting adults and prohibited the legislation of any laws that might interfere with the private sexual conduct of adults. As a result, Rodney Croome, an Australian LGBT rights activist, brought a case at the High Court of Australia that the Tasmanian sodomy laws were against federal legislation. The *Croome v Tasmania case*[21] forced the Tasmanian government to finally give in and repeal the laws in question.

The Family Law Act of 1975 already recognised *de facto* unions, whereby couples who are living together on a domestic basis could register their situation in a manner similar to a civil union or domestic partnership. This is applicable to both same-sex and opposite sex couples, and affords most of the rights of married couples. From 2008 onwards, a spate of legislative changes were brought about following the Australian Human Rights Commission's 2007 report "Same-Sex: Same Entitlements." 85 Federal laws were reformed, leading to the elimination of discrimination from the various legislations.[22] Several states have passed regional laws on civil unions and domestic partnerships, with some cities even going above and beyond the state legislations.[23] However, till date, there has been no national or federal consensus on same-sex marriage.

New Zealand inherited an archaic colonial law that punished homosexual acts with death from as early as the 1840s. Yet, the country became one of the most progressive when it came to LGBT rights. It decriminalised homosexual acts between consenting adults in 1986, and criminalised discrimination on the basis of sexual orientation through amending the Human Rights Act of 1993. It was the first country on the continent to pass same-sex marriage laws in 2013, but not without a decade of strategic litigation behind it.[24]

Nepal, a geographical and cultural neighbour of India, has gone way beyond its continental (and sub-continental) neighbours. Nepal was a monarchy throughout the days of the British Empire, and was never under British administration, being mostly a buffer ally.[25] For most of the period of monarchic rule, homosexuality was a crime. However, the 1990s saw a patent rise in civil society organisations and advocacy in the country, owing to the various steps undertaken to democratise the governance of the country. Due to several political upheavals, the incipient democratic process came to a halt and absolute monarchy was restored. This pushed forward further political dissent. In 2007, a revolution in Nepal overthrew the monarchy and established a secular democratic government.[26]

The revolution allowed for the greater participation of several civil society bodies, including LGBTQI organisations. However, soon enough many LGBTIQ groups felt side-lined by the new government, and thus moved the Supreme Court of Nepal in 2007 with a writ petition.[27] This legal claim brought about a change in the stance of the Nepalese government, leading to the decriminalisation of homosexuality along with the introduction of several laws guaranteeing the rights of the LGBTQI community.

The 2015 constitution contains provisions against discrimination on any ground, including sex or sexual orientation by the State or anyone else. This includes one's right to use one's preferred gender on identity cards, as well as the usage of gender-neutral terms where the gender binary was earlier the norm. While the constitution does secure equal rights for all marginalised communities in the country, which includes the LGBTQI community, it does not specifically address the issue of marriage outside the gender binaries.

Going beyond the traditional Western blocs

Within BRICS, fellow-countries of the Global South, South Africa and Brazil, are the only two to have decriminalised homosexuality and gone so far as to admit civil unions of same-sex couples equal and equivalent to marriage. After the fall of apartheid, the "new" democratic South Africa entrenched non-discrimination based on sex, sexuality and gender in its constitution.[28] Through judicial activism, various laws criminalising same-sex behaviour were struck down in 1997-1998, as they were made unconstitutional.[29] Following further judicial activism, in 2006, civil unions equal and equivalent to marriage were instated. While the Acts governing marriage and civil unions are different, the rights and duties are the same, and civil unions may be referred to as marriage by the parties.[30]

Brazil has had a somewhat unique colonial past. It went from being a colony to the capital of the Portuguese Empire in 1808. In 1822, it became independent as an empire unto itself, with the Portuguese monarch Dom Pedro I being crowned its first emperor. As early as 1830, the Imperial Penal Code ruling the country did not include sodomy as a punishable offence.[31] The fall of the monarchy and the rise of the Republic in the late 19th century did not significantly change this situation.

After much turmoil throughout the 20th century, including the institution of a military dictatorship in 1964, Brazil democratised in 1988. The new federal constitution, while not specifically prohibiting discrimination based on sexuality, does set several overarching protections, including the inviolable right to privacy.[32]

Brazil is organised in a federal structure with a federal constitution as well as state constitutions. This allowed the states of Mato Grosso and Sergipe to promulgate their own constitutions prohibiting discrimination based on sexual orientation in 1989. However, it was only in the 1990s that a movement towards legalising civil unions and gay marriages took place, with the politician Marta Suplicy proposing a bill on civil unions in 1995.[33] Till date, that bill has not been approved.

However, in 2004 the situation of sexual minority rights took a juridical turn. The Highest Court of the state of Rio Grande do Sul approved same-sex civil unions, allowing state notaries to start registering such unions.[34] Yet, it was not until 2011 that the Supreme Federal Court extended the institution of "união estável" (or stable unions) to same-sex couples nationwide. This was a rather significant move, for it required the definition of family to be changed in national legislation.[35] In the same year, the state courts in São Paulo changed civil unions into same-sex marriages, setting the trend for the future. In 2013, Brazil legalized same-sex marriage across the country.[36]

Russia has a very conservative stance on homosexuality. While consenting sexual behaviour between two adults of the same sex was decriminalised in 1993,[37] there has been no progress beyond that to afford same sex couples similar protections to opposite-sex couples. In fact, there has been a spate of legislation across various regions that ban any kind of same sex sexuality or advocacy as "propaganda."[38] There has also been a rise in violence against the queer community along with a strong resistance against pride marches or parades.

China, with the abolition of the Hooligan laws in 1997,[39] essentially decriminalised homosexuality. However, there has hardly been any movement beyond that. Special areas in China, like Hong Kong and Macau, have specific laws which extend limited protection to same-sex couples, but both are yet to legally validate same-sex unions.

Europe and the United States of America – differences galore

In Europe, countries have come around to accepting homosexuality and same-sex relationships at different times in history, while not necessarily with universal acceptance. Under the European Convention of Human Rights (ECHR), Article 14 prohibits discrimination, stating that "[t]he enjoyment of the rights and freedoms set forth in [the] Convention shall be secured without discrimination on any ground such as sex, race, colour, language, religion, political or other opinion, national or social origin, association with a national minority, property, birth or other status."[40] Thus, same-sex sexual activity is legal in all 28 countries of the EU. However, there is still disagreement in issues of civil unions and same-sex marriages.

Western European countries seem to have been the most forward when it comes to decriminalising same-sex relations, which in some cases took place even prior to the rights movements of the 20[th]century. In Belgium, same-sex sexual activity has been legal since 1795, and France since 1791. In the United Kingdom, however, the process started only from 1967, with England and Wales being the first in recognising male same-sex sexual activity as legal, and then in 1981 and 1982 respectively with Scotland and Northern Ireland. Ireland legalised same-sex sexual activity in 1993.[41]

Belgium has also had same-sex cohabitation or unions from 2000, France from 1999, the UK from 2005, and the Netherlands from 1998. However, when it comes to same-sex marriage, the UK legalised it as late as 2014, but it is still illegal in Northern Ireland. The Republic of Ireland, on the other hand, legalised Civil Partnerships from 2011 to 2015, and graduated to marriage from 2015. The Netherlands has had same-sex marriage from 2001, Belgium from 2003 and France from 2013. The latest in this group is Germany, which had same-sex partnership from 2001, and finally legalised same-sex marriage in 2017.[42]

Without going into detail about all 28 countries within the EU, in certain cases, there have been tendencies of regressing as well. For instance, in Slovakia, a referendum was held in 2015 to invalidate, among other things, gay marriage, as marriage was to be defined as a union only between a man and a woman. While the question whether there should be a referendum about the definition of marriage and other related aspects was approved, the referendum itself was invalid due to a poor voting turnout.[43] France, too, saw a large anti-gay marriage protest in October 2016, with the demonstrators hoping that a new conservative government would repeal the same-sex marriage legislation of 2013.[44]

The United States of America witnessed major social changes in the 20[th]century. The civil rights movement, for instance, did not stop with the extension of equal rights to the black population, or with the legalising of interracial marriages. It carried to the streets of San Francisco in the 1970s, which marked the beginning of gay rights movement – the Stonewall riots– and, in many ways, continues today.[45] With a federal system similar to Australia, every state has different standards of recognition of LGBTIQ rights. It was with the landmark case of Lawrence v. Texas[46] as late as 2003 that the Supreme Court of the US legalised same-sex sexual behaviour across the entire US between consenting adults and consenting adolescents of a close age. Marriage laws, too, were different in different states. It took another decade for the US v. Windsor[47] to strike down the definition of marriage as a union between a man and a woman. However, there is no comprehensive legislation on discrimination on the basis of sexuality in the US – each state has its own laws around it, and some of them are utterly regressive even today, and somewhat representative of the social settings and circumstances.

Conclusion – changing opinions, but are they changing fast enough?

As seen above, the journey has been conflicting, and paths to equal rights have been daunting and challenging. There are many differing opinions on who deserves what rights around the world. Even in countries where LGBTIQ movements started decades ago, they have borne fruit quite recently. However, we are in a day and age when minorities have an agentic voice that can no longer be silenced and pushed into the margins.

There are currents flowing both for and against LGBTIQ recognition. Countries that hold hands within geo-political bodies, despite having several interests in common, and sometimes being quite vociferous about minority rights, often differ when it comes to LGBTIQ rights. Unsure of what morality to follow – constitutional or populist- and whether to give in to what may be considered as an invisible minority in many cases, there is no consensus on the matter. Many governments and judiciaries have tried to side-step the matter, or if they do engage, they keep it in limbo till they feel the time is right. They fear that upholding constitutional morality would upset the societal fabric and populist sentiments.

However, given that most countries mentioned above are signatories of the Universal Declaration of Human Rights, having differing standards of equality for their own citizens seem to go directly against what they initially signed up for. Seemingly, some people have more entitlement to the same rights that are supposedly available for everyone – or in Orwell's famous words, "All animals are equal, but some animals are more equal than others".

Endnotes

[1] An acronym widely used as an umbrella for the Lesbian, Gay, Bisexual, Trans/Transgender, Queer and Intersex communities.

[2] Intersectionality was a term coined by Kimberlé W. Crenshaw to describe overlapping factors which are related to systems of oppression, domination and discrimination. For a detailed reading into it, refer to Kimberlé W. Crenshaw, "Mapping the margins: Intersectionality, identity politics, and violence against women of color." *Stanford law review* (1991), pp.1241-1299.

[3] While it is a growing trend, it is slow. There are several countries across the world where homosexuality is still criminalised and LGBT people are severely persecuted, where religious fundamentalists host anti-gay rallies and protests. Even the Global North has its fair share of discrimination against the LGBTIQ community, despite being the charge-bearer of change. However, when a legal system is in favour of a minority population in general through anti-discrimination laws, equality laws, etc., it helps in redressing the wrongs and to give justice to those discriminated against.

[4] Perhaps the divergence between constitutional morality and populist/social morality has seldom been more apparent than in India. The constitution of India was at best a compromise between various political factions of the time. The constituent assembly debates are proof of the frictions between the different parties and their varied political agendas. Dr. B. R. Ambedkar, one of the founding fathers of the Indian Constitution, and a man who was highly critical of the caste system, understood how important it was to separate the democratic policy being set up through constitution-making from the highly undemocratic institution of caste. His speeches about the need for constitutional morality and the lack of the understanding of the same by the masses is reflected in his speeches in *The Constitution and the Constituent Assembly Debates* (Lok Sabha Secretariat, Delhi, 1990). However, while this barely touches the tip of the iceberg, this is a matter to be discussed at length another time.

[5] An acronym for Brazil, Russia, India, China and South Africa, it is a grouping of some of the world's largest developing economies, with its primary focus on non-interference and collaboration on mutually beneficial programmes.

[6] In fact, it wasn't until 1994 that people who refer to themselves as *Hijras* (more generally known as one of the indigenous transgender groups) were given voting rights, with the Supreme Court of India granting them the third gender status as late as 2014 in the *National Legal Services Authority v. Union of India*, WP (Civil) No 604 of 2013.

[7] Chapter XVI of the Indian Penal Code, Act No. 45 Of 1860 by the British Parliament, carrying on as the primary criminal law in India till date, albeit with a few amendments. It is to be noted that this Act was only meant for the British dominions, and not the Princely States, which had their own legal systems. However, it was adopted in its entirety by both India and Pakistan (as the Pakistan Penal Code) after the independence of both countries.

[8] In a few instances, Section 377 has been used in filing cases against domestic violence against women. One such instance was reported in *Staying Alive: Evaluating Court Orders: Sixth Monitoring & Evaluation Report 2013 on the Protection of Women from Domestic Violence Act, 2005* by Lawyers Collective (Women's Rights Initiative) New Delhi, 2013, page 48.

[9] Ironically, neither in legislation governing marriage, nor in legislation governing divorce. For instance, in the Hindu Marriage Act, Section 5 states "a marriage may be solemnised between two Hindus" and lays out various conditions. Even where it delineates the ages of the bride and the bridegroom, it does not refer to the bride and the bridegroom marrying each other.

[10] For instance, the marriage of Madhuri Sarode, a transgender person, with her partner Jay, at a temple in Mumbai, details of which can be found at *http://*

timesofindia.indiatimes.com/articleshow/56256604.cms (last accessed July 25, 2017). This isn't the first time such a marriage was conducted, but it is one of the first to be publicly declared and celebrated.

[11] *Naz Foundation v. Govt. of NCT of Delhi* at the Delhi High Court, 160 Delhi Law Times 277 (2009).

[12] Paragraph 56, *Suresh Kr. Kaushal v Naz Foundation* (Civil Appeal No. 10972 of 2013), (2014) 1 SCC 1.

[13] Amended in 1986, and in the same form since.

[14] Decriminalised under the Sexual Offences Act 1967 for England and Wales, under the Criminal Justice (Scotland) Act of 1980 for Scotland and under the Homosexual Offences (Northern Ireland) Order 1982. I have discussed same-sex marriage in the UK later in the article and the citations are given there.

[15] Female homosexuality was never considered illegal, so this pertains only to male homosexuality. Prima facie this might seem strangely liberal, but it was primarily because women were not considered to be of political importance

[16] All the countries mentioned here are discussed in detail later.

[17] The original Section 377 of the Penal Code of Singapore, which was similar to the one in India, was repealed and replaced in 2007 by a law on sexual intercourse with a human corpse. Currently there is ongoing research on why Section 377A had to be introduced. It has been conjectured that with the rise of transvestite sex workers in Singapore at the time, a law had to be brought about to criminalise sexual acts through commission between two men.

[18] *Tan Eng Hong v Attorney-General* [2012] SGCA 45.

[19] Although it was initially proposed in 1973, it only came into power in 1976.

[20] Communication No. 488/1992, whereas the complaint was filed initially by Nicholas Toonen in 1991, with admissibility being granted in 1992, and date of adoption of views (decision), March 1994 – available online at http://hrlibrary.umn.edu/undocs/html/vws488.htm

[21] [1997] HCA 5 (26 February 1997)

[22] A National Enquiry into Discrimination against People in Same-sex Relationships: Financial and Work-Related Entitlements and Benefits, published by the Human Rights and Equal Opportunity Commission of Australia in 2007 - available online at http://www.humanrights.gov.au/samesex/index.html

[23] In 2004, the Howard Administration amended the Marriage Act of 1961, to include a definition of marriage as the union of a man with a woman, thus tacitly establishing that unions of any other sort are not marriages. In November 2016, the Australian Government proposed to hold a plebiscite on the issue of same-

sex marriage. However, the opposition vetoed this move in the Parliament, saying that this would be playing with the rights of LGBTQI population.

[24] The legal battle started with *Quilter v Attorney General* ([1998] 1 NZLR 523) wherein three female couples were denied the license to marry by the Registrar-General as the common law understanding of marriage is that between a man and a woman. This case went to the High court, and later the Court of Appeal (the then-apex Court of New Zealand), which upheld the ruling of the High Court, siding by the definition of marriage being that between a man a woman. Two of the couples involved in the earlier case sued New Zealand a the United Nations Human Rights Committee (*Ms. Juliet Joslin et al v New Zealand*, Communication No. 902/1999) but the Committee rejected the case in 2002. It was in 2013 that MP Louisa Wall introduced a Bill, which led to the Marriage (Definition of Marriage) Amendment Act of 2013, giving same-sex couples the right to marry by defining marriage for the first time in the legislative history of New Zealand, and by stating it to be the "union of 2 people, regardless of their sex, sexual orientation, or gender identity" (Section 5).

[25] Nepal and the British Empire fought against each other in the bloody Anglo-Nepali war between 1815-1816. This led to the signing of the Sugauli treaty of 1816, which made Nepal cede various regions of what is now a part of India, as well as give the British the right to recruit soldiers, as the British East India Company was highly impressed by the valour of the Nepali soldiers (which led to the rise of the Gorkha Regiment). This started the alliance between Nepal and the British empire, which carried on through both World Wars as well.

[26] *For a comprehensive analysis of the events in Nepal since 1990, refer to Mahendra Lawoti and Susan Hangen (eds.), Nationalism and Ethnic Conflict in Nepal: Identities and Mobilization After 1990, Routledge Contemporary South Asia Series (Routledge: London, 2013).*

[27] *Sunil Babu Pant and ors. Government of Nepal and ors.*, Writ No. 917 of 2007.

[28] Section 9 (3), the Constitution of South Africa.

[29] *National Coalition for Gay and Lesbian Equality and Another v Minister of Justice and Others* [1998] ZACC 15 – the Constitutional Court of South Africa struck down laws prohibiting consensual sexual acts between men, basing it on the Bill of Rights in the Constitution, stating that it went against the prohibition of discrimination based on sexual orientation as given in the Constitution.

[30] *Minister of Home Affairs and Another v Fourie and Another,* [2005] ZACC 19 – after a unanimous decision by the Constitutional Court stating that same-sex couples have the constitutional right ot marry, the Civil Union Act was promulgated in November 2006, which gives same-sex couples the right to either "marriage or civil partnership" as per the description of the Act. All rights and duties of marriage are equal in a civil partnership. However, the Marriage Act of 1961 carries on side by side.

[31] For a better understanding of Brazilian history from the time of Portuguese colonisation, please refer to Boris Fausto, A Concise History of Brazil (Cambridge University Press, 1999).

[32] Chapter 1, Article V(X), Constitution of Brazil.

[33] Brazilian Congressional Bill No. 1151, which aimed to change Article 1723 of the Civil Code to define a civil union as between two people irrespective of the gender of either party. Because of the positive stance of the Brazilian apex court on the matter, mentioned later in the paper, the Bill may have a greater chance in the Senate.

[34] "Notary of Rio Grande do Sul accept registration of same-sex civil union" (translated from Portuguese), *Terra*, March 4, 2004, available online at http://noticias.terra.com.br/brasil/interna/0,,OI275352-EI306,00.html

[35] Decision by the Supreme Federal Tribunal of Brazil on ADI 4277 and ADPF 132, May 5, 2011

[36] Resolution of the National Justice Council, No 175 of May 14, 2013

[37] Update to resolution RUS33940.E, whereby the Yeltsin Government repealed Article 121.1 of the Russian Federation Criminal Code criminalising same-sex behaviour between men (similar behaviour amongst women wasn't criminalised), and Article 132 criminalises any non-consensual sexual behaviour, irrespective of the genders of the people involved.

[38] The Russian federal law "for the Purpose of Protecting Children from Information Advocating for a Denial of Traditional Family Values", passed on June 11, 2013, banning all "propaganda" on gay rights or exposing minors to homonormative literature.

[39] It was removed from the list of mental disorders in China in 2001. For a brief overview of the situation in China around LGBTQI rights, please look at *The Economist explains: Chinese attitudes towards gay rights* available online at *https://www.economist.com/blogs/economist-explains/2017/06/economist-explains-2* (last accessed on July 25, 2017)

[40] Available online at *www.echr.coe.int/Documents/FS_Sexual_orientation_ENG.pdf* (last accessed on July 25, 2017)

[41] Female same sex activity was always legal in the countries in the UK and the Republic of Ireland.

[42] Italy deserves a special mention here, as, despite being the bastion of Roman Catholicism, it has started recognising same sex civil unions as of 2016. For a comprehensive overview of gay marriage and civil unions in countries within the European Union and Europe at large, please refer to Michael Lipka, "Where Europe stands on Gay Marriage and Civil Unions", *Fact Tank: Research in numbers,* Pew Research Center, June 30, 2017, available online at *http://www.pewresearch.org/*

fact-tank/2017/06/30/where-europe-stands-on-gay-marriage-and-civil-unions/ (last accessed on July 25, 2017).

[43] It was disguised under the garb of protecting family and children. For more details please refer to Ben Tufft, "Referendum to entrench gay marriage ban in Slovakia overwhelmingly supported but fails due to low turnout", *The Independent*, February 8, 2015, available online at *https://www.independent.co.uk/news/world/europe/referendum-to-entrench-gay-marriage-ban-in-slovakia-overwhelmingly-supported-but-fails-due-to-low-10031769.html* (last accessed on July 25, 2017).

[44] "French anti-gay marriage protesters march to revive issue before polls", *Reuters*, October 16, 2016, available online at *https://www.reuters.com/article/us-france-politics-gaymarriage-idUSKBN12G0T9* (last accessed on July 25, 2017).

[45] Several counter-movements in the form of anti-equality protests and riots occurred around the time of these changes, and still carry on through protests, rallies and bills. In 2017 alone, more than 100 bills have been tabled across the USA – Susan Miller, "Onslaught of anti-LGBT bills in 2017 has activists 'playing defense'", *USA Today*, June 1, 2017, available online at *https://www.usatoday.com/story/news/nation/2017/06/01/onslaught-anti-lgbt-bills-2017/102110520/* (last accessed July 26, 2017)

[46] 539 U.S. 558 (2003).

[47] 570 US (2013).

A Critical Analysis of
Section 377 of Indian Penal Code

Gowthaman Ranganathan

The previous section outlined the international human rights perspective on human sexuality and morality. In this section, we will have a closer look at how the law regulates human sexuality; in particular we will look at the infamous section 377 of the Indian Penal Code. At the outset, it is pertinent to note that the discussion on section 377 or the discussion on non-normative sexualities (Lesbian, Gay, Bisexual) is not an exhaustive discussion of human sexuality. Human sexuality is a vast area of study under which legal regulation of non-normative sexualities and gender identities (Transgender, FTM, MTF, etc) is only a part of. The reason why discussions on non-normative sexualities are equated to human sexuality is because of the onus placed on LGBTIQ persons to speak about sexuality. Thus, this discussion is restricted to the impact that the law has on the lives of LGBTIQ persons and not to the impact on human sexuality per se.

While speaking of law's regulation of sexuality, Section 377 finds a central place but this is not the only way in which sexuality is regulated. Provisions of law pertaining to obscenity, nuisance and local police acts have been used to persecute LGBTIQ persons. However, section 377 has been an important issue around which social, as well as legal action, has been arrayed to speak against the violence faced by LGBTIQ persons. Hence, this section will focus on section 377 of the Indian Penal Code while acknowledging the fact that law by itself in other forms is also used to regulate, control and penalise sexuality. Filing of kidnapping charges against one of the partners in a lesbian relationship by the parents of the other partner, using obscenity laws to obstruct information of safe sex are illustrative of instances where law other than section 377 is invoked. This piece is insufficient to explore the impact of other laws which will at best find a mention in passing.

Before setting out on an analysis of juridical response to section 377, it is important to gain clarity on what the section states. The wording of the section is as follows:

> "Unnatural offences: Whoever voluntarily has carnal intercourse against the order of nature with any man, woman or animal shall be punished with imprisonment for life, or with imprisonment of either description for term which may extend to ten years, and shall also be liable to fine

> Explanation.—Penetration is sufficient to constitute the carnal intercourse necessary to the offence described in this section."

Three key problems with the section maybe pointed out at this juncture. First, it does not take into consideration the consent of the parties involved. Thus, there is no distinction between consensual and non-consensual acts. Criminal law is premised on the harm principle which is to say that when a person is harmed, the state steps in to prosecute the harm doer. However, in the case of consensual sexual acts, there being no harm, the state should have no role to play. Second, the section does not take into account the age of the parties involved. In the absence of a separate law punishing child sexual abuse, section 377 was the only recourse to prosecute children who were sodomized. As a result child rights organization argued for the retention of this section to prosecute perpetrators of child sexual abuse. However, in 2012, a separate law has been enacted to punish perpetrators of child sexual abuse rendering the use of section 377 for non-consensual sexual acts on minors redundant. Third, the section embodies a certain Victorian morality imposed by the colonisers on the colonised. It is important to note that England decriminalised homosexuality in 1967 even as we hold on to this colonial legacy till date. These are a very brief sketch of the problems with section 377.

The section has been used to both prosecute and persecute LGBTIQ persons. Prosecution involves a criminal trial being carried out against a person for indulging in acts prohibited under the section. This may lead to an acquittal where a person is held not guilty. However, the process of undergoing trial in itself is a punishment. In the event of a conviction, the accused may serve a prison term up to a period of ten years or life imprisonment. Persecution is when a person threatened with a prosecution under section 377 and is exploited or extorted. Prosecution and persecution leaves a person scarred and adversely affects his physical and mental well being.

One of the earliest cases where section 377 was invoked was against an anonymous hijra who was only identified as Khairati. She was picked up because she was "found singing dressed as a woman among the women of a certain family". It was suspected that she would have allowed someone to commit sodomy to herself thus abetting (facilitating) an offence under section 377. The following passage from the Human Rights Watch report titles 'This Alien Legacy:[1] The Origins of "Sodomy" Laws in British Colonialism' aptly summarizes what transpired in the case:

> "The trial court stated that"he is shown to have the characteristic mark of a habitual catamite - the distortion of the orifice of the anus into the shape of a trumpet ... which distinctly points to unnatural intercourse within the last few months." Thus Khairati was not tried for any particular incident of sodomy: the only clue was clothing-substantiated by later medical examination. The lower court stated that "the three facts proved against the accused-his appearance as a woman, the misshapement [of the anus], the venereal disease-irresistibly lead to the conclusion that he has recently subjected himself to unnatural lust." The appeals court set aside the conviction because there was no specificity about the act: time, place, and identity of the "accomplice" were unknown. However, the judge called official attempts at "checking these disgusting practices ... laudable."[2]

Thus, though the hijra in the case was acquitted, she was subjected to demeaning medical processes and was picked up only on the basis of a perception that she maybe indulged in acts that constitute 'unnatural offences against the order of nature'.

The jurisprudence on what constitutes 'carnal intercourse against the order of nature' continues to stay a puzzle. In the past, courts have held it to be non-procreative sex or sexual acts that are imitative of penovaginal sex.[3] More recently, the Supreme Court in *Suresh Kumar Koushal* v *Union of India*[4] (which will be discussed in some details later) has made the puzzle further complicated by providing no conclusive test to determine what constitutes carnal intercourse against the order of nature.

In more contemporary times, section 377 was used to attack organizations working on HIV prevention in Lucknow. In 2001, the office of the Bharosa Trust was illegally raided and materials on safe sex, HIV prevention were seized. Further, four health care workers were arrested and kept in custody of forty seven days.

Naz Foundation India approached the High Court of Delhi in 2001 stating that the section is a violation of fundamental rights under Part III of the Constitution of India. After eight years, the Delhi High Court gave its verdict in 2009 in the case of *Naz Foundation India* v. Government of *NCT of Delhi*.[5] The court read down the section so as to not apply to consensual sex between adults in private. The court arrived at this conclusion on the basis that criminalisation of consensual sex between adults in private violates the fundamental rights under Article 21, Article 14 and Article 15 that guarantees the right to live with dignity, the right to equality and the right against discrimination respectively. While upholding the right to live with dignity and the right to privacy, the court states:

> "In the Indian Constitution, the right to live with dignity and the right of privacy both are recognised as dimensions of Article 21. Section 377 IPC denies a person's dignity and criminalises his or her core identity solely on account of his or her sexuality and thus violates Article 21 of the Constitution. As it stands, Section 377 IPC denies a gay person a right to full personhood which is implicit in notion of life under Article 21 of the Constitution."[6]

While holding that Section 377 was against the right to equality enshrined in the Constitution, the court held that:

> "When everything associated with homosexuality is treated as bent, queer, repugnant, the whole gay and lesbian community is marked with deviance and perversity. They are subject to extensive prejudice because what they are or what they are perceived to be, not because of what they do. The result is that a significant group of the population is, because of its sexual non-conformity, persecuted, marginalised and turned in on itself."[7]

The Court is aware that the larger public opinion maybe against LGBTIQ persons. Realising this, it places reliance on constitutional morality as opposed to popular or public morality. In the words of Justice A P Shah who along with Justice Muralidhar heard the arguments in the case and authored the judgment:

> "Popular morality or public disapproval of certain acts is not a valid justification for restriction of the fundamental rights under Article 21. Popular morality, as distinct from a constitutional morality derived from constitutional values, is based on shifting and subjective notion of right and wrong. If there is any type of 'morality' that can pass the test of compelling state interest, it must be 'constitutional' morality and not public morality" It was further stated that, "Moral indignation, howsoever strong, is not a valid basis for overriding individual's fundamental rights of dignity and privacy. In our scheme of things, constitutional morality must outweigh the argument of public morality, even if it be the view of the majority."[8]

The decision was received with celebration from the LGBTIQ community across the country with the Queer Pride marches in three cities *viz.* Bengaluru, Delhi and Kolkata which were organized within a few days of the judgment. The judgment was applauded by many for being counter-majoritarian and upholding the rights of minorities. It is pertinent to note that most countries where anti-sodomy laws were struck down, it has been through judicial intervention and seldom through legislative processes.

The judgment paved way for many to assert their identities and come out in the open. The emancipatory potential of the judgment was demonstrated among others in three instances which are outlined below.

The first is the case of Professor Ramchandra Siras who was the chairman of the department of Modern Indian Languages at the Aligarh Muslim University. On 09.02.2010, newspapers widely reported that Prof. Siras was filmed having consensual sex with another adult male. Subsequently, Prof.Siras was suspended from the University where he was working for over twenty years. Along with the suspension, Prof. Siras was asked to vacate the premises he was residing at and electricity and water supply were severed for his house. Prof. Siras approached High Court of Allahabad against these orders by the University.[9] Advocate Anand Grover appearing for Prof. Siras submitted before the court that, "the petitioner is entitled to the fundamental rights to his privacy, dignity, equality and non-discrimination on the basis of sexual orientation, and freedom of movement". On 01.04.2010, the High Court set aside the orders of the University. This was possible only because of the Delhi High Court judgment that enabled Prof. Siras to appear before the court. Though this was a positive development, the incident met with a tragic end with the death of Prof. Siras on 07.04.2010 which was just a few days before his retirement.[10]

Another positive judicial response post the judgment of the Delhi High Court was when the News Broadcasting Standards Authority took *suomoto* cognizance (took notice on their own accord) of a sting operation conducted in Hyderabad by TV9 a news channel. The channel carried a programme that contained a story relating to the mushrooming of the gay culture in Hyderabad. The programme showed unmorphed videos of men purported to be gay which is in violation of their right to privacy. The agency then headed by Justice Verma concluded that, "in effect what the content of the programme clearly did was; instead of carrying a 'crime story' it merely carried evidently a gratuitous depiction and reportage of homosexuality among men without any underlying serious message for the society; the programme needlessly violated the right to privacy of individual's with possible alternate sexual orientation, no longer considered taboo or a criminal act; and the programme misused the special tool of a 'sting operation' available only to subserve the larger public interest."[11] The news channel was fined a sum of rupees one lakh and was ordered to publish an apology for three days expressing regret for the telecast. Yet again, this success was possible as a result of the enabling environment created by the Delhi High Court decision.

The two cases above show that despite the legal change having occurred, instances of homophobia continues. In the intervening night of November 03 and November 04, 2013, 13 men were arrested at Hassan in Karnataka under three different FIRs for an offence under Section 377 of the Indian Penal Code.[12] The arrests were made under three different FIRs, one of which alleged non-consensual sex by a person who was well known to some of the arrested men. The other FIRs were filed by the police on their own accord. The arrests were in clear violation of the guidelines for arrest set out by the Supreme Court in *D K Basu* v. *State of West Bengal*.[13] Interviews with men arrested show that they were subjected to harassment during and after the arrest and their families continue to face harassment. However, since the cases were registered post-2009 after Section 377 was read down, it will play a role in reducing the impact of the case at least on those who have been accused despite consensual sexual acts. Criminal law cannot be retrospectively applied i.e. it cannot apply with effect from an earlier date. Since the Supreme Court decision reinstated Section 377 only in 2013 after the arrests were made, the decision will not apply to this case.

The three cases above demonstrate that the judicial response in reading down Section 377 has helped in reducing fear and challenging homophobic acts. Since 2009, many supports groups and events with focus on LGBTIQ persons have come into existence creating a safe environment for LGBT persons to freely express themselves.

However, a major setback for the rights of LGBT persons came on December 11, 2013. Within a few days after the Delhi High Court's decision, an appeal against the judgment was made by Suresh Kumar Koushal, an astrologer by profession. He was joined by various religious groups in seeking a reversal of the Delhi High Court's decision and reinstating Section 377 of the Indian Penal Code. Four years after the appeal, the Apex Court reversed the decision of the Delhi High Court and held that there was no flaw in Section 377 and if there is any change needed, it should be through the Parliament. While overturning the Delhi High Court's decision, the Supreme Court noted:

> "While reading down Section 377 IPC, the Division Bench of the High Court overlooked that a miniscule fraction of the country's population constitute lesbians, gays, bisexuals or transgenders and in last more than 150 years less than 200 persons have been prosecuted (as per the reported orders) for committing offence under Section 377 IPC and this cannot be made a sound basis for declaring that section ultra vires the provisions of Article 14, 15 and 21 of the Constitution."[14]

The court further noted that, "in its anxiety to protect the so-called rights of LGBTIQ persons and to declare that Section 377 IPC violated the right to privacy, autonomy and dignity, the High Court has extensively relied upon the judgments of other jurisdictions."

The court concluded by stating that, "We hold that Section 377 does not suffer from the vice of unconstitutionality and the declaration made by the Division Bench of the High Court is legally unsustainable."

LGBT persons were dismissed with one stroke as being a miniscule fraction. Such a rationale goes contrary to the principle that even if the rights of one person was violated, it would still be a violation to be remedied by the constitutional court. Some commentators have marked this decision as one of the darkest hours of the Indian judiciary.[15] The reaction to the judgment of the Supreme Court can be summarised in the words below:

> However, after momentary despair, anger, and fear, LGBTIQ people took to the streets in an unprecedented show of dissent and defiance to the regressive verdict of the Apex Court. Activists, allies, and members of the community were clear that all that was done after 2009 when the Delhi High Court granted full and complete citizenship to queer persons will not be undone by the Supreme Court. The community showed a complete refusal to be pushed back into the closet or be dismissed as the "miniscule minority".[16]

With the reinstatement of Section 377 in the law books there is a lot of fear and anxiety amongst LGBTIQ persons. They are susceptible to extortion, exploitation and discrimination. A review petition before the Supreme Court seeking a review of the case was also dismissed. Subsequently a curative petition has been filed before the Apex Court which is pending. In a recent development, the case has been referred to a larger bench.

Subsequently, in April 2014, the Supreme Court affirmed the rights of transgender persons. This was a historic judgment. In *National Legal Services Authority (NALSA)* v. *Union of India*,[17] the court affirmed the rights of transgender persons under Article 14, 15, 19 and 21 and recognized the rights to self identification.[18] The court did not go into the details of Section 377 as Suresh Kumar Koushal was already decided. However, in a passing observation, the court did refer to Section 377. A reference was made to *Queen Empress* v. *Khairati*[19] discussed above and stated that, "even though he was acquitted on appeal, this case would demonstrate that section 377, though associated with specific sexual acts, highlighted certain identities, including Hijras and was used as an instrument of harassment and physical abuse against Hijras and transgender persons."

Many have argued that the rights of transgender persons would not be completely realised as long as section 377 is present. While LGBTIQ

persons await the decision in the curative petition pending, the struggle
for decriminalisation continues.

Endnotes

[1] Alok Gupta. This alien legacy: The origins of" sodomy" laws in British
colonialism. Human Rights Watch, 2008.

[2] Alok Gupta, This alien legacy.

[3] *Khanu* v. *Emperor*, 1925 High Court of Sind, p.286; *Lohana Vasantlal Devchand*
v. *The State*, 1968 All India Report, High Court of Gujarat, p.252 and *State of
Kerala* v. *K.Govindan*, Criminal Law journal (1969) p.20 as cited at supra Note 1.

[4] *Suresh Kumar Koushalv. Union of India* (2014) 1 SCC 1.

[5] *Naz Foundation India* v. *Government of NCT of Delhi*, 160 Delhi Law Times 277

[6] *Naz Foundation India* v. *Government of NCT of Delhi*, 160 Delhi Law Times 277
at Para 48.

[7] *Naz Foundation India* v. *Government of NCT of Delhi*, 160 Delhi Law Times 277
at Para 94.

[8] *Naz Foundation India* v. *Government of NCT of Delhi*, 160 Delhi Law Times 277
at Para 86.

[9] *Dr. Shrinivas Ramchandra Siras & Ors.* Vs. *The Aligarh Muslim University*, Civil
Misc. Writ Petition No.17549 of 2010 accessed from *http://
elegalix.allahabadhighcourt.in/elegalix/WebShowJudgment.do.*

[10] 'Aligarh', a biopic of Prof. Siras was released on February 26, 2016.

[11] Copy of Order issued by NEWS Broadcasting Standards Authority, New
Delhi to TV9, Hyderabad about TV9's Homophobic story "Gay culture rampant
in Hyderabad" accessed from *http://gaysifamily.com/wp-content/uploads/2011/03/
TV9_NBA_Order.pdf.*

[12] 13 People arrested under Section 377 of the Indian Penal Code in November
2013 accessed from *http://altlawforum.org/gender-and-sexuality/13-people-arrested-under-
section-377-of-the-indian-penal-code-in-november-2013/.*

[13] *D K Basuv State of West Bengal* (1997) 1 SCC 416.

[14] *Suresh Kumar Koushalv. Union of India* (2014) 1 SCC 1 at Para 43.

[15] Suresh Koushal v. Naz Foundation: Pratiksha Baxi accessed from *https://
kafila.online/2013/12/16/suresh-koushal-v-naz-foundation-pratiksha-baxi/amp/.*

[16] Ruling in India not the last word, Gowthaman Ranganathan, Gay and Lesbian
Review, June 25, 2014 accessed from *http://altlawforum.org/publications/ruling-in-india-
not-the-last-word/.*

[17] *National Legal Services Authority (NALSA)* v. *Union of India* WP (Civil) No 604 of 2013.

[18] The decision has triggered law making initiatives. The report of the standing committee on Social Justice and Empowerment on the Transgender Persons (Protection of Rights) Bill, 2016 is the most recent development towards the full realization of the NALSA judgment. Even as the implementation of the judgment progresses haltingly, the community is hopeful.

[19] (1884) ILR 6 ALL 204.

Legal Perspectives with Reference to Transgenders

Sandhya Raju

Laws are a reflection of society. Law is enacted to maintain law and order. In simple terms it lays down the norms with the sole objective of maintaining order in the society wherein the society would constitute a collection of people under a common system of governance

Transgenders, as we know, are people who identify themselves to a gender they are not born with. Some of them are called as transsexuals if they desire medical assistance to transition from one sex to another. "Transgender" is an umbrella term which in addition to people whose gender identity is the opposite of or different from their assigned sex may also include people who are gender queer bi-l-gender, pan gender, gender fluid or agender. Being transgender is independent of sexual orientation.

There is a constant struggle to establish their identity. In our existing vocabulary, one finds an absence of recognition of this facet. In a uni-dimensional manner, the norm is that a person through their biological characteristics is identified as a male or a female based on the- sexual organs they are born with. The fact that there could be a possibility that a person may not identify with the gender he is born with was not really envisaged. Consequently, people who came within this realm remained in the fringes. The norm is that one is identified as belonging to a particular sex if he/she is born with the corresponding sexual organs. Consequently, it follows that they would have to follow the gender identities ascribed to that particular sex. Thus a person coming within the male sex will have to conform to the characteristics of the male gender and that of a female sex will have to conform to the norms ascribed to a female gender. This in turn is consequent to the patriarchal mores and notions.

Remaining in the peripheries brings its share of discrimination and stigma as in the perception of - society one neither belongs to the male gender nor the female gender. A society which does not want to think beyond the male and female gender stereotypes, would find it difficult to comprehend the existence of transgenders and their adoption within its fold.

In the context of law, there is a binary concept of man and woman and the legal relations are identified and specified on this basis. Law laid down the rules on the basis of the current morality of the period in which the law was drafted. The concept of sexual orientation is seen in a restricted linear manner within the purview of man –woman within the legal framework. It necessarily excludes the concept of a LGBTIQ concept thus excluding an entire section from the purview of sexuality and consequently marginalising an entire section of the society on the gates of sexual morality. The Indian Penal code which is representative of a Victorian morality clearly excludes the idea of sexuality which does not fall within the traditional linear models of morality. It is through this Prism of binary identity of gender that the law addresses sexuality. Even within the personal laws one finds that the concept of marriage is couched in a man woman relationship. The reason being that there was no concept of a third gender till the NALSA[1] judgement came out.

Sexuality as a concept is not talked about as it's a taboo. Sexuality, as defined by the Oxford dictionary means a person's capacity for sexual feelings or a person's sexual preference. The stigma and discrimination faced by the transgender community is primarily on account of the concept of sexuality as the norm is of being heterosexual. Anything opposed to the norm becomes deviant and hence immoral. This coupled with the patriarchal attitudes embedded in society makes it extremely difficult for transgenders to exercise their sexual identities. There are huge barriers of stigma, discrimination perceptions, myths when a person comes within the framework of a transgender.

For example in the Indian Penal code[2] section 8[3] defines Gender wherein "the pronoun he and its derivatives are used of any person whether male or female. Further Section 10[4] defines "Man, Woman" wherein man denotes a male human being of any age: - the word Woman denotes a female Human Being of any age. Again in section 11, the word person includes any company or association or body of persons, whether incorporated or not. It is pertinent to note that the Indian Penal code which lays down the provisions of various offences committed against an individual or the state was enacted in 1860. There is no concept of Transgender or other gender having been included either in Section 8, 9 or 10 for that matter. This gains significance while we look at offences against the human body in Chapter XVI wherein specifically offences relating to hurt, assault and sexual offences are mentioned, one finds that offences due to the limitation of the definition, they would be excluded and consequently outside the ambit of protection. There is an explanation to include *she* within *he* but not *other*. This is a peculiar notion as it excludes the possibility of a category of people who may not come within the folds of the definition of he or she. On a Perusal of the code, one finds that reliefs are available only to a HE or a SHE. The most damaging would be section 377[5] which clearly states that *whoever voluntarily has carnal intercourse against the order of nature, with any man, woman or animal shall be punished with imprisonment for life or with imprisonment of either description for a term which may extend to 10 years and shall also be liable to fine.* The Explanation states further that penetration is sufficient to constitute the carnal intercourse necessary to the offence described in this section. On examination of section 377, one finds that the sexuality is limited to a man _woman relation. Anything beyond would go against the natural order and would come within the purview of section 377. Consequently, it follows that notion of transgenders does not come within its purview at all as a victim but would come within its purview as an offender. Section 377 was challenged on the grounds of being violative of constitutionality in *Naz foundation & others Vs Governemnt of NCT Delhi & others*[6] by way of a public interest Litigation. This judgment laid down the following:-

> We declare that section 377 IPC ,in so far as it criminalises consensual sexual acts of adults in private, is violative of Articles 21, 14, and 15 of the Constitution.[7]

It was a reading down or article 377 to exclude consensual sex among adults in private. This was a landmark judgment as it preserved the sexual autonomy of sexual minorities and a major breakthrough for exercising the rights of sexual identities of sexual minorities. This was challenged in Appeal in *Suresh Kumar Kaushal Vs Naz foundation and others Civil Appeal no: 10972/2013*.[8] It is submitted that while dismissing the Appeal the Honble Court held as follows:-

> Those who indulge in carnal intercourse in the ordinary course and those who indulge in carnal intercourse against the order of nature constitute different classes and the people falling in the latter category cannot claim that Section 377 suffers from the vice of arbitrariness and irrational classification. What Section 377 does is mere to define the particular offence and prescribe punishment for the same which can be awarded if in the trial conducted in accordance with the provisions of the Code of Criminal Procedure and other statutes of the same 8 Page 83 family the person is found guilty. Therefore, the High Court was not right in declaring Section 377 IPC ultra vires Articles 14 and 15 of the Constitution 43. While reading down Section 377 IPC, the Division Bench of the High Court overlooked that a minuscule fraction of the country's population constitute lesbians, gays, bisexuals or transgenders and in last more than 150 years less than 200 persons have been prosecuted (as per the reported orders) for committing an offence under Section 377 IPC and this cannot be made a sound basis for declaring that section ultra vires the provisions of Articles 14, 15 and 21 of the Constitution 44.

> The vagueness and arbitrariness go to the root of a provision and may render it unconstitutional, making its implementation a matter of unfettered discretion. This is especially so in case of penal statues. However while analysing a provision the vagaries of language must be borne in mind and prior application of the law must be considered.[9]

Clearly, the Hon'ble Supreme Court adopting a restrictive interpretation declined to expand the ambit. This was a great step back for the proponents of establishing the rights of the sexual minority community primarily on the footholds of sexual identity.

Constitutional Rights[10] are guaranteed for all citizens and consequently the rights for the transgender community can be seen enshrined in the framework of Article 14, 15, 16, 19 and 21.

Article 14 of the Constitution states that the state shall not deny to any person equality before the law or equal protection of Laws within the territory of India. The basis of the equality doctrine is non-discrimination. Non discrimination in all spheres of an individual's life. The equality clause contained in article 14 requires that all persons subjected to any legislation should be treated alike under like circumstances and conditions. Equals have to be treated equally and unequal's ought not to be treated equally.

Article 19 which deals with Protection of our rights to Freedom is a crucial section which creates the basic fundamental rights of citizens. Two of these are relevant here namely Article 19(1a) which lays down that All citizens shall have right to freedom of speech and expression and 19 (1d) to move freely throughout the territory of India. Going into Art 19 (1)(a) it was laid down in *Indian Express Newspapers Vs Union of India (1985)1scc 641* that freedom of expression has four broad social purposes to serve (i) it helps an individual to attain self-fulfilment, (ii) it assists in the discovery of truth (iii) it strengthens the capacity of an individual in participating in decision making and (iv) it provides a mechanism by which it would be possible to establish a reasonable balance between stability and social change.

Article 21 guarantees that no person shall be deprived of his life or personal liberty according to the procedure established by law without due process of the law. In this context, Article 21 has been widely expanded to include all aspects leading to ensure a life with dignity. It emphasizes that dignity is an integral part of the right to life and any anything which compromises the same will amount to denial of the right to life and consequently violation of a fundamental right.

It is in this context that identity is an important feature wherein, sexual identity forms a crucial content. Acceptance and recognition of the sexual identity becomes an integral part of life to ensure the dignity of an individual. For a transgender person, the freedom to express sexual identity is the crux of human dignity. This was recognised and established by the Supreme Court judgement in NALSA vs Union of India and other.[11] This was a path breaking judgement which identified the transgender community as an entity having the right to express as they desired within the framework of fundamental rights in the Constitution.

It very clearly underlined the recognition of a third gender taking it beyond the parameters of male and female binary. It observed thus,

the emphasis is on the development of an individual in all respects. The basic principle of dignity and freedom of the individual is common to all nations particularly those having a democratic set up. Democracy requires us to respect and develop the free spirit of human beings which is responsible for all progress in human history. Democracy is a method by which we attempt to raise the living standards of the people and give opportunities to every person to develop his or her personality. It is founded on the personal coexistence and cooperative living. If democracy is based on the recognition of the individuality and the dignity of man, as a fortiori we have to recognise the right of a human being to choose his sex/gender identity which is integral to his / her personality and is one of the most basic aspects of self-determination dignity and personality and is one of the most basic aspects of self-determination,dignity and freedom (Emphasis added) In fact there is growing recognition of the fact that the true measure of development of a nation is not economic growth but human dignity.[12]

This judgement opened quite a few doors for transgenders and a new lease of life from the disappointment of the judgment in Naz foundations case[13] as it gave them the freedom to express themselves in the identity which they were comfortable with and gave a window of opening for coming within the mainstream. For an effective implementation of this judgment, it therefore, becomes imperative that there needs to be a pressing move to amend the existing laws to be in conformity with the NALSA judgement[14] encompassing spheres of marriage, adoption, employment etc. This judgement though it recognized their right to express their sexual identity was silent on the correlation with Section 377 as it would contradict the notions of the right to marriage which necessarily involved the sexual content. Explaining that the transgenders have the right to express their identities and could not be discriminated, it stopped short of verbalising the right to found a family.

It was further observed in Shivani Bhat Vs State of NCT of Delhi and ors[15] it was observed that "Every human being has certain inalienable rights. This is a doctrine that is firmly enshrined in our Constitution. Gender identity and sexual orientation are fundamental to the right of social self-determination, dignity and freedom. These "freedoms" lie- at the heart of personal autonomy and freedom of individuals. A transgenders sense or experience of gender is integral to their core personality and sense of being".

Within the International legal frameworks too, it has not been a smooth ride to ensure that sexual minorities with specific reference to transgenders. It was only in December 2008 that there was a specific reference to the protection of the right of sexual minorities and that of sexual identities. Before this the concept was sought to be read into the right of life and human dignity component and further read into the provisions relating to the right to marry and establish a family. It was on the 18th of December 2008, a landmark statement was issued at the United Nations (UN) General Assembly. Supported by 66 member states the UN Declaration on Sexual Orientation and Gender Identity affirmed that "all human rights [must] be applied to all human beings, regardless of their sexual orientation or gender identity", and "condemned all human rights violations based on sexual orientation or gender identity, whenever or wherever they might occur,"16 . Unfortunately, India is not a signatory to this declaration. The declaration is yet to be adopted by the UN General Assembly but until then the existing provisions exist in Article 6 of the Universal Declaration of Human rights which mentioins the Right to Life, Article 16 of the International Covenant on the Civil and political rights (ICCPR) highlights the protection of the right to life, the right of recognition before the law. Further Article 17 of ICCPR offers a non-subjection to arbitrary or unlawful interference with his privacy, family, home or correspondence, nor unlawful attacks on his honour and reputation and everyone has the right to protection against these attacks.

The key specific declaration on sexual orientation and gender identity can be traced to the Yogyakarta principles. In its introduction it states" Many States and societies impose gender and sexual orientation norms on individuals through custom, law and violence and seek to control how they experience personal relationships and how they identify themselves. The policing of sexuality remains a major force behind continuing gender-based violence and gender inequality" These principles were an outcome of a project by the International Commission of Jurists and the International Service for Human Rights, on behalf of a coalition of human rights organisations, to develop a set of international legal principles on the application of international law to human rights violations based on sexual orientation and gender identity to bring greater clarity and coherence to States' human rights obligations. There were 29 principles adopted of which the key principles formulated were on the right to Universal enjoyment of Human rights, Right to Equality and non-discrimination. Right to recognition before Law, Right to Life, Right to Privacy and Right to found a family. It is submitted that that right to found family involves the sexuality component. When marriage is identified with heterosexuals, those coming outside the framework are excluded from founding a family. This would then become a violation of one of the integral fundamental rights.

Finally though a window of opportunity has been provided by the NALSA judgement which can be taken forward to expand the rights, there is still a long way to go. This has already led to the bringing out of a Transgender Policy,[17] a first by the State of Kerala. The goals and the objectives of TG policy supports the attainment of:-

a)   A just society where men, women and TG's have equal rights to access development opportunities resources and benefits.

b)   The Right to live with dignity and enjoy a life free from all forms of violence.

c)   The right to freedom of speech and expression in all matters that affect them.

d)   And right to equal voice and participation in key development decisions that shape their lives, communities and the state.

As a result the framework on its implementation - notes the statutory requirements for ensuring the Right to dignity and life without violence by bringing into conformity the laws relating to domestic violence, sexual violence and enabling the right to marriage.

The Transgender persons (Protection of Rights) Bill 2016 introduced by the Ministry of Social Justice and empowerment had several lacunas as it was felt that many discriminatory provisions had crept into it. As per an Indian Express report[18] the bill was stated to protect transgenders from discrimination in education, employment, and the right to rent or buy property. Offenders could be jailed for 6 months to 2 years, and fined. The Bill paved the way for a comprehensive healthcare strategy for transgenders, including mandating that the government should provide for sex reassignment surgery, hormonal therapy, counselling, separate HIV sero-surveillance centres, and insurance schemes. It aimed to ensure that such children were not separated from their families due to social stigma. In cases of abandonment, the state would provide rehabilitation centres. The Bill required the government to create vocational training and welfare schemes for such persons. It made no commitments on transgender student's scholarships or pensions for the elderly, but left it to the state government to formulate such schemes from time to time." This totally excluded the right of the person to found a family or adopt children for that matter. The sexuality aspect was totally ignored in so far as their sexual relations a key component in the pursuit of the right to life. It is presumed through the bill that the person would be a sexual. This was strongly objected to by the standing committee.[19]

The Present discourse on - Human Sexuality and Sexual Morality with respect to transgenders is hinged on their freedom to express themselves in the identity they choose. The deviation from the norm of heterosexual sexuality coupled with the existing patriarchal norm leads to - immense stigma and discrimination. There needs to be a concerted action and movement leading to an attitudinal change on the bedrock of constitutionality to guarantee the rights granted through the NALSA judgement which is a window of immense opportunity.

Endnotes

[1] *NALSA vs Union of India and other wpc (civil)* 400/2013.

[2] Padala Rama Reddi, *Criminal Major Acts*, (20th Edition, Hyderabad, Asia law house).

[3] Padala Rama Reddi, *Criminal Major Acts.*

[4] Padala Rama Reddi, *Criminal Major Acts.*

[5] Padala Rama Reddi, *Criminal Major Acts.*

[6] Naz foundation Vs Govt Of NCT delhi & others, WPC 7455/2001.

[7] Naz foundation Vs Govt Of NCT delhi & others, WPC 7455/2001.

[8] *Civil Appeal no: 10972/2013.*

[9] *Civil Appeal no: 10972/2013.*

[10] Gopal Sankaranaryanan, *The constitution of India* , (7th edition, Lucknow: Eastern Book company , 2014).

[11] wpc (civil) 400/2013.

[12] NALSA Vs U/I wpc (civil) 400/2013.

[13] Suresh Kaushal &others Vs Union of India civil Appeal no: 10722/2013

[14] Supra vii.

[15] WPC (crl) 2133/2015.

[16] *https://ses.library.usyd.edu.au/bitstream/2123/5323/1/DISSERTATION_LMorgan.pdf* accessed on 31 May 2017.

[17] State Policy for Transgenders in Kerala 2015.

[18] *http://indianexpress.com/article/explained/transgenders-persons-bill-provisions-explained-2952316/* accessed on 31 May 2017.

[19] *https://www.telegraphindia.com/1170722/jsp/nation/story_163285.jsp* accessed on 31 May 2017.

Towards a Liberative Theology of Human Sexuality

Born Again: The Untold Story of Selin

Santosh Koshy Joy

"I don't believe in second birth, but if given a choice I would like to be born a cow. These days cows are more revered than us."

Abstract

This article is a short biography of Ms Selin Laxmi, a transgender based in Delhi, as narrated to the author. Due permission to share this story with her true name has been taken. Through the sharing of this experience, the author tries to give a glimpse of some of the real life challenges that a transgender person goes through in India, particularly giving insights to some of the unique practices that are followed in some of the *hijra* communities. In spite of being born in a Christian family, Selin finds spiritual solace in Christian prayers as well as other faith practices.

Amid pouring rain and approaching darkness, she stood in front of her mother's fresh grave and grieved her heart out. She was here only some hours ago for the burial but that was not enough for her ailing heart. She wanted solitude to cry and confess away from the din of the relatives and other mourners. For hours she lamented and cried aloud till she fell down on the grave unconscious. The child was back on the bosom of her mother after a long wait. Her despair had some relief, her prayers for some moments of an unrestrained company with her mother was answered.

In the evening of 24th of May in 2001, SelinLaxmi was informed of her mother's passing away with an advice to avoid attending the funeral. Only six months ago, Selin got lucky to share a breakfast with her mother after sixteen years of staying apart. She got in touch with her family in 1998 but was strongly told to stay away from them for the sake of societal norms. Selin longed for the company of her mother but her rekindled happiness could not last much.

Laxmi, the influential transgender community leader of Delhi was born the youngest 'son' in the Syrian Christian family of Pathanamthitta district in Kerala. He[1] was fondly called Aniyan, meaning the younger brother in Malayalam. He had four siblings including an elder sister.

Aniyan grew up to become a transgender community leader passing through –much trauma, tests and now is a living testimony to the world for the "challenges" which a third gender faces. Being spiritually anchored helped her fight many odds. Armed with the Bible by her side, she proudly quotes the verses from the book of Isaiah which is a promise of the God to render the transgender people an "everlasting name." She reads the verse aloud to me from a leather bound Bible with a lot of small chits and bookmarks inside *Isaiah 56:4-5 "To the eunuchs who keep my Sabbaths, who choose what pleases me and hold fast to my covenant—to them I will give within my temple and its wallsa memorial and a name better than sons and daughters;I will give them an everlasting name which will endure forever."*

Revealing Aniyan

Aniyan was born in the year 1967 on 24th of Oct. Aniyan, now called Laxmi Selin, recalls her mother was only 33 when her father passed away leaving the family in peril and all four kids were toddlers. They had to shift to Madras, now Chennai, in search of a living when she was just nine. Her brothers worked to make ends meet while she was encouraged to study by the family.

Aniyan was an intelligent boy in the class since the family days in Kerala. He completed his education till the fourth standard in the local Pazhakulam primary school before getting admission in Adoor High School for further studies. Aniyan was liked by his classmates for his honesty and cooperative attitude.

He had many friends and most were girls as he liked their company. Those girls used to tell me, "You are more like us. You are not Aniyan, we will call you Selin. Infact, I also liked the name Selin more," says Laxmi Selin.

Aniyan was in 6th standard when the family moved to Chennai and he joined a school there to further his education. Aniyan was metamorphosing as Selin in the din of the Chennai town. Comparative anonymity in the metropolis gave Aniyan the opportunity to explore more and to know that there was a whole transgender community which was like her. The female inside her male body was dominating her thoughts. She agreed though reluctantly but glad that she was a girl. Selin now preferred the pronoun 'she' for herself.

Transgenders who frequented her colony often caught up with her and told her she was beautiful and a few times took her to their fold to introduce to the transgender kinnar community in Chennai. There she dressed at her will and spend the day like a soul independent of worldly manifestations. Back home, for her family, Selin was still Aniyan.

Selin Excels

Circumstances forced her to be sent back to Kerala to finish her 10th class from Adoor government school. Her mother shifted from Chennai to Kerala to help her in studies while they lived in a rented accommodation. Selin topped the class in the secondary school examinations. Owing to her scholarly accolades and 'meek' behavior, she was chosen to be trained to become a Malankara Catholic priest. Stranded in a dichotomy which only she knew apart from her Chennai transgender friends, Selin completed her pre-degree studies while living in the seminary.

Destiny took a turn when she was asked by the seminary authorities to 'change her feminine ways' or leave the place. She tried her best to 'adjust' but was asked to leave. Selin was back in Chennai with the family. For her, the rejection from a church institution was traumatic owing to the fact that now she was back to the world where she had to struggle. As she recollects,

> One of the reason for me to join the seminary was the fact that now I could serve God and the community without the bias of the gender. I was

leading a life which I knew cannot lead me to a family life. Life had to be tough and full of struggle outside and dedicating myself to the service of God was my aim. But it was not permitted by the authorities.

Her rendezvous with education though did not last here. Selin once again had a chance to be sent to a Catholic institution in Bangalore to pursue her studies in Medicine. The Church-run-hospital was attached to a seminary where brothers were trained for the Lord's ministry. Here she completed her first year in MBBS while working rest of the time in the Seminary as the pharmacist. Her second stint in a seminary also ended the same way as before. She was sent back home after more than a year as she was not found suited to be trained to grow a 'brother' in the Church. She had to come to Chennai and this time the stay with family lasted only for three days.

Coming Out

After experiencing rejection from the Bangalore seminary, living with family became a tough task as she recollectswhile not completely accepting or denying whether she liked the gaze of - those soliciting boys and men,

> *One day I was standing in front of our home and a boy passed by mocking me. I did not respond to him though I felt irritated. He passed by again and I had to run inside to hide while he stood in front of my house as if waiting for me. My mother was somehow watching this and that evening I was brutally beaten up by my brothers. I left home to escape any further wrath.*

I think my family tried twice to find a "solution" for me by sending me to the Church institutions. "Coming back home meant now a life-long burden for them, " Selin adds.

It was during the time between the two seminaries that Selin was taken to meet Muthamma by her transgender friends who visited her colony. As a practice, Muthumma agreed to adopt Selin as her Shishya. Selin fondly remembers the day, "I wore Sari and took photographs and felt like a complete lady after meeting Muthamma."

Out of home, many nights were spent on roads and hungry days were a routine. "Once walking from Purushuvakom to Thiruvottiyur during night I was chased by men and for the first time I felt the vulnerability of being a female," says Selin who was by now wearing a sari and a female attire as a habit while not living with the family.

Out of home, Muthumma seemed to be her obvious shelter but it could not last long beyond four days. In the slums of Thiruvottiyur in Chennai, Mutthumma was finding it tough to manage her existing flock and hence Selin chose to move to a rented room. Her source of livelihood was grim. She recalls having worked in the garden of an Armenian Church and the priest paying her a one rupee coin for her labour. Things improved when Selin made the smart move to sublet her small room for fellow transgenders some of them men who worked as sex workers. With the money earned from her 'tenants', Selin paid her rent and sustained her living. Her tenants were men dressed up as women and engaged in sex work. With the rent money in her hand every month and self-dependent she was Selin now, unquestionably.

Bombay Beckons

Kajal, eye liners, turmeric fairness cream and things that she loved were all that a lady loved and she was now liked by many. She was cordial with her fellow transgender community. She was amongst them but was different and unique. Her dense black hair and mannerism were popular with people. She was more educated, informed and read than many of them. She now had to move out and see the world of her likes. She left for Mumbai.

A Nagercoil native Tamil speaking transgender Manjulamma ran a prostitution home in Kamatipuram area of Mumbai. Selin reached there with some recommendation from a common contact. The place had around 20 girls and Selin had no choice but to be there for a while till she could think of some alternative avenues for survival.

A defining experience of Selin's stint in Mumbai was the trip to Mumbai with Manjulamma's girls. While the whole group was enjoying their trip on a cruise, a foreigner sought the company of Selin from Manjulamma. It was surprising for Selin but also revealing that she was attractive to men. Another milestone experience for Selin to define her sexuality was the insistence of a client in Kamatipuram to sleep with her. Reluctantly she agreed.

"I can't express those experiences in words but it was a mix of guilt, eagerness and enthusiasm," says Selin, adding that physically, it was impossible for her to manifest her feminine sexuality with her underdeveloped organs and beliefs which trained her to be 'pious'. The meeting in the bed ended abruptly as pain and remorse overwhelmed Selin in that tiny cell of flesh trade. A friendly known girl in the house replaced Selin for the client without Manjulamma knowing the turn of events. Mumbai, then Bombay, now seemed enough for Selin. She chose to be back in Chennai after six months.

Recollecting Mumbai, Selin says that all through her Mumbai experience she was in burden because she was taught during childhood that the "body was the temple of God." Her memories of praying with her family and never missing the opportunity to close the door and pray every day with the Holy Bible as her companion filled her with guilt, as she recollects, "Prostitution in Mumbai was not just sinful but the place was pathetic with cries, agony and pain. I wanted to run away from that place but survival was my primary concern those days."

Nirvana

The ritual of performing Nirvana, as referred among the *kinnar*[1] communities, is an important process which helped them in affirming their identity as a *kinnar*. Selin had taken the help of another *Kinnar*, to perform the 'Nirvana' operation domestically with country tools to get rid of her under-grown male sex organ. She shares,

> *That little flesh above my vagina was a stigma, I had to remove it and enter into a new life and we in our community call the 'progression' as 'Nirvana' " The ritual was dedicated to a deity called Bahuchrajji with its temple in Mehsana in Gujarat. It was a painful but a definitive step and was a must to be completely in the fold of the transgender world By Nirvana a person who lacked any identity became an ardhnari or kinnar.*

Kinnars-irrespective of their caste or religion believe in Bahuchrajji temple and its authority in being the deity which helped them in achieving the 'Nirvana'.

Cold Delhi

After the Nirvana process, Selin now travelled alone to Delhi which was a city much talked about money earning destination for *kinnars* during those times. Armed with some meagre savings from her Kamatipuram spell she reached Shalimar Bagh area in the National Capital.

"Delhi was known as a place of opportunity for us. But things here were pathetic. The place was filthy and fearful," Selin explains who now had a new name, Laxmi. Selin was not a common name in this part of the country and she chose to introduce herself to be more a commoner. Later in life when Aadhar cards were made, she insisted that her name be written as Selin alias Laxmi but the officer denied her the alias tag and her documents today read "Laxmi Selin".

Begging was an immediate option available along with spending nights in the streets of Delhi. Regular molestations and abuses left her mentally weak and physically tired. It was vulnerable for her especially in the nights. In the freezing winter of 1984, in the month of September, Laxmi decided to jump before an approaching train and end her life for good.

Sustaining further became challenging and she chose to end her life instead as she recalls,

You may choose to call me a coward but I just thought why should I live any more. My Church had no place for me, my family thought that I was a lifelong burden. I decided to earn bread for myself and tried several things and Delhi was the last option and here things were really cruel.

It was while walking down the tracks from Shalimar railway crossing and as she was waiting for the next approaching train that she met Shobha. "She was a beautiful Kinnar and sympathetic to me like a sister," says Laxmi who was then introduced to the Pushpa Toli (group) by Shobha. While North Delhi burned in the aftermath of the Indira Gandhi assassination, Laxmi was slowly growing roots in the complex transgender world of Delhi with her beautiful looks and interaction skills among her transgender community. Azadpur was their area of work where Pushpa and Laxmi went for money collection for their Toli. Selin chooses to stop here without further elaborating her traumatic incidents in Delhi and insists that only good things are meant to be remembered.

Transgender Leader

Today, she is guarded day and night and a high security residence is her abode with modern safety equipment. Visitors have to verify their credentials through a camera in the gate before Laxmi herself takes the call to open the gate or deny entry. Her movement in the city is swift and in a cascade of her followers. The local politicians and police administration frequent her 'Dera' or the abode of the leader of the cult seeking help of all sorts from election support to assistance in dealing with a local law and order issue. Meet Laxmi, the didi (elder sister) for many and a help to the people in need.

During elections the local politicians want her to accompany them for campaigning. "The fact that our community is well connected in the area is helpful to the politicians. They seek our help in approaching the new families. Police and administration take our help when needed."

About her political views, she shares

> Politically, I was a bit confused. I became the vice-president of my ward for the BSP party first. Later, I had an active role in BJP and former Delhi Chief Minister Saheb Singh Verma was very sensitive to the cause of our community and hence we chose to be at his party's side. Now things have changed. Politics today is of hatred and I prefer to stay away from it.

Slowly but steadily, Laxmi, who now proudly displays her name as LaxmiSelin, grew up to become the *Naik Sardar* of the *Dheeraj Pahadi* cult. *Dheeraj Pahadi* is a cult prevalent in the North India with around 10,000 followers and a *NaikSardar* is a leader of a designated area. Laxmi has the area of Patel Nagar, Ranjit Nagar, South Patel Nagar of Delhi in her 'control'. She is one of most respected *Naik Sardars* in the *Dheeraj Pahadi* panchayat (administration) set up. The 'panchayat' of the cult recognizes her as a learned *Kinnar* who can speak chaste English and can sort out things amicably within the community if any dispute arises. She owns five multistoried homes side by side in Jahangirpuri locality with many of her 'chela' or followers living with her.

She formed the Buniyad Foundation to help her community members and to treat them for Tuberculosis, HIVand AIDS. With funding from International agencies she ran the Community Based Organisation(CBO) for around a decade till her work got stopped due to a medical emergency.

"I had to undergo a hip surgery and with that a lot of activities within our Dera stopped forever. I want to start them all once again but health does not allow," she says.

A Malayalee transgender with Chennai upbringing is a darling of the press in Delhi. Her antecedents are exposed while she ventures on her weekly fish purchase in the INA market along with her followers who guard her. The press in Delhi often talk of her in high regard and she is undoubtedly a position which Selin with her hard work and passion towards the community which she belongs to. She was featured on CNN in a program and that brought her international fame. Local papers and Malayalam dailies often quote her on issues concerning her communities. "I neither like nor dislike the press. I just want them to quote us correctly. Once a Malayalam newspaper called us Hijras. That's a word full of contempt. I objected and wrote a letter to them. They obliged by correcting themselves"

Familial Identity

The journey of Aniyan to Selin and from Selin to Laxmi has been an expedition of personal crisis for her with moments and experiences which challenged her own perceptions and expectations. Failed attempt to marry a lover and multiple attempts to adopt a child are few of them. "Like everyone, I love to be cared and want to belong to a family," says Selin whose only dream now is to be buried in the family grave along with her mother. "But that seems impossible, they won't allow it to happen as they did not allow me to be with my mother when she was alive," she emphasizes.

A street child grew up with her in the family and she taught him to hotel management diploma before getting him married. Selin feels that after marriage the boy purposely ditched her and the 'dera' and chose to live separately with his wife.

Selin adopted a son from a known single mother who was about to abort the child after conceiving. She completed the legal formalities and organized a baptism ceremony for the child. The event was a huge show with local bigwigs attending the function. The happiness was short lived and the biological mother challenged Selin's authority over the child in just few months. The case was argued and decided in favour of Selin in the lower court while the High Court took a different view although the child was ruled to be with Selin for life. The High Court asked Selin to handover the child to his biological mother at regular intervals for the purpose of feeding and nursing. The decision hurt Selin and for her, it was akin to challenging her credentials to bring up a child. She gave up on her legal guardianship and handed over the child to the mother completely.

Her experiment to live with a man was also short-lived. A drummer in a music group fell in love with her and rebelled with his family for Selin. She was unperturbed but suicide bid by the boy made her accept him to her house. They planned to live like husband and wife for life. The pain did not deter Selin to perform all her sexual duties to satisfy her 'husband'. Around after a year, things changed and the man decided to step out of her embrace.

Owing to her Syrian Christian background and may be assured by the fact the Selin's maternal uncle was an Orthodox priest, she applied for membership in an Orthodox Church in Delhi in Rohini area. The parish rejected her request without stating a reason. She did not give up on the quest for a religious identity and finally took membership in the Malankara Catholic Church. The parish arranged for the baptism of her adopted son and now the local area prayer meets at her residence at regular intervals.

The drawing room of her palatial 'Dera' is adorned with portraits of bishops and Mother Mary has a prominent place along with a life size portrait of her own departed mother. 'Dera' is a place for everyone and we have transgender from all faith and caste, Selin says while explaining that how the part earning of each eunuch is collected to arrange for an annual grand gathering of Eunuchs .

The entrance to her home has an ornamentally casted Sai Baba statue with a garland over it. Her spiritual experiences vary from her vision of Lord Shiva guarding her while on her journey to Amarnath cave with his Shivbhakt transgender 'guru' to Mother Mary and saints guiding her when she suffered in loneliness on several occasions.

Coping Mechanism

"I cry with my room closed and lighted. I pray often but when alone. Every time I pray with tears my requests are answered. I see God and talk to him," says Selin with a heavy heart when asked if she feels that her relationship with God has been uninterrupted all through her journey. She feels sorry that her identity as a Christian has been challenged many a time.

On her recent tour of the South-East Asia, she saw women in cities carrying puppy and cats along in public places. Reaching back to India, the first thing she did was to adopt a foreign breed dog which she flaunts to the visitors. She claims animal are more loyal to human beings than fellow men and women. This birth has been really painful. This is really bad of God to have sent someone to this earth in this form as I am. I should have been either a boy or a girl. I wish I was born again.

"I don't believe in second birth, but if given a choice I would like to be born a cow. These days cows are more revered than us," says a well-informed Selin with a tinge of her political maturity.

> Religious tags matter a lot but in our Dera we celebrate Eid with the sacrifice of a goat. Holi and Deepawali are a huge feast. Amid all these festivities, I remain a private Christian. I am respected as a follower of Christ and although I don't go out to evangelise I wish to set an example for others to follow. Prayer is a regular companion of mine and Sunday without Church is difficult. You can call me a struggling Christian.

Endnotes

[1] *Kinnar* is a popular name for Transgenders in India, mainly used in the Northern states. Selin preferred using this terminology.

An LGBTIQ-Inclusive Christian Anthropology and Public Theology[1]

Jacob Mathew

Introduction

Theology, as we understand, is expected to deal with the faith motives along with the subsequent convictions to strengthen the believer involving in 'public sphere' with an intention to transform it in the light of the Gospel of Christ. In its discourse about *the world within the Church* and its discourses that are understandable and *sharable to the wider society*,[2] the Church is expected to spread its creative wings. Here in this briefing we deal with how the theologians, the leaders and pastors of local parishes & organizations can be equipped along the lines of Christian anthropology and public theology, in its engagement with the LGBTIQ.[3]

Confirming the role of the family, of the closed society and of the Church, as 'the place that provides warmth when the whole world is so cold,' such never had been so to the LGBTIQ, who face triple alienation: neither the Church/its outfits or the wider society, nor the family has been kind or even courteous to the LGBTIQ community. Every now and then we see or listen to stories of such treatment meted out to the sexual/ gender minority; from the frisking gate at the airports to the other public transport facilities and from the workplaces, the worship centres & hostels/ medical centres we hear such 'meta-narratives'[4] of being ill treated. In the midst of such unending discrimination and cruelty meted out to them and since we claim to follow the faith and the biblical tradition for such a perspective and pejorative attitude here is an invitation for a revision along with a spirit of the Bible. The following lines we perceive as giving endorsement for a revised attitude to the sexual/gender minorities:

A.   Christian Anthropological endorsement

i.   Human: Created in the Image and Likeness of God

What is the credential of being human? How is human dignity valued in the society? This is the area of analysis in anthropology. There comes up the idea of a human as being created in the image of God[5] and declares a human as the 'manifest presence'[6] of God among the rest of creation. Even when this esteem for human is accepted, many are reluctantto assign such status unto the fellow human beings who are being branded under the mnemonic LGBTIQ. Do we not consider them as human by any parameter? Or do we reject such persons as sub human/non-human? Do we accept their right to live in the face of the earth?[7]

ii.   Prophetic anthropological endorsement

The aforestated anthropological placement becomes important to be reconsidered as evident from the Messianic Prophecy (Is. Ch. 56), which categorically includes 'eunuch' for a responsible place in relation with the 'people of God [v.3].[8] Inclusivity in the Messianic Prophecy continues with its openness for the 'eunuchs' for its leadership [v.5, 10], across its boundaries [v.5]. Inclusivity for the sexual minority is allowed with the granting of permission for leadership in 'the Temple of the Lord' [v.5], the important day/time of observation of 'Sabbath' [v.4], and in their association with 'the Law' [v.4]. Those are observed in the prophetic anthropological endorsement as in line with the 'will of God' [v.4]. Also, it is prophesied as acceptable upon the 'Mount of God' [v.7] & endowed with the 'Name of God' [v.5].

Categorical inclusion for the 'eunuch' continues with their association with the Sacrifices at the Altar of the Lord [Is. 56:7]. The hope in fruitfulness is also offered graciously for the Transgender, but expressed laconically at verse three: 'Let not the eunuch say, "Behold, I am a dry tree." This gets intensified with the right revealing of its purpose as, "for mine house shall be called a house of prayer for all peoples" (Is.56:7c). The Lord God who gathers the outcasts of Israel saying, 'Yet I will gather *others* to him, beside those that are gathered unto him already' (v. 8). All these, according to the prophetic eschatology, work along with the fact that the concept of 'image of God' is associated not only with the inward human, but also with the external physique of the person: the diversity of which could never be a basis of discrimination.[9]

iii.   Biblical endorsement of Kinship and Kindness

The concept of Image of God flows into the idea of 'sisterhood' or 'brotherhood' based on the common paternity of God. Accordingly, the entire created world including all other creatures is to be treated as created together. Also since all human beings share the image of God, they are to be treated as sisters and brothers. If one to look for a biblical paradigm, Jesus treated and received people as they are: the 'sinners,' 'the tax collectors' and the women enjoyed acceptability and mutual respect [Lk.15:1ff.]. This being so, how can one Christian, knowing that 's/he is the disciple of the Lord' [Jn.13:35], disobey the divine command to 'love one another'? 'Honor everyone and love the brotherhood' is the endorsement from the disciple of Jesus Christ [1Pet.2:17].[10] Therefore 'let brotherly love continue' [Heb. 13:1] is the standing instruction and mandate. The 'new commandment' which Jesus gave unto his disciples to 'love one another' [Jn. 13:34] is to be furthered with all the fervour to reach out to the sexual minorities. One needs to be open to the fact that there is no kindredhood when it is not extended for the sexual and the gender minorities.

It is true that there is no question of Jesus receiving/not receiving any one of those who are referred in this article. However, Jesus always embraced the people at the margins: he was declared as a friend even to the tax collectors and the sinners. The idea of human sisterhood/ brotherhood needs to be further in relation to the gender/sexual minorities: a natural outcome of understanding that humanity is created in the image of God. Thereby human beings are able to get in touch with and can help any section of the society including the socially ostracised like the LGBTIQ.

B.   Public Theological Endorsement

Along with the realm of Christian Anthropology and kindred-hood, the issue of unending discrimination meted out to the LGBTIQ in the society and cruelty against them needs to be seen along the lines of Public Theology.[11] Since some of the professed Christians claim to follow the faith and the biblical tradition with a derogatory perspective and attitude, here is an invitation for revision along with a spirit of the Bible to be prompted for public intervention. This becomes significant since such a prejudiced attitude has attained mounting proportion these days and has become an issue of public and judicial attention.[12]

As we presume, *'Public theology'* focuses on issues of public concern, by drawing the 'resources, insights and compassionate values of the Christian faith to contribute to the welfare of society.'[13] The *meta* [small] narratives which we receive from the LGBTIQ community [about their struggles] should be taken as a basis to create a forum with an opportunity to emerge public theological deliberations.[14]

Issue of 'Homophobia' and Forum of Public Theology-Reasons

When there is an attempted interpretation to bring out the spirit of the Biblical text for a healthy society with a meaningful engagement with the life situation of the LGBTIQ, there is need and scope for public theology. This could be pursued with the probing, how will we direct the society to live with an active participation of the challenged community too? Also, how the theologians and ministers of the word of God are able to uphold the integrity of creation and formulate a creative and sensible deliberation on the issues of justice, equality, human dignity and welfare for the challenged members of the human family? The issue of 'homophobia'[15] comes [needs to come] to the forum of public theology in this context. It needs to be successfully attempted because of several reasons:

   a. Since the churches are becoming more and more compartmentalized and closeted on this issue of common interest, public theological attempts could provide resources for people *to make connections between their faith and this practical social issue.* The strong hatred against such minorities sometimes assumes justification [Biblical ratification] for violent action against 'homosexuals,'[16] and for cruel sidelining of the transgender. The churches are either incapable or reluctant to venture on such occasions of mistreatment, which have assumed damaging proportions. Since religious worshippers are sometimes highly prejudiced not even permitting the Transgender to stand along with others during worship, some public theological attempts could give openness for the good of the society. In one dialogue session at Tiruvalla in Kerala organized by the Kerala Council of Churches, one Transgender shared the anxiety saying, "in our life time will we be permitted to participate in public worship in our place without any fear of rejection or ousting?" This points to the reality that many of the Christian Churches are yet to become 'Christ-like ' to support a person who wishes to come out with their physical diversities & distinct sexual orientations.

b. Since *discrimination* against people of different sexual orientation comes in many forms and *affects all walks of life*, gender/sexual minorities are discriminated against at work places, at schools, at clubs, places of worship, at airports, trains or similar public transport facilities, and in many other areas as well. This creates tension at those contexts, and it turns out dreadful for many. It affects the peaceful coexistence in the society by creating a traumatic situation with depletion of identity for many. It negatively affects the presentation of the affected and those at the giving edgewhich prompt to be attended at the level of Public theology. A simple attitudinal change for the better could solve this problem

c. Since *discrimination* against people of different sexual orientation is more intense *among the churches* and religious groups, who consider homoerotic 'behaviour'[17] as a sin and transgender as a misfortune, and there by it becomes a target of bias, public theological engagement could change the situation for the better. Many researchers claim that homoerotics still find themselves the target of bias within institutions like churches and professional organizations.[18]

d. Since it is often claimed by the religiously pious that the faith and the biblical tradition demands a punitive perspective and attitude [towards LGBTIQ], there occurs the *need for a balanced interpretation* to bring out the spirit of the Biblical text for a healthy society. Within the Bible we meet plurality of images; images of peaceful coexistence to that of military take-over of nations, worship-centered piety to that of secular wisdom, pessimistic world view of Ecclesiastes to the optimistic submission to the will & justice of God as expressed in the of Book of Job. It has the tenderness of Psalms to that of prophetic protest, expressions of commitment and dedication. This plenitude gives us space to think of the 'eroticism' and the prophetic idealism as to be balanced with secular idealism.[19]

e. Also since homophobia with the strong hatred could assume the justification for violent action against 'homosexuals,' such dangerous divides in the society need to be curbed. It is being observed that, attacks on sexual minorities have risen in recent years.[20] If the biblical interpretations also contribute to our homophobic mindset, we need to boldly apply the hermeneutical principles of Public Theology and contextual theology[21] to deal with the issue. It should become an immediate initiative on our part probing, 'how do we theologically and pastorally engage with these siblings of ours who have been brutally abused?'

f. Public Theology-apologetic/confessional approach: Public Theology being involved in 'theological articulation for finding a rationale for public engagement,' could be endorsed as a means and measure to enrich our endorsement of the cause related to the LGBTIQ.[22] But since it is theological, its method and means need to be seen against the tracks of theology and public theology as well. Just as stated by Vincent E. Bacote 'theological matters to be made comprehensible/even digestible for the public.'[23] Any public theological articulation needs to be more of an apologetic approach[24] and not just for the sake of pursuing any confessional approach,[25] which unlike the other will be more accommodative to the culture and to the personal categories of life.[26] This will more or less be an ecumenical approach in general and will be congenial both for biblical interpretation and also for following a culturally accommodative and inclusive stand point.[27]

g. Equally significant is the mixed attitude to the interpretative attempts in favour of the LGBTIQ to overcome 'homophobia' and 'TG phobia. A clear example is the interpretation given for the text on the 'sin of Sodom' [Gen. 19:1-29], in relation to the words of Classical Israelite prophets, where they emphasize on the moral and ethical demands of the covenantal relationship of the people of Israel [Ezek.16:49; Amos. 4:1, 11; Is.1:10-17]. For Ezekiel, the sin of Sodom has nothing to do with homosexuality, rather with covenantal incontinence. For Amos, the prime cause for the destruction of Sodom and Gomorrah was oppression meted out to the poor and the needy. Similarly, the Isaianic text appears as God convicting the people of the twin cities because of their reluctance to abide by the covenantal demands. Can the Prophetical emphases be confused as literal interpretations of the earlier biblical traditions or as customizations/new mutations in the contextual eventualities? Nevertheless, more than mere enthusiasm to support or reject the sexual minorities, it is a possibility and challenge for the biblical interpreters to customize the world as congenial for the LGBTIQ.[28]

Conclusion

The analysis so far has proceeded with the acknowledgement that there is need to equip the theologians, the leaders and pastors of local parishes and organizations along the lines of Christian anthropology. An awareness of the biblical idea of kinship and along the line of public theology, in formulating its treatment meted out to the LGBTIQ. Having the intrinsic worth of being moulded by the very hands of God [Gen. 1:27] and human being declared as the 'manifest presence' of God among rest of the creation, it does not provide any ratification for the triple alienation that the LGBTIQ community face in today's context. How ridiculous is it for the triple agents, the families, the churches and the wider society to continue in their pejorative attitude? Along with the realm of Christian Anthropology and brother/sisterhood [kindred-hood], the issue of unending discrimination meted out to the LGBTIQ in the society and the cruelty against them need to be seen along the lines of Public Theology. With its focus on issues of public concern, by drawing the 'resources, insights and compassionate values of the Christian faith to contribute to the welfare of society,' Public Theology brings out public theological deliberations in favour of the sexual and gender minorities. Christian anthropological understanding and the track of public theology endorses inclusivity to the LGBTIQ.

Endnotes

[1] Christian Anthropology has the concern to see how the biblical tradition treats human with regard to the origin, existence and destiny of a human. Public Theology

as we understand involves the theological articulations to promote public engagements both within the church and in the wider society.

[2] When Felix Wilfred responded on the future of Asian Theology, he tried to systematize it by incorporating these two aspects of Public Theology. Felix Wilfred, "On the Future of Asian Theology: Public Theologizing," *Theology to go Public*, edited by Felix Wilfred (Delhi: ISPCK, 2013), 35.

[3] The mnemonic, LGBTIQ has become a construct to point to the required affirmation of human rights, democratic freedom and social change for the Lesbians, the Gay, the Bisexual, the Transgender [TG], the Intersex and the Queer.

[4] Denotes small & simple narrations that legitimizes power, authority and social customs. It could also be grand overarching narrations. Anyway here it is taken to point to simple narrations from the weaker/minority sections in the society.

[5] This is the Biblically endorsed understanding of intrinsic worth of human being moulded by the very hands of God [Gen. 1:27]; became a living being when 'God breathed into the nostrils'[Gen.2:7]. Instead of narrowing down the understanding of 'image of God to certain physiological, intellectual or procreative faculties in human, image of God is to be seen as everything in human that originated and culminates in the divine personhood. Gregory of Nyssa, one of the Patristic writers, pointed to the wisdom of God, the love of God and the freedom of God as the three basic elements in the image and likeness of God in Human.

[6] The usage 'manifest presence' was introduced to the theological world by Rev. Fr. Paul Varghese, who subsequently became bishop and principal of the Orthodox Theological Seminary, Kottayam. Paulos Gregorios, *Cosmic Man. The Divine Presence Divine Presence* [New Delhi: Sophia Publications, 1980], 225.

[7] Let us promote the repeated idea of human created in the image of God. Therefore I need to reflect on the mentality, truth, justice, love and kindness which the Lord has shown to the whole creation. My attitude to the Lord, the society and all creation should be in this perspective which should become a directive principle rather than a goal that is to be achieved. I share in the glory of the Lord, which therefore cannot permit to go for any kind of parochial, selfish thinking /action.

[8] This becomes progressive when one considers the legislation to shut out the eunuchs from the congregation of Israel (Deut. 23:1) or from the Levitical priesthood (Lev. 21:20). Such thoughts and not such persons are to be excluded because this is in the promise & hope in the Messiah who is to come.

[9] Personal interview with Mathews Severios, [Professor, Orthodox Theological Seminary, Kottayam] on 23.08.2016, 4pm.

[10] The other strong endorsement on the idea of 'Christian brotherhood' is to be seen in the following biblical portions too [Eph. 4:29; Gal. 3:28].

[11] Following Felix Wilfred, the world of deliberations within the Church should be understandable and sharable to the wider society [two aspects of Public Theology]. Felix Wilfred, "On the Future of Asian Theology............," *Theology to go Public*, 35.

[12] Bears in mind the whole lot of discussion related to Art. 377 of IPC, judgements from the Supreme Court and the much referred verdict from the Delhi High Court [2009] revoking 377, and the cry of the victims and the cry for the marginalised sexual minorities.

[13] 'Public theology' is a form of Applied Theology, which itself is one of the three branches of Christian theology: next to the other two branches, Historical theology and Systematic theology. 'Public theology' reflects critically on the ethical and political implications of religious faith and witness, and does so in the public sphere, in publicly accessible ways. http://www.otago.ac.nz/ctpi/otago032508.pdf. Accessed Saturday, 20.08. 2016, 8am.

[14] When there is a detrimentally evil some silence on the issue of society's attitude to any section of the marginalized in the society, societal forces should be monitored to bring out discussions in its public sphere, having concern for everyone and in search of 'common good.' Shashi Ratnakar Singh, "People and public sphere in India," *Social Change*, [2009] vol.39, 270-80; *http://www.environmentportal.in/ files/People %20and%20public %20sphere%20in%20India.pdfs*.

[15] Homophobia refers not only to mere pejorative attitudes towards the people who are identified as being LGBTIQ, rather it is the hatred or fear of people of such sexual inclinations [the lesbian women and the gay men] which sometimes lead to expressions of hostility, aggressive mentality and acts of violence. Paola Bacchetta, "Queer Formations in (Hindu) Nationalism," *Sexuality Studies*, edited by Sanjay Srivasta, [Oxford, U.K.: Oxford University Press, 2013], 121-140.

[16] If we were to say the same thing about the many instances of the 'homosexuals' & the transgender being alienated in our society, sometimes because of the superior spirit of 'the normal' [having the awareness of being created in the image of the Lord and as having hetero-sexual orientations], we would be regarded as narrow-minded/even ruthless to the core. By no means, we could write off a transgender as simply subhuman with many vices. Any concept of superiority for the 'normal human' and the doctrine of exclusive grace of 'image of the Lord' go both against our experience and the spirit of our age. Rather we should be ready with our interpretation of the biblical text to accept their identity as human. Inclusivity in the use of words & phrases are explained in the next foot note, numbered 18.

[17] The theological students at the 'Serampore University circle' might be familiar with the request for needed inclusivity in the use of words & phrases, which

endorses to consider homosexuality as a sexual orientation rather than an intentional preference. For such inclusive words & phrases, Santhosh S. Kumar, *A Guide to Inclusive Language for theological students, Christian ministers and lay leaders* [Bangalore: United Theological College, 2012].

[18] Even though medical professionals, at least from 1980's, began changing their attitude towards the sexual minorities, stigmatization among the 'religious' continues worsen. When groups maintain homosexuality as sexual preference rather than an orientation, such 'behaviour' becomes a sin and runs counter to the will of God.http://archive.adl.org/hate-patrol/homophobia.html#.V7fGeFt97IU. Accessed Saturday, 20.08. 2016, 9am;   Parmesh Shahani, *GayBombay: Globalization Love and Belonging in Contemporary India* [USA, India: SAGE (2008); http://www.indianpsychiatry.org.

[19] Queer refers to the concept and phrase 'gender queer,' an umbrella term covering those who fall outside the non-binary gender identity of male & female. It points to the sexual/gender minorities who are not either hetero-sexual or hetero-gender.http://genderqueerid.com/gq-terms. Accessed 10.12.2016, 8pm. The queer reading of the bible [*queering*] is to be treated as a Christian counterpart to the secular trend to read texts as congenial and friendly to the people with different sexual orientations. Just like what had happened at the third quarter of twentieth century in the case of 'feminist reading,' the 'queer reading' of the Bible could be treated [at least out of curiosity for the same] as a diverse option for biblical understanding. Reading of the Bible could be in the strict religious way, the artistic way, the scholarly track and could be approached strictly as a literary piece. There are certain readings that could be seen as having openness in understanding [David Carr, *The Erotic Word Sexuality, Spirituality and the Bible* (Oxford: OUP, 2004)]; Willard M. Swartley, *Homosexuality: Biblical Interpretation and Moral Discernment* (Scottdale, Pennsylvania: Herald Press, 2003)]. When one is interested in 'queering' the passages on Jesus as 'the friend of the tax collector and of the sinner [Lk.15:1-10],' what the Gospel narrator puts emphasis on 'rejoicing' among the friends, as the narration is retold it as an occasion where friends of the shepherd who found out the lost sheep [Lk.15: 4-7] and that the lady who retrieved her lost coin are called to 'rejoice' with them [Lk.15: 8-9]. The subsequent passage on 'the prodigal son' [Lk.15:11f.] also proceed along to the rejoicing within their families.

[20] As per the Latest Hate Crime Statistics Report Released [2013] anti-gay crime is on the rise. Accordingly, of the 5,928 incidents reported, six were multiple-bias hate crime incidents involving 12 victims. Of the 5,922 single bias incidents reported, the top three bias categories were race (48.5 percent), sexual orientation (20.8 percent), and religion (17.4 percent). *https://www.fbi.gov/news/stories/latest-hate-crime-statistics-report-release, accessed 2016, March 5, 7pm.*

[21] Feminist hermeneutical principles of 'silence' & 'suspicion' could be applied to selected texts to elaborate & motivate the readers to have a preferential option

for the sexual minorities. Anyway this is not attempted, since it may appear as unwieldy at this point, but it is a potential area to be discussed.

[22] Vincent E. Bacote, *The Spirit in Public Theology* [Michigan: Baker academic, 2005], 22.

[23] Vincent E. Bacote, *The Spirit in Public Theology*, 22-23.

[24] Ronald F. Thiemann, who defined public theology as "faith seeking to understand the relation between Christian convictions and the broader social and cultural context within which the Christian community lives," conceives of an apologetic approach as more accommodative to the culture and other societal aspects. [Ronald F. Thiemann, *Constructing a Public Theology*, (Louisville: Westminster John Knox, 1991), 21; Mack Stackhouse, *Public Theology and Political Economy: Stewardship in Modern Society,*(Grand Rapids: Eerdmans,1987, xi].

[25] The confessional approach will be normative to a great extent, simply directing with strict religious principles and moral judgments in the communication of Christian doctrines and stand points [Ronald F. Thiemann, *Constructing a Public Theology*, Louisville, 1991].

[26] Max L. Stackhouse, *Public Theology and Political Economy*, [Michigan: Grand Rapids, 1987].

[27] Quoting materials from a different context, but of the same category could relate with what is stated here. The major apologetic challenges in the pluralistic context of India include Faith, Practice and Identity, where the contradictions in lives & churches invalidate the Christian claims of Gospel and the Bible. Just similar to that the non-accommodative approach of the so called 'religious' against the sexual minorities in putting Christian Faith, Practice and Identity. [C.V. Mathew, "Apologetic Challenges in India," Editors. Grace Jacob & Paulson Pulikottil, *Beyond Borders. Challenging Boundaries of Philosophy, Faith & Education*, (Bangalore, India: Primalogue, 2010), 151-160].

[28] Nevertheless, the biblical interpretations also contribute to the punitive mindset in the society, we need to boldly apply to the biblical text the principles of Christian anthropology, and the hermeneutical principles of Public Theology and Contextual Theology [like feminist hermeneutic principles of silence & suspicion] to deal with the issue. How can we, with the interpretation of the biblical texts provide an antidote by bringing out the theological categories and theological strands, to work for such minorities, and motivate both the Christian and the secular minded readers of the Biblical text to come out of any punitive attitude towards the sexual minorities.

Towards an affirming
Sexual Ethics and Spirituality

Lai-shan YIP

Abstract

In order to propose for Queer, affirming sexual ethic and spirituality and identify related spiritual resources, this paper first examines the causes for condemnation of homosexuality and the denigration of LGBTIQ persons and their sexualities, namely heterosexism and the devaluation of sexual pleasure. Then, an ethical model of just good sex is used to address the challenges to a queer-affirming sexual ethics and exemplify a spirituality of sexual-justice and sexual integrity, merging individual pleasure with common good. Finally, examples of spiritual resources for queer-affirming and body-affirming spirituality are explored in the biblical, mystical and liturgical traditions.

The oppression towards LGBTIQ people is rampant. Over eighty countries still criminalize homosexuality while Muslim *Sharia* law in ten countries sentence homosexuality with a death penalty.[1] Most intersexual babies, who are both male and female, or, neither male nor female, are forced to undergo "corrective surgery" to fit into the binary gender categories.[2] Bisexual people, whose fluid sexual attraction to both same and different gender does not fall into the compulsory heterosexual norm, are thus denigrated as promiscuous.[3] The hatred of gay men for being womanized is cultivated from a macho-masculine culture that serves militaristic and violent agendas.[4] The heterosexist official teaching of the

Catholic Church on banning the condom use also accentuates the AIDS crisis particularly among the vulnerable groups in some developing countries.[5] All these violations of the equal dignity of LGBTIQ people and other underprivileged groups pose a legitimate charge against the official sexual ethics of the Church, in which heterosexuality as the moral norm denies, denigrates and discriminates - sexual diversity expressed by LGBTIQ people. This calls for a sexual ethics and a spirituality that can affirm the sexualities of LGBTIQ people and pursue equality and justice for all.

Robert E. Goss contests that from early Church teachings on controlling the sexual desire to the current Religious Rights mentality on gay sex as self-indulgence, "sexual pleasure remains at the heart of charges against same-sex sexuality."[6] In addition, Patricia Beattie Jung finds that in sexual teachings based on the experiences of the heterosexual male, the sexual pleasure of women is devalued and is disqualified for any intrinsic value to good sex, except for unitive and procreative functions. This denial of sexual pleasure explains the condemnation on (queer) LGBTIQ sex, which is basically for mutual pleasure in order to be good.[7] While the moral ideal for sex has shifted from procreation to intimacy within marital sex nowadays, Grace M. Jantzen notes that sexual pleasure is increasingly treated as a private issue and public policies related to sexual morality are overlooked. For example, pharmaceutical companies and beauty industries bolster intimacy of private sexual pleasure and powerfully shape the consumption of new reproductive technologies and the construction of womanhood. Commodification of sex also leads sexual exploitation of poor women and children.[8] While the HIV/AIDS virus has killed millions of lives and some gay men prefer the anal-receptive sex without condoms, Mary E. Hunt urges the need for balancing private choice in sexual life with communal well-being as a matter of justice.[9]

Both sexual pleasure, sexual justice (right to express one's sexuality) and social justice are important elements for sexual ethics that can affirm the sexual diversity expressed by LGBTIQ people and, at the same time, promote the well-being of all. In this paper, I will argue that sexual pleasure as a moral good is the basis for a sexual ethics for LGBTIQ people and all others. I will integrate it with the model of "just good sex" proposed by Hunt as the connotation of just good sex explicitly tells the core elements of a relevant sexual ethics. Just good sex is a right to sex that is "safe, pleasurable, community-building and conducive to justice."[10] I will first discuss the Catholic Church teachings on sex, in particular their treatment of sex as vice, and their relationships to heterosexism. Then, I will discuss the mystic tradition and the sacramental life as resources for Catholics to redeem sexual pleasure, sexual diversity and sexual justice and for the theological input on just good sex.

Heterosexism and devaluation of Pleasure

Fear and devaluation of sexual desire and pleasure has embedded in the long history of Church teachings on the rejection of sexual pleasure and the compulsory heterosexuality in the form of a life-long, monogamous, heterosexual marriage. In addition, when the Church has also feared for sexual sins in all-male celibate life and paid strong efforts to construct the sin-identity of sodomite, the condemnation of male-male sex and masturbation of the sodomites continues in its current strong condemnation of homosexuality and its pursuit for sole pleasure (without any procreative purpose). While the Church currently does not preach about the second coming of Christ to come to our earthly life, it has fixated in its suspect of sex and continued to uphold the virtue of virginity and chastity and the condemnation of sodomites. Hunt defines heterosexism as "the attitude and ability to enforce the notion that heterosexuality is normative to the exclusion of the full flowering of same-sex possibilities."[11] The fear of sex and sexual pleasure alone cannot lead to heterosexism. It is the bias, attitude and the power of the dominant groups over the sexual minorities that heterosexism executes sexual oppression.

Nowadays, many Christian communities still condemn homosexuality due to heterosexism, denigrating the personhood of LGBTIQ people. For example, for the Roman Catholic Church, although the same-sex orientation is no longer regarded as sin, "homosexual acts are intrinsically disordered and can in no case be approved of."[12] In the 1986 document, a homosexual tendency is regarded as "ordered toward an intrinsic moral evil as an objective disorder", though it is not a sin.[13] Till today, the same view continues. Despite its condemnation of violence against homosexuals, the Church justified such violence in banning the civil rights pursuit of the LGBTIQ people due to its unchecked heterosexism.[14]

There are several factors shaping heterosexism. Hunt asserts that heterosexism of the current Catholic teachings is "rooted in an outdated anthropology that claims sexual complementarity between males and females as natural law", and seeks to implement the teachings in public policies.[15] Christine E. Gudrof points out that the sexual dimorphism is challenged by the diverse understandings of gender across different cultures, the continuum of sexual orientations as in the Kinsey scale and the existence of intersexuals—all these point to the multiplicity of sexualities.[16] The Church also operates its teachings in a patriarchal culture in which ownership of women conferred to men and the headship of men in the family are romanticized and people with colour are over-sexualized. Heterosexism together with racism and sexism keeps the gendered social hierarchy in control and marginalizes the minorities.[17] Hunt calls for the need to name heterosexism as sin for its eradication.[18] I find that, at the same time, it is necessary to redeem sexual pleasure from demonization in the pursuit of sexual integrity and justice.

Pleasure as a Moral Good

Gudorf in "Body, Sex and Pleasure" argues that sexual desire should be suppressed, but to be understood and that sexual pleasure should be recognized as a moral good and affirmed as part of God's creation. Pleasure and bodily pleasure help to cultivate our humanness whereas pain and suffering can distort it. While noting sexual pleasure of women as being long neglected and suppressed, Gudorf asserts that masturbation helps women to understand their own bodies for sexual fulfillment and to know later how to enjoy partnered sex. In this case, masturbation is not necessarily evil and self-interest does not exclude the interest of others.[19]

Gudorf maintains that pleasure, though it is necessary, alone does not constitute sufficient condition for goodness. There are different levels of pleasures, some higher and some lower. Higher ones may confer benefits to others. Sexual pleasure does not necessarily belong to the lower ones as sex can communicate love to our loved ones. Body pleasure is good as it can convey to us our own goodness. The problem arises when human connection is lacked in the pursuit of pleasure. Moreover, sexual pleasure should be established as the primary reason and criteria to judge the goodness of sex while, simultaneously, intimacy and bonding are indirect ends. Sex can convey and mean love. The pleasure in orgasm is beyond pleasure effecting changes in one's relation with a partner and the society as one can learn to trust and reach out more. In good sex, we learn that it is mutual satisfaction, which further extends to just, loving union in community under the reign of God. We also learn inclusiveness that is a basic human value. Commitment to the partner's pleasure teaches us to eroticize mutuality, instead of dominance. Sex can also symbolize union with God implying the Trinitarian intimacy. [20] The power of sex is symbolic like the sacraments. The emotional intensity in sex can function to affirm the existence of sexual partners under the threat of death. Sexual intimacy and bonding provide insights and energy for community-building.[21] Hence, establishing sexual pleasure, as a moral serves to affirm the sexualities of LGBTIQ people.

Just Good Sex

Although sex can sustain life through its ability to bond, it is insufficient to create community and ensure communal well-being. In the construction of a new sexual ethic, we cannot stop at the affirmation of sexual pleasure. Therefore, I suggest using Mary Hunt's model of just good sex. This connotation is wide and deep enough to integrate communal and societal dimensions of sexuality. In an increasingly global, pluralistic and violent context where women's sexuality suffers domestication, framing in individualistic terms, Hunt in her conception of just good sex defines sexuality in its broadest sense as "the range of ways in which embodied beings, namely, people, interact in physical – sometimes, though not always, genital – fashion, as a means of self-expression and communication."[22] This broadening serves to extend sexuality to all in a non-discriminating manner and stop privileging heterosexuality. Moreover, the positive connotation of just good sex values moral agency in making responsible choices for the well-being of oneself and the community. This is a marked difference from the official sexual teachings that concern about prohibitions of individual acts and overlook the dynamics of contextual factors playing into these private acts.[23] In other words, the goodness of sexual activities is defined not only by an individual sense of sexual fulfillment, but also be judged by its capacity to promote both individual and communal justice.

Three major tenets of just good sex are as follows:

1. Affirm sex as a basic human right that calls for public and communal
    support and responsibility:

This points to the profound relationality of right relationships within a
unified cosmic whole.[24] While different cultures may have different
understandings of universal human dignity, the use of the model of just
good sex should encourage communal dialogue and delineation on the
more detailed moral content of just good sex within a particular culture
and among different cultures. The fluidity and its interplaying dynamics
on the substances of just good sex can serve to facilitate and highlight
moral agency of both individual and collective levels and prevent moral
hegemony of any groups, religious or secular.

2. Call for social change that renders body-spirit connections in sexual
    pleasure, linking individual good to communal good:[25]

Queersexuality affirms the goodness of the sexual body. The erotic
becomes the site of sacredness and revelation of God. Sex is gift and
grace from God.[26] Experiencing God as our passionate lover, we are
empowered by God's erotic love to the integration of love-making and
justice-doing.[27] Full embodiment of sex also means transforming the
genital-focused orgasm (balloon sex) to full-body pleasure, which enhances
connection to God, partner and life.[28] Furthermore, under the threat of
AIDS, safe sex is a major concern in good sex. Safe also means one's right
to maintain own boundary with the freedom to be alone and without
coercion. In the deepest sense of the erotic, good sex also extends to
cover other pleasures comprising of a safe, caring and just world.[29]
Moreover, social recognition of body right is needed to affirm the
development of full personhood and moral agency.[30]

I will like to add one more aspect, inspired by John J. McNeil, who
points out that sex is for fun. Human playfulness reveals God's creativity
and expresses our humanity to the fullest extent, in terms of human
freedom. It also enhances the quality of interpersonal relationships.[31]

3. Make sex and sexuality conducive to community building without any
    emphasis on multiple relationships:

It is the creation of a network of loving relationships. Right relationships
with oneself, others, cosmos and God serve to combat all forms of

oppression from racism to sexism, to heterosexism, to narrow hedonism. The erotic power also generates fierce and tender friendships, all caring relationships and responsible choices on procreation.[32] The fierce tenderness among women enhances liberative struggles and communal survival.[33] The erotic also expresses its fullest extend to include the eros of the earth and our intimate connection to the earth and God. Earthly delight of all and the pursuit of ecological justice cultivate a cosmic communion.[34]

Hence, this model of just good sex not only affirms sexual pleasure as a moral good and sexual justice for all (the right one' sexual expression including the diverse sexualities of LGBTIQ people), but also ties personal pleasure to communal well-being (social justice). It is a relevant sexual ethic for the current situation of heterosexism, privatizing sexual pleasure, AIDS crisis and sexual exploitation of poor women and children.

Catholic Sources for a Right to Just Good Sex

Although the right to just good sex should be regarded as a universal right and should not exclusively be applied to Catholic sexual ethics, I will identify some sources from the Catholic tradition to ground this model as a valid Catholic sexual ethics. While acknowledging the negative language of Church teachings on sex, Jordan asserts that the mystic tradition and the liturgical tradition provide sources for redeeming pleasures from demonization and creating pleasurable identities linking sex to salvation.[35]

Regarding the mystic tradition, Jordan finds that the highly erotic language is used by the mystics to express the intensity of their union with God and that mystical experience gives similar physiological effects as those of sexual pleasure and orgasm. Our prayer experiences can provide insights and guidance for sexual ethics. In the reverse direction, sexual intimacy also teaches us how to pursue the pleasure of union with God. Personally, I find this challenging as we, Catholics, have been taught to venerate God and have never flirted with God. The erotic identities and language of the mystic are really important insights.

For example, Bernard of Clairvaux in *On Loving God* drew on the Book of Song of Songs to write about the love between God and us, "…There she will receive the long desired caresses and say, 'His left hand is under my head and his right hand has embraced me.' Then she will feel and esteem all the signs of love she had received during her lovers' first visit, as coming from his left hand, altogether inferior and of little value in comparison with the infinite delights of his right hand's embrace…"[36] Desire is also a major theme in Bernard's work. He wrote,

> *The third kiss takes place when the mind, having been consumed by penitential sorrow and having received the gifts of the virtues, is inspired by heavenly desire, and desires to be led into the secret joys of the inner chamber and is impatient in its love. Then, with sweet sighs, breaking into the words of the soul, it cries out with all the affection of its heart, 'It is your face, O Lord, that I seek.*"[37]

He also taught how to grow intimate with God starting like Mary Magdelene kissing Jesus' feet and, therefore, instructed that "the kiss of God is the gift of the Holy Spirit."[38] Although the metaphors used in Bernard's works are the love between a man and a woman, any of us can imitate the bride because the erotic love between God and us transcends gender or sexual orientations. This fits the new sexual ethics here that excludes no one.

Another example is from a beguine mystic, Mechtild of Magdeburg during 13th century Germany. She used the metaphor of the passion between two women, Lady Love and Lady Queen (Soul) to talk about how to the soul empties herself to achieve intimacy, "Love who wounds and binds her devotees, who sickens them and slays them and asks everything of them in order that she may bring them to an undivided will and a mutual interchange of desire, to make love manifest."[39] On one hand, I find that the two feminine figures stimulate the fierce tenderness of women's relationships. Again, the erotic intimacy transcends any gender or social hierarchy. On the other hand, I find that the feminine imagery of the Divine may imply a fluid diversity of the sexual or gender identity of God, an Omni- gender God. This diversity reflects in the multiplicity of human sexual expression.

The Song of Songs has seldom been quoted by the official Church teachings. Marvin Ellison draws on the hermeneutics of feminist, womanist and gay scholars on this love poem to uncover its liberating ethic. The passion of a man and a woman cross the patriarchal sex that aims for procreation and control on women's bodies. Erotic pleasure and sexual body are affirmed. The passionate love of the two violates the dominant cultural norms. The dark skin colour and small breasts of the female love are highly appreciated challenging the dominant norm on beauty. Both body goodness and sexual pleasure are emphasized and affirmed. The bold expression of the sexual desire of the woman and her critique on the perspectives of her audiences show an assertion of her right to love across possible social and racial boundaries and an accusation against sexual oppression. The affirmation of beauty and moral integrity of love and sexual justice offers a biblical ground for a sexual ethic that values bodily pleasure and affirms the sexuality and love of LGBTIQ people and all other sexual minorities.[40]

Regarding the liturgical tradition, Jordan points out that liturgy as a communal prayer arouses pleasurable feelings of the participants with a glimpse of heaven, hymnody and sonority of the Scripture, etc.[41] Moreover, he in *The Silence of Sodom* points out that in the homoerotic liturgy of the homophobic Catholic hierarchy, the celebrant of the Eucharist does not only hold the Body of Christ in hand, but also becomes the Jesus himself. This is "the most physical elevation" of the body.[42] On one hand, I find that the Eucharist as one of the most symbolic features of the Catholic faith can ironically be used for affirming homoerotic and queer love. On the other hand, the venerated Body of Christ calls for an affirmation of the body goodness.

Examples of gay and lesbian saints also provide inspirations for same-sex love and relationships. For example, Saints Sergius and Bacchusare, popular in Christian gay communities, were Roman soldiers in the fourth century. After being discovered as Christians, they were tortured to abandon their faith. After Bacchus had died in the torture, he returned as a spirit to support Sergius so that the latter would strive on till they would be together one day. Some ancient text named them as lovers.[43] These saints lived out a spirituality of faith and fidelity to God and that of deep love to his own lover.

Nancy Wilson makes a connection between sexuality and Sabbath. She claims that "sexuality was made for humanity, not humanity for sexuality', a paraphrase of Jesus' teaching on Sabbath. Sabbath is a gift to humanity, so is sexuality. Sabbath is an equalizer that all can come to share the communal meal. So is sexuality that all should be equal for all to enjoy. All who share the Eucharist are called to do justice and promote equality in the society like Jesus whose life is an example of compassion and justice, especially engaging the minorities for a better community life. Like Sabbath, sexuality functions as refreshment. We need Sabbath for a good adult play (sex). Sabbath is for healing, so is sexuality, which can give healing touch.[44] Goss also sees making love on Sabbath as blessed so that sex can be claimed as sacred. He strengthens his argument by the fact that sex is the only activity not prohibited on Sabbath.[45] I find that both the analogy of Sabbath to sexuality and the Sabbath sex redeem the dignity of human sexual pleasure and its relation to justice.

Regarding the creation of pleasurable identities, Jordan points out that the successful projection of sexual identities in pastoral practice relies on the substitution of gendered roles performed in preaching, praying, rituals, and theology. For example, in Latin liturgy, there are multiple substitutions of identity — the celebrant priest becomes Christ or changes to the spouse of Christ.[46] With her veiling, a nun may become the virgin martyr Agnes as well as the bride of Christ. During Eucharist, one takes Christ as wine and bread to attain union with Christ.[47] When the priest serves Eucharist, he takes up the role of a woman in serving the meal. I also find that when the priest conducts foot-washing in the Holy Thursday liturgy, this act makes him like the woman who washes Jesus' feet with her tears to express her love for Jesus. If we try to project alternate identities, in which the capacity for erotic pleasure is integrated, perhaps the communion of the Eucharist community is an erotic union of queer people or drag queens whose erotic connections with one another allow one to become another and passionately get into union with the same or different gender. This erotic communion of the Eucharist community can serve as the basis for the cosmic communion in the model of just good sex.

Conclusion

The long history of Church teachings on sex builds on demonization of sexual pleasure, control of desire, devaluation of body and policing on sexual deviations. Moreover, the issue of social justice is seldom addressed in official sexual teachings. Eventually, such kind of sexual teachings gives its harmful expression in heterosexism and the body-spirit dichotomy that seriously afflicts suffering on LGBTIQ people and other sexual minorities. The right to just good sex is an attempt to build a body-affirming and justice-seeking sexual ethics for all. The consciousness of the sexual minorities will continue to contribute for a more comprehensive understanding of "just good sex." While homosexuality has a deep root in Catholicism, recovering Catholic sources will be one important antidote to heterosexism and is complementary to an inter-religious, inter-cultural and inter-disciplinary effort over the world to implement the universal right to just good sex.

Endnotes

[1] Vanessa Baird, *The No-Nonsense Guide to Sexual Diversity* (Oxford: The New Internationalist, 2007), 15-6.

[2] Virginia Ramey Mollenkott, "Crossing Gender Borders: Toward a New Paradigm," in *Body and Soul: Rethinking Sexuality as Justice-Love*, ed. Marvin Ellison and Sylvia Thornston-Smith (Cleveland, OH : Pilgrim Press, 2003), 187-8.

[3] Susan HalcombCriag, "Bisexuality: Variations on a Theme," in *Body and Soul: Rethinking Sexuality as Justice-Love*, ed. Marvin Ellison and Sylvia Thornston-Smith (Cleveland, OH : Pilgrim Press, 2003), 115-7.

[4] Daniel C. Maguire, "Men, Male Myths, and Metanoia," in *Body and Soul: Rethinking Sexuality as Justice-Love*, ed. Marvin Ellison and Sylvia Thornston-Smith (Cleveland, OH : Pilgrim Press, 2003), 178-80.

[5] Catholic For Choice, *Truth and Consequence, A Look behind the Vatican's Ban on Contraception* (Washington D.C.: Catholic For Choice, 2008), 10-5, *http://www.catholicsforchoice.org/topics/reform/documents/TruthConsequencesFINAL.pdf* (accessed 15 May 2008).

[6] Robert E. Goss, "Gay Erotic Spirituality and the Recovery of Sexual Pleasure," in *Body and Soul: Rethinking Sexuality as Justice-Love*, ed. Marvin Ellison and Sylvia Thornston-Smith (Cleveland, OH : Pilgrim Press, 2003), 201-6.

[7] Patricia Beattie Jung, "Sanctifying Women's Pleasure," in *Good Sex: Feminist Perspectives from the World's Religions*, ed. Patricia Beattie Jung, Mary E. Hunt and Radhika Balakrishnan (NJ: Rugters Univ. Press, 2001), 77-86.

[8] Grace M. Jantzen, "Good Sex: Beyond Private Pleasure," in *Good Sex: Feminist Perspectives from the World's Religions*, ed. Patricia Beattie Jung, Mary E. Hunt and Radhika Balakrishnan (NJ: Rugters Univ. Press, 2001), 6-13.

[9] Mary E. Hunt, "AIDS in a Globalized Economy: A Religious Reality Check," in *Body and Soul: Rethinking Sexuality as Justice-Love*, ed. Marvin Ellison and Sylvia Thornston-Smith (Cleveland, OH : Pilgrim Press, 2003), 258.

[10] Mary E. Hunt, "Just Good Sex: Feminist Catholicism and Human Rights," in *Good Sex: Feminist Perspectives from the World's Religions*, ed. Patricia Beattie Jung, Mary E. Hunt and Radhika Balakrishnan (NJ: Rugters Univ. Press, 2001), 158.

[11] Mary E. Hunt, "Eradicating the Sin of Heterosexism," in *Heterosexism in Contemporary World Religion: Problem and Prospect*, ed. Marvin M. Ellison and Judith Plaskow (Cleveland, OH: Pilgrim Press, 2007), Ch 6.

[12] Congregation for the Doctrine of the Faith, *Declaration on Certain Questions Concerning Sexual Ethics*, (Vatican: CDF, 1975), no. 8.

[13] Congregation for the Doctrine of the Faith, *Letter to the Bishops of the Catholic Church on the Pastoral Care of Homosexual Persons* (Vatican: CDF, 1986), no.3.

[14] Congregation for the Doctrine of the Faith, *Considerations Regarding Proposals to Give Legal Recognition to Unions Between Homosexual Persons*, (Vatican: CDF, 2003, no. 7, 10).

[15] Hunt, "Eradicating the Sin of Heterosexism," Ch. 6.

[16] Christine E. Gudorf, "The Erosion of Sexual Dimorphism: Challenges to Religion and Religious Ethics," *Journal of the American Academy of Religion 69*, No. 4 (December 2001), p.863-891.

[17] Marvin M. Ellison, "Facing the Moral Problem: The Eroticizing of Power and Control," in *Erotic Justice: A Liberating Ethic of Sexuality* (Louisville, KY: Westminister John Knox Press, 1996), 40-58.

[18] Hunt, "Eradicating the Sin of Heterosexism," Ch. 6.

[19] Christine E. Gudorf, "Sexual Pleasure as Grace and Gift," in *Body, Sex and Pleasure: Reconstructing Christian Sexual Ethics* (Cleveland, OH: 1994) 81-97.

[20] Gudorf, "Sexual Pleasure as Grace and Gift," 97-124.

[21] Gudorf, "Sexual Pleasure as Grace and Gift," 127-38, 161.

[22] Hunt, "Just Good Sex," 158-9.

[23] Hunt, "Just Good Sex," 160-9.

[24] Hunt, "Just Good Sex," 160-70.

[25] Hunt, "Just Good Sex," 170-1.

[26] Goss, "Gay Erotic Spirituality," 206.

[27] Robert E. Ross, "God as Love-Making and Justice-Doing," in *Jesus Acted Up: A Gay and Lesbian Manifesto* (San Francisco: Harper, 1993), 166.

[28] Robert E. Goss, "Finding God in the Heart-Genital Connection," in *Queering Christ: Beyond Jesus Acted Up* (Cleveland, OH: Pilgrim Press, 2002), 56-68.

[29] Hunt, "Just Good Sex," 171-2.

[30] Gudorf, "Sexual Pleasure as Grace and Gift," 160-2.

[31] John J. McNeil, "The Freedom to Play," in *Taking a Chance on God: Liberating Theology for Gays, Lesbians, and Their Lovers, Families and Friends* (Boston: Beacon Press, 1996), 110-20.

[32] Hunt, "Just Good Sex," 172.

[33] Mary E. Hunt,*Fierce Tenderness: A Feminist Theology of Friendship* (New York: Crossroad, 1994), 51, 69, 148-9.

[34] Daniel T. Spencer, "Keeping Body, Soul and Earth Together: Revisioning Justice-Love as an Ecological Ethic of Right Relation," in *Body and Soul: Rethinking Sexuality as Justice-Love*, ed. Marvin Ellison and Sylvia Thornston-Smith (Cleveland, OH : Pilgrim Press, 2003), 319-333.

[35] Jordan, *The Ethics of Sex*, 155-72.

[36] Bernard of Clairvaux, "On Loving God," in *The Works of Bernard of Clairvaux*, *Treatises II*, Cistercian Father Series, Vol. 5, ed. M. Basil Pennington (Washington, D.C.: Consortium Press, 1974) 120.

[37] Cited from Bernard of Clairvaux, *Sancti Bernardi Opera*, ed. Jean Leclercq, henriRochais and C.H. Talbot (Rome, EditionesCistercienses, 1957-1977) by Michael Casey, *Athirst for God: Spiritual Desire in Bernard of Clairvauz's Sermons on the Song of Songs* (Kalamazoo, MI: Cistercian Publications, 1987) 126-7.

[38] John Michael Talbot and Steve Rabey, "The Way of Love: Bernard of Clairvaux," in *The Way of the Mystics: Ancient Wisdom for Experiencing God Today* (San Francisco: Jossey-Bass, 2005) 38.

[39] Cited from Barbara Newman, *Gods and the Goddesses: Vision, Poetry, and Belief in the Middle Ages* (Philadelphia: Univ. of Pennsylvania Press, 2003) 157 by Beverly J. Lanzetta, *Radical Wisdom: A Feminist Mystical Theology* (Minneapolis, MN: Augsburg Fortress, 2005) 54.

[40] Ellison, *Erotic Justice*, 71-73.

[41] Jordan, *The Ethics of Sex*, 169.

[42] Mark D. Jordan, *The Silence of Sodom* : Homosexuality in Modern Catholicism (Chicago: Univ. of Chicago Press, 2000) 207-8.

[43] John Boswell,*Same-Sex Unions in Premodern Europe* (New York: Villard Books, 1994), 154.

[44] Nancy Wilson, "A Queer Theology of Sexuality," in *Our Tribe: Queer Folks, God, Jesus, and the Bible* (San Francisco: Harper, 1995), 266-76.

[45] Robert E. Goss, "Gay Erotic Spirituality," 210.

[46] Jordan, The Ethics of Sex, 170-2.

[47] Mark D. Jordan, "Sodomites and Churchmen: The Theological Invention of Homosexuality," in Michel Foucault and Theology: The Politics of Religious Experience, ed. James Bernauer and Jeremy Carrette(Aldershot, Hants, England; Burlington, VT :Ashgate, 2004), 240.

Masculinity and Justice

Philip Vinod Peacock

Abstract

This paper attempts to look at how patriarchy intersects and interconnects with other social structures to not only oppress women as a class but also to construct particular forms of masculinity. It particularly looks at how patriarchy combines with race, caste and communalism to construct both feminine and masculine ideas of gender. It further fleshes out why and how men can be involved in the struggle for gender justice.

Patriarchy, Race and Caste

Patriarchy does not exist in a vacuum. Rather we find that patriarchy co-exists and operates along with other mechanisms of organizing power. Therefore we find that patriarchy coalesces with capitalism and economic globalization in a manner which invisibilizes and trivializes women's labour. Therefore within the gendered division of labour, a primary way of the division of labour across cultures, we find that that which is considered to be 'women's work' is trivialized and not considered work at all. Within capitalist constructs which account for work only that which is paid for, women's labour within the context of the household is not counted as work thereby invisibilizing women's economic contribution.

In a likewise manner we find that patriarchy also coalesces and interconnects with issues of race, caste, religious affiliation and regional location. This coalescing and interconnections, of course, ensure that it is not necessarily true that all women and are powerless when compared to all men. A poor black man in rural Uganda, for example, has much less access to resources and privilege as compared to a middle-class white woman living in New York. Of course, I would have to add a caveat here because any man can sexually assault any woman. The idea of using bodies as weapons is of course frightening.

Yet the fact that patriarchy as a structure must be seen along with other structures has deep implications for how we consider masculinity itself. The point that I am making is that precisely because there is an intertwining of mechanisms of organizing power our masculinities are not only formed by gender and gendered relations but also by several other factors. Dale Bisnauth, one of those who journeyed with us in the process of developing the gender manual *From Hegemony to Partnership*[1] offered an analysis of the construction of the masculinity of the black man in the Caribbean. Bisnauth prised open the nexus between race, slavery and masculinity when he suggested that the present situation of the Caribbean male is historically rooted in the black slave being treated as chattel for the production of more slaves through reproduction. Further slave men were shunted from one woman to another so as to be able to impregnate as many as possible for the creation of as many slaves as possible. For Bisnauth then this historical connection between gender and slavery plays itself out in the present construction of Caribbean male masculinity, where sexual prowess is valorized and there exists a disconnect between the male and the rearing roles of children. While Bisnauth's contention is problematic, it offers us certain possibilities in uncovering multilayered structures, which go to create the understanding of maleness in the Caribbean today.

Yet at the same time we should not consider these historical circumstances as offering men loopholes out of which they can condone destructive and violent behaviour. Swathy Margaret, the Dalit feminist, however calls Dalit men out on this very issue. While recognizing the dominant caste males desire of the possession and control of the body of the Dalit males, what Margaret also asserts is that this is what drives the Dalit males desire to possess the Dalit woman's body as his own, his contention being if they can have her why can't I? This combination of caste, class and patriarchy, however, condenses its violence on the body of the Dalit woman herself. Where in the case of competitive masculinities it is the Dalit woman who is the loser and the Dalit man instead of being a support winds up being the victimizer.

Perhaps there is nowhere more evident the issues of competitive masculinities than in the cases of ethnic and religious based conflict. I would perhaps like to reflect on this from the experience of what we specifically refer to as communal violence in India. Communal violence is a quintessentially Indian term for religious sectarian violence. I draw particularly from the previous research I have done in the area.

Sex, Sexuality and Communalism in the Indian Context

While there has always been a connection between sex, sexuality and violence against women this has taken a particular direction in the history of communal violence in India. There exists among the followers of the Sangh Parivar today an almost unnatural fear of the sexual prowessof the Islamic male that is most apparently reflected in the myth of the ever-increasing Muslim population. This is not only manifested in the oft-quoted myth of the enormous increase in the Muslim population in the country but also in overtly sexual language and symbols used by the Hindu right. In an article entitled The Feminization of Violence: Women in the Politics of the Shiv Sena by Sikata Banerjee, the author quotes an interview with a Shiv Sena activist who makes the point that when the news of Hindu households being burned in Mumbai reached the ears of his wife, she remarked that "I should offer you bangles now. What are we? In our own country Hindus are being burned."[2] The sexual overtones are very clear – The 'manhood' of the activist is being put into question here, it is as though he has been emasculated. It is also interesting to note that the question "What are we?" is posed instead of 'who are we?' The obvious innuendo being made here is that the activist is a eunuch and not a man. The same sexual overtone was once again seen in the post-Godhra chants of the ABVP on the JNU campus who chanted *"Jis Hinduon ka Khoon na Khola, voh Hindu nahin, voh hijra hai."*[3] This feeling of emasculation is usually built up by myths and legends, namely the rape of Hindu women during the partition, rapes of Hindu queens by Muslims and abductions of women by Muslims right throughout history. The penal envy is further perpetuated by the loss of the Indian 'Hindu' cricket team to 'Muslim' Pakistan. One can begin to understand then why Cricket becomes such a bone of contention for the *Sangh Parivar*. The politics of sex and sexuality also comes clear in the reaction of the *Shiv Sena* towards Valentines Day, after all, love is something that has to be countered for the fear of Hindu girls falling in love with Muslim boys. The anger against cross-cultural marriages can also be evaluated as a response to the same to the same phenomenon.

The loss of virility and impotence then has to be compensated by overt signs of maleness, it is no wonder then that the BJP tested nuclear weapons as soon as it came into power, a sure sign of male aggressiveness, Pakistan's follow up of a greater number of nuclear tests was just another way of comparing size! Even more overt is the innumerable number of missiles that have been tested so far; the phallic symbolism of a missile should not go unnoticed. Communal Violence against women then has to be begun to be read within the framework of men regaining their lost virility by overt acts of aggression towards others and towards the women of the 'other' community in particular. The form that this aggression takes is of course rape and other forms of sexual violence towards women. Similar examples can be seen in other areas in which ethnic violence has taken the form of rape and sexual assault of women and actually of men as well.

On the surface level, of course, the simple politics of rape is to revenge the lost honour of one community by the dishonouring of another. The most obvious way of doing this is by violating the 'honour' of the women of the other community. On another but a related level rape in the context of communal violence is also related to destroying the purity of another community. A woman's body and sexuality is often referred to as her honour or her purity and is under the protection of her husband or father. In the process of rape, the perpetrator defiles this purity and in the process humiliates her father or husband. Perhaps the recent spurt of protests against rape and sexual assault against women have to also be read within the logic that men are no longer able to protect the women, the anger against the patriarchal state, epitomized as the father as against Mother India is only an extension of this logic.

But the politics of pollution go further than this, communal violence requires the existence of two or more communities that perceive themselves as distinct. In the process of rape, the perpetrator, in fact, plants his seed in the woman thus polluting the lineage and claiming it as his own. He has in fact subjugated the entire race.

In several cases, however, as we have already heard, the sexual organs of the women were severely injured and women were murdered, the effort was no doubt to hit at the demographic and the economic status of the community. The seemingly obvious response to the myth that Muslims were over populating the country was that their numbers had to be reduced. The pogrom was carried out by bringing injury to the reproductive organs of the women who were and would be bearing the children to ensure that the population would not grow. While the economic enterprise of the Muslims in Gujarat were affected by the burning of their shops, restaurants etc. the possibility of an economic regeneration was negated by the killing of foetuses, children and of course the murder of women and the destruction of their reproductive organs.

It has also not gone unnoticed that the fundamental organisations are also extremely patriarchal and often seek to confine women to the private realm under the control of men. The Hindu right wing therefore, sees as the ideal Indian women the *Sati Savitri* whose life's fulfilment is in fulfilling the desire of her husband. Similarly, the Islamic right wing prescribes severe restrictions on women including dress codes and injunctions on education. The appeal to revivalist notions of bringing back the golden age also has connotations of returning to a time when women were docile and could be easily controlled. While what we have to recognize is that while certain markers of masculinity and femininity had its relevance in a particular context, with the onslaught of modernity much of these have lost their often nurturing roots.

Obviously the intersectionalities between religion, gender, globalization and modernity in India have risen to horrendous levels leading to monstrous masculinities.

We are here today to speak of redemptive masculinities though and I would like to suggest five ways of moving forward.

1. We need to move beyond gender binaries to rediscover the fluidity of gender

2. We need to be able to recover a way of seeing and doing that which is based on justice and which would seek to not just dismantle patriarchy but to dismantle and delegitimize all hierarchy.

3. We need to recognize, interrogate and flesh out the complexity that is to be found within the various ways injustice combines and struggle to find ways of not just being men, but being human and humane

4. We must recognize that we cannot easily fashion the world in the way in which we want to. We need to desperately discombobulate ourselves

5. We need to love dangerously. We have too many social and religious norms which tell us how to love, we need to find ways to transgress, and in this transgression find our common salvation.

Endnotes

[1] Dale A. Bisnauth in Patricia Sheerattan-Bisnauth & Philip V Peacock (eds) *Created in God's image: From hegemony to partnership,* A Church manual on men as partners: Promoting positive masculinities, (Geneva 2010: World Council of Reformed Churches, WCC).

[2] Sikata Banerjee, "The Feminization of Violence: Women in the Politics of the Shiv Sena" in *Asian Survey* Vol. 36, Issue 12 Dec 1996 p.1214. It should be pointed out that it is the man who is putting these words into the woman's mouth

[3]*Op. Cit.* Tanika Sarkar p. 2875.

Queer Identities and the Bible

L. Jayachitra

Gender identity, sexuality, and sexual orientation are subjects of great interest for contemporary readers of the Bible. 'Genderqueer' is an umbrella term that covers non-normative gender identity and gender expression, i.e., non-binary gender that falls outside the gendered male-female binary model. Gender queer is also known as gender-variants. Apart from the most familiar gender category of transgender (trans-women and trans-men), there are 26 more gender queer identities - they are Androgyny, Pan-gender, Bi-gender, Tri-gender, A-gender, Neutrois, Retransitioners, Appearance gendered, Trans-binary, Trans-crossdressers, Binary's butch, Fancy, Epicene, Intergender, Trans-masculine, Trans-feminine, Demi girl, Demi guy, Girl fags, Guy dykes, Gender fluid, Tomboy, Sissy, Non-binary butch, Non binary femme, and Cross dresser. Can biological sex be understood fully in a simple female-male binary in the context of about 28 gender-queer possibilities being scientifically identified? Can hetero-normativity continue to lead the field of interpretation when there are more than 15 possible sexual attractions possible outside heterosexuality?[1]

Human sex is more complex than a simple female-male binary where every individual is solely and unambiguously male or female. However, the common notion of the 'hermaphrodite' as an individual with a full set of both male and female organs is also inaccurate and misleading. When the human foetus misses the demarcating difference between typically male-related and typically female-related genitals, they cross over the strict binaries of female and male genitalia and sexes. Across the various conditions, the external genitalia can appear typically male, typically female, in between, or mostly absent; internal genitalia and reproductive organs can include testes, ovaries, one testis and ovary, or an ovotestis. Chromosomes can be XX, XY, XXY, XX/XY or a range of variations. Therefore, when we try to categorize biological sex, it could only be female, male or intersex.

Now the question of 'third gender' arises as to how we understand transgendered people. Trans-women are born with male genitals and later through sex-corrective surgeries try to conform to female bodies. In the same way, trans-men are born with female genitals and prefer to conform to male bodies. But such surgeries are expensive in countries like India. There are also transgender persons who opt to live without sex-corrective surgeries with the genital organs they are born with. Once the genitally-ambiguous possibilities are understood, it may help us to explore the various sexual expressions of queer persons including trans-women, trans-men and intersex people apart from homosexuals in general. Here it must be noted that the word 'queer' denotes more than homosexual issues, though queer discussions have developed, in the course of the history of LGBTIQ concerns.

The word 'queer' is used as an umbrella term to refer to various non-heterosexual and non-hetero-normative sexualities:

> To queer means, to make strange - and Queer interpretation is precisely a practise of making strange that which has been assumed to be familiar. (It) challenges domesticated constructions and interpretations... and wonders about who such constructions and interpretations have closeted. As a strategy of liberation, Queer interpretation seeks to expose and to challenge the violence that such constructions and interpretations have done to people's identities, experiences and bodies.[2]

Queer Bible Commentary published in 2006 has opened up new vistas for exploring various biblical interpretation from queer perspectives. Prior to this, the first wave of queer interpretation was political in approach especially to interrogate the difficult texts prohibiting LGB expressions. Genesis 19 on Sodom's act of homosexual violence is a prominent text which has been used vehemently against homosexual practices. The Levitical laws against homosexuality in Lev. 18:22 ("You shall not lie with a male as with a woman; it is an abomination.") and 20:13 ("If a man lies with a male as with a woman, both of them have committed an abomination; they shall be put to death; their blood is upon them.") are questioned as to very biased against people of homosexual orientations. Deuteronomy 22:5 ("A woman shall not wear a man's apparel, nor shall a man put on a woman's garment, for whoever does such things is abhorrent to the Lord your God.") is a terror text to trans-gendered persons for it prohibits cross dressing.

The second wave of queer interpretation applies the traditional tools of biblical criticism, including the historical-critical method, to texts that appear to condemn same-sex sexuality. These approaches emphasize the historical contexts of the biblical texts, thus offering an implicit (or explicit) argument against using these texts to adjudicate modern sexual practices, homosexual or otherwise. Such modes of interpretations challenge texts like Genesis 19 asking if homosexuality or homosexual rape is the real issue in the text.

The Bible is not silent about queer identities. To start with the second creation narrative, "And the rib that the Lord God had taken from the man he made into a woman..." (Gen 2:22), separating woman from the body of Adam had raised interpretations in favour of the first human as a hermaphrodite in the hermeneutical circles.

Later on, as we consider specifically the exilic and post-exilic period, many Jewish men functioned as eunuchs in the palace of Babylon (2 Kings 20:18; Isa. 39:7; Jer.29:2). In Isa. 56:3b-5: "...and do not let the eunuch say, "I am just a dry tree." For thus says the Lord: To the eunuchs who keep my Sabbaths, who choose the things that please me and hold fast my covenant, I will give, in my house and within my walls, a monument and a name better than sons and daughters; I will give them an everlasting name that shall not be cut off." This is a post-exilic affirmation or a corrective to Deuteronomic law of keeping men with defective genitals away from the house of Yahweh. Also in the New Testament, Jesus makes a reference to eunuchs in Mt. 19:12: "For there are eunuchs who have been so from birth, and there are eunuchs who have been made eunuchs by others, and there are eunuchs who have made themselves eunuchs for the sake of the kingdom of heaven."

The biblical texts that may not have explicit mention of homosexual practices, but homoerotic expressions have highlighted the queer presence in the Hebrew Bible. The filial relationship between David and Jonathan is a very good literary narrative of homoeroticism. In 1 Sam 18:1, it reads, "The soul of Jonathan was bound to the soul of David, and Jonathan loved him as his own soul." The phrase, "he loved him as his own soul" appears again in v.3 and in v.4, as the sign of covenant made with David, Jonathan gave away his robe, armour, sword, bow and belt. This covenantal act could be interpreted as a political allegiance or an act of personal affection. 1 Sam. 19:1 expresses that "Jonathan took great delight in David," and therefore pleaded with Saul to spare his life in vv.2-7. 1 Sam. 20 is a detailed narrative of the emotional friendship between Jonathan and David which is based on "faithful love" (vv.14,15) and the narrative goes on to state that they "kissed each other and wept with each other" while parting. When they meet again at Horesh in 1 Sam.23:16-18, there again they make a covenant with each other. When David mourns over the death of Jonathan, he comments as in 2 Sam. 1:26, "I am distressed for you my brother Jonathan; greatly beloved were you to me; your love to me was wonderful, passing the love of women." The filial relationship between David and Jonathan could express their love for each other much beyond the normal parameters of hetero-normativity.

References are also made to female homoeroticism. The story of Naomi and Ruth is most commonly an identified case for female homoeroticism. In Ruth 1:16-17, Ruth says to Naomi, "Do not press me to leave you or to turn back from following you! Where you go, I will go; where you lodge, I will lodge; your people shall be my people, and your God my God. Where you die, I will die - there will I be buried. May the Lord do thus and so to me, and more as well, if even death parts me from you!" This statement and the way Ruth and Naomi spent the rest of their life together, according to queer interpretation, may allude to erotic love (Lesbianism of Naomi and bisexuality of Ruth) between them.

There are three New Testament passages, which are generally used to allude to same-sex relations. They are Romans 1:26-27; 1 Cor. 6:9; and 1 Tim. 1:10. The Greek word *malakoi* in 1 Cor. 6:9 could be translated as 'effeminate' and *arsenokoitai* in both 1 Cor. 6:9 and 1 Tim. 1:10 as a male sexual pervert. The word *malakoi* may refer to a trans-woman or a man behaving like a woman in sexual intercourse. The word, *arsenokoitai* is translated in certain English versions as homosexuals. This may rather refer to male prostitution or any kind of promiscuity or pederasty (a male having sex with a minor boy). The Roman passage may be more clearly indicating same-sex relations than the Greek words *malakoi* and *arsenokoitai* in other two passages. These New Testament passages pose the danger of queerphobia.

Towards a Queer-friendly Biblical Interpretation with Special reference to Romans 1:26-27

Romans 1:26-27 projects a homophobic passage which raises a number of questions in relation to how these verses may be understood in a context where queer relations are viewed more sympathetically by a minority group of scholars and activists. How would Pauline homophobic passage be re-read to address the valid human rights concerns of queer community today? If the Roman passage condemns homosexuality, what kind of attitude would a New Testament interpreter adopt to relate such texts to contemporary concerns of queer realities? How would an interpreter attempt an inter-cultural reading of Paul of Jewish and Greco-Roman cultures?

A household in first century C.E. is a microcosm of all three societies of Jews, Greeks and Romans, where the male head holds control over sexual rights of all subordinate members, the only difference being that Jews did not exercise control over male sexuality. This indicates that Jews were against homoerotic relations. However, Greek and Roman households extended different ways of exercising homoerotic and homosexual relations.[3] In these two cultures, men entertained sexual relations with male and female slaves and prostitutes. "It is arguable that similar assumptions may have prevailed in Jewish society, but restricted to heterosexual relations, though there were voices warning of the dangers of engaging prostitutes."[4]

James D.G. Dunn draws our attention to the following:

In the Greco-Roman world homosexuality was quite common and even highly regarded, as is evident from Plato's Symposium and Plutarch's Lycurgus. It was a feature of social life, indulged in not least by the gods (e.g., Zeus' attraction to Ganymede) and emperors (e.g., Nero's seduction of free-born boys was soon to become notorious). The homosexual reputations of the women of Lesbos was well established long before Lucian made it the theme of his fifth Dialogue of the Courtesans (second century A. D.)[5]

Nevertheless, "Roman law rejected same-sex intercourse among its citizens (and also intercourse with unmarried women citizens) as a criminal sexual act and despised it as a Greek disease."[6] Dunn comments that the description of same sex tendencies in vv.26-27 "is a characteristic expression of Jewish antipathy toward the practice of homosexuality so prevalent in the Greco-Roman world."[7] And Paul's remarks concerning the giving up of "natural" (heterosexual) intercourse (1:26-27) in favour of "unnatural" (1:26) understands homosexuality as a violation of the natural order.[8] Here Paul emphasizes a clear distinction of Jews from gentiles.

The Greek term παρὰ φύσιν (against nature) has particular reference to sexual relations such as pederasty. But abhorrence of homosexual practice as such is particularly Jewish. The word φύσις is not a Hebrew concept. "The concept is primarily Greek, typically Stoic - to live in harmony with the natural order and its divine rationality being the Stoic ideal."[9] According to Greek philosophy, sex is primarily meant for procreation and any kind of sexual act that lacks procreation is unnatural. For Philo sexual intercourse which is not for the purpose of procreation is contrary to nature.[10] Philo understands nature as a divinely created order. For Paul as for Philo nature is a creation and its order, God's order. For procreation, heterosexual consummation was deemed as inevitable. Josephus also holds similar idea that the only place for sexual intercourse is the natural union of man and woman and only for the procreation of children. For him, "Same-sex relations do not procreate and they are unnatural in the sense of being abhorrent to the (heterosexual) beholders. In addition effeminacy rates as shameful for a man, because it makes him less than a man."[11] The viewpoints of Philo and Josephus clearly exhibit hellenistic Jewish homophobic approach to same-sex relations. Dunn reiterates that

> *Homosexual practice is characterized with the emphasis of repetition as "unnatural," where Paul uses very Greek and particularly Stoic language to broaden the appeal of the more characteristically Jewish rejection of homosexuality, and where he in effect appeals to his own reader's common sense to recognize that homosexual practice is violation of the natural order (as determined by God).*[12]

Charles D. Myers Jr. slightly differs from Dunn in denoting the free will and mutual involvement that

Paul's choice of the active verbs, "exchanged" (1:26) and "giving up" (1:27) assumes that homosexuality is an activity freely chosen. Paul's use of the phrase "consumed with passion" (1:27) reveals the belief that homosexual behaviour is associated with insatiable lust and unbridled passion. [13]

The phrase ἐξεκαύθησανἐντῇὀρέξει αὐτῶνεἰςἀλλήονς (burned in their lustful passion to one another) in v.27 indicates that their passions were mutually attested to one another. When Paul refers to same sex relations between women in v.26 in the words αἵ τεγὰρθήλειαι αὐτῶνετήλλαθξαν τήνφνσικήνχρῆσινεἰςτήν παρὰφύσιν, what is natural intercourse is intercourse with the opposite sex and what is contrary to nature refers to same sex relations between women. Female to female eroticism was more widely condemned in the Greco-Roman world than male erotocism.[14] When Paul refers to same-sex relations between males in 1:27, using the phrase "leaving the natural intercourse of women" (τὴνφνσικὴνχρῆσιντῆςθηλείας) what is intended is vaginal intercourse and when he writes literally of "males in males" (ἄρσενεςἐνἄρσεσιν), the reference is most likely to anal intercourse.

As du Toit observes, in Paul three lines converge:

> what the normal, heterosexual majority of his readers, on account of their own sexual orientation, would regard as natural, then "what the conservatives in the Greco-Roman world, as represented by their moralists, would view as 'natural'" and thirdly "and decisive would be conformity to the will of God. ...for Paul the decisive indication of what would be 'natural' is the man-woman relationship as ordained by God, the creator … the term 'unnatural' is here, at the deepest level, a theological judgment.[15]

Interestingly enough, Paul does not term this unnatural act as sin. William Loader cites William Countryman that

> Paul concedes that same-sex acts are seen by Jews as dirty practices, reflected in his use of the word, ἀκαθαρσα "impurity" in 1,24, but does not condemn them morally. "While Paul wrote of same gender sexual acts as being unclean, dishonourable, improper, and 'over against nature,' he did not apply his extensive vocabulary for sin to them. It was not in itself sinful, but had been visited upon Gentile culture". He concedes that Paul "is no doubt looking askance at it here", but the target of his condemnation is not same sex relations but idolatry and the sins listed in 1,29-31. It is because of these that God handed people over to engage in same sex relations. Thus he reads πεπληρωμένινς (1,29) as "having been filled", indicating

that Paul refers to people's sins only in response to which God let people be dirtied by unclean actions. Engaging in same sex relations is "unnatural" in the sense that it is in "notable discontinuity from what would previously have been expected", but is not itself sin.[16]

"Paul may have had in mind hypocrisy among some Roman Stoics who promulgated self-discipline and restraint of passions, condemning same sex relations, while at the same time engaging in them with their students."[17] As Jewell suggests, Paul may refer to homosexual acts in an imperial household as in the case of Nero.[18] Elliot alludes to a similar imperial background by referring to Caligula's death- he was stabbed through his genitals.[19] Therefore, it becomes dubious to pass judgment by the word play of τὴνφυσικὴν and παρὰφύσιν upon the wilful and mutual same-sex acts in Rom 1:26-27.

Conclusion

The Bible is a book of its own times, in the sense that, it deals with faith expressions and socio-cultural contexts of a group of people of a particular time in history. A contemporary topic such as queer identity may not find a direct links to the Bible for the kind of support it expects from religion as such. However, a liberation oriented reading of the Bible may help us to understand how inadequate it would be to do a literal reading of the passages that deal with homophobia in the Bible. The passage that is exegeted from the book of Romans, in this paper is a model one. The overarching biblical principles of love and justice may help us to find the various sympathetic and empathetic readings of the Bible in favour of queer persons. The fact remains true that the Bible provides sufficient amount of pointers to queer agents and advocates to formulate theological articulations.

Endnotes

[1] See http://genderqueerid.com/gq-terms viewed on 12th September 2016.

[2] Robert E.Goss and Deborah Krause cited by Susannah Cornwall, *Sex and Uncertainty in the Body of Christ. Intersex Conditions and Christian Theology* (London: Equinox, 2010), 200.

[3] William Loader, *The New Testament on Sexuality* (Grand Rapids: Eardman, 2013), 83.

[4] Loader, *The New Testament on Sexuality*, 90-91.

[5] James D. G. Dunn, *Word Biblical Commentary Volume 38A Romans 1-8* (Dallas, Texas: Word Books, 1988),65.

[6] Loader, *The New Testament on Sexuality*, 86.

[7] Dunn, *Romans 1-8*,74.

[8] Charles D. Myers, Jr., "Epistle to the Romans," in *The Anchor Bible dictionary, Volume 5*, edited by David Noel Freedman and others (Doubleday: New York), 827.

[9] Dunn, *Romans 1-8*, 64.

[10] William Loader in his book *Philo, Josephus and the Testaments on sexuality. Attitudes towards Sexuality in the Writings of Philo and Josephus and in the Testaments of the Twelve Patriarchs* (Grand Rapids: William B. Eerdmans Publishing Company, 2011) deals extensively with Philo on sexuality in the first century. See pp. 204-216.

[11] Loader, *Philo, Josephus and the Testaments on sexuality*, 354.

[12] Dunn, *Romans 1-8*, p.74.

[13] Myers, Jr., *Epistle to the Romans*, 827.

[14] Brooten cited by Loader, *Reading Romans 1 on Homosexuality* , p.17.

[15] duToit cited by Loader, *Reading Romans 1 on Homosexuality* , 15.

[16] L. William Countryman, *Dirt, Greed, and Sex: Sexual Ethics in the New Testament and Their Implications for Today*, Minneapolis, 2007 cited by Loader, *Reading Romans 1 on Homosexuality* , 1.

[17] Swancutt cited by Loader, *Reading Romans 1 on Homosexuality*, 3

[18] Jewell cited by Loader, *Reading Romans 1 on Homosexuality*, p. 3.

[19] Elliott cited by Loader, *Reading Romans 1 on Homosexuality*, p. 3.

Towards a Liberative Christian Sexual Ethics

Rethinking Body and Gender, Sexuality and Sexual Differences

Ronald Lalthanmawia

Sexual Orientation

Sexual orientation refers to the sex of those to whom one is sexually and romantically attracted.[1] Sexual orientation refers to an enduring pattern of emotional, romantic and/or sexual attractions to men, women or both sexes. Sexual orientation also refers to a person's sense of identity based on those attractions, related behaviours and membership in a community of others who share those attractions. The terms 'lesbian' and 'gay' are used to refer to people who experience attraction to members of the same sex, and the term 'bisexual' describe people who experience attraction to members of both sexes. Sexual orientation is distinct from other components of sex and gender, including biological sex (the anatomical, physiological and genetic characteristics associated with being male or female), gender identity (the psychological sense of being male or female) and social gender role (the cultural norms that define feminine and masculine behaviour).

A sexual orientation does not always appear in definable categories and, instead, occurs on a continuum and people perceived or described by others as Lesbian, Gay and Bisexual may identify in various ways.

Etiology and Mental Health Perspective

There is no consensus among scientists about the exact reasons that an individual develops a heterosexual, bisexual, gay or lesbian orientation. Although much research has examined the possible genetic, hormonal, developmental, social and cultural influences on sexual orientation, no findings have emerged that permit scientists to conclude that sexual orientation is determined by any particular factor or factors. Many think that nature and nurture both play complex roles; most people experience little or no sense of choice about their sexual orientation.

Research has found no inherent association between any of these sexual orientations and psychopathology. Both heterosexual behaviour and homosexual behaviour are normal aspects of human sexuality. Both have been documented in many different cultures and historical eras. Despite the persistence of stereotypes that portray lesbian, gay and bisexual people as disturbed, several decades of research and clinical experience have led all mainstream medical and mental health organizations in this country to conclude that these orientations represent normal forms of human experience. Lesbian, gay and bisexual relationships are normal forms of human bonding. Therefore, these mainstream organizations long ago abandoned classifications of homosexuality as a mental disorder.

In 1952, the American Psychiatric Association published its first edition of the Diagnostic and Statistical Manual (DSM-I), in which homosexuality was considered a "sociopathic personality disturbance." In DSM-II, published in 1968, homosexuality was reclassified as a "sexual deviation." However, in December 1973, the American Psychiatric Association's Board of Trustees voted to remove homosexuality from the DSM.[2]

It was only in 1992 that the World Health Organization (World Health Organization, 1992) removed "homosexuality" from the International Classification of Diseases (ICD-10), which still contains a diagnosis similar to "ego-dystonic homosexuality."[3]

Treatment related to Homosexuality and Bisexuality

All major national mental health organizations have officially expressed concerns about therapies promoted to modify sexual orientation. To date, there has been no scientifically adequate research to show that therapy aimed at changing sexual orientation (sometimes called reparative or conversion therapy) is safe or effective. Recent systematic review of the peer-reviewed journal literature on sexual orientation change efforts concluded that "efforts to change sexual orientation are unlikely to be successful and involve some risk of harm"[4]. Furthermore, it seems likely that the promotion of change therapies reinforces stereotypes and contributes to a negative climate for lesbian, gay and bisexual persons. This appears to be especially likely for lesbian, gay, and bisexual individuals who grow up in more conservative religious settings.

Helpful responses of a therapist treating an individual who is troubled about her or his same sex attractions include helping that person actively cope with social prejudices against homosexuality, successfully resolve issues associated with and resulting from internal conflicts, and actively lead a happy and satisfying life. Mental health professional organizations call on their members to respect a person's (client's) right to self-determination; be sensitive to the client's race, culture, ethnicity, age, gender, gender identity, sexual orientation, religion, socioeconomic status, language and disability status when working with that client; and eliminate biases based on these factors.

Sexual Orientation and Sexual Activity

The types of sexual activities performed often follow the sexual orientation of an individual. However, it is not unusual for heterosexual people to have some sexual experience with people of their own gender. Thus, for example a man who defines himself as having a heterosexual orientation may be attracted to other males (have "homoerotic" interests) and have sexual contact with men.

Heterosexual, bisexual and homosexual orientations often overlap, and Kinsey proposed a continuum of sexual orientation. However, this approach has been recently challenged, as it suggests that heterosexual and homosexuals are polar opposites. Some researchers have suggested that gay and heterosexual orientations are independent dimensions, thus one can be simultaneously high or low in both dimensions.[5]

Prevalence

Studies on sexual behaviour are subject to considerable methodological difficulties. In particular, people are often reluctant to reveal stigmatised thoughts and activities.

However, international research indicates the following approximate levels:

Males who identify as gay   3%
Females who identify as lesbians   2%
Sexual behaviour with own gender ever - UK males   8.4%
Sexual behaviour with own gender in past 5 years - UK males   2.6%
Sexual behaviour with own gender ever - UK females   9.7%
Sexual behaviour with own gender in past 5 years - UK females 2.6%

The Australian Study of Lifestyle and Relationships is the most comprehensive study to date addressing this question.[6] This study reports:

	Male	Female
Identify as gay	1.6%	0.8%
Report same sex sexual experience ever	6%	8.5%

Gender Identity

Sex is assigned at birth, refers to one's biological status as either male or female, and is associated primarily with physical attributes such as chromosomes, hormone prevalence, and external and internal anatomy.

Gender refers to the socially constructed roles, behaviours, activities, and attributes that a given society considers appropriate for boys and men or girls and women. These influence the ways that people act, interact, and feel about themselves. While aspects of biological sex are similar across different cultures, aspects of gender may differ.

The term transsexual refers to people whose gender identity is different from their assigned sex. Often, transsexual people alter or wish to alter their bodies through hormones, surgery, and other means to make their bodies as congruent as possible with their gender identities. This process of transition through medical intervention is often referred to as sex or gender reassignment, but more recently is also referred to as gender affirmation.

People who were assigned female, but identify and live as male and alter or wish to alter their bodies through medical intervention to more closely resemble their gender identity are known as transsexual men or transmen (also known as female-to-male or FTM). Conversely, people who were assigned male, but identify and live as female and alter or wish to alter their bodies through medical intervention to more closely resemble their gender identity is known as transsexual women or transwomen (also known as male-to-female or MTF). Some individuals who transition from one gender to another prefer to be referred to as a man or a woman, rather than as transgender.

People who cross-dress wear clothing that is traditionally or stereotypically worn by another gender in their culture. They vary in how completely they cross-dress, from one article of clothing to fully cross-dressing. Those who cross-dress are usually comfortable with their assigned sex and do not wish to change it. Cross-dressing is a form of gender expression and is not necessarily tied to erotic activity. Cross-dressing is not indicative of sexual orientation.

The diversity of transgender expression and experiences argues against any simple or unitary explanation. Many experts believe that biological factors such as genetic influences and prenatal hormone levels, early experiences and later adolescence experiences or adulthood may all contribute to the development of transgender identities.

Gender Identity and Sexual Orientation

Gender identity and sexual orientation are not the same. Sexual orientation refers to an individual's enduring physical, romantic, and/or emotional attraction to another person, whereas gender identity refers to one's internal sense of being male, female, or something else. Transgender people may be straight, lesbian, gay, bisexual, or asexual, just as non-transgender people. Some recent research has shown that a change or a new exploration period in partner attraction may occur during the process of transition. However, transgender people usually remain as attached to loved ones after transition as they were before transition. Transgender people usually label their sexual orientation using their gender as a reference. For example, a transgender woman, or a person who is assigned male at birth and transitions to female, who is attracted to other women would be identified as a lesbian or gay woman. Likewise, a transgender man, or a person who is assigned female at birth and transitions to male who is attracted to other men would be identified as a gay man.

Gender Identification

The term 'transgender' is sometimes used to refer to someone whose identity or behaviour falls outside the stereotypical gender norm. The terms 'male to female' (MTF) and 'female to male' (FTM) transgendered persons are used to refer to individuals who have undergone a process of gender affirmation.

Transgender people experience their transgender identity in a variety of ways and may become aware of their transgender identity at any age. Some can trace their transgender identities and feelings back to their earliest memories. They may have vague feelings of "not fitting in" with people of their assigned sex or specific wishes to be something other than their assigned sex. Others become aware of their transgender identities or begin to explore and experience gender-nonconforming attitudes and behaviours during adolescence or much later in life. Some embrace their transgender feelings, while others struggle with feelings of shame or confusion. Those who transition later in life may have struggled to fit in adequately as their assigned sex only to later face dissatisfaction with their lives. Some transgender people, transsexuals in particular experience intense dissatisfaction with their sex assigned at birth, physical sex characteristics, or the gender role associated with that sex. These individuals often seek gender-affirming treatments[7].

A psychological state is considered a mental disorder only if it causes significant distress or disability. Many transgender people do not experience their gender as distressing or disabling, which implies that identifying as transgender does not constitute a mental disorder. For these individuals, the significant problem is finding affordable resources, such as counseling, hormone therapy, medical procedures and the social support necessary to freely express their gender identity and minimize discrimination. Many other obstacles may lead to distress, including a lack of acceptance within society, direct or indirect experiences with discrimination, or assault. These experiences may lead many transgender people to suffer from anxiety, depression or related disorders at higher rates than non-transgender persons.

Transsexualism is a relatively rare phenomenon. An exact prevalence data is not available, partly because of the lack of a good, verifiable definition. The best data suggest that:

Definition	Proportion of general male population	Proportion of general female population
Those identifying strongly as an opposite-gendered individual	1 in 11,000	1 in 30,000
Those seeking gender reassignment surgery	1 in 30,000	1 in 100,000

Interventions

Hormonal Therapy

Oestrogen therapy

In progressively higher doses in MTF transsexuals. This results in:

- Reduced hair growth on the face & body
- Some breast tenderness & growth
- Decreased libido
- Testicular shrinkage
- Decreased muscle strength
- Less aggressive behaviour.

Anti-androgens (cyproterone acetate) is also sometimes used.

Side effects are relatively uncommon & people are monitored every 6-12 months

Androgen injections (testosterone)

Is used in progressively higher doses for FTM transsexuals. This results in:

- Facial andbodily hair
- Male pattern baldness
- Deepening of the voice
- Enlargement of the clitoris
- Redistribution of body fat

- Increased muscle strength
- Increased libido
- Cessation of menstruation

Surgery

This is essentially an irreversible step and so is only contemplated after thorough psychological preparation. It is usually preceded by many months living in the new gender role. Surgical techniques are highly specialized and are still evolving. The aim is to enable the transsexual to live more fully as their preferred gender, and to function sexually in that role. Procedures have now been developed to enable the construction of functional vaginas & creation of a penis.

Most people who undergo gender re-assignment are much happier and can participate more fully in society.

Terminologies

- **Asexual:** A person who generally does not feel sexual attraction or desire to any group of people. Asexuality is not the same as celibacy.

- **Bisexual**: A person who is attracted to both people of their own gender and another gender

- **Gay**: A person who is attracted primarily to members of the same sex. Although it can be used for any sex (e.g. gay man, gay woman, gay person), "lesbian" is sometimes the preferred term for women who are attracted to women.

- **Gender expression**: A term which refers to the way in which we each manifest masculinity or femininity. It is usually an extension of our "gender identity," our innate sense of being male, female.

- **Gender identity**:The sense of "being" male, female, gender queer, agender. For some people, gender identity is in accord with the physical anatomy.

- **Heterosexual**: A person who is only attracted to members of the opposite sex.

- **Homosexual**: A clinical term for people who are attracted to members of the same sex.

- **Homophobia**: A range of negative attitudes and feelings toward homosexuality or people who are identified or perceived as being lesbian, gay, bisexual or transgender (LGBT).

- **Intersex:** A person whose sexual anatomy or chromosomes do not fit with the traditional markers of "female" and "male."

- **Lesbian**: A woman who is primarily attracted to other women

- **Queer**: An umbrella term sometimes used by LGBTQA people to refer to the entire LGBT community.

- **Questioning:** For some, the process of exploring and discovering one's own sexual orientation, gender identity, or gender expression.

- **Pansexual:** A person who experiences sexual, romantic, physical, and/or spiritual attraction for members of all gender identities/expressions, not just people who fit into the standard gender binary (i.e. men and women).

- **Sexual orientation**: The type of sexual, romantic, and/or physical attraction someone feels toward others.

- **Transgender**: This term has many definitions. It is frequently used as an umbrella term to refer to all people who do not identify with their assigned gender at birth or the binary gender system.

- **Transphobia**: The fear or hatred of transgender people or gender non-conforming behaviour.

- **Transsexual**: A person whose gender identity is different from their biological sex, who may undergo medical treatments to change their biological sex, often times to align it with their gender identity, or they may live their lives as another sex.

- **Transvestitism:** Transvestism is a fetish in which a person repeatedly cross-dresses to achieve sexual arousal or gratification

Endnotes

[1] American Psychological Association (2012). Guidelines for psychological practice with lesbian, gay, and bisexual clients. Am. Psychol. 67 10–42. 10.1037/a0024659.

[2] Spitzer R. L. (1981). The diagnostic status of homosexuality in the DSM-III: a reformulation of the issues. *Am. J. Psychiatry* 138 210–215. 10.1176/ajp.138.2.210.

[3] Cochran S., Drescher J., Kismödi E., Giami A., García-Moreno C., Atalla E., et al. (2014). Proposed declassification of disease categories related to sexual orientation in the international statistical classification of diseases and related health problems (ICD-11). Bull. World Health Organ. Bull. 92 672–679. 10.2471/BLT.14.135541 [PMC free article].

[4] American Psychological Association (2009b). Report of the American Psychological Association Task Force on Appropriate Therapeutic Responses to Sexual Orientation. Available at: *https://www.apa.org/pi/lgbt/resources/therapeutic-response.pdf*.

[5] Storms MD Theories of sexual orientation. Journal of Personality & Social Psychology 1980;38:783-92.

[6] Smith A et al Aust & NZ Journal of Public Health 2003; 27(2):138-45.

[7] Sue D. W. (2010). Microaggressions in Everyday Life: Race, Gender, and Sexual Orientation. Hoboken, N.J: Wiley.

Queer Ethics

Arvind Theodore

Introduction

What is the need to talk about sexual ethics or queer ethics? Why is there a need for us to conduct an ethical enquiry about sexuality? While such questions are unsurprising, there are a number of reasons as to why we must talk about sexuality. First, we are all sexual beings as sexuality is a fundamental aspect of our personhood. Being sexual beings that we are, it is normal to talk about sexuality. Secondly, for most Christians the mention of sex or sexuality brings to mind images of sexual sin or sexual prohibitions, as sin is conveniently defined in sexual terms. In more ways than one, we tend to cringe at the mention of sexuality. Hence, sexuality is moralized and morality is sexualized. Thirdly, because of the moralization of sexuality and sexualisation of morality, sexuality finds itself to be in a crisis. But what is this crisis? As Marvin M. Ellison puts it, "The crisis of sexuality is… (the) highly negative attitudes about sex, the human body, women, and other marginalized people […] pornography industry, pervasive patterns of sexual assault and abuse, the ordinaries of antigay/ antilesbian violence […]"[1] The crisis of sexuality can also be observed in eroticizing dominant/subordinate social relations, valorising gender roles, and distorting love and desire by casteism, racism, sexism and other forms of injustices. While this crisis forms and determines the social world around us, wecannot help but concede that the social world in turn shapes and regulates sexual morality. This sexual morality, however, is fraught with problems as it aims at controlling bodies and desires.

Having established this background, this paper will elaborate on the need to conduct an ethical enquiry about sexuality and the need for queer sexual ethics. It will further address what sexual ethics and queer ethics are and then delineate certain fundamental propositions of queer sexual ethics.

Sexuality and Ethics

It is important that one addresses these questions: What does ethics have to do with sexuality? Can ethical reflections on sexuality be of any help? Speaking on sexual ethics, Elizabeth Stuart and Adrian Thatcher in their book, *People of Passion: What the Churches teach about Sex*, differentiate morality from ethics. This is significant. To them morality, which comes from the Greek word *mores* means a custom or a way of life which, in a restricted sense, describes people's behaviour – right or wrong conduct. With or without our knowledge, a lot of customs (those related to sex and sexuality) are presented as products of (Christian) morality. But morality cannot be confined to the personal domain alone; it has social, economic, political and environmental implications.[2] Ethics,which comes from the Greek word *ethos*, implies a critical reflection on assumptions, justifications, consequences and explanations offered that has a moral dimension.[3] Ethics reflects critically on morality itself, thereby making ethics a reflective task. As Enrique Dussel points out that morality denotes the prevailing system while ethics reflects the oppressed community's future order of liberation.[4] Since the LGBTIQ[5] persons are not merely located at the peripheries of the society but also of our consciousness,their desire and hope for liberation are often ignored completely or deemed "immoral" by the morality of the prevailing order. But the oppressed community's yearning for liberation includes an ethically critical and reflective task of the dominant morality. Hence, for those who have been victimized by an imperious sexual morality that the Church proudly holds on to, the only way for them to make sense of their oppressive past, present and hope-filled future is by treading on the path of ethics. Perhaps that is why Anthony Weston categorically states that people come to ethics to live life meaningfully.[6]

Sexual Ethics

Sexual ethic is an ethic that relates to community and personal standards of conduct in interpersonal relations, sexual relations, issues of power and consent, and how individual behaviour aspects impacts society.[7]Quite contrary to what most of us would expect, sexual ethics does not seek to provide answers and solutions to issues surrounding sexuality, but rather seeks to remove confusions and clarify issues by being viable, sustainable, and life-affirming.[8] Elizabeth Stuart and Adrian Thatcher opine that a sexual ethic takes into consideration the wider social and political contexts and can be applied to all people no matter who they are in a relationship with.[9] The two also observe that sexual ethics cannot ignore the body – its sensations, desires, ecstasies, and pains – nor can it colonize and desexualize it. To Marvin M. Ellison sexual ethics critiques outmoded assumptions on sex, gender, family and sexual difference, and argues that sexual sin has more to do with issues of power rather than sex itself.[10] It espouses principles of human freedom, friendship, intimacy, love, goodness of a human body, sensual joy, and uniqueness of the human person and personal conscience.[11]

Sexual ethics is imperative because of the need for just love and just sex. The traditional Christian ethical framework on sexuality is outmoded and insufficient as it governs bodies and idolizes libidinal sexual repression.It rests on the understanding of sexuality, body and desire that stands in contrast to that of contemporary times. Therefore, to speak of sexual ethics today is to have an ethic that is based on the principles of love and justice (embodying freedom and relationality) and one that is built on the modern understanding of sexuality, sex and gender.

Defining Queer

Over the decades the term queer has become popular and hence has been used as a prefix to methodologies, theologies, ethics, theories, and scientific studies. Traditionally, the term has been used in a negative way. Often interpreted as "strange," "odd," "peculiar," "to spoil" and so forth, the term was hurled as an insult at one who didn't fit in.[12] Finding the term offensive, the queer community began to subvert and define it by what it rejected, using it as a sign of pride, representing their desires and interests.[13] Queer, if personified, is a person who stands in opposition to fixed normative sexual and gender categories and the dominant hetero-patriarchal culture. If used as a methodological approach, it questions the existence of and disembowels social normative claims, hierarchies, and power relations.As Theodore W. Jennings states, "… the term "queer"" does have a certain utility in expanding the horizons of inquiry with respect to marginalized sexualities."[14]

Queer Ethics

When one speaks of sexual ethics, the general notion is that it concerns only a certain group of people, namely the heterosexuals, thereby ignoring the sexualities of non-heterosexuals. Moreover a circular look at (traditional) sexual ethics suggests to us that they are products of arrogant male heterosexual reason. Therefore, there is a need for a sexual ethic that allows respectable space for each sex, body and flesh to inhabit and that, according to Luce Irigaray, can be done only when sexual ethics is 'queered.'[15] So, queer ethics brings to light issues concerning the sexuality of the queers, addressing their sexuality not as something inferior or an alternate version of sexuality, but rather as a variant expression of sexuality demanding equal attention and 'status.' Such an ethic affirms diversity in voices, identities, and practices (open marriage, sex work, kinky sex and so on), and grants a certain privilege to the sexualities, perspectives, and experiences of the wider queer community.[16]

Propositions of Queer Ethics

Jennings in his book, *An Ethic of Queer Sex: Principles and Improvisations*, lists out few ethical themes of queer ethics that are important for our consideration. Three of his themes will be briefly mentioned while I add two more to the list in order to help us understand the foundational propositions of queer ethics.

The first theme Jennings mentions is, "Justice and Mercy as Meaning of Love of Neighbour." With justice being one of the foremost principles when it comes to ethics *per se*, it is no surprise that the concept of justice has become foundational for queer ethics as well. Jennings states that queer ethics should be committed to going beyond feelings to a pattern of action. When Jesus spoke of loving the neighbour and enemy, he invoked as a correlative ethical guide the prophetic call of justice and mercy.[17] The concepts of justice and mercy would draw us to be attentive to the vulnerabilities of all individuals, particularly the sexual minorities. This implies that the welfare and dignity of all are pivotal. On the same lines, Ellison adds that only an ethic founded on the principle of justice (and mercy) would honour the goodness of bodies; pay gratitude to diversities (age, gender, sexual orientation and so forth); espouse concern for the sexually abused, exploited, and violated; and, lay emphasis on accountability.[18]

When sexuality is looked through the lens of justice issues of power, sexual hierarchies, and sex-negativity can be ethically and critically looked at. And when that is done the moral nature of sexual acts, subordination of women, and queer phobia as justice issues become more perceptible and discernible.[19] When queer ethics is founded on the principle of justice, our understanding of sexuality will begin to reorient and remodel in accordance with justice-bound ethical principles.

The second theme is, "Improvisation rather than Rules." Many Christians argue that an ethic of sexuality has to prescribe certain fixed and non-negotiable codes that prohibit certain sexual acts. But to Jennings this is not the task of queer ethics. To him queer ethics goes beyond rules, regulations and prohibitionslooking for continual improvisation. It requires responsible freedom where each one's decisions will be responsible decisions and where there would be constant invention of ways to respond to people, issues, and contexts.[20] This is precisely what makes such an ethic to be constantly on the move and not remain stagnant. To have a closed ethic is to limit the mystery of sexuality itself. Miguel A. De La Torre opines that sexual ethics needs to keep changing.[21] And that is why any ethical system must be ever ready to meet the needs and challenges of societies and communities. To remain relevant queer ethics embodies the principle of improvisation.

The third theme that Jennings lists out is, "The Ethical and the Political." Speaking on the pitfalls of sexual ethics, Jennings asserts that sexual ethics has the tendency to focus only on the private, ignoring the public, thereby ignoring any form of activism towards the disenfranchised.[22] But all relationships and all peoples are set within contexts of sexism, racism, classism, ageism, casteism or some form of injustice. Queer ethics in being ethical must also be political - to advocate for the rights of the excluded. Social forces and institutions that perpetuate marginalization need to be contested. To be ethical one must be critical of the role law, politics and culture play in defining queer people and relegating certain expressions of sexuality to the base. Therefore, this ethic envisions the re-structuring of relationship models, re-ordering of communities and identities and re-visioning of sexuality within its contextual and relational challenges. To be ethical is to be political. Queer ethics is then both ethical and political.

The fourth theme added to the list is, "Significance of the Sexual Body." One of the main contributions of queer ethics is the recognition of the body, the sexual erotic body. While much was spoken and written on the creation of the body, disciplining the body, sanctifying the body, healing of the body, and death of the body throughout Christian history, the human body as a sexual body was less discussed and far from being affirmed. Too often the Church has treated the body as a source of problems (illness, disability, lust, violence, etc.) and not as a source of pleasure and sensuality.[23] If sexuality is a justice issue, violation of the body and denial of body right is an issue of sexual injustice.[24] Queer ethics accords power, in this case, "erotic power," to the body. Speaking of the eroticizing power of the body, Ellison states that this erotic energy is ethical when it is experienced between two bodies with a sense of freedom, respect, playfulness and intimacy.[25] It is important to allow individuals to discover their own means and ideas of the erotic through their bodily experiences and not normalize the power of the erotic. Queer ethics therefore resists the phenomenon of normalization of the body and allows the body to assume its potentialities as a sexual erotic body.

The fifth and final theme is, "Recognition of Sexual Diversity." What does sexual diversity mean? Does it mean diversity unlimited? Must we give blanket affirmation to all sexual practices? Certainly not! To affirm sexual diversity is to affirm sexual expressions that involve responsibility, consent, faithfulness, intimacy and safety. Jennings quotes Gayle Rubin where she asserts, "A democratic morality should judge sexual acts by the way partners treat one another, the level of mutual consideration, the presence or absence of coercion, and the quantity and quality of the pleasures they provide."[26] Therefore, one cannot condone sexual expressions if it betrays rights of sexual minorities, women and children. That being said, it is important for us to understand that sexual variation is not a perversion of sexuality; sexual homogenization is. We must realize that each person is different to the other and that each person is sexually attracted by different things, to different persons, by different means and for different reasons. Hence, queer ethics provides enough space for discovery, wonder, celebration and affirmation of various expressions of sexuality. By resisting the homogenization of sexuality and normalization of heterosexuality, queer ethics quell the power of heteronormativity over human persons and relationships and makes the sexual expressions and experiences of all persons valid and telling.

Conclusion

The dominant understanding of sexuality has prevailed and infiltrated the minds of the common people, the laws of the state, and official statements of the Church. This surely needs change. The social and political power of ethics needs to be exercised to alter the power residing in the hetero-patriarchal systems. It is important to reiterate that we are living at a time when sexuality is being moralized and morality is being sexualized. We are living at a time when sexual injustice is on the rise. We are living at a time when sexual injusticeis taking place right next to us. Are we able to discern these injustices? The need to counter and challenge sexual injustice is imperative. Queer ethics, in some sense, allows us to do that. It allows us to question the sex-negativity within faith communities and belief systems; it allows us to recognize the spiritual and divine power of sexuality; it allows us to affirm the body in all its sensations and experiences; it allows us to regard and respect diversities in sexualities; and it allows us to view and understand sexuality within its social, economic and political contexts.

Endnotes

[1] Marvin M. Ellison, *Erotic Justice: A Liberation Ethic of Sexuality* (Kentucky: Westminster John Knox Press, 1996), 16.

[2] Elizabeth Stuart and Adrian Thatcher, *People of Passion: What the Churches teach about Sex* (London: Mowbray, 1997), 26.

[3] Hunter P. Mabry, "What is Christian Ethics?" in *Christian Ethics - An Introductory Reader*, ed. Hunter P. Mabry (Delhi: ISPCK, 2013), 213.

[4] Enrique Dussel, *Ethics and Community*, trans. by Robert R. Barr (New York: Orbis Books, 1986), 28.

[5] LGBTIQ is the acronym for Lesbian, Gay, Bisexual, Transgender, Intersex and Queer. *Lesbian* is a woman who is sexually attracted to another woman. *Gay* is a man who is sexually attracted to another man. *Bisexual* is a person who is sexually attracted to both a woman and a man. A bisexual is also known as "bi." *Transgender* is a person whose self-identified gender does not match the sex assigned at birth. *Intersex* is a person who has characteristics or genitalia of both the sexes. *Queer* is

used as an umbrella term for LGBTI and is often also used to refer to an ethical norm of transgressing sexual and gender binaries. "Q" also stands for *Questioning* referring to those individuals who are unsure of or are still exploring their own sexual orientation and/or gender identity. See, Eva Apelqvist, *LGBTQ Families: The Ultimate Teen Guide* (Plymouth: Scarecrow Press, Inc., 2013), 8-9.

[6] Anthony Weston, *A Practical Companion to Ethics*, 3rd ed. (New York: Oxford University Press, 2006), 2. Ethics also becomes a process by which the marginalized communities overcome oppressive or controlling societal mechanisms. See, Miguel A. De La Torre, *Doing Christian Ethics from the Margins* (New York: Orbis Books, 2014), 21.

[7] Presbyterian Church of Aotearoa New Zealand, *Sexual Ethics* (Wellington: Presbyterian Church of Aotearoa New Zealand), 5.

[8] *http://www.iep.utm.edu/sexualit/#H13* (accessed June 26, 2017).

[9] Elizabeth Stuart and Adrian Thatcher, *People of Passion…*, 191.

[10] Marvin M. Ellison, *Making Love Just: Sexual Ethics for Perplexing Times* (Minneapolis: Fortress Press, 2012), 3.

[11] Kevin T. Kelly, *New Directions in Sexual Ethics: Moral Theology and the Challenge of AIDS* (London: Geoffrey Chapman, 1998), 139.

[12] Gerard Loughlin, "Introduction: End of Sex," in *Queer Theology: Rethinking the Western Body*, ed. Gerard Loughlin (Victoria: Blackwell Publishing, 2007), 7.

[13] Gerard Loughlin, "Introduction: End of Sex," in *Queer Theology: Rethinking the Western Body*, 8.

[14] Theodore W. Jennings, Jr., *An Ethic of Queer Sex: Principles and* Improvisations (Illinois: Exploration Press, 2013), 14.

[15] Luce Irigaray, *An Ethic of Sexual Difference*, trans. Carolyn Burke and Gillian C. Gill (New York: Cornell University Press, 1993), 18.

[16] Theodore W. Jennings, Jr., *An Ethic of Queer Sex: Principles and Improvisations*, 193.

[17] Theodore W. Jennings, Jr., *An Ethic of Queer Sex: Principles and* Improvisations, 200.

[18] Marvin M. Ellison, *Making Love Just: Sexual Ethics for Perplexing Times*, 33.

[19] Lisa Sowle Cahill, "Sexuality and Christian Ethics: How to Proceed," in *Sexuality and the Sacred: Sources for Theological Reflection*, eds. James B. Nelson and Sandra P. Longfellow (Kentucky: Westminster/John Knox Press, 1994), 25.

[20] Theodore W. Jennings, Jr., *An Ethic of Queer Sex: Principles and* Improvisations, 201.

²¹ Miguel A. De La Torre, *A Lily among the Thorns: Imagining a New Christian Sexuality* (San Francisco: John Wiley & Sons, 2007), 73.

²² Theodore W. Jennings, Jr., *An Ethic of Queer Sex: Principles and* Improvisations, 201.

²³ Davina Cooper, "Speaking beyond thinking: Citizenship, governance and lesbian and gay politics," in *Sexuality and the Law: Feminist Engagements,* ed. Vanessa E. Munro and Carl F. Stychin (New York: Routledge-Cavendish, 2007), 184.

²⁴ Marvin M. Ellison, *Erotic Justice: A Liberation Ethic of Sexuality*(Kentucky: Westminster John Knox Press, 1996), 40.

²⁵ Marvin M. Ellison, *Erotic Justice: A Liberation Ethic of Sexuality,* 80.

²⁶ Gayle Rubin, "Thinking Sex: Notes for a Radical Theory of the Politics of Sexuality," in *Pleasure and Danger: Exploring Female Sexuality,* ed. Carole S. Vance (Boston: Routledge & K. Paul, 1984), 15, quoted in Theodore W. Jennings, Jr., *An Ethic of Queer Sex,*17.

Just Love: Constructing a New Framework of Christian Sexual Ethics

Miak Siew

The conventional framework of Christian sexual ethics today is simple - sex is only ethical within the confines of marriage. Few people question this framework, even though many Christians have been known toviolate this bond. This absolutist approach is often presented in churches today, and any further investigation and discussion are cut off. Those who differ, suggesting other approaches, are often accused of moral relativism. There is just no room to talk about sex in the church other than prohibitions. Christian sexual ethics is often limited to prescriptive or normative ethics. Even more concerning is together with the exporting of United States' "culture war" along with the spread of the Evangelical Christianity globally that one's stand on sexual ethics becomes a litmus test whether one is a "true Christian," regardless whether one practices what one professes.

On the other hand, the secular moral approach to sexual ethics – that sex acts between consenting adults in private, barring a few exceptions, should be nobody else's business – is also inadequate, given that this approach of reasoning often fails to consider the constellations of relationships we are embedded in, and the impact of our actions – be it sexual or otherwise – go far beyond our personal and private realms.

Neither the conventional framework of Christian sexual ethics nor the secular moral approach to sexual ethics is adequate today. We desperately need to revisit and rethink our frameworks of Christian sexual ethics today so that instead of parading around the conventional framework of sexual ethics that is out of touch with modern times, we find ways of constructing ethical frameworks that are just, loving, appropriate and life-giving.

In the past half a century, many Christian ethicists and theologians have offered new perspectives on Christian sexual ethics. Margaret Farley writes, "Theology, too, has offered important insights regarding human sexuality and behaviour. Some of this work in North America began among Christian theologians in the 1960s with the Roman Catholic debate on artificial contraception. Soon after, significant publications by Anthony Kosnik and his colleagues in the Roman Catholic tradition, and James Nelson in the Protestant traditions, marked the start of a whole new era for Christian sexual ethics. The contributions of Charles Curran, André Guindon, Philip Keane, Giles Milhaven, Lisa Sowie Cahill, Beverly Wildling Harrison, Carter Heyward, Christine Gudorf, and many others have been invaluable in the search for sexual understanding within Christian communities. Biblical scholars have joined with theologians in attempting to interpret the tradition. Phyllis Trible, Mary Rose D'Angelo, William Countryman, Robin Scroggs, Richard Hays, and Dale Martin, among others, have provided approaches to exegesis and interpretation important for questions of sexual ethics. Jewish theologians, too, have provided significant studies on many of the same issues. Writers such as Eugene Borowitz, David Feldman, David Novak, Judith Plaskow, David Biale, and Elliott Dorff, have critically engaged the questions of sex and sexuality in ways of immense importance for the Jewish community and beyond."[1]

In the course of my ministry as a gay pastor, I have found several books very helpful in critically examining, deconstructing and reconstructing frameworks of Christian sexual ethics – L. William Countryman's *Dirt Greed and Sex: Sexual Ethics in the New Testament and Their Implications for Today*,[2] Margaret A. *Farley's Just Love: A Framework for Christian Sexual Ethics*,[3] Mark D. Jordan's *The Ethics of Sex*,[4] Marvin M. Ellison's *Making Love Just: Sexual Ethics for Perplexing Time*[5] and *Sexuality and the Sacred: Sources for Theological Reflection*.

Margaret Farley states that her book "does not aim to provide a complete or specifically comprehensive sexual ethic" but rather include "some of the elements for a comprehensive sexual ethic."[6] Likewise, in this article, I hope to address two questions — why a new framework of Christian sexual ethics is needed, and how do we construct such a framework. It is important to help individuals learn to examine for themselves the issues and considerations involved sexual ethics, so they can learn the spirit of the law, instead of just obeying the law.MarvinEllison argues that "any ethical guide about human sexuality worth its salt should assist readers in making sense of a broad range of sexual issues and also help them generate effective action responses."[7]

Basis for the conventional framework of sexual ethics

Not only is the conventional framework of sexual ethics inadequate in addressing our realities today, how this framework is derived also needs to be critically examined. What ethical principles lie behind this framework? Are these principles still valid in today's world?

A.   Purity & pollution

William Countryman proposes purity as a dominant theme in how Scripture addresses sexual morality. He states that "all regulations dealing with human sexual activity… are related to purity ethics, since they deal with the body's boundaries." He argues that the principle of purity's"particular affinity for sexual rules tends to mislead us in our reading of other aspects of sexual ethics."[8] Countryman draws from Mary Douglas' argument that "dirt can be understood only in relation to a system that excludes it." Dirt, according to Douglas, is essentially disorder and "the old definition of dirt as matter out of place."[9] Countryman notes "a system that divides clean from dirty is a way of understanding and defining what it is to be human — or, more specifically, what it is to belong to a particular human group that so defines purity.[10] Purity is about maintaining clear boundaries between categories based on assumptions about the created order of things. The prohibitions against interbreeding of different kinds of cattle, sowing fields with two kinds of seeds and wearing garments made of mixed materials in Leviticus 19:19 come from the same emphasis on purity — that is about order, about how everything must be in place instead of being out of place. Likewise, arguments against same-sex acts and relationships that draw from the account of the creation of humankind in Genesis is based on assumptions on how things are to be ordered.

Just as the prohibitions found in Leviticus 18 which begins with the instruction, "You shall not do as they do in the land of Egypt, where you lived, and you shall not do as they do in the land of Canaan, to which I am bringing you" is about distinguishing the Jewish people from the other people in that time, the "culture war" today on the issues of same-sex marriage and LGBTQ inclusion in churches is about distinguishing "true" Christians from the rest. One's stand on these issues has become a litmus test of belonging and allegiance to the Christian faith.

Is purity an important principle in constructing a new framework of sexual ethics? After all, we now largely ignore concerns with impurity with regards to prohibitions with regards to intercourse with a menstruating woman (Leviticus 18:19, 20:18). I would argue that there are other more important principles that require our attention.

Countryman highlights that the genealogy of Jesus in the beginning of the Gospel according to Matthew is radical in its inclusion of four women who share with one another two disreputable qualities: all four were Gentile and all four were involved in some kind of violation of the sexual codes." They were Tamar, the Canaanite woman who pretended to be a prostitute to trick her father-in-law Judah into having sex with her so that she could beget a son in the name of her deceased husband; Rahab, the Canaanite woman who aided the Israelite spies in Jericho; Ruth the Moabites, who initiated sexual relations with Boaz so that he can be the kinsman-redeemer for her mother-in-law Naomi and herself; Bathsheba, who was referred to as "the wife of Uriah," which Countryman argues "underlines the act of adultery by which David first took her."[11] What does their inclusion in Jesus' genealogy mean?

B.   Private Sexual Property

The other dominant principle that governed sexual morality in early Christian communities was the idea of private sexual property. Countryman writes "on the whole, however, Christians held firmly to the notion of private sexual property and made this the foundation for constructing their sexual ethic. If impurity or dirtiness no longer served to define sexual sin, greed, the desire to have more than one's own fair share of goods did."[12] Women and children were seen as the property of the patriarch and our modern understanding of marriage is very different from the understanding in the ancient Mediterranean world. Countryman points out that "Biblical Hebrew and ancient Greek felt no need, it seems, to make the distinction between "woman" and "wife"" and "marriage was not equivalent to a blood relationship, though it did alienate a woman to some degree from her own blood kin. The Torah gives a good illustration of the ambiguity involved, in the form of restrictions imposed upon priests in the matter of mourning. A priest is allowed to mourn only for members of his immediate family, and this included neither his wife nor his married sister (Lev.21:1-4)."[13] Hence, adultery was seen as a crime against sexual property – the concern here is the patrilineage –the legitimacy of heirs and the purity of the family line. Countryman's close examination of the laws against incest reveals that incest is less about inbreeding than it is about property and hierarchy – "the language makes clear that the incest was an offence not so much against the woman violated as against her husband."[14] The absence of any explicit prohibition against intercourse between a man and his daughter is odd especially when the code is very detailed and Countryman suggests that this may be "because a patriarch had to be recognized as owning the female members of his household, so that in some sense this would be an exercise of his rights."[15]

This idea of sexual property is preserved to this day even though it may not be obvious. The National Council of Churches of Singapore has not issued any statement in response to the review of reviewing the issue of marital immunity for rape in Singapore and the silence is disturbing. The counselling supervisor and coordinator of Grace Counselling Centre, Kirby Chua, said in an interview that "as a Christian counsellor, he was himself "very torn" about how he felt about abolishing the marital immunity for rape because marriage was a "sacred sacrament" to him.[16] Chua's view, whether he realises it or not, is not so much about the sacredness of marriage but the rather the patriarchal nature of marriage. The basis of marital immunity for rape is property – the wife is the property of her husband. We need to revisit the conventional framework of sexual ethics that sex is only ethical within the confines of marriage again because sex can be unethical even in the confines of marriage.

Most of us would be familiar with the order of service for a heterosexual marriage. What we may not realise is that this idea of sexual property is also preserved in the liturgy when the woman is given by a male, usually the patriarch, from the woman's family to the groom.[17] While most Christians in the modern context no longer see marriage the transfer of property of one male to another, the hetero-patriarchal roots of marriage are still obvious. It is imperative that we recognise the patriarchal systems that undergird the conventional framework of sexual ethics today.

Instead of seeing marriage as a transfer of sexual property, most of us would view marriage as a mutual ownership as the couple are asked as part of the liturgy if they will have each other as their spouse and live together in the covenant of marriage. They would "belong" to each other, and are called to be "faithful" to each other and we see this as fidelity. How do we understand fidelity? Rabbi Richard Address' article "Is it still adultery if the spouse has Alzheimer's?"[18] exposes the complexity we find ourselves in that cannot be easily moralised. Address shares, "a healthy spouse – let's call her Sarah – caring for her husband, who is restricted to an Alzheimer's facility. Sarah must deal with the extended institutionalisation of her spouse. She cares for him with love and dignity, but also feels that he is not really her spouse." Address concludes his article stating, "we are once again confronted with the challenge of having our religion adapt to new realities. It is an opportunity to teach our values in unprecedented ways and to let our values speak to the realities of an ever-expanding life.How do we tease out how we understand fidelity in our context today as we deconstruct and reconstruct Christian sexual ethicsfor people who are married and people who are single?

Just Love as a new framework of Christian sexual ethics

In 1991, the Special Committee on Human Sexuality, "Keeping Body and Soul Together: Sexuality, Spirituality, and Social Justice," the Presbyterian Church of the United States of America (PCUSA) published the report *"Presbyterians and Human Sexuality."* Although PCUSA did not adopt the report in their 203rd General Assembly, it serves as a helpful reference as we discuss a new framework of Christian sexual ethics.

The report elaborates:

"As James B. Nelson notes, "One of the basic challenges to church and synagogue… is to change the sexual hegemony of the nuclear family and the resulting temptation to police the sexuality of everyone who does not fit that mould." Coming of age requires us to recognize and honour the

rich variety of family patterns which persons construct to meet their needs
for intimacy and interpersonal communication.

At the same time, the church also needs to confront its own myopia and
exclusivism in sacralising one form of family. "In doing so," Nelson
observes, "we have elevated a relative historical (and bourgeois) social
structure to ultimacy, and we have enforced a sexual model which excludes
and devalues countless persons."

It is vital that a constructive reformation of Christian sexual ethics
happen. The report argues that "traditionally, sexual ethics have focused
on questions of the form rather than the substance of sexual relationships.
Preoccupation with form, however, has led to an unfortunate neglect of
some rather fundamental ethical considerations." Like what I have noted
earlier in the silence of the National Council of Churches of Singapore
in response to the review of reviewing the issue of marital immunity for
rape in Singapore, the report notes that "very important questions about
the presence or absence of mutual consent, respect, and commitment in
sexual relations, as well as the distribution of power, have been downplayed
or simply ignored."[19]

Ellison points of that the report "takes a pro-sex, feminist, and gay-
affirming stance and offers a radically different ethical framework about
sex and sexuality" and "it provides an alternative perspective by mapping
out a progressive Christian ethic of sexuality grounded in the central
affirmation that "a gracious God delight[s] in our sexuality and call[s] us
to wholeness in the community." A life of holiness manifests itself in the
promotion of human well-being and justice in the community. Faithfulness
is exemplified in an ongoing commitment to embody justice-love in all
connections. "Such love, such justice, such passion for right-relatedness,"
the report affirms, "seeks to correct distorted relations between persons
and groups and to generate relations of shared respect, shared power, and
shared responsibility."[20]

How do we work out a new framework of Christian sexual ethics?

At the heart of Christian ethics, I believe, are the two commandments
that Jesus said are the foundation of all the law and the prophets in Matthew
22:37-40. How do we interpret as loving God and loving our neighbour
in the context of Christian sexual ethics then?

Just love emerges as the empathic answer – a love that does not objectify the beloved, a love that does not coerce, a love that is not romanticised or distorted, a love that is vulnerable, a love that is about intimacy and connection. Karen Lebacqzwrites "sexuality is therefore a form of vulnerability and is to be valued as such. Sex, eros, passion are antidotes to the human sin of wanting to be in control or to have power over another." She argues that "the desire to have power over, or control over another is a hardening of heart against vulnerability. When Adam and Eve chose power, they lost their appropriate vulnerability and were set against each other in their sexuality. Loss of vulnerability is paradigmatic of the fall. Jesus shows the way to redemption by choosing not power but vulnerability and relationship."[21]

The PCUSA report also calls for justice-love as the fundamental principle in its proposal for a new Christian sexual ethic. Ellison describes the five value commitments that undergird the reports' call for a justice-love social ethic as "(1) honouring the goodness of bodies and of sexuality, "our capacity to give as well as receive pleasure and comfort; and the power of intimacy to build mutual respect and well-being"; (2) gratitude for diversities of age, gender, sexual orientation, and so forth; (3) special concern for the sexually abused, exploited, and violated; and (4) accountability not only to our partners, but also in terms of the well-being of the whole community. A fifth commitment is distinctive to a liberatory ethical methodology: to learn from the marginalized, "those relegated to the underside of history, theology, and ministry [who] have unique angles of vision from which to estimate how faithful, just, and loving the church is in its internal life, as well as in its engagement with the culture.""[22]

Margaret Farleyalso proposes "just love" as key consideration in sexual ethics. She argues that "not all our loves are good, even though they are loves. There are wise loves and foolish, good loves and bad, true loves and mistaken ones. The question is ultimately, what is a right love, a good, just and true love?"[23] She concludes that "love is true and just, right and good, insofar as it is a true response to the reality of the beloved, a genuine union between the one who loves and the one who loved, and an accurate and adequate affective affirmation of the beloved."[24] From the basis of just love, Farley proposes seven norms for "a contemporary human and Christian sexual ethic." They are:

1. Do No Unjust Harm
2. Free Consent
3. Mutuality
4. Equality
5. Commitment
6. Fruitfulness
7. Social Justice[25]

At Free Community Church where I serve, we have adapted Farley's seven norms as well as included the eighth norm. We further elaborated on these norms.

1. Always Do No Harm – Our sexual behaviour must always do no harm to ourselves or our partner(s).

2. Always Honour Free Will and Consent – Our sexual acts and relationships must always honour a person's free will and understand that sex is only ever ethical when one's partner(s) is able to truly give free consent.

3. Value Mutuality – learn to give and to receive, not just one or the other but both.

4. Ensure Equality of Power in the sexual act and relationship, otherwise the sex is abusive or manipulative.

5. Be Committed and be Truly Intimate with the other in the sexual act and relationship

6. Be Enriching – good sex leaves the partner and the self with a sense of goodness and wholeness.

7. Sex must be Socially Just and Responsible – as strange as this may sound, sex must make our lives, the lives of our partners and the lives of our communities a better place.

8. Be Redemptive and Liberating – Our sexual acts and our sexual relationships should bring us, our partner(s) and our communities back closer to God's intentions for sex (including self-honesty and

authenticity, intimacy and acceptance by others, an outpouring of self for others, creativity and play, and spiritual development) and should be a freeing experience for us, our partner(s) and our communities.[26]

Similarly, the LGBT Catholic group Dignity USA cite seven values in sexual behaviour which promotes "creative growth and human integration" from the report, "Human Sexuality: New Directions in American Catholic Thought," a study commissioned by The Catholic Theological Society of America. Instead of statements, they have offered questions based on the values for reflection. They are:

1. Self-liberating: Does it express one's authentic self and wholesome self—interest as a source and means of growth toward maturity? Does it enslave the self with bonds of compulsion and selfishness?

2. Other-enriching: Does it express a generous interest in, and concern for, others' well-being? Does it coerce or violate another person or show cruelty?

3. Honest: Does it express the real relationship that exists? Does it seduce and manipulate behind a facade of pretence?

4. Faithful: Does it express a consistent pattern of interest and concern that can grow deeper and richer? Does it refuse to let intimacy grow?

5. Socially responsible: Does it express a realization of relationship to wider communities and of service to their interests? Does it contribute to an atmosphere of exploitation or depersonalization?

6. Life-serving: Does it express a willingness to share and promote life as well as fulfil one's own needs? Does it allow a relationship to become a mutual or shared selfishness?

7. Joyous: Does it express appreciation for the gift of life and the mystery of love? Does it weaken the other person's self-esteem or ability to enjoy sex and relationships? Does it weaken the other person's self-esteem or ability to enjoy sex and relationships?[27]

I have found these values extremely helpful in helping people construct a framework of sexual ethics that is authentic and life-giving, grounded in just love. Contrary to what many believe, instead of lowering the bar of morality, the new frameworks of Christian sexual ethics above call for more accountability, authenticity, reflexivity and commitment to work out for ourselves how our lives, relationships and sexual behaviours are just and loving and faithfully responding to the commandments to love God and to love our neighbours. It is not to give license or justification to do as we please, but, like what Ellison articulates succinctly, "to equip people with skills and insight for assessing the quality of their intimate (and other) relationships and for negotiating how their needs and the needs of others will be fairly met. A justice-centered ethical framework can, in fact, give pride of place to mutually shared pleasure, as well as responsible freedom, as moral resources and guides."[28]

Ellison compares ethics to art, stating that "ethics, like art, is about figuring out where to draw one's lines," and "sometimes the effort still goes awry. Whenever that happens, bad ethics, like bad art, must be critiqued, packed up and discarded. However, good ethics, like good art, requires public display and deserves wide public engagement because of its power to stimulate our imaginations and enrich community life."[29] Good art, I would add, challenges us to examine and re-examine ourselves, our circumstances and environments and our relationships.

Endnotes

[1] Margaret Farley, A. *Just Love: A Framework for Christian Sexual Ethics*. Reprinted. London: Continuum, 2012, p 9-11.

[2] Louis William Countryman, *Dirt Greed and Sex: Sexual Ethics in the New Testament and Their Implications for Today*, 1st pbk. ed (Philadelphia: Fortress Press, 1990).

[3] Margaret Farley, Margaret A. *Just Love: A Framework for Christian Sexual Ethics*, (Reprinted, London: Continuum, 2012).

[4] Mark D. Jordan, *The Ethics of Sex*, New Dimensions to Religious Ethics (Oxford, UK/ ; Malden, Mass: Blackwell Publishers, 2002).

[5] Marvin Mahan Ellison, *Making Love Just: Sexual Ethics for Perplexing Times* (Minneapolis, Minn: Fortress Press, 2012).

[6] Margaret A. Farley, *Just Love: A Framework for Christian Sexual Ethics*, Reprinted (London: Continuum, 2012), 16.Farley, *Just Love*, 16.

[7] Ellison, *Making Love Just*, 2.

[8] Countryman, *Dirt Greed and Sex*, 11.

[9] Mary Douglas, *Purity and Danger: An Analysis of Concepts of Pollution and Taboo*, Collected Works, Mary Douglas; Vol. 2 (London: Routledge, 2003), 12.

[10] Countryman, *Dirt Greed and Sex*, 12–13.

[11] Countryman, *Dirt Greed and Sex*, 90–91.

[12] Countryman, *Dirt Greed and Sex*, 148.

[13] Countryman, *Dirt Greed and Sex*, 151.

[14] Countryman, *Dirt Greed and Sex*, 161.

[15] Countryman, *Dirt Greed and Sex*, 162.

[16] Melissa Zhu, "Behind Closed Doors: Rape and Marriage in Singapore," *Channel NewsAsia*, http://www.channelnewsasia.com/news/singapore/behind-closed-doors-rape-and-marriage-in-singapore-7931028   accessed on August 20, 2016.

[17] Episcopal Church, ed., *The Book of Common Prayer and Administration of the Sacraments and Other Rites and Ceremonies of the Church: Together with the Psalter or Psalms of David According to the Use of the Episcopal Church* (New York/ : [Greenwich, Conn.]: Church Hymnal Corp./ ; Seabury Press, 1979), 424.

[18] Richard Address, "Is It Still Adultery If the Spouse Has Alzheimer's? – The Forward,", http://forward.com/opinion/11387/is-it-still-adultery-if-the-spouse-has-alzheimer-0030/ accessed on May 12, 2017.

[19] "Presbyterians and Human Sexuality 1991," Report of Special Committee on Human Sexuality, Presbyterian Church USA, (Louisville: Presbyterian Church USA, n.d.), 19.

[20] Ellison, *Making Love Just*, 32.

[21] Karen Lebacqz, "Appropriate Vulnerability." In *Sexuality and the Sacred: Sources for Theological Reflection*, edited by James B Nelson and Sandra P Longfellow, 1st ed. Louisville, Kentucky: Westminster/John Knox Press, 1994, p 259.

[22] Marvin M. Ellison, *Making Love Just*, p32–33.

[23] Farley, *Just Love*, p196–97.

[24] Farley, *Just Love*, 198.

[25] Farley, *Just Love*, 216–32.

[26] Free Community Church, "Christian Sexual Ethics,", http://www.freecomchurch.org/christian-sexual-ethics/ accessed June 17, 2017.

[27] Dignity USA, "Sexual Ethics," 2017, https://www.dignityusa.org/book/sexual-ethics-experience-growth-and-challenge/sexual-ethics,   accessed June 17.

[28] Ellison, *Making Love Just*, 71.

[29] Ellison, *Making Love Just*, 2.

Marriage and Family –
The Traditional View

Phanenmo Kath

INTRODUCTION

Marriage and family in the Bible refer to a covenant, a sacred bond between man and woman instituted by and publically entered into before God. A central feature of all human societies is an institution composed of a culturally accepted union of a man and a woman in husband-wife relationship as well as roles that recognize an order of sexual behaviour and legalize the function of parenthood. The most modern definition tends also toward a dynamic description of marriage as process [1] or as companionship.

A family is the very first cell in the social structure, the very first social bonding. Without family, there exist no children or human society of this nature. It is said, "As the families are, so be - humankind". [2] "A family comprises of people living together in an environment, which can be a centre of healing where one can open up frustrations, confess stupidities, and express anger without anyone retaliating." Here one can be oneself without make-believe.[3] Family plays a very important role in the holistic development of individuals and through them the transformation of society. A family that prays together stays together. What contributes to the strength of the family is the right relationship it holds.[4]

A family provides the initial learning experiences that make one genuinely a human, and moulds children into ideal people. Children grow in an atmosphere of security and affection, and material attributes replace true love and concerns of parents. Home is the place where the others in the family understand us. Family is the focus of the social, political, psychological and religious spheres of our lives. Families have always been the wellsprings of strength and stability to the society. God has planned the human race with a mysterious chemistry which draws two volatile people to each other, the fusion of temperaments and the fascinating biology necessary for building up a home. There is nothing on earth that can substitute the rich relationship which is nurtured inside the family.[5]

A family is an institution that plays a major role in exerting influence in the attitude, personality and - behaviour of its members. Hence the responsibility of the family in the context or environment for the growth and development of the members cannot be overlooked.[6] The family is conceptualized as a system of interconnected relationships whereby the quality of the relationship between spouses is-likened to the quality of care parents provides their offspring and vice-versa.[7] "Our existence commences in the family. The family is where life begins and love never ends. Families are the heart and soul of human society." Family also constitute the basic social unit, basic sexual unit, the basic child-raising unit, the basic communication unit, and the basic all-around fun and friendship unit."[8] These relationships are special because they both form and express an individual's identity and character.

1.   FAMILY

Family is a group of persons united by the ties of marriage, blood or adoption, constituting a single household; interacting and intercommunicating with each other in their respective social positions of husband and wife, mother and father, son and daughter, brother and sister, and creating and maintaining the common culture. It is a group of the community living together, sharing and having mutual understanding, love, care, respect, and creating and maintaining common culture.[9] There are many types of families in modern society – traditional two-parent families, single-parent families, couples without children, three-generation families, gay family, etc.[10]

The family is a social organism, or system. The term 'organism' connotes the biological core of the family, its qualities of a living process and functional unity, and its natural life history. Whatever affects one part of the family organism automatically affects all parts, just as an infected, injured, or well-functioning hand influences the entire body. It is one of the oldest primary social institutions, which keep on changing throughout the changing time and place.[11]

The family is the garden of human personality – the primary place where persons are formed, deformed, and transformed. Parents are the architects of family. Thus, marriage and family counselling and enrichment can focus a healing, growing light on the very roots of personal health and illness. The family is a social system of primary relationships from which individuals derive their major sources of psychological and spiritual nurture. A loving, mutually nurturing family is a place of emotional nourishment and spiritual renewal- an interpersonal garden where mutual growth is nurtured.

John Bowring said, "A happy family is but an earlier heaven." Michael J. Fox said, "Family is not an important thing, it's everything." And Mother Teresa said, "What can you do to promote world peace? Go home and love your family." And it was Albert Einstein who said, "Rejoice with your family in the beautiful land of life!"[12]

The family, as a social institution, is being challenged by several contemporary crises. All families have their own problems. Present day family is going through a period of transition from a traditional way of life to a techno-conscious way of life. There is a trend towards removal from the family of the traditional functions of work, religious worship, the nursing of the sick, and education.[13]

We also recognize the greater mobility of the family, the tendency to family breakdown, the rise in divorce, the change in sexual morality. The instability of the family is characterized by the downgrading of the authority of parents, a trend toward -egalitarianism in the relation between male and female, the parental uncertainty of roles and responsibilities; decline in the importance of grandparents; and the irresponsibility of children. It seems that people are unsure of what their family stands for- its strivings, standards, and values. Mother, father, and children each perceive differently what the family is or ought to be.[14] Therefore, there is an urgent need for pastoral care and counselling for the families in present day context.

2.   BIBLICAL CONCEPT OF MARRIAGE

The Christian concept of marriage is based on the teachings of the Bible. In the Old Testament, marriage is expressed through words of actions like 'take (*lakah*) a wife' (Gen. 24:2, 67, Hos. 1:2), 'covenant' (Jer. 2:13) 'go in' (Gen. 16:2) and *yada* (knowing intimately-Gen 4:1). The frequently used expression for marriage is 'taking a wife' which implies arrangement with the family of the girl that their daughter can be taken as a wife for another man and not stealing or driving her by force. The New Testament uses the Greek term *gamous* (meaning 'marriage -Jn. 2:1) and it became the root word for English monogamy or polygamy.

3.   NATURE OF BIBLICAL MARRIAGE

The various texts in the Bible give us some important theological aspects of marriage as pointed out below and challenge Christians to follow the teachings of the Bible when they plan out a Marriage.

1. Marriage is Instituted by God

God the creator does not want - man to be alone in the Garden of Eden. He cannot relate meaningfully with the animals and plants. He needs another human being to relate, interact and share his views, joys and sorrows. God's plan for Adam is expressed by the words, "It is not good for the man to be alone. I will make a helper suitable for him" (Gen. 2:18). Since living alone' can mean loneliness, the view of the creator emphasizes living in relation with other avoiding individualism. This concern of living in families and thus making a wider community is expressed in different parts of the Bible (e.g. Eccl. 4: 9-12).

2.   The Permanence of Marriage

Marriage is intended to be permanent since it was established by God. Matthew 19:6, Mark 10:9). Marriage represents a serious commitment that should not be entered into lightly or unadvisedly. It involves a solemn promise or pledge, not merely to one's marriage partner before God and among the witnesses of the host of believers.

3.   The Sacredness of Marriage

Marriage is not merely a human agreement between two consenting individuals (a civil union) it is a relationship with God (Gen. 2:22) under whose authority a covenantal pledge and vow is made. The marital relationship between husband and wife is therefore considered as holy and pure, as it has God's sanction with promise for blessed life.

4. The Intimacy of Marriage

Marriage is the most intimate of all human relationships, uniting a man and woman in "one Flesh" union (Gen 2:22-23). Marriage involves leaving one's family or origin and being united to one's spouse, which signifies the establishment of a new family unit-distinct from the two originating families. Uniting of two new kinship relationships between two pure unrelated individuals by the most intimate of human bonds.

5. Marriage is a Joint Responsibility

In creating and uniting Adam and Eve, God has given them a joint responsibility. God told both of them to till the ground and keep it (Gen. 2:15). This command indicates a joint responsibility for humanity in developing and taking care of the creation. However, man is given a basic responsibility to support the family by earning and working on the ground to produce food for the family. Family on the other hand, has a biological function of conceiving - and raising children. Each of their roles is valuable and needed for the family and society.

The differences in gender role need not be used for gender inequality and discrimination. Rather husband and wife should complement each other through their various contributions to the family.

CONTEMPORARY TRENDS IN MARRIAGE

There are certain issues concerning the religious principles and traditions of marriage. An age old traditional practice- which existed for centuries is been challenged among today's generation. while many of our youth believe that marriage is between a man and a woman, a lot of changes have come in the way they select the bride or groom, their preference of gender (Man to man or woman to woman) as they arrange their marriage.

1. Arranged Marriage-Consent and conversation

In India, 80% of the marriages are arranged by the parents for their sons and daughters. Usually families ask their relatives or brokers to collect details of the bride and groom and pay the brokers some commission if the selection and dowry deals work out satisfactory. With the modern communication facilities, families have turned to use matrimony columns in newspapers, TV and internet dot coms. But the way the marriage is arranged is slowly changing due to increasing travel, economic opportunity and globalization. In the previous decades, the sons or daughter had to accept the selected partner for their wedding without seeing the partner or talking to him or her.

Whatever their parents and elders do, they had to simply accept and marry that person whether he or she is suitable or not. The values in this kind of arranged marriages are to maintain caste and dowry system, agricultural land, property, and income. But today, the literacy and awareness about human rights are increasing among girls and they want to have a say in their marriage. Some boys and girls want to know each other before giving their consent.

2.   Extra Marital Affairs and Separation

Having extra marital affairs by a married person with another man or woman is not new to Indian society. But this is increasing today because of the influence of mass media particularly TV serials and commercial advertisements . As society is getting more modernized and secularized, some people irrespective of age indulge in developing a relationship with the other sex outside their marital bond. Other reasons for this trend are loneliness of the spouse, lack of love and concern from the spouse, the need for an extra income from the other partner, and alienation of husband or wife from the spouse for the sake of job in other countries or states. The authority and roles of families and churches are challenged to intensify their teaching, counselling and guidance to youths and married couples.

Reflection and Conclusion

Change is the only constant in the world today, and it is happening at an increasing pace in Indian society. Many inventions and discoveries in the fields of science and technology, facilitation of education for all, advancement in the information technology and mass media, acceptance of democratic ideals- all have had a tremendous influence on marriage and family life in India. Accordingly, age-old-notions and values regarding marriage has undergone a sea change.

Thus efforts must be made to enable young men and women to meet life with more adequate knowledge and resources, especially with regard to the establishment and maintenance of their own marriage and family.

Endnotes

[1] Carl Ransom, Rogers, The necessary and sufficient conditions of therapeutic personality change. *Journal of Consulting and Clinical Psychology*, 21: 1957. 95-103.

[2] Simon, K.V., *Family God's Design and Destiny*: Hyderabad Authentic Book. 2009, 11.

[3] Mascarenhas, Marie Mignon, *Family Life Education: Value Education*. Bangalore: Centre for Research Education and Training for Family Life Promotion. 1993, 17.

[4] Isaac, Mar Philoxenos, *Family God's Design and Destiny*, edited by Simon, K.V, Hyderabad Authentic Book. 2009, Forward Page.

[5] Simon, K.V., *Family God's Design and Destiny*: Hyderabad Authentic Book. 2009, 17.

[6] Stuart, T. Hauser, *Adolescent and Their Families*, New York: The Free Press 1991, 17).

[7] Deborah, B. Jocobvitz and Nell F. Bush, Reconstruction of Family Relationship: Parent-Child Alliances, Personal Distress and self-Esteem" *Developmental Psychology*, Vol. 32, No. 4.732-743, 1996.

[8] Kath, Phanenmo, *The Impact of Select Correlates on Naga Family System: Implications for Family Counselling Models*. D.Th Unpublished Thesis, Kottayam: FFRRC, 2014, 19-20.

[9] B.C., Rai, 1998, *Sociological Foundation of Education*. Lucknow: Prakashan Kendra,1998, 185).

[10] Mishra, G., "Reflection on Continuity and Changes in the Indian Family System." in *Trends in Social Research*, 2 (1), 1995, (27-30).

[11] Mascarenhas, Marie Mignon, *Family Life Education: Value Education*. Bangalore: Centre for Research Education and Training for Family Life Promotion. 1993, 19.

[12] Kath, Phanenmo, *The Impact of Select Correlates on Naga Family System: Implications for Family Counselling Models*. D.Th Unpublished Thesis, Kottayam: FFRRC, 2014, 21.

[13] George, Joseph, "The Changing Pattern of Family in India. Exploration in Postmodern Age" in *Ripples*. 1/1, 2008, (11-19).

[14] Jacob, P. Thomas, "Steward in Family" in *Christian Family in Transition: Continuity and Discontinuity*, Edited by Koshy P. Varughese, Faridabad: Dharma Joyti Peeth, 2012, 9.

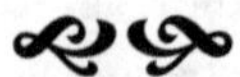

A Response to Kath's Traditional View on Marriage and Family

Miak Siew

While I do not challenge the importance of family in society today, I do not fully agree with Phanenmo Kath's perspectives on marriage and family. Dale Martin warns that "identification of anything but God at the centre of Christian faith is idolatry" and "contemporary Christianity in the United States – whether Protestant or Catholic, liberal or conservative – has so closely aligned the basic message of Christianity with the family and "traditional family values" that it is in a state of idolatry. Martin states, "though most Christians assume that the current centrality of marriage and family represents a long tradition in Christianity, it is actually only about 150 years old. One could even make the argument that the current focus on the heterosexual nuclear family dates back only to the 1950s."[1]Martin highlights "how wrong modern Christians are when they claim that their own ideology, and idolatry, of the family, is simply "the biblical" or "the traditional" position." It is important to understand that the high valuation of marriage and the family runs counter to the teachings of Jesus, authors of the Gospels, Paul, and other biblical writers, as well as most of the church "fathers," popes and saints... In fact, there are more resources in Scripture and tradition to critique marriage and the family rather than support it."[2]

Jesus himself, as Martin points out, "refused to identify with his traditional family and instead substituted for it the eschatological community that shared his vision of a new, divinely constituted family."[3]

Jesus asks "who is my mother and who are my brothers?... Whoever does the will of God, that one is my brother and sister and mother" (Mark 3:33-35; cf Matt. 12:46-50; Luke 8:19-21). Martin states "all our Gospels present Jesus as creating and living within an alternative to the household: an itinerant group of men and women unrelated to one another by blood or marriage, most of whom had also apparently separated from their families. Jesus called his disciples away from their households. Although perhaps teaching the commandment to honour one's parents should still be obeyed (the evidence is either non existent or inconclusive), he told one man not even to bury his father – a teaching that would have been perceived as an incredible and offensive affront to family values in ancient Palestine (Luke 9:59-60, Matt. 8:21-22). In another saying, passed on by Luke, Jesus says, "If anyone comes to me and does not despise [or hate: *miseo*] his own father and mother and wife and children and brothers and sisters, and yes his own life, he is not able to be my disciple" (Luke 14:26).[4]

Marriage was not accorded the same level of importance and significance as Kath suggests. It is important to highlight that Kath's suggestion that marriage is instituted by God is tenuous at best. There is no Hebrew word for wife. The Hebrew word *ishshah* often translated as "wife" in Gen 2:24 is the same word translated as "woman" in Gen 2:22 and Gen 2:23. We need to find the historical influences that shape this translation that now become the "evidence" for the divine sanction of marriage. Marriage in Biblical times has been about the transfer of property as women then were considered chattel – they were the property of the patriarch of the family, usually their fathers. Marriage then was the transfer of ownership from the patriarch of the woman's family to her husband.

The Apostle Paul believed that "marriage was something of a concession to human frailty, to save from fornication those who could not be content, so it was better to marry than burn with lust."(1 Cor 7:8-9).[5] It would be hard to argue that Paul would consider marriage to be divinely sanctioned.

While many Christians regard marriage as a sacrament today, no Christian wedding ceremony existed before 1000CE and marriage was not an ecclesial matter. Even the Protestant Reformers, including Martin Luther, "rejected the scriptural basis for declaring marriage a sacrament" based on the scholarship of Valla and Erasmus, stating that "mystery" is a better translation of the term in Eph 5:32.[6] What was the Church's changing attitude towards marriage?

The Church's interest in regulating marriage, Diarmaid MacCulloch suggests, could be the Church's "wish to see property left to churches rather than a large range of possible heirs in the family." He points out "the more limits placed on legal marriage, the more chance there was of there being no legal heir, so that land and wealth would be left to the Church, for the greater glory of God." An alternative perspective Mac Culloch suggests for this new concern for marriage and its boundaries is that this is "another response to new arrangements which were emerging for land ownership in the eleventh-century society where landed estates were not broken up by the old custom of dividing the estate between the members of the family, but rather the emergence of primogeniture where "the eldest take all." This became widely established by the twelfth century, and the Church and its concern for legitimate marriage is seen by the nobility as being helpful to identify the true heir under the law of primogeniture. The Church's interest in regulating marriage also comes partly from "the loss of ecclesiastical estates to possession by families" as many clergy then who were not monks were married, and they "might therefore be inclined to make Church lands into hereditary property." This resulted in the declaration in the second council called at the Pope's residence in Rome, the Lateran Palace, in 1139 that declared all clerical marriages not only unlawful but invalid.[7]

I, like Martin, am concerned that "the modern emphasis on marriage and the nuclear family... fools people into thinking that the modern family can do what it cannot do. The modern family simply cannot bear the weight placed on it; it cannot deliver all the goods demanded of it, whether social, economic, emotional, or psychological. Conservatives and liberals who focus on the family, therefore, are allowing the state to shirk its own responsibilities. They are attempting to push off onto the fragile modern family the responsibilities that only the state in the modern world can really bear: for universal child care and education, health care, care for the elderly and disadvantaged."[8]

I would even go as far as suggest that the family is the source of dysfunction of many people today. All families are dysfunctional in some way – and it is the family that perpetuates the cycle of dysfunction as children inherit the brokenness and dysfunction of their elders. As Martin points out, Jesus "taught people to forsake those institutions and enter into an alternative, eschatological society. The household was part of the world order he was challenging. It, along with other institutions of power, would be destroyed with the coming kingdom. The household, moreover, represented traditional authority, which he was challenged at every turn. The household was implicated in the cycle of death. Indeed, the household, as the site of procreation, birth, and burial, was the very technology of life and death in the ancient world. For the historical Jesus, the rejection of marriage and the family was as necessary as the proclamation of the resurrection and the eternal kingdom of God."[9]

It is the Church, the Body of Christ, that is this eschatological society. It is the Church that is the new family – a people related not by blood, but by seeking and doing the will of God. The Church, too, can easily become an idol – it is by remembering to place God and God's will in the centre of what we do as Church that we avoid idolatry. At its best, the Church is the embodiment of this eschatological society that turns traditional authority upside down – where "the first shall the last, and the last shall be first." I find that echoed in Martin Luther King Jr.'s notion of the "Beloved Community" described by the King Center, the memorial institution founded by Coretta Scott King as"a global vision in which all people can share in the wealth of the earth. In the Beloved Community, poverty, hunger and homelessness will not be tolerated because international standards of human decency will not allow it. Racism and all forms of discrimination, bigotry and prejudice will be replaced by an all-inclusive spirit of sisterhood and brotherhood."[10]

There are certain issues concerning the religious principles and traditions of marriage. An age old traditional practice- which existed for centuries -has been challenged by today's generation. While many of our youth believe that marriage is between a man and a woman, a lot of changes have come in the way they select the bride or groom, their preference of gender (Man to man or woman to woman) –to arrange their marriage.

Endnotes

[1] Dale B Martin, *Sex and the Single Savior: Gender and Sexuality in Biblical Interpretation*, 1st ed (Louisville, Ky: Westminster John Knox Press, 2006), 103–4.

[2] Dale B Martin, *Sex and the Single Savior*, 122.

[3] Dale B Martin, *Sex and the Single Savior*, 106.

[4] Dale B Martin, *Sex and the Single Savior*, 104.

[5] DiarmaidMacCulloch, *Christianity: The First Three Thousand Years*, 1st American ed (New York: Viking, 2010), 119.

[6] Daniel Patte, ed., *The Cambridge Dictionary of Christianity* (Cambridge; New York: Cambridge University Press, 2010), 763.

[7] MacCulloch, *Christianity*, 372–73.

[8] Martin, *Sex and the Single Savior*, 123.

[9] Ibid., 106.

[10] Jeff Ritterman MD, "The Beloved Community: Martin Luther King Jr.'s Prescription for a Healthy Society," *Huffington Post*, January 19, 2014, http://www.huffingtonpost.com/jeffrey-ritterman/the-beloved-community-dr-_b_4583249.html.

Towards a Responsible and Life-giving Ministry in the Context of Sexual and Gender Diversities

A Biblical Response to Homophobia: Genesis 19:1-11

Rosy Zoramthangi Ralte

Abstract

One of the most hotly debated issues in the contemporary Christian and secular world is the subject that surrounds LGBTIQ. This pressing issue has been received with mixed feelings. There is an outright rejection and sometimes an expression of sensitivity towards them. All these diverse receptions find inspiration and clues from the Bible and from what God had said! The paper aims at challenging those prejudiced reading and interpretation of texts so as to break down prejudice reading, and use of the Bible.

Introduction

The Bible has been one of the most abused and (mis)quoted texts wherein people from all walks of life read and quote to suit their needs or support their cause. Titles like 'Texts of Terror,'[1] 'The Savage Text,'[2] 'Bible Trouble'[3] vividly portrays the many nuances in the use and abuse of the Bible in the past and present. As such, the Bible whose core message is liberation and salvation has been reduced to an intimidating text. In so doing, the Bible has been forced to become an instrument of oppression, text that validates and legitimate exclusion, violence and oppression.

Queer[4] Theory[5]/ Reading/ Interpretation

Two things become strikingly apparent when the Scriptures are studied for guidance on sexuality. One is how different the cultural and societal world of the Bible was from that of the contemporary world. The other is how infrequently issues that pertain to sexuality are mentioned in the Bible. With respect to the first difference, the very words used in the Scriptures often have meanings different from their current usage, if only because they refer to different institutions and different realities.[6] Gay spirituality, the acknowledgement that there are experiences of being gay, of being part of a gay community and culture, that can give rise to spirituality, deserves mention in this context. The often fraught relationship which homosexuals have had with institutional religion and the exclusion they have encountered left many feeling alienated by 'religion'.[7] The expression of this sexuality can be an attempt at transcendence, even self-transcendence.

With the many painful experiences of exclusion and isolation, Queer reading is the use of the libertine hermeneutical circle in an intertextual reading... searching for a way to read the Bible which will displace its heterosexual core in a deconstructionist fashion, the hermeneutical proposal is a libertine one. That is to say, it displaces the reader of the Bible to bedrooms, dungeons and other unusual locations which will enable her to have different and embodied points of view and perspectives.[8]

Negotiating LGBTIQ and the meaning making practice of the Bible

The reason reading Scripture involves issues of text (what God said) and reader (how we know what God said) is because like all reading, Scripture involves a transaction between God's word and the reader's ability to understand and apply that word. This is reiterated clearly in the words of Farnsworth who said, "Unlike the common assumption that the Bible just sits there like "pre-arranged alphabet soup," understood through an act of "immaculate perception."[9] Scriptural understanding actually involves an interactive process between the text and the cognitive and affective structures the reader brings to the text. This is not to say that God's word changes, but rather what changes the reader's ability to understand the text or accommodate the interpretive schemas to a more accurate understanding of the text. Reading involves the whole person of the reader, the personal experiences, cultural background, cognitive beliefs and presuppositions are all brought in, and this in turn makes the understanding of the text diverse.[10]

We find in scripture reading "a counter-'as' to the long accepted 'as' that is widely and uncritically accepted as objectively real" (and that, presumably, often goes under the name, "Christianity").[11] Likewise, human lives and social relationships are made possible and significant and effective, in other words, they are structured by the stories, ordinances, procedures, practices, signs, habits, and so on that create the shape, nuance, and possibility of our lives.[12] Much of the "as structure" of experience comes from the shape given life by these stories, ordinances, procedures, practices, signs, and habits.

To a large degree, we see the world as it is given to us by the society which we live in, as such meaning/s conveyed and how it is signified, is as important as the text itself to an individual reader or the community reading it. Thus, texts are no longer isolated but alive and communicative with the reader. To keep the text alive, there should be ample space for reading exercises, and if there is no space to signify the Scripture in the lived realities of an individual or the community the future of Scripture's transformative power is uncertain.

The history of LGBTIQ biblical interpretation can be traced through the preaching and scholarship that has taken place in Metropolitan Community Church (MCC), a denomination founded in 1968 by Rev. Troy Perry. In the MCC, the Bible has been read and interpreted consistently and intentionally in the classrooms and pulpits since its inception. Unlike other communities, the members of MCC have brought their particular life experiences to bear on reading and interpreting scripture in liberating ways for LGBTQ.

Over the years, the LGBTIQ biblical interpretation has moved from a defensive stance to an offensive stance. More recently LGBTIQ has moved toward embracing the Bible as a friendly text. It assumes that there is more to the Bible than silencing the clobber passages. It identifies texts that affirm same sex love and the goodness of human sexuality. The stories of Jonathan and David, Ruth and Naomi are often taken as examples of same sex love. The Song of Songs has been lifted up as a text that celebrates the joy of human sexuality which is not measured by marital or procreative status by challenging sex that does not procreate. Traditions and teachings like ancient rabbinic teaching[13] that condemn sexuality are also critically analysed. The first consideration is recognition that Judaism placed high value upon procreation as the visible fulfilment of the sexual relationship (Gen. 1:27-28; Ps. 127:3-5; Ps. 113:9; Prov. 17:6). To be without children and descendants was to experience leanness in God's favour, even disfavour (Gen. 16; 30:1-8). The corollary to this understanding of sex, Israel regarded man *and* woman as the highest gift of God's creation (Gen. 1:26-27; 2:18-24).[14] Thus for a man to spurn sexual relationship with a woman for homosexual relations was viewed as refusing God's treasured gift of creation and the blessing of offspring (cf. Rom. 1:18-29). A second consideration is that Israel (and the church) developed its morality in the context of its relationship with pagan nations.[15] The most important consideration is that the genius of the biblical message is not upon "classifying the vices" of humans, but in beckoning men and women into God's community of love, healing, and forgiveness.[16]

If the biblical condemnation of sex without procreation is to be taken seriously as a rule of exclusion for LGBTIQ community, then, the postmodern world where contraceptive measures are taken liberally would also fall under the 'immoral' category!

The Text in its Context 'Gen 19:1-14'

There are a handful of scriptures that are used against the LGBTIQ community to promote homophobia and violence. These texts are called 'clobber passages' because of the abusive way they have been used. Genesis 19 is regarded as one of the 'clobber passages', but it will be critically analysed from the literary, sociological, and theological perspective to identify whether it could be termed 'clobber passage'.

The stories narrated in Gen. 12-50 are put together to reflect Israel's faith. They are neither pure fiction nor pure history[17] but historicized prose fiction.[18] It contains four units: Gen 18:1-15, 18:16-33, 19:1-29, and 19:30-38.[19] The tradition of Lot and the evil city of Sodom: Genesis 18-19.1 is found within this block. These narrative blocks are told in such a way that they could become the story of each ensuing generation. The readers could participate in a great, yet often quite hidden drama of divine action and human response.[20] The custom of hospitality in Ancient West Asia (AWA) is presented in these two chapters of the Abraham narrative.

Chapter 18 and 19 records the visitation of Abraham and Lot by messengers, and the way hospitality is extended towards them.

The whole chapter is a continuation of Gen. 18, 'the men' in 18:16, 22 has become the 'angels/messengers' in 19:1, 15. The strange appearance of messengers was with a clear purpose; one is to promise a beginning 18:1-15, and to affect an ending 19:1-28.

The primary interests of the stories in Genesis and Judges is hospitality to strangers, an indispensable custom in the ancient world. Lot's offer of his two betrothed daughters as sexual objects for the citizens of Sodom suggests the extreme to which he will go to be hospitable, particularly under duress. While the story is interested in the code that enables foreigners to travel to distant lands, it treats homosexual rape, and does so most unapprovingly.[21] Another problem with the text according to Brueggemann is that it does not seem to belong to the historical narratives of Israel. It is more akin to the comprehensive statements about human history found in Gen 3-11, Lot is the only connection which has dictated its placement in the Abrahamic materials...its purpose and structure is to show the tension between the faith of Abraham and the waywardness of humanity.[22]

Verses 1-3 The messengers reached Sodom by the evening, which is likely the same day as in 18:1. *Malakim* is often translated as 'messengers' or 'angels' in reference to supernatural messengers.[23] The text stands as a clear parallel to the 'welcoming scene' of the 18:1-5 linking the two narratives. Narration of the confrontation between the city's men and Lot and his guests provides specificity to the evaluation of Genesis 18:20 and sets the stage for the anticipated cities' destruction.[24]

Verses 4-5 reveal the nature of Sodom's sins. Gen. 13:13 portrayed the Sodomites as "evil" and sinners"[25] but leave out neither detail explanation nor discussion of how and what kind of sin qualifies them as evil and sinners, likewise, the much-needed explanation is missing from these verses. If mention is not made of the exact sin committed that qualifies the Sodomite as evil and sin then why is this text generally quoted to condemn homosexuality? The problem of interpreting these verses rests heavily on the translation of the Hebrew word *ya'da*[26] (perceive, know) used in reference to the men of Sodom who demanded 'to know' Lot's guests. *Ya'da* manifests a rather broad semantic scope in the OT usage, its different usage indicates-[27]

a) A sensory awareness of objects and circumstances in one's environment attained through involvement with them and through the information of others.

b) To describe the recognition that results from the deliberate application of the senses, from investigation and testing, from consideration and reflection.

c) It indicates the knowledge that results from realisation, experience, and perception and that one can learn and transmit.

Besides these, *ya'da* also points to the knowledge of 'good and evil' in the context of decision making, sexual experiences, a legitimate or an illegitimate manifestation of sexuality. In some passages it describes sexual intercourse: a man with a woman (Gen. 4:1, 17, 24:16, 38:26; Judg. 19:25; I Sam 1:19; I Kgs. 1:4), woman with man (Gen. 19:8; Judg. 11:39), and homosexual intercourse (Gen. 19:5; Judg. 19:22).[28]

Verses 6-8 see Lot persuading and reasoning with the 'men' by using ploys.[29] First, he pleads them urgently saying, "My friends, don't do this wicked thing" emphasizing his brotherhood with the citizen of Sodom. Second, he offers his virgin daughters in place of his two guests and makes it appealing to the 'men' by pointing out his daughters' sexual innocence. Lastly, he argued that if they carry out such contemptible behaviour, it would be an appalling breach of hospitality.

Hospitality in the context of the AWA requires 'protection' and at Lot's invitation the strangers had received sanctuary 'under his roof,' violation of this custom would brand the city lawless. To be inhospitable was not only to be despicable but irreligious.[30] Lot, as portrayed in v.6, is most hospitable and very solicitous of his visitor's welfare and his attempt at persuading the men of Sodom picturised him as a man of no mean courage. True to the cardinal principle of Oriental (sic) hospitality that protecting your guests is a sacred duty, he bravely goes out to face the mob alone.[31] His acts of hospitality towards his guests did invite criticism especially from the feminist, as he offered the safety and protection of his guests at the cost of sacrificing his daughters. However, the main intention and emphasis of the text is 'Lot as a good host.'

Verses 10-11 reveal the scuffle between Lot and the mob. When Lot's attempt to persuade turned ugly and violent, the guests interfered on behalf of Lot and revealed their true nature by striking the men with sudden blindness. Wenham takes the action of the angels putting out their hand and brought Lot inside was no doubt an echo of Noah who took care of the dove. As Noah's power and wisdom exceeded the doves', so does angelic protection exceed human. The angelic act of striking the men with sudden blindness recurs in I Kings 6:18. The act of blinding or blindness does convey symbolic meaning, thus, physical blindness in this case may well refer to spiritual blindness.[32] The men of Sodom cannot see physically or spiritually where they are going, the same blindness is seen in Lot's sons-in-law. The men fumbling for their home in their blindness might be an indication of how deep rooted their sin was! Divine judgment often induced repentance but here in this narrative, it does not have the desired effect.

This narrative is relaying to us the retributive judgment of God, the role of Abraham, and how God remembered the Abrahamic covenant. Though Lot and Sodom figured prominently here, the main emphasis is on Abraham, the mediator. Abraham's presence may seem elusive, but he is still the hero.

Is Genesis 19 a Clobber Passage?

From the discussions on the text it is obvious that the interpretation process can take on a more general route or being embroiled in a divisive path. The choice we are confronted with is- are we going to make the scripture a 'text of terror' that alienates or a text that untie? The general understanding and interpretation of this passage always lean towards homophobia because most interpreters focussed solely on the interpretation of the word '*ya'da*' with its sexual reference. This type of closed and biased reading needs to be rectified.

In order to let the text speak inclusivity to a wide range of readers, the whole corpus needs to be taken into serious consideration as to recognize why and how the 'Lot's narrative' is inserted in the 'Abrahamic Narrative'. As Mathews has put, "the presentation of God as the One who honoured the promises made to Abraham, a picture of a hope that 'all people will be blessed."[33] This means that this narrative is still very much interested in presenting Abraham as the chosen One with whom the blessing of 'others' is rested. Critical glance at the narrative discloses that the main motif of the whole narrative do rest on the tradition of hospitality in Ancient West Asia, wherein 'Gods in disguise reward hospitality and punish inhospitality,'[34] thrived.

Boswell suggested that "the essential sin at Sodom was not homosexuality but a lack of hospitality, a virtue that was much valued then than today. Lot has violated custom at Sodom by entertaining foreign guests without permission of the city elders, and so they came, not wanting to 'know' the guests sexually but to know who they were."[35] This argument seems appropriate as the list of Sodom's sins given in Isaiah 1:10; 3:9; Jer. 23:14; Ezek 16:46-48 did not contain homosexuality. What is more challenging is the way how Jesus reflected on Sodom. Boswell claims that Jesus, who mentions Sodom in conjunction with the failure of cities to receive his disciples also interpreted this narrative as a lack of hospitality and that this story is at most tangentially related to sexuality.[36] If the offense of Sodom is understood with specific reference to sexuality, the turbulent mood could well "suggest gang-rape rather than a private act of either 'sodomy' or any specific sexual act."[37]

The Bible is silent regarding the particularization of Sodom's sin as homosexuality, and for this reason, there are so many varieties of conjecture revolving around the exact nature of 'Sodom's sin'. What the text did record is simply a general disorder of a society organized against God.[38] The use of the term "outcry" in 18:20-21 and 19:13 argues in the direction of a general abuse of Justice (Isa. 5:7 without any explicit indictment. Cf. Luke 10:8-12). It may be sexual disorder is one aspect of the general disorder but that issue is presented in a way scarcely pertinent to contemporary discussions of homosexuality.[39]

The Bible contains different types of literary devices, Gen 19 also contains **'hyperbole'** one of the most common and widely used literary device. In hyperbole, the writer or speaker exaggerates to create a strong effect.[40] Gen 19:4 presents a clear example and use of hyperbole. The text reads, "But before they lay down, **the men of the city, the men of Sodom, both young and old, all the people to the last man**, surrounded the house". As highlighted in the text, 'all'/'every' are used excessively to convey the totality of something in a positive or negative way. Is it possible to take these as it is? The practicality of the text is doubtful. Was Lot's house big enough to accommodate all the men of the city, men of Sodom, both young and old, all the people? Just by reading it without any proper reasoning, it is clear that it was impractical. To assemble all the men would require a big convention hall or ground instead of just a mere 'house'.

Another literary form present is repetition of words, in Biblical Hebrew, repetition is often taken as referring to an 'emphasis' or 'stress' on what the writer deemed important. Isaiah 40 begins with a call for 'comfort' for the exiles, wherein the word 'comfort' is repeated twice, emphasising the message of 'comfort' as the need of the hour.

The question we must deal with is what the writer seeks to convey and try to deconstruct them in ways understandable to the present reader. The pressing concern of this text to me is not so much about homosexuality but of God's retributive justice, and the totality and the deep influence of sin on the citizens of Sodom irrespective of their age.

Concluding Remarks

Once we acknowledge the ways texts have hurt and still hurt people, we can see how it might contain a surplus of experience that can inform our lives. Experiences and practices that condition our perspective should be changed if it promotes division and exclusion.

What kind of religion and faith are we professing?[41] Reflecting faith as proposed by Kant seems viable in a world where there is so much violation of goodwill toward others and the politics of difference.[42]

The interpretation and reading of the Bible especially the OT must be carried out in such a way that it is not just employing the different available methods but to break barriers that divide people in terms of gender, sexual orientation, social status etc.

If Scripture has been used to dominate, exclude, and promote hatred the same scripture could be used to fight back for the core message of the Bible is not of dominion but justice, love, peace and harmony.

More than that, our beliefs about the Bible as denouncing certain groups of people must be changed in the postmodern society where identity and boundaries are becoming very fluid. Reading and the interpretation process of the Bible must take into consideration the presence of the LGBTIQ, where the quest to find God in the lived experiences is urgent. God and the Scripture must not be alienated from the experiences that the community is dealing with; instead, Scripture must be released from the traditional divisive clutches that it may transcend rigid boundaries.

Endnotes

1 Phyllis Trible, *Texts of Terror: Literary-Feminist Reading of Biblical Narrative* (Minneapolis: Fortress Press, 1984).

2 Adrian Thatcher, *The Savage Text: The Use and Abuse of the Bible* (Malden, MA: Wiley-Blackwell, 2008).

3 Teresa J. Hornsby and Ken Stone, *Bible Trouble: Queer Reading at the Boundaries of Biblical Scholarship* (SBL Semeia Studies 67. Atlanta: SBL, 2011).

4 Once the term 'queer' was, at best, slang for homosexual, at worst, a term of homophobic abuse. In recent years 'queer' has come to be used differently, sometimes as an umbrella term for a coalition of culturally marginal sexual self-identifications and at other times to describe a nascent theoretical model which has developed out of more traditional lesbian and gay studies. Annamarie Rustom Jagose, *Queer Theory: An Introduction* (New York: New York University Press, 2005), 1.

5 Queer theory is first coined by Teresa de Lauretis, a feminist film critic.

6 Frederick W. and Hannah A. Keene, *The Bible and Human Sexuality.* Theology Forum Adult Sunday School Class. Redland, California: The First Baptist Church, 1992. 301

7 Clemens N. Nathan, *The Changing Face of Religion and Human Rights A Personal Reflection.* Boston: Leiden, 2009), 60.

8 Marcella Althaus-Reid, *The Queer God* (New York: Routledge, 2003), 3.

9 David J. Cranmer and Brian E. Keck, "God Said it: Psychology and Biblical Interpretation, How Text and Reader Interact through the Glass Darkly" in *Journal of Psychology and Theology* (22: 3, 1994), 207.

10 David J. Cranmer and Brian E. Keck, "God Said it", 207.

11 Walter Brueggemann, *A New Ways of Looking at Scripture Texts under Negotiation: The Bible and Postmodern Imagination* (Philadelphia: Fortress Press, 1993), 15.

12 Walter Brueggemann, *A New Ways of Looking at Scripture*, 27.

13 Rabbi Steven Greenberg, *Wrestling with God and Man: Homosexuality in the Jewish Tradition* (Wisconsin: Wisconsin University Press, 2004), 3.

14 Willard M. Swartley. *Homosexuality: Biblical Interpretation and Moral Discernment* (Scottdale, Pennsylvania: Herald Press, 2003), 93.

[15] J. M. Sprinkle, "Sexuality, Sexual Ethics" in *Dictionary of the Old Testament Pentateuch* Eds. T. Desmond Alexander and David W, Baker (Secunderabad: OM Authentic Books, 2003. 741-753), 747.

[16] Willard M. Swartley. *Homosexuality*, 94.

[17] Frank S. Frick, *A Journey Through the Hebrew Scriptures* (Fort Worth, Texas: Harcourt Brace & Company, 1995), 161.

[18] Robert Alter, *The Art of Biblical Narrative* (New York: Basic Books, 1981), 24.

[19] Ed Noort, "For the sake of Righteousness Abraham's Negotiations with YHWH as Prologue to the Sodom Narrative: Genesis 18:16-33" in *Sodom's Sin Genesis 18-19 and its Interpretations*. Eds. Noort And Eibert Tigchelaar. Themes in Biblical Narrative Jewish and Christian Traditions Vol. VII (Leiden: Brill, 2004), 3.

[20] Terence E. Fretheim, "The Book of Genesis" in Leander E. Keck Ed. *The NIB Old Testament Survey* (Nashville: Abingdon Press,2005), 19.

[21] James L. Crenshaw, "It's All About a Missing Rib: Human Sexuality in the Bible" paper presented at the Faith and Scholarship Colloquium at Florida Southern College on October 27, 2005.

[22] Walter Brueggemann, *Genesis: Interpretation A Bible Commentary for Teaching and Preaching* (Atlanta: John Knox Press, 1980), 163.

[23] A, Boling, "Mal'ak" in *TWOT*: 1, 464-465.

[24] J. I. Lawlor, "Lot" in *Dictionary of the Old Testament Pentateuch* Eds. T. Desmond Alexander and David W. Baker (Secunderabad: OM Authentic Books, 2003), 558.

[25] Victor P. Hamilton, "The Book of Genesis 18-50" in *NICOT* 1B, 33

[26] It can be translated and understood depending on its occurrence and context. It could mean know, understand, perceive, observe, care about, become acquainted with, have sexual relations with, it also convey meanings like cause to know, brought to awareness etc. Terence E. Fretheim, "Ya'da" in *New International Dictionary of Old Testament Theology and Exegesis* Vols. 2 ed. Willem A. Van Gemeren (Cumbria, UK: Paternoster Press, 1996), 410.

[27] W. Schottroff , "Ya'da to perceive, know" in Ernst Jenni and Claus Westermann Eds. *Theological Lexicon of the Old Testament* Vol. 2 hesed-siyyon. Trans. Marl. E. Biddle (Peabody, Massachussets: Hendrickson Publishers Inc., 1997), 511-513.

[28] 'Know' (sexually) is a euphemism, like the analogous usage of Arab, *arafa* and Akkadian *elidu(m)* 'to know sexually' or *lamadu(m)* 'to come to know (sexually)'. See W. Schottroff , "Ya'da to perceive, know" in Ernst Jenni and Claus Westermann Eds. *Theological Lexicon of the Old Testament* Vol. 2 hesed-siyyon. Trans. Marl. E. Biddle (Peabody, Massachussets: Hendrickson Publishers Inc., 1997), 515.

[29] Kenneth A. Mathews, "Genesis 11:27-50:26" in *The New American Commentary An Exegetical and Theological Exposition of Holy Scripture* Vol IB (Nashville, Tennessee: Broadman and Holman Publishers, 2005), 236.

[30] Edward Day, *The Social Life of the Hebrews* (Oxon: Routledge Revivals, 2011), 170.

[31] Gordon Wenham, "Genesis 16-50" in *WBC* Vol. 2 (Dallas, Texas: Word Book Publisher, 1994), 55.

[32] Gordon Wenham, "Genesis 16-50" in *WBC* Vol. 2, 56.

[33] Kenneth A. Mathews, "Genesis 11:27-50:26" in *The New American Commentary An Exegetical and Theological Exposition of Holy Scripture* Vol. I B (Nashville, Tennessee: Broadman and Holman Publishers, 2005), 231.

[34] Weston W. Fields, *Sodom and Gomorrah: History and Motif in Biblical Narrative* JSOTSS 231 (Sheffield: Sheffield Academic Press, 1997), 55

[35] J. Boswell, *Christianity, Social Tolerance, and Homosexuality: Gay People in Western Europe from the beginning of the Christian Era to the 14th Century* (Chicago: Chicago University Press, 1980), 91-117.

[36] J. Boswell, *Christianity, Social Tolerance, and Homosexuality*, 117. Cf. The absence of homosexuality as Sodom's sin is supported by Walter Brueggemann, *Genesis: Interpretation A Bible Commentary for Teaching and Preaching* (Atlanta: John Knox Press, 1980), 164.

[37] Walter Brueggemann, *Genesis: Interpretation A Bible Commentary for Teaching and Preaching* (Atlanta: John Knox Press, 1980), 164.

[38] *4Q172 fragment 4 of* DSS a small, and yet unassigned fragment presents the only case in the Dead Sea Scrolls where a relation between (Sodom and) Gomorrah and sexual sins is suggested. Eibert Tigchelaar, "Sodom and Gomorrah in the Dead Sea Scrolls" in *Sodom's Sin Genesis 18-19 and its Interpretations*. Eds. Noort And Eibert Tigchelaar. Themes in Biblical Narrative Jewish and Christian Traditions Vol. VII (Leiden: Brill, 2004), 52.

[39] Walter Brueggemann, *Genesis*, 164.

[40] Kenneth Boa, "Literary forms in the Bible". https://bible.org/seriespage/iv-literary-forms-bible. Accessed on 1st August, 2016.

[41] Jacques Derrida, *Acts of Religion* Ed. Gil Anidjar. (Madison Avenue, New York: Routledge Taylor and Francis Group, 2010), 49.

[42] Miroslav Volf, *Exclusion and Embrace: A Theological Exploration of Identity, Otherness, and Reconciliation* (Nashville: Abingdon Press, 1996), 10.

Towards a Responsible and Life-Giving Ministry with and Among Sexual and Gender Minorities

Pauline Ong

Abstract

In recent decades, Christian churches in the Western world have seen much progress in integrating gender and sexual minorities within their communities. Asian churches, on the other hand, seem to be mired in trepidation, suspicion and hesitation. This article explores how we, as pastors and ministers, play a vital role in speaking up for those who have no voice and the importance of our self-awareness, understanding and empathy in nurturing life-giving ministries with and among gender and sexual minorities.

Introduction

Over the past two decades or so, many churches around the world have been grappling with the challenging task of coming to a decision as a community how we are to respond pastorally, ethically and lovingly towards sexual and gender minorities in our midst. The struggle has been especially difficult in Asia because many Christians remain uninformed about LGBTIQ persons and issues, and old stereotypes continue to misinform church policy and practices. The reasons are manifold and interrelated. Many LGBTIQ Christians in Asia are afraid of coming out to their church communities for fear of being ostracized or shamed, especially in communities that pride themselves on upholding "conservative" values. So while there are undoubtedly LGBTIQ Christians in every church, many feel the need to hide important parts of themselves from their Christian siblings and remain invisible for reasons of personal safety and belonging. Because LGBTIQ Christians do not feel safe coming out to their faith communities, many of their Christian siblings do not have access to hearing the stories or participating in the journeys of LGBTIQ Christians. So debates and dialogues regarding sexual and gender minorities have often bordered on the theoretical instead of being rooted in real facts and struggles faced by real-life people. In fact, in my conversations with various churches, I have heard quite a number of Christians tell me they do not personally know someone who is both Christian and LGBTIQ, and I am the first one they have met. I often smile in response and tell them they probably do know a number already but those persons have just not come out to them yet. We may not be aware of it and perhaps it is not our intention but unwittingly, many of our church communities have created or maintained an unwelcoming environment of fear, especially for our Christian siblings who identify as LGBTIQ.

Three crucial pastoral issues would be explored in this article with regards to how we can grow responsible and life-giving ministries that support sexual and gender minorities more effectively. These issues include understanding the wide spectrum of views Christians currently hold regarding faith and sexuality; understanding identity formation, its impact on relationships and how this affects LGBTIQ persons; and the immense potential the Church has for harm and healing with respect to sexual and gender minorities. Before I explore these topics, I would like to state that LGBTIQ covers a very wide spectrum of people and I am aware of the potential biases and limitations of this article. For example, the issues faced by a transgender man may be very different from that of a lesbian woman. I have tried my best to cover issues that may apply across the board to most sexual and gender minorities. I must state though that there are disproportionately a lot more books written on the issue of homosexuality and faith as compared to transgenderism and faith, or bisexuality and faith. So while I refer to such books and discuss the issues mainly from the perspective of homosexuality, I do so hoping that the general principles still apply to various sexual and gender minorities.

Understanding the Wide Spectrum of views Christians hold regarding Faith and Sexuality

Often in public discourse, there is a tendency to only see two moral stances on homosexuality or any other gender and sexual minority issues: acceptance or rejection. In reality, the debate is far more complex than that. Whatever view one holds, it is important to realize that appreciating the different views and teaching others there is a spectrum of views, instead of just propagating one view as valid and acceptable, opens up the way towards more expansive dialogue and a deeper understanding between each other. More importantly, for many LGBTIQ Christians who for their whole lives have probably only heard they are at best, a contradiction, or at worst, an abomination, just the knowledge and acknowledgement by other Christians that there is a spectrum of views can itself be life-giving. On a deeper level, reflecting on where we stand and why we believe what we do will also open up the way for God to move, enlighten and challenge us towards more loving and inclusive policies.

L.R. Holben's *What Christians Think About Homosexuality: Six Representative Viewpoints*[1] provides a helpful summary of this spectrum of views, and this article will briefly summarize the six viewpoints-

Condemnation

The "condemnation" camp believes that the Bible is the ultimate moral authority and the literal text is above all scrutiny. Scripture is the only source for our understandings about homosexuality, and thus any psychological or sociological perspectives are rejected as promoting non-Christian worldviews. Some see homosexuality as a form of demon possession that requires exorcism. It is noted that the Bible contains no positive references to homosexuality so it is regarded that same-sex desires are as sinful as same-sex acts. In this approach, there is no distinction between homosexual orientation and homosexual acts. Proponents of this camp do not generally discuss trying to turn a homosexual into a heterosexual. However, it is often assumed that, were a homosexual person to convert to Christianity, he or she would cease to experience same-sex desires.

A Promise of Healing

The "healing" camp says homosexual orientation is real, even if its origins remain mysterious and debated. While viewing all sex outside of marriage as sin, they stress that same-sex desires, alone, are not sinful and that homosexual sin is no worse than other sins. While same-sex desires are not considered sinful, they are viewed as psychological impairment or immaturity, from which one can and should undergo mental and spiritual recovery. The homosexual orientation is seen as unnatural and it may develop through an inadequate or immature bond with the same-sex parent. Thus, same-sex relationships are unfulfilling and unstable, because they are broken imitations of failed parent-child relationships.

As with "Condemnation" proponents, the moral authority is the Bible, which negatively judges same-sex acts. Moreover, the Bible specifically endorses the positivity of male-female relationships. Maleness and femaleness are meaningful because of their juxtaposition and "Promise of Healing" proponents strongly advocate for sexuality-conversion programs.

A Call to Costly Discipleship

Many groups, including the Vatican and some mainline Protestant denominations, believe that same-sex orientation is an imperfection or impairment, but rarely the result of a conscious choice. Since healing does not always occur, many who experience same-sex attraction face the choice of "costly discipleship". This camp urges all who experience same-sex attraction to be chaste and not act on their inclinations. To them, faithful discipleship means a commitment to lifelong celibacy. This approach emphasizes that life in a sinful, fallen world is often painful and complex. This view strives to take into account the actual situation and life experience of homosexual people, and relevant science. This view ask that homosexual Christians practice sexual abstinence and understand their sexual orientation to be a disability.

Pastoral Accommodation

Proponents of "pastoral accommodation" characterize same-sex sexual activity as inherently imperfect, rather than entirely sinful. They note that humans make moral decisions and act within a context of ambiguity. "Pastoral Accommodation" proponents attempt to discern universal truths, taking into account the cultural and historical context of situations in the Bible. Although the writers of the Bible were divinely inspired, they could not have had scientific knowledge of things like genetics or sexual orientations. Modern understanding of the world requires us to nuance our ethics based on a contextual reading of the Bible. According to this perspective, when healing or celibacy is impossible for a gay person, a homosexual monogamous relationship that demonstrates fidelity should be morally tolerated.

Affirmation

The fifth viewpoint on homosexuality takes a significant leap beyond the previous position of qualified acceptance. "It does not merely tolerate gay and lesbian relationships, it affirms them as positively good. Committed homosexual relationships are seen as holding all the same potential for a self-transcending exchange of love as heterosexual relationships."[2] Proponents of this view argue that sex is primarily giving love to another, growth in relational intimacy, and the development of mature selfhood. Homosexual relations can achieve this equally as well as heterosexual ones. They believe that the morality of same-sex sexual activity is to be evaluated exactly on the same terms by which heterosexual acts are evaluated – the quality of relationship they express. Sexuality is not a degraded part of human nature but a gift from God that allows us to grow in love. If both partners are consenting, non-exploitative, mutually committed and faithful, then the relationship is a moral one. Monogamous, committed, homosexual relationships are considered truly sacred unions.

When it comes to interpreting the biblical texts, proponents of "affirmation" contend that we must examine what the author was intending to say, and in most cases, the text was not primarily about same-sex relationships as we understand them today. Peter Gomes, the chaplain of Harvard University reflects this position and those who share these sentiments: "Given the appeal to the Bible in the case against homosexuality, one would assume that the Bible has much to say on the subject. It has not. The subject of homosexuality is not mentioned in the Ten Commandments, nor in the summary of the Law. No prophetic discourses on the subject. Jesus himself makes no mention of it."[3] Proponents understand the Bible's overarching message as twofold: God is love, and God is just. As Christians, we are called to enact that love and justice. What kind of justice and love would condemn one for his or her immutable sexual orientation, or deny this person the fullness of human experience because of it? Advocates of this viewpoint contend for full membership of practising gays and lesbians in the church, including the affirmation of ordination. Most support laws that would uphold marriage equality and they believe in the full legal recognition of same-sex marriages.

Liberation

This final perspective builds its ethic from the fundamental principle of justice and the affirmation that no one is outside the embrace of the Creator's love. Moreover, "it is not for the heterosexual majority in the church to dictate to gays and lesbians what they can and cannot do with their sexuality. The relevant moral issue for Christians lies elsewhere: in a biblically based call to struggle against all forms of oppression and domination, including homophobia."[4] Advocates call for church and society to move beyond the specific biblical injunctions about homosexuality to the broader themes of justice and liberation. Christian ethicist Marvin Ellison believes that some biblical texts serve patriarchal and homophobic sentiments. He argues that all reading of Scripture is political and "either supports or challenges unjust power structures." Thus, "a hermeneutics of suspicion is necessary to discern the racist, sexist, and heterosexist character of sexual injustice," which, he believes, we sometimes find in the Bible itself.[5]

The Bible's comprehensive call is to struggle against all oppression and domination. In that light, homosexual Christians are at the forefront of a new Christian faithfulness, proclaiming Jesus' radical message: that nobody is outside of God's love. Because homophobia, transphobia, and similar prejudices are the last acceptable forms of discrimination inside the Church, God is that much more in solidarity with LGBTIQ. From this perspective, to truly understand the Bible, one must read it through the eyes of the oppressed. Advocates of this perspective set forth a full embrace of inclusion in society for all LGBTIQ.

Our Reflections for Action

Holben's summary of the spectrum of views is just a basic framework for us to reflect upon and perhaps take into further discussion with our various church communities. As we read through these positions and identify where we stand personally on the issue of homosexuality and the faithful Christian, we need to first be aware of our own prejudices and preferences. There are limits to our knowledge of what it means to be a LGBTIQ person navigating through life in our society. So it might be helpful to listen to the stories and journeys of LGBTIQ before we decide on our stance on this issue. Secondly, our views can and do evolve as we open up our hearts and minds and let the Holy Spirit guide, enlighten and challenge us. The more deeply and personally we know a LGBTIQ Christian person as a friend, the less we are tempted to fall back on the easy way out. If we want to grow a more responsible and life-giving ministry, we need to first commit to studying the various interpretations of Scripture and other literature more comprehensively and deeply knowing the people we want to minister to. Each person is a complex human being, a soul with longings for love and belonging, a deep capacity to love and be loved, and a call to grow according to God's image and purposes.

As pastors and ministers, the best thing we can offer LGBTIQ is to guide them towards understanding God's heart for them. We do not prescribe what they should believe or how they should think. We help them understand they are loved and accepted by God fully and unconditionally, and we encourage them to discover what that means with the guidance of the Holy Spirit. We walk with them, cry with them, listen to them, struggle with them in prayer, and hold sacred space for them. In presenting the spectrum of views, we acknowledge that there may be different ways of looking at and responding to this issue, and we open up a safe space for expansive dialogue and deeper understanding.

Understanding Identity Formation and Its Impact on relationships for LGBTIQ Persons

In the past, many people argue that there is something inherently wrong or defective with LGBTIQ and that is the reason why many LGBTIQ are unable to have healthy and sustainable intimate relationships. The blame is placed squarely on their shoulders and what is worse, it is explained in a way that attacks their inherent worth and dignity, diminishing their value as sacred beings created in the image of God. It is appalling that such baseless conjectures continue to peddle around, masquerading as undisputed truths to the unsuspecting. What is even more heartbreaking is that conversing with some LGBTIQ revealed that this argument might be true because they have been hurt numerous times in their romantic relationships and have not heard a different or more compelling reason for why they are unable to sustain healthy relationships.

There are many factors that influence relationships, and society actually has a large part to play in its success or failure. Heterosexual couples enjoy tremendous support from their families, governments, faith communities, friends and society to succeed in building and nurturing their relationships. Even so, divorce rates are still climbing. On the other hand, most LGBTIQ couples do not enjoy the same support from their families, friends or society at large. Instead, they face opposition, criminalisation, disapproval, discouragement, indifference, the threat of violence or being disowned by the very people whom they need support and love from as they navigate through the joys and challenges of nurturing an intimate relationship. Many feel the need to keep their relationships a secret from their families or to isolate themselves from segments of society in order to protect themselves from hurt or harm. As one can imagine, it is extremely difficult to maintain a healthy and loving relationship in a social vacuum or within a negative, unsafe or oppositional environment.

There is another reason why it has been so hard for many LGBTIQ to maintain and nurture healthy intimate relationships. Erickson[6] proposed the view that one develops his or her unique identity separate from one's parents during adolescence. This is crucial to the next stage of development because identity formation will influence how healthily one attaches to another person in an intimate relationship as one grows from adolescence to adulthood. I realized that for a LGBTIQ, the challenge of building intimate relationships does not just begin during that stage of life, but way before one enters adulthood. Most LGBTIQ struggle with understanding and accepting themselves from a relatively young age when they start perceiving that they are different from their peers, and this difference is one to be feared because they know it may lead to rejection and ostracism. Many become aware of this difference as they are growing up and because there are societal pressures to be or act a certain way depending on one's gender, young LGBTIQ tend to struggle to understand why they are different from their peers and how they can conform to societal expectations in order to belong. They question their own identity, often in secret and feeling alone, and increasing societal pressures causes many

LGBTIQ to go into hiding or denial. Some are so fearful of the consequences of being different and ostracised that they develop self-hatred or are unable to accept themselves wholly. Many continue to live fragmented and secret lives even as they enter young adulthood as they struggle to align various parts of themselves in an authentic and meaningful way.

Being secure in one's own identity and being able to be oneself freely and authentically is a very important step to successfully build an intimate relationship with another person. However, given the current climate of many Asian societies today, it can be very difficult for young LGBTIQ to have a safe environment to even explore and understand the difference they perceive about their own identities or sexualities. Having responsible adults in the families or faith communities with whom they can talk openly and honestly is paramount to healthy identity development and subsequently, to healthy relationship formation. A responsible and life-giving ministry to sexual and gender minorities requires education and information about psychosocial issues and how these play out in the lives and development of LGBTIQ under our care. Creating safe bastions where LGBTIQ can ask questions and share honestly about their journeys is an important first step. Walking with and helping them along in their journey in an open, supportive and loving way would significantly improve their well-being and in turn, influence the long-term health of their relationships. Knowing there are trusted adults who accept them as they are would ease the sense of loneliness and alleviate the fear of not belonging. That is what we can do on a one-on-one level as ministers and pastors. But we have the potential to do so much more.

The Immense Potential the Church has for Harm and Healing

On a much larger scale, churches are agents of change among faith communities and society. Are there ways we can speak up against myths, stereotypes, prejudices and misunderstandings based on ignorance and fear? Are there arenas where we can take a loving stand against hate and violence, and make a stand for love and equality? We have a special role as leaders in faith communities because events around the world have shown that it is often people in faith communities who oppose most strenuously to the right of LGBTIQ to love or even to exist. Even as I write this article, news have been streaming in over the past week of a teenager, T. Nhaveen, being beaten, burnt and sodomised by his schoolmates for being effeminate. He later died from his injuries. The heartbreaking plea of his mother resonates a call to action, "My son is dead. Don't let this happen to anyone else's child."[7] Standing up and speaking out is crucial because it will save actual lives.

If we were to take a poll of the churches in Asia currently and ask them how they would respond pastorally to someone who is seeking advice about being gay and Christian, I would venture to guess that about 80% or more of pastors or ministers would probably prescribe something along the lines of "A Call to Costly Discipleship" or "A Promise of Healing" as explained in the summary earlier. The general response of mainstream churches have been telling LGBTIQ persons of faith that while they may not be able to do anything about their same-sex attraction (or the need to align with their true gender identity for transgender persons), they should not act on this attraction or impulse. In other words, for people experiencing same-sex attraction, the recommended model for coping is life-long celibacy. Basically, what churches are asking of LGBTIQ persons is that they be alone for life, whether they have the gift of celibacy or not. Live alone, die alone, and unlike single people, do not even think about dating. Be alone. This sounds like the opposite of what God declared in Genesis 2:18, "It is not good for the human to be alone." So is this the best we can do as followers of Christ? Do we truly think this is the only acceptable response the God of love expects of us?

Fear begets fear. As human beings, we tend to fear what we do not know, fear mixed with a lack of understanding has resulted in many Christians reluctant or unwilling to engage deeply on the issue of reconciling faith and sexuality for LGBTIQ Christians. It is sometimes far more convenient to hold to a more traditional stance and not rock the boat, so to speak. Silence for some is due to fear of displeasing God or their church leaders, questioning God or the Bible, or worse, that they might be pro-gay or possibly gay themselves. Some to uphold traditional "family values" as against what they believe are "sinful lifestyles". Others are more informed and sensitive to the nuances of this issue but remain on the fence because they fear taking a stand or bringing it up for discussion might be potentially divisive and contentious. So for various reasons, many Christians either choose to be especially vocal against this issue, or choose to remain silent.

It is impossible to remain silent because lives are at stake, silence perpetuates the environment of fear within our faith communities, and LGBTIQ can assume that silence means agreement with the current climate of disapproval and even hate in some quarters. Perhaps what would truly displease God is if we do not take a deeper and more careful look at this issue for the sake of justice and love for our LGBTIQ siblings, and consider how we can develop a more loving, just, wise and balanced perspective that would bring life, not death. It would be a remiss not to mention with gratitude, the growing number of Christians in Asia who are seeking to stand alongside and bring life to LGBTIQ who face great odds in the current environment. It is with deep courage, love and determination that they challenge existing norms and rock the proverbial boat in their communities as they gently forge a way forward even in the face of resistance or opposition. They are the ones who inspire and move me as I write this article.

Conclusion

It is undeniable that the meta-narrative of the Bible moves towards more inclusion, not less, culminating with every tribe, every tongue, every nation. How are we moving towards more inclusive policies and practices in our faith communities? How are we practising Christ-like love in all we do and say? In summary, we as ministers first need to be aware of our own prejudices and preferences. Once we are able to accept and acknowledge the limitations of our knowledge and experience, we are taking the first step towards truly listening and understanding with our hearts, minds and souls. The more deeply and personally we know a LGBTIQ Christian person as a fellow human being and friend, the more we will be able to minister pastorally in a life-giving way. As pastors and ministers, the best thing we can offer LGBTIQ people is to guide them towards understanding God's heart for them. We recognize that each person is a complex human being, a soul with longings for love and belonging, a deep capacity to love and be loved, and a call to grow according to God's image and purposes. We help them understand they are loved and accepted by God fully and unconditionally, and we encourage them to discover what that means with the guidance of the Holy Spirit. We walk with them and hold sacred space for them. Most importantly, we do not allow fear to keep us silent. We speak up on behalf of those who have no voice. Giving voice to those who have been kept silent is our calling and responsibility. We speak up because of love. How will history remember us as we strive towards justice and inclusion? May the Holy Spirit guide, enlighten and empower us as we together seek to bring about change and transformation.

Endnotes

[1] L.R. Holben, *What Christians Think About Homosexuality: Six Representative Viewpoints*, (D & F Scott Publishing Inc., 1999)

[2] L.R. Holben, *What Christians Think About Homosexuality*, 153.

[3] D.P. Hollinger, *The Meaning of Sex: Christian Ethics and the Moral Life.* (Grand Rapids: Baker Academic, 2009), 178.

[4] L.R. Holben, *What Christians Think About Homosexuality*,199.

[5] M.M. Ellison, *Erotic Justice: A Liberating Ethic of Sexuality*,(Louisville: Westminster John Knox, 1996), p70, 73.

[6] E.H. Erikson, *Identity and the Life Cycle*, (New York: W. W. Norton,1980).

[7] Malaysian teen Nhaveen dies after brutal assault by bullies (2017, 16 June), *The Straits Times, http://www.straitstimes.com* accessed on 25 June, 2017.

Church, Homophobia and Heterosexuality

Wati Longchar

Medical professionals and psychiatrists opine that homosexuality is not a disease or a disorder but another expression or an orientation of human sexuality and therefore cannot be categorized as criminal, sinful and a mental disorder. It is said that a vast majority of human sexuality researchers, therapists, physiologists generally agree that a person's sexual orientation is determined before reaching the school age. Some researchers even argue that homosexual orientation takes place very early in the life cycle, possibly even before birth.

Many religious leaders all over the world are in the forefront aggressively challenging legalization of same sex marriage in the name of culture, tradition, and values. Opinions are divided. Churches also hold conflicting opinions and some churches have been divided over the issue, and some brothers and sisters who revealed their identity have been ostracized and excluded from the community. Therefore the ostracization and exclusion are justice issues. We hear justice voices in India, Taiwan and many countries in Europe and North America demanding approval of their sexual orientation socially, legally, morally and even spiritually. Different sexual orientation is a reality and it is God given. How then do we address this issue? What is the role of the church and theological education?

Homophobia – A Heterosexual Problem?

The society is sick of homophobia. It has become like a disease which is discriminating many people. Let me highlight how family, church and society treat LGBTIQ community by sharing a testimony:

> My name is Sani (name is changed) and I was born in a Christian family. As I grew older, I felt different in my behavioural pattern. I became more attracted to men, admired heroes and always wanted to get married to a hero. I started hating my body when I saw hair on my face and body. Seeing my behaviour, my parents thought that I am possessed by the devil and took me to a Revival camp. My parents even took me to a psychiatrist. My parents and I prayed to God but my feeling remained the same. My parents were worried and thought that I am a burden and shame to the family and openly said that I am possessed by an evil spirit. Many people tried to avoid me. I felt very depressed and struggled alone. Since I did not change my behaviour, my parents, brothers and sisters started torturing and abusing me. Sometimes I was beaten and was threatened that I will be sent to jail. I also experienced discrimination in school. My fellow students always teased me. It became unbearable and thus I decided to leave both school and home without knowing what future lies ahead of me. I wandered here and there begging for food, sometimes slept in the street, bus and railway stations. After a few days of wandering hopelessly, I met a trans-gender friend. I explained to her my problem. She was kind enough to give me shelter and food at her place and she asked me to work in her beauty parlour. It was a great relief for me. However, I discovered that the work place was also not safe either. The police personnel verbally abused and tried to sexually molest us from time to time; sometimes they would ask irritating and irrelevant questions. Though we had to face such cruel acts almost every day, we had no choice since that was the only means of living. When we complained to local authorities, their answer was "you are a man and why are you wearing a female attire. Change your lifestyle and after that nobody will harass you." Realizing that God is the only answer for my life, I went to a Revival Camp again. I prayed and fasted for days. The counsellor asked me to repent and, as a sign of repentance, was asked to return to my parent's home, cut my hair like men, and wear men's clothing. I did as advised and gave testimony to many churches how God changed my life. But my feeling remained the same though I prayed every day. I always wanted to undergo sex reassignment and settle with a man and work in the church.

After speaking in an awareness seminar on human sexuality, Sani raised many questions: I always feel that "I am a woman"- Is this feeling because of sin? Am I possessed by the devil? Is my faith in God not strong enough because my feeling of being a woman remains unchanged? Did God create only male and female in the beginning? Am I not created in the 'Image of God'? Does the 'Image of God' include "feeling"? I want to be a woman- Is it a sin if I undergo sex re-assignment surgery? After my sex-reassignment, will the church accept me for marriage? Can I study theology and serve in the church? Will the church ordain me? Can we say that God intends all human beings to be only heterosexual?

I asked Sani, "do you feel discriminated in the society and church?". Sani replied,"Yes, very much. I always experience frequent tortures and stigmatization. No one likes me including my parents and friends because they think that I am abnormal, and possesses by an evil spirit. Everyday I experience mental distress and sometimes I ask God why He created me like this and at times I even think that ending my life is the best solution." I did not know what to tell Sani. I just said "you are beautiful, strong, creative and God's special creation. The world is richer and more beautiful because you are a special gift of God to the world. You are unique and you can make a lot of contributions to the world. Those who discriminate against you, abuse you and torture you are doing so against the will of God because the Bible teaches about love, compassion and care for one another. Rather, they are sinners because they are acting against the will of God. Your feeling of wanting to be a woman is not because of your faithlessness or sin but because God created you in a special way. God loves you and you are a precious child of God. Give thanks for your special body, your physical and emotional make up."

Attitudes of the dominant Heterosexuals

The testimony of Sani speaks about the attitude of the many heterosexuals; the confusion of parents, family members and even the pastor who are all heterosexuals. The various reactions can be summarized as: (1) Outright denial: Same sex relation is unnatural and unacceptable. It is immoral like prostitution and spreads HIV which brings a curse to society. It is not only against the cultural norm, but also against biblical teaching. God created man and woman for the purpose of reproducing, homosexuality will not fulfil God's command because it is contrary to biblical mandate; (2) Expectation of *divine* intervention – God is the creator and he has the power to change persons, if one comes to him with true repentance. Prayer and repentance are the solution. (3) Attempt for

Psychological/medical intervention – Homosexuality is a mental illness and is a product of the environment. Homosexual behaviour can be corrected medically and psychologically; (4). Harassment, rejection, isolation and exclusion usually happens as it is sinful and shame to the family. The last resort is inflicting pain physically or uttering abusive language and creating psychological fear. Sometimes, the family sever relationships to avoid shame and influence on other family members.

These reactions portray ignorance and unpreparedness of the parents, relatives and pastors. Sani attended the Revival Camps, prayed, fasted but God did not change her. This attempt further marginalized her, created guilty feeling because she was told that it is due to lack of faith that she is not getting cured. Since divine intervention failed, her parents opted for a medical/psychological intervention, but Sani still experienced the inner affectional orientation. Human beings do not choose their sexual orientation, but they discover it as something given by God. Prayer, psychological treatment, or even inflicting torture cannot change the sexual orientation of a person. It is heterosexuals who want homosexuals to change in their way. Heterosexuals are not prepared to accept them because homosexual do not come under the "norm" of their defined marriage and sexual relationship. This irrational prejudice, Max Stackhouse said that is nothing but "bigotry, ignorance, repressive authoritarianism, sexual chauvinism ("heterosexism"), or psychological pathology ("homophobia").[1] He wrote:

> *It is certainly true that some who call themselves Christian have confused the tradition they confess with ideas that derive from prudish denials of sexuality as a gift of God, culturally established gender roles, arrogant self-righteousness, or psychosocial pathologies …. Some versions of the faith have been repressive of wholesome sexual impulses and have wrongly condemned other people to second-class citizenship. These betrayals of Christianity deserve severe condemnation – not only because they have broken faith with the tradition in the name of the faith but also because they unlovingly distort what is true about the human condition.[2]*

Exclusion – A Structural Problem

Who are excluded and by whom? Like other forms of marginality, the issue of LGBTIQ is a structural problem. The present social, cultural, religious, economic and political structures and ideologies are created by the majority people. Anything that does not conform to their norms is considered as evil and to be discarded. Society is structured in terms of normal-abnormal, natural-unnatural, superior-inferior and clean-unclean. In this view of life the latter is seen as a burden to society because they are considered to be cursed by God; they are wrong and need to be corrected. These false presuppositions and beliefs, created by the majority people that inflict injustice and misery to many people, constitute the definition of structural sin. Dominion and unjust social relationships are often legalized and supported by the Constitution of the countries or customary laws and practices, traditions and social arrangement and further sanctioned by religion as in the case of LGBTIQ and patriarchy. Excluded people are left to live in unbearable misery and humiliation in many ways. Today one major marginalized community who are excluded from dominant power structures is the LGBTIQ community. They are seen as psychologically imbalanced in their character, abnormal and indulging in sinful same-sex relations and acts.

We need to understand the reality of structural injustices by dominant power and majority. We can understand the seriousness of discrimination only from the experience of the excluded, but not from the experience of the majority. That means one has to judge the social dynamics from the perspective of people in the periphery. It is the marginalized groups suffering that provide criteria to judge the inherited social structures and eventually struggle for the humanization of the social reality. Therefore, any analysis of social reality has to take the point of view of the excluded ones, demanding conscious rejection of unjust and oppressive system in society. Similarly, the church needs to listen to the cries of LGBTIQ, if she wants to create a just society.

The LGBTIQ community lives a life of misery, due to judgemental attitudes of the majority society. They face exclusion, disappointments, rejection from their family, society and friends. They are subjected to many forms of violence. Violence could be physical, verbal, emotional or sexual. Perpetrators of this violence are anyone on the street, teachers, office staffs, maintenance staff, classmates, neighbours, domestic maids, drivers, parents, etc. In some societies, once the family discovers that their son/ daughter or sibling is gay, lesbian or bisexual, emotional blackmailing begins. Parents threaten to disown them, threaten to send them out of the house especially when they are still minors and are unable to fend for themselves, threaten them to cut-off from inheritance, force the son/daughter to marry and cajoling. Sadly, this is happening in our church and society due to the lack of understanding of LGBTIQ by the majority society.

We live in a patriarchal society where female inferiority is affirmed and a wife is seen as mere 'children bearer'. Discussion about sex is taboo - silence and shame - even between the spouses. Same clan marriage is considered as incest in some society. Children outside of marriage are considered as illegitimate. In this kind of society, LGBTIQ community suffers more because parents and elders are not in a position to openly discuss and give guidance on their sexuality. The presence of LGBTIQ is a reality. They are in our family, church and society and they are our brothers and sisters. We need to accept them –with an open mind, like our Lord Jesus.

Re-orienting our Theological Assumptions

We need to challenge some of the traditionally held theological assumptions on sexuality. A major reason for exclusion of LGBTIQ by the church leaders is that such relationship is not natural, it is not blessed by God, it will not bear offspring, thus it is against God's command to humans "be fruitful and multiply". (Genesis 1:22). A homosexual relationship cannot transmit the gift of life to the next generation. They also argue that if LGBTIQ persons are allowed to adopt children, they will grow in a dysfunctional family, because children will be raised by two fathers or two mothers, instead of having a male father and female mother. Sani's question raises many theological issues. Does God intend all people to be heterosexual, or does God also intend, and so create, some people to be homosexual? How do we interpret Christian understanding of the image of God, sin, faith, marriage and family, and the right to ministry in the church?

Image of God – Some of the early theologians thought that 'men' alone are created in the 'image of God'. They understood it in terms of intellectual capacity and moral discernment. This one-sided construct is challenged by feminists saying that both male and female together reflect the image of God. Again, upholding the beauty and perfection of God's creation, disabled people were seen as a distorted image of God. Today, with the rise of disabled movements, the image of God is no longer seen in terms of beauty and perfection, but interpreted in terms of 'giftedness.' The LGBTIQ community is asking a new theological question does 'feeling' reflect-the image of God? How do we interpret the 'image of God' in the context of diverse expression of sexuality? It is said that always and everywhere a certain percentage of men and women develop as homosexuals or lesbians- can we deny that they are not part of God's creative plan? Or can we say that homosexuality is a distorted creation of God? Christian affirms that all human beings are made in the image of God and thus all must be equally respected by an individual and by laws. Oppression, victimization and denial are contrary to biblical affirmation.

Sin and punishment –The moral teaching of the church towards homosexuality has been negative for many centuries. Homosexual behaviour was seen as contrary to the will of God. For example, John Chrysostom, a brilliant and influential theologian of the fourth century, said that homosexual intercourse is sin- worse than fornication, worse even than murder.[3] Affirming prosperity theology, some Christians tend to see suffering, diseases, failures, poverty, disability and homosexuality as cursed by God. They are viewed as a consequence of sin committed by parents or by themselves. Destruction, punishment, suffering and sin are interrelated. To justify this argument as in the case of homosexuality, Christian often refers to the story of Sodom and Gomorrah (Genesis 19: Jude 1:7). It is argued that Sodom and Gomorrah were destroyed because of the practice of homosexuality. However, biblical scholars[4] today are of the opinion that Sodom and Gomorrah were condemned not because of homosexuality but due to their selfishness; they did not practice kindness as demanded by God (Micah 6:8) They were proud of their increasing numbers and the wealth they enjoyed. "They had wealth and food in plenty, comfort and ease, but never help the poor and wretched."[5] They hated foreigners and refused to extend help to others. God punished them because of their arrogant, selfish, unkind and in- hospitability towards strangers. In addition, they were also involved in various crimes. In the New Testament, Jesus did not interpret the sin of Sodom as sexual. Not a single verse in the Gospels record Jesus specifically referring the sin as homosexuality. He did speak of sexual sins, but in reference to all, regardless of sexual orientation. When Jesus instructed his disciples to preach in the towns of Israel, he warned that those who do not receive them peacefully will be judged more harshly than the people of Sodom and Gomorrah

(Matt. 10: 5-15). Then, do we have the right to condemn homosexuality? Are they sinners? Are they not part of God's creation? John Mcneill argued that there is no connection between sexual orientation and sin, sickness, or failure; rather, it is a gift from God to be accepted and lived out with gratitude. God does not despise anything that God has created.[6] Abuse and misuse of the gift of sexuality is a sin. Sin involves selfishness, pride, neglect of the needy, and in-hospitability to strangers. Biblical scholars argue that scripture does not condemn homosexual orientation, but the lustful sexual activity of both heterosexual and homosexual which include idolatry, prostitution, promiscuity, violent rape, seduction of children, or violation of guests' right.[7]

Marriage and family – The universal assumption is that marriage is a life-long union only between a man and a woman; blessed by God and together they fulfil God's command to humans "be fruitful and multiply" (Genesis 1:22). What about couples who do not have children? Couples who do not wish to have children due to various reasons? They are not fulfilling God's command, "be fruitful and multiply" do we have right to condemn them? Do we have to look upon them as disobedient to God? There are also, many same sex couples who have lived together for many years and adopted many children, and their children are making significant contribution to society. Do we have the right to condemn them as sinners? With the medical advancement, multiple organ transplants like liver, kidney, eyes, etc., are possible, What about sex re-assignment surgery? Can we justify ethically? Can we deny Christian marriage to them? The Bible speaks of God calling different people and community for his service. God commanded them to maintain holiness and do justice. Along with upright morality, commitment, dedication, sacrifice and willingness to serve God are the basis for Christian ministry. Can we deny them from Christian ministry on the basis of same sex marriage? Can you say that sexual fulfilment is exclusively the rights of the heterosexual?

Natural and unnatural sexual relationship –Citing a Scripture passage like Jude 1:7 "Just as Sodom and Gomorrah and the surrounding cities, which likewise indulged in sexual immorality and pursued unnatural desire; serve as an example by undergoing a punishment of eternal fire." Similarly, Romans 1:26-31 also says,

> For this reason God gave them up to degrading passions. Their women exchanged natural intercourse for unnatural, and in the same way also the men, giving up natural intercourse with women, were consumed with passion for one another. Men committed shameless acts with men and received in their own persons the due penalty for their error. And since they did not see fit to acknowledge God, God gave them up to a debased mind and to things that should not be done. They were filled with every kind of wickedness, evil, covetousness, malice. Full of envy, murder, strife, deceit, craftiness, they are gossips, slanderers, God-haters, insolent, haughty, boastful, inventors of evil, rebellious toward parents, foolish, faithless, heartless, ruthless.

What is meant by "unnatural sex"? The original text in Greek is *sarkos heteras*. In various other translations, the word used is *perverted sensuality, unnatural lust, unnatural sex, the lust of men for other men, pursued unnatural desire, sexual sin*. These words refer to the desire for an unusual sexual intercourse. This desire for unnatural sex should not be limited to only a homosexual. It refers to heterosexual relationship too. For example, 70 years old man getting married with a 25 years old girl is unnatural, or European or African tourists seeing the body of Asian women look exotic and tempting, and they would like to try them and enjoy this unusual sexual relationship. It is unnatural behaviour. The church must stand for the sanctity of morality, but it should not narrow down the issue of morality to homosexual relationships alone.

The Gift of Sexuality

Human beings are inescapably and irreducibly sexual being. It is natural and instinctive. Sexuality is one of the greatest gifts of God. Since human sexuality is a divinely-ordained gift of God, we should not be ashamed and apologetic. It is not inherently evil. God has created the human with the body and the body is the temple of God There is an essential goodness in the creation and God has an affirmative relationship with the whole created order. Adam was incomplete without Eve and vice-versa. This complementarily is not just physiological but it is a true being-with-another. Human beings exist in this self-conscious differentiation. Sexuality is a divine gift, and hence God intends us to celebrate this divine gift in committed and monogamous relationships, we should challenge any immoral sexual relationship whether heterosexual or homosexual. However, the Church should not demonize, criminalize, and exclude from the fellowship of God on the basis of one's sexual orientation. The church must be supportive by encouraging the families not to force them into getting married. Motivate people to be honest about who they are and initiate healthy discussion about/one's sexuality.

Negative attitudes towards sexuality and our body-denying spirituality stem from distorted understanding of God's purpose. The embodied God who embraced flesh in Jesus Christ is the ground for loving our bodies and to celebrate life and sexuality without abuse and misuse. Instead of stigmatizing and demonizing, the church is called to be a sanctuary where love, compassionate care and justice minister to all. Therefore, with open mind and prayer, let us:

- Affirm that human sexuality is God-given and good. Human sexuality is a good thing and sacred, a gift from God, the Creator, so that human beings become co-creator with God.

- Safeguard respect of diversity in a responsible manner within responsible relationships. Misuse and abuse of sex and sexuality is condemned in the Bible

- Consider sexuality within a broader framework of understanding the human being as a relational being that relates to others, and not only in terms of single acts that are evaluated in isolation. Hence, sexuality would be assessed with regard to how it serves and contributes to such relationships.

- Affirm that responsibility and mutuality are the basis for how we shape and live in sexual (as well as family) relationships with others.

- Address misuse of sexuality as in prostitution, pornography, promiscuity, trafficking, incest and other forms of sexual exploitation;

- Affirm all human beings, irrespective of sexual orientation, as created in the Image of God.

- Encourage churches to advocate for the dignity and the rights of those who risk being criminalized because of their sexual orientation.

- Continue the open, honest and self-critical talk about family, marriage and human sexuality.

- Given the seriousness of the issues of homosexuality, encourage the churches not to disregard either the issues or the presence of LGBTIQ within the Church.

Endnotes

[1] Max L. Stackhouse, "The Heterosexual Norm" in *Homosexuality and Christian Community*, ed. Choon-Leong Seow (Louisville: John Knox Press, 1996), p. 12.

[2] *Ibid.*, p. 134.

[3] Richard B. Hays, "Awaiting the Redemption of Our Bodies: The Witness of Scripture Concerning Homosexuality" in *Homosexuality in the Church: Both Sides of the Debate*, eds. Jeffrey S. Siker (Louisville: Westminster John Knox Press, 1994), p. 11.

[4] Please refer to Gerald West, Reconfiguring a biblical story (Genesis 19)...... in Unit 2 p of this book for more details.

[5] Alan A. Brash, *Facing our Differences: The Churches and Their Gay and Lesbian Members* (Geneva: WCC Publication, 1995), p. 36.

[6] John J. Mcneill, "Homosexuality: Challenging the Church to Grow" in *Homosexuality in the Church, op.cit.*,p. 50.

[7] John J. Mcneill, "Homosexuality: Challenging the Church to Grow," 56.

Advocacy Work with LGBTIQ Communities

Anshi Zachariah

Abstract

This article focuses on the situation of the LGBTIQ community, their difficulties and need for advocacy and the role of faith groups in this scenario.

The LGBTIQ communities face challenges by being part of a society, which by and large follows a binary understanding of gender. This understanding is also derived from traditional interpretations of biblical texts (Adam - Eve). While newer biblical interpretations as well as a broadened definition of gender support an understanding of everyone as equal creations of God and equal members of society, in reality, many members of the LGBTIQ community do not experience this equality in their li-lives.

Though entitled to basic human rights as everyone else, people with a LGBTIQ background faces undue hardships. These include hurdles and threats by the existing legal framework, lack of support by their families, teachers and peers, resulting in dropping out of school, which in turn leads to disadvantages in the job market, apart from the anyway existing discrimination at the workplace. They comprise of biased portrayal in the media sustaining the view of and dealings with the LGBTIQ community in public places or by the police. And they also include challenges with access to and availability of appropriate health care.

This article invites faith groups to join in the efforts for advocacy for the LGBTIQ community in the described areas. Foremost, faith groups can impact a change of perception in society by an open discourse on sexuality allowing a transformation of the overall view of patriarchal heterosexism. The article concludes that church as a community of equals is called to engage in LGBTIQ advocacy as part of her call to a ministry of compassionate justice and healing.

Introduction

The biblical accounts of creation found in the first three chapters of Genesis influence our understanding of gender roles and concepts of sexuality. These familiar stories of the creation of Eve and Adam in the Garden of Eden has a long and varied history of interpretation within the Christian tradition to demonstrate that there are only two genders-male and female, and among them, women are inferior and/or subordinate to men. However, it is important to investigate the patriarchal and heteronormative biases of the original authors of the biblical texts and their interpreters.

Phyllis Trible, a feminist Biblical scholar, clarifies that it is not until after the 'fall' that hierarchical distinctions between man and woman come about. Before their banishment from the garden there is a high degree of equality between the sexes that is demonstrated in the text. She notes that "God first made the human (*Adam*) without gender, since, although a masculine pronoun is used for the new creature, it is not until the woman is made from this creature that the sexes are differentiated"[1] What is significant here is to understand how the biblical story of Eve and Adam is helpful in constructing an inclusive and gender-neutral notion of human sexuality and gender which rejects the binary thinking and accepts the spectrum of gender identities and sexual orientations that constitute the whole being of a person.

Challenging the Gender Binary

It is a fact that we are conditioned to believe that there are only two genders, but it is not so. To discuss more gender identities, we need to reinvent our understanding of gender. "It seems clear that gender is not fixed at birth, nor is it limited to just two categories. In addition, gender cannot be defined as biological, one's genitalia, appearance, natural, only male or female, fixed or non-changing because gender is a cultural construct, not a physical reality."[2] The gender binary identity is forced on us through a socio-cultural reinforcement which begins right from our family, education systems, work, religious groups as well as the larger society. Hence, this article aims to affirm that gender is not a binary and that there can be as many variations of gender as possible due to our desire to be who we are which is very much shaped or influenced by the larger society. Hence, the question of inclusion and exclusion does not occur as all of us are God's creation, and no one can feel superior over the other. It is the basic right of each individual, irrespective of gender, sexuality, race and caste to be who they are, and enjoy their rights and privileges as God's creation. It is the basic right of every person to live with self-esteem and right to live with dignity.

Are the Basic Human Rights at Stake?

Though the Universal Declaration of Human Rights acknowledges and affirms the "inherent dignity and of the equal and inalienable rights of all members of the human family,"[3] an explicit articulation of declarations, conventions and treaties of the LGBTIQ communities is lacking, and their human rights are at stake. The LGBTIQ communities are denied basic civil, political, social and economic rights either by law or practices. The violations of basics rights like right to life, non discrimination, the freedom of movement, right to privacy, the right to practice any religion etc. from all parts of the world are documented in a study guide prepared by Human Rights Education Associates (HREA).[4] However, such violations still exist in a world which is no shortage of declarations of human rights and other constitutional provisions to safeguard every citizen.

Article 14 of the Indian Constitution ensures citizens equality before the law. *Article 15* (1) prohibits the state from discriminating any citizen on ground of any religion, race, caste, sex, place of birth or any of them. How far such provisions are helpful for the LGBTIQ communities is contentious and complex. The Indian Penal Code has criminalized same sex practices as it is "against the order of nature" under sec 377. (Section 377, IPC). Though the Delhi high court judgment (2009) decriminalised same sex practices, the 2013 judgement of the Supreme Court reverted it. Later, the 2014 NALSA Judgement has directed Centre and State Governments "to grant legal recognition of gender identity whether it be male, female or third gender."[5] There are also other provisions like 36A of the Karnataka Police Act, which gives the Commissioner of Police the power to control and maintain a register to scrutinize the whereabouts of the transgender community. The Immoral Traffic Prevention Act, 1986 which intends to stop the trafficking and sexual exploitation of women and children are used to criminalise male, female and transgender sex workers. As per this Act, though prostitution is not an offence, practising it in a brothel or within 200m of any public place is illegal.[6]

Realities to Live with.....

Lack of family support

A gender non conforming child, experiences discomfort in their gender assigned at birth starting from early childhood. However, they are likely to assert their identity once they reach puberty. Once they disclose their discomfort to the assigned gender these children experience rejection, discrimination and even threats, and are not even safe in their own families. It is not easy for them to leave their family and move out, but situations force them to leave their loved ones and go out into the world which they have absolutely no idea about. The significant role which family plays in the marginalization of gender non confirming children is a serious concern. Female born minorities face further discrimination within their families due to patriarchal norms and controls. A study by LABIA highlighted that the families emerge as the extremely violent and non supportive structures that maintain the hierarchy. "Considering the patriarchal nature of society, all People Assigned Gender Female at Birth tend to face greater violence and discrimination within the family. And when the non-normative gender and sexuality arise, things become even worse".[7]

Dropouts

The gender non-conforming children are teased -, bullied and are met with silence as well as physical assaults for the very reason that they are not able to cope with the societal expectations on how to talk, dress, appear and the like. Many of the gender nonconforming persons are unable to complete their education due to such negative experiences in school. The LABIA[8] study also highlighted the fact that for several respondents, school was a place that negated the very sense of self. This is also a very tough phase for them personally as they themselves have not dealt with it or do not know how to deal with it. They face humiliation from friends and teachers and they are not in a position to share information with their family members, resulting in dropping out of the school and migrating to urban areas where they come in touch with people with similar experiences. Sport is another area where many participated and found safe space for self-expression. On the other hand, there is also differential treatment for boys and girls playing sports or an attitude that certain sports are boy's sports.[9]

Lack of employment and discrimination

Discrimination in terms of employment for the gender and sexual minority communities happens in different forms. For many of them being drop outs from school and unable to complete their education; the opportunities for employment are very limited. Denial of a job despite being qualified is common. In most cases, LGBTIQ employees may be underemployed or paid less than non-LGBTIQ employees, despite having a similar qualification and experience. Some of them work at IT sectors, NGOs and CBOs while a good number of transgender continue with begging and sex work. The lack of Identity documents in their preferred gender is another challenge; however, the NALSA judgement ensures the right to self-identification. There are ways one can change it, at the same time there are many ways such requests can be rejected in spite of having legal provisions.

Health

Health care is a challenge to the LGBTIQ communities right from the beginning. Most of the time, their health is reduced to HIV and AIDS and to sex reassignment surgery. Their general health and wellbeing, emotional and physical needs are not given enough attention. Also, most of the religious leaders look at HIV and AIDS only as a sexual aberration which is spread only through the bad and immoral practices. This dominant understanding of HIV as an issue of immorality and sexual promiscuity and also automatically ascribing the negative labelling to these communities should be condemned.

There are several instances of denied treatment and unwarranted behaviour to the transpersons. In spite of being dressed in a certain gender, the gender marked in the registration counter may not match with their preferred gender. This creates much discomfort and frustration. Once they move out of the immediate family, the daily struggles for sustenance keeps them involved in tedious tasks, which results in ignoring health or denying health needs. Even the response of the health system is so negative that they keep on postponing their health care needs.

The sex reassignment surgery (SRS) is one of the lifelong dreams for many a transgender. Some of them opt out of that also because the medical system which in spite of many advanced techniques and research is not in a position to provide accurate, efficient surgeries. The doctors are not trained enough, or they are still learning by experimenting on the trans community, putting the lives of the trans community in danger. Also, the treatments are very expensive. Hence the trans-community is still hoping for an efficient, subsidised SRS surgery. In a recent discussion on the official YouTube channel of Manorama News "Is there human experiment in Trivandrum medical college,"[10] a trans man raised the hardships that he suffered while undergoing the SRS procedure. The Government should set this on a top priority and allocate more grants and fellowships for advanced research and training to do such complicated but crucial procedures.

Media

The media many time gives less or distorted coverage to the LGBTIQ issues. There is also a tendency to portray a negative picture. The recent sting operation conducted by TV9 in Bangalore was an example. Dayamma Nirvana is an age old traditional method of castration among the transgender community. TV9 has released a video projecting such a Dayamma nirvana to be a kidnapping and forced castration of a youth who was part of the community for the past three years, this resulted in the arrest of 5 transgenders.

Public space

Accessing public spaces is a challenge to the trans-genders. They face silent and loud physical and sexual abuses while using public spaces like malls, metros, shops, bus stands, religious spaces and the like. Using toilet is one of the difficult challenges for students who are gender non conforming.[11] For a trans-man, if he goes to a men's toilet, chances are that he is abused sexually or physically. At the same time, if he goes to a woman's toilet, the women will scream and call people's attention that may land him being physically assaulted. There are instances where transmen used bathrooms reserved for persons with disabilities as they were unsure and not comfortable to use either men's or women's toilet. This is also a major health hazard which transmen face on a day to day basis.

A recent announcement by the water and sanitation ministry of the central government which allows members from the third-gender to use washrooms meant for both men and women in the community and public toilets raises certain questions.[12] Though it is a welcoming move the question is what guarantee is ensured for the safety of the person and who will be held responsible if they experience social discrimination by using either male or female rest rooms. It also is contrary to the NALSA judgment which opts for separate facilities for transgenders.

Housing

The absence or inadequate housing is one of the serious problems faced by the transgender community. In most cases, the family deprives the trans-community from having any share in the property with the excuse that the transgenders cannot run a family and also cannot reproduce. In spite of making an advance payment and higher rents than usual, the transgenders find it difficult to get housing due to the objections raised by the neighbours and the landlords based on the stereotype that they are frauds and they will create trouble! The Jogappa research study conducted by Aneka exposes a range of issues around housing. "The issue of housing is not merely having a place to reside: it includes a range of subsidiary themes within its ambit, such as accessibility to housing, security, availability of resources and so on."[13] However, - housing is a basic need once a transperson is out of their family homes.

Police Harassment

The police harass and discriminate transgenders for no reason for any issues in the community. Karnataka Police Act 36A and other discriminatory laws are often used to charge them. In 2002, four kothi sex workers were picked from the streets by the police and severely beaten up and harassed. An enquiry of this event came out as a report[14] and such incidents continue to happen even today. Rapes in jails are common, *kothis* and *hijras*[15] are always at a greater risk of mistreatment by authorities and inmates[16] and are sexually violated.

How do we advocate in such a context?

Legal Advocacy

In spite of all the apprehension about the legal system, the legal system with the constitutional guarantees ensures powerful tools for the community to move forward. First of all, it is very important to mobilize the existing legal frame work. Many of the constitutional provisions guarantee and affirm the space and rights of the gender and sexual minorities as the citizens of the country. There are procedural safeguards such as Criminal Procedure Code 1973 which can safeguard and ensure the rights. "A citizen is entitled to file a case in the High Court for violation of their fundamental rights."[17] It is very crucial to take as many steps as possible to repeal Art 377 and repeal 36A of Karnataka Police Act and review other judgments and bills. Human rights groups have protested against this Act as well as Sec 377, which has been used by the police to persecute transgenders. However, the government of Karnataka told the high court that "it would delete the word "eunuchs" from Section 36(A) of the Karnataka Police Act, which gives powers to the police to "regulate eunuchs."[18] Though this petition has not yet gained the achieved goal, but still a step forward in the life of the movement of the transgenders in Karnataka. This petition was filed by the Karnataka Sexual Minority Forum demanding the constitutional right to equality granted to the third gender.

The task is to make sure that bills which ensure dignity and rights for the trans-communities like Nalsa Judgment shall be implemented. The pro-community provisions of the Social Justice and Empowerment Bill, Tiruchi Siva Bill, The Transgender Bill 2015 and 2016 are another area of crucial Intervention. The recent Anti-discrimination and Equality Bill 2016 introduced by Dr Shashi Tharoor, MP on 10 March 2017 puts the need for an anti-discrimination legislation back on the political agenda. "The Bill clubs people under various groups- protected, and disadvantaged; and defines what would constitute discrimination, both direct and indirect. The Bill clubs following characteristics – sexual orientation: gays, lesbians, bisexuals, kothis and other sexual minorities; and gender identity: transgendered persons, hijras and gender-non-conforming persons; under disadvantaged groups, along with caste, race, disability, HIV-status, marital status etc. It further prescribes forming of a Central Equality Commission by both Centre and State Governments to "exercise the power conferred on, and to perform the functions and duties assigned to it under this Act."[19]

The legal battle is one of the keys to ensure equality for the LBGTIQ communities. It is very important for the faith communities to endorse such efforts. The faith groups should stand with the community based groups and other networks who take lead in such struggles rather than sabotaging it. When the Delhi High court decriminalized same sex relations through a petition filed by the NAZ Foundation, many of the religious groups came to the street and stood united and joined together in filing an appeal to the Supreme court which resulted in re-criminalizing sexuality based on sec 377 of the IPC. Hence, it is very important to create and strengthen larger networks of faith groups to reject homophobia and transphobia and to create a welcoming and safe space for the transgender and transsexuality communities.

Advocacy from an Interfaith Perspective

Sexuality is a subject treated with a 'Don't ask, Don't say' attitude in the family, educational institutions, faith groups and in the larger society. All sectors of society, ranging from religious institutions to small families, avoid and actively discourage the discussion of gender and sexuality. Thus, we are severely ill-equipped to nurture authentic sexual health in our communities. At the same time, our understanding of the issue is distorted with dominant heteronormative and patriarchal notions of gender and sexuality. Religion plays a significant role in perpetuating patriarchal heterosexism as the "natural" and "normal" order of sexuality. The complex and controversial nexus between gender, sexuality and religion forms the basis for this distorted understanding. It is the very reason, the churches and faith groups have the mandate to initiate and encourage discussions around sexuality as part of the very mission of the church/faith group. The attitude towards gender and sexual- minorities should be addressed and challenged so that we can get rid of such imbibed notions about a group of people who are very much part of God's creation.

Advocate for educational rights and employment opportunities

Many of the gender non-conforming children could not continue or complete their education due to lack of acceptance they experienced at home and in school. Sensitizing and equipping the school teachers and their immediate community to the needs of these children should be prioritized and implemented. Specific advocacy efforts must be worked out to ensure education rights of the LGBTIQ communities. Educating the family, peer group etc are mandatory to make sure there are enough support groups.

Employment opportunities are also related to completion of education as well as professional, technical and skill based training. Companies and institutions must adopt careful recruitment strategies as well as in job training to encourage and equip more LGBTIQ members to enter the work force. Sensitization programmes must be conducted in such institutions to avoid insensitive and discriminatory practices. Every person has to be given equal opportunity for employment in any institution.

Towards a holistic approach to health

A holistic approach to the health and well being of the LGBTIQ communities is to be promoted. Religious institutions should take the lead in de-linking the existing nexus of gender and sexual minorities with sin and immorality. This enables the individual to come out and affirm one's identity free of guilt and shame and to get access to the health care services.

Sensitization of the health care providers at all levels is a crucial step and this should be maximized. The Medical Council of India should make and issue guidelines every year, to ensure that there is no discrimination in treatment at any level. To understand and access health care as a right and not as benevolence is essential. The level of discrimination is such that many LGBTIQ members postpone or cancel their health requirements. For those who opt for sex re-assignment surgery, proper information and guidelines should be provided by the health fraternity. It is also important to scale up the debate on gender identity and sexual orientation as a choice and orientation rather than a disorder.

Media Advocacy

Media plays a major role in erasing the stigma the LGBTIQ people go through. It should help enhance media coverage of the community in local, national and global context. The media should also help to enhance a favourable public opinion, support and social inclusion to develop a deeper understanding of the diversities of sexuality. Media interventions should also facilitate legal support and counsel in ensuring their legal provisions. It is also important that Media gain a deeper awareness and knowledge about the community that Media can transmit right knowledge to the general population. The social media, both print and electronic etc should follow sensitive and respectful guidelines to be closely incorporated in the treatment of these issues. Short documentaries on gender and sexual minorities could be made to expand the visibility of the community. Public meetings with various Civil Society Organisations, activists and progressive leaders from political parties, as well as cultural activists, could also be done to increase visibility and acceptance.

Action Research

Ongoing Action Research is needed to generate insights, facts & figures on the needs, challenges of the community as well as the biases and prejudices of the general public for better understanding and for highlighting accurate and authentic information to plan out further advocacy strategies for future interventions.

Police Reforms

The police administration should work in consultation with a local standing committee comprising of social activists and human rights activists to investigate cases of abuse and illegal cases against the community. The police should be transparent and careful in dealing with all procedures and penalties and even better to consult with a standing committee. Measurements should be taken to ensure protection and safety in all dealings especially custody and in prisons. Another caution is to make sure that the transperson is not sent to the prison cell with other men to prevent harassment, abuse and rape.

Conclusion

The Church as the Community of Equals

The church is a community of equals and hence there is no room for domination by any. The church ceases to be a church if it engages in any act of dehumanization of any individuals based on their gender identity, sexual orientation, caste, class or of any differences whatsoever. Religion plays a major role in reinforcing the moralistic perception of sexuality. Hence, it is the responsibility of the religious/faith groups to promote an understanding of sexuality which is body affirming, inclusive and which celebrates differences. The Church, as the body of Christ, is a community called out to continue the ministry of compassionate justice and healing. The Church can no longer remain a silent spectator while the LGBTIQ community is facing discrimination and marginalization from within the church. Rather, the church needs to boldly affirm, acknowledge and welcome the presence of the LGBTIQ community in the whole life of the church.

Where is the Church in their experiences of utter God forsakenness? Where is the body of Christ when people are discriminated and rejected? Is there any hope for justice from the faith communities. A new discernment of the rejected communities entering the place of healing and restoration within the church community is the ministry of the church and all our advocacy efforts should lead to creating a community of equals.

Endnotes

[1] "Did Man or God Create Woman? Feminist Interpretations of the Story of Eve and Adam", by theyellowdart, Author at Faith Promoting Rumor 2009 *http://www.patheos.com/blogs/faithpromotingrumor/2009/06/did-man-or-god-create-woman-feminist-interpretations-of-the-story-of-eve-and-adam/* accessed on June 12, 2017.

[2] Berkely Hermann, 2016 , "Challenging the Gender Binary" in Academia *https://www.academia.edu/6736395/Challenging_the_Gender_Binary* accessed on May 30, 2017.

[3] h*ttp://www.ohchr.org/EN/UDHR/Documents/UDHR_Translations/eng.pdf* accessed on July 26, 2017.

[4] Study Guide: Sexual Orientation and Human Rights Copyright © Human Rights Education Associates (HREA), 2003, *http://hrlibrary.umn.edu/edumat/studyguides/sexualorientation.html* accessed on June 6, 2017.

[5] The Supreme Court judgement on Transgender Rights(NALSA vs Union of India): A summary of the 15th April 2014 judgement, by Danish Sheikh P1*http://*

/orinam.net/content/wpcontent/uploads/2014/04/nalsa_summary_danish.pdf accessed on June 6, 2017.

[6] "The Immoral Traffic (Prevention) Act, 1956" Human Rights Law Network http://www.hrln.org/hrln/child-rights/laws-in-place/1715-the-immoral-traffic-prevention-act-1956.html accessed on June 12, 2017.

[7] "Breaking the Binary: A study by LABIA-a Queer Feminist LGBT Collective, Published by LABIA, a Queer Feminist LGBT Collective, Mumbai, April 2013, p.40.

[8] Breaking the Binary, p.43.

[9] Breaking the Binary, p.44.

[10] "Is there human experiment in Trivandrum medical college" Published on May 1, 2017 ,Counter Point, Manorama News, *https://www.youtube.com/watch?v=_Deae3zfgp4* accessed on May 3, 2017.

[11]A Tool for legal Empowerment of Transgender Persons in India, Tweet Foundation, Published on May 11, 2017 *https://www.youtube.com/watch?v=vW_pItl7m4A&feature=youtu.be* accessed on May 15, 2017.

[12] US dithers but India aids third gender with bathroom bill Dipak K Dash| TNN | Updated: Apr 5, 2017, 01.27 PM IST *http://timesofindia.indiatimes.com/india/ensure-toilet-access-to-3rd-gender-centre-tells-states/articleshow/58018540.cms accessed on June 12*, 2017.

[13] Jogappa: Gender, Identity, and the Politics of Exclusion ,Aneka/HBF, Bangalore 2014, p.49.

[14] Human Rights violations against the transgender community: A study of Kothi and hijra sex workers in Bangalore, India, Report by People's Union for Civil Liberties, Karnataka (PUCL-K)September 2003.

[15] Human Rights violations against the transgender community, 17-19.

[16]Human Rights violations against the transgender community, 37.

[17] Human Rights violations against the transgender community, 68.

[18]Krishnaprasad, "Will delete word 'eunuchs' from police Act: State", 201 *http://www.thehindu.com/news/cities/bangalore/Will-delete-word-%E2%80%98eunuchs%E2%80%99-from-police-Act-State/article13996218.ece* accessed on January 26, 2017.

[19] "After Two Failed Attempts at Amending Sec 377 in Parliament, Dr. Shashi Tharoor introduces Anti-Discrimination And Equality Bill", Gaylaxy.March 16, 2017 *http://www.gaylaxymag.com/latest-news/two-failed-attempts-amending-sec-377-parliament-dr-shashi-tharoor-introduces-anti-discrimination-equality-bill/#gs.EW7piZA* accessed on March 20, 2017.

Gay Rights: Bridging Science, Society, Religion and the Church

K.S. Jacob

Abstract

The persistence of conservative heterosexist ideals and norms within religion and society encourage homophobia, prejudice and bigotry. Despite major changes in society the bias related to human sexuality continues, albeit in sophisticated forms in today's world. The discordance between positions held by science, medicine, psychiatry on one-hand and religion and conservative cultures on the other will take time to converge. We should be aware of the issues and should strive to measure our own goodness and humanity, not by the people we exclude, but rather by the attitudes we embrace and those we include.

Modern medicine and psychiatry abandoned pathologizing same-sex orientation, behaviour and life style many decades ago.[1] The World Health Organization accepted same-sex orientation as a normal variant of human sexuality in its International Classification of Diseases 10 in 1992.[2] The United Nations Human Rights Council values Lesbian, Gay Bisexual and Transgender (LGBT) rights.[3] LGBTIQ orientation, behaviour and lifestyles have been accepted in many western nations, which have equal legal status; civil partnerships are recognised as a marriage in some countries.

This chapter summarises perspectives based on science, medicine and psychiatry, discussed in detail elsewhere.[4-9] It also examines the issues from a Biblical point of view with a focus on India.

Medicalization of homosexuality

Early 19th century understanding of homosexuality was religious. The shift in ideas from sin to medical pathology occurred in the late 19th and early 20th centuries.[10,11] Early etiological speculations included genetic, endocrine and anatomical differences, which were said to produce a particular orientation. Others argued for imperfect sexual differentiation, immaturity and pathology as causal. These beliefs led to claims that homosexuality could be cured.

These explanations also led to the removal of the responsibility of defining homosexuality from the realm of religion and secured it within science and medicine. However, it also created a category of persons — the homosexual. This was in stark contrast to the religious belief that homosexuality was a behaviour rather than identity. It also perpetuated the social stigma by moving it from the domain of sin to that of pathology.[10,11] The term "homosexual" became and is pejorative. However, it considers only one aspect of a person and tends to sum up his or her entire identity.

Normalization of homosexuality

The work of Kinsey and his colleagues in the mid-20th century was a scientific and cultural watershed.[4-11] They documented a high prevalence of same-sex feelings and behaviour in men and women. Many researchers documented homosexuality across cultures and among almost all non-human primate species and argued that it was natural and widespread. Investigations using psychological tests could not differentiate between heterosexual and homosexual orientation in men. Research also demonstrated that people with the homosexual orientation did not have any objective psychological dysfunction or impairments in judgment, stability and vocational capabilities. This led to a movement within American psychiatry, which argued against the a priori assumption that homosexuality is pathological. Psychiatric, psychoanalytic, medical and mental health professionals now consider homosexuality a normal variation of human sexuality.[4-11]

On the origins

Medicine and science continue to debate the relative contributions of nature and nurture, biological and psychosocial factors, to homosexuality.[4-11] The proposed biological models argue for genes and hormones organizing brain circuits that mediate sexual orientation with biology playing a permissive role by providing neural circuits through which neuronal connections are inscribed or through indirect effects working through temperament and personality. Despite many hypotheses and much research, there is no definite evidence to suggest specific genetic, neural or hormonal differences that determine sexual orientation.

Anthropologists have documented significant variations in the organization and meaning of same-sex practices across cultures and changes within particular societies over time.[4-11] The universality of same-sex expression co-exists with variations in its meaning and practice across cultures. Cross-cultural studies highlight the limits of any single explanation of homosexuality within a particular society.

Classical theories of psychological development hypothesize the origins of adult sexual orientation in childhood experience.[4-11] However, recent research argues that psychological and interpersonal events throughout the lifecycle explain sexual orientation. It is unlikely that a unique set of characteristics or a single pathway will explain all adult homosexuality.

The debate on homosexuality is polarized with arguments for it being innate and fixed, versus constructed and mutable.[4-11] The essentialist theory argues that it is innate and an expression of biological factors. Constructivists argue that homosexuality is a result of social and external influences. The argument that homosexuality is a stable phenomenon is based on the consistency of same-sex attractions, the failure of attempts to change and the lack of success with treatments that attempt to alter sexual orientation. There is a growing realization that homosexuality is not a single phenomenon; that there may be multiple phenomena within the construct of homosexuality.

However, classical theories of psychological development employ untestable conjectures. They argue without proof that the origins of adult sexual orientation lie in childhood experience and development. Similarly, genetic and biological theories are reductionistic. They do not explain complex aspects of human behaviour, including natural inclination and choice. The universality of same-sex orientation and behaviour and variations in its meaning and practice across cultures undermine single and simplistic explanations.

Human sexuality is complex and diverse.[4-11] The recognition of the distinction between desire, behaviour and identity acknowledges the multidimensional nature of sexuality. The fact that these dimensions may not always be congruent in individuals suggests complexity. Bisexuality and discordance between biological sex and gender role and identity add to the conundrum. Medicine and psychiatry continues to employ terms like homosexuality, heterosexuality, bisexuality and trans-sexuality to encompass all related issues. However, current social usage argues for lesbian, gay, bisexual and transgender (LGBTIQ) terminology, which focuses on identities.

Culture

Anti-homosexual attitudes, once considered the norm, have changed over time in many social and institutional settings in the West.[4-11] However, heterosexism, which idealizes heterosexuality, considers it the norm, and denigrates and stigmatizes all non-heterosexual forms of behaviour, identity, relationships and communities, is also common. However, the anti-homosexual attitudes of many religions and communities reflect the existence of widespread prejudice.

Many conservative and tradition-bound societies continue to be ruled by religious and social orthodoxy and patriarchy.[4-11] In fact, many of the difficulties faced by LGBTIQ people are a result of stigma and discrimination they face in our heterosexual world. However, those opposing these views argue that heterosexuality has been the norm throughout history and in different cultures. They are not willing to accept homosexuality as part of a normal identity. They suggest that it will lead to the breakdown of the family.

The prevalence of homosexuality is difficult to estimate for many reasons including the associated stigma and social repression, the unrepresentative samples surveyed and the failure to distinguish between desire, behaviour and identity. The figures vary among age groups, regions and cultures. Western figures are said to approach 10 per cent.[10,11]

Medicine and society

Medicine has a complex relationship with culture, society and governments.[12] Michel Foucault recognised knowledge structures, which enhance and maintain the exercise of power.[13] He argued that the religious practice of confession, secularised in the 18th and 19th centuries, allowed people to confess to their innermost thoughts. These became data for the social sciences, which used the knowledge to construct mechanisms of social control. Medicine in the 19th and early 20th centuries medicalized sexuality, switching the emphasis from sin to pathology. However, the vibrant Gay Rights movements of the mid-20th century forced medicine to re-examine the issues. A critical review and analysis of the evidence did not suggest pathology, impairments or reduced capabilities, resulting in the deletion of homosexuality from psychiatric classifications.

Clinical approaches

In most circumstances, the psychiatric issues facing LGBTIQ people are similar to those of the general population.[4-11]However, the complexities of these identities require tolerance, respect and a nuanced understanding of sexual matters. Clinical assessments should be detailed and should go beyond routine labelling and assess different issues related to lifestyle choices, identity, relationships and social supports. Helping people understand their sexuality and providing support for living in a predominantly heterosexual world is crucial and mandatory. People with LGBTIQ orientation, behaviour and lifestyle face many hurdles, including the conflicts in acknowledging their homosexual feelings, the meaning of disclosure and the problems faced in their coming out.

There is no definitive evidence of the effectiveness of sexual conversion therapies.[4-11]In fact, there is evidence that such attempts may cause more harm than good. Such attempts at conversion may result in increased mental distress including inducing depression and sexual dysfunction.

With the acceptance of homosexuality as a normal variant by mainstream health professionals, there has been a reduced emphasis on using and evaluating sexual conversion therapies within medical and psychiatric circles. However, faith-based groups and counsellors pursue such attempts at conversion using yardsticks, which do not meet scientific standards.[4-11,14] Clinicians should keep the dictum "first do no harm" in mind. Physicians should provide medical service with compassion and respect for human dignity for all people irrespective of their sexual orientation. Training physicians, psychiatrists, psychologists and counsellors in the assessment of sexuality is mandatory.

Indian context

India has had a liberal tradition and attitude to sex and sexuality as evidenced by the treatise, the *Kamasutra*. Temple sculpture in Konark and Khajuraho and other temples also suggest similar liberal and diverse position on sex and sexuality. However, more recently the British government, during their colonial rule of the Indian subcontinent, criminalised homosexuality based on Victorian attitudes and morality. They introduced laws to punish same sex behaviour.

After Indian independence, the Indian Penal Code included these laws as Section 377, which included incarceration for same-sex behaviour. The police often used the law to harass, threaten and blackmail people with homosexual orientation. The Delhi High Court, in a landmark judgment in 2009 read down Section 377.[15] However, the Supreme Court of India reinstated the law in 2013.[16] The response from mental health and legal establishment to restoring Section 377 of the Indian Penal Code was weak.[17-18] Conservative theologians and religious leaders in India celebrated the verdict, revealing their deep-seated intolerance and bigotry. It betrayed a poor understanding of the issues and reflected deeply ingrained prejudices. The Indian medical, legal and religious establishments, steeped in traditional, social and cultural tenets, hesitate to support LGBTIQ rights, while accepting many other western-international legal, medical and psychiatric standards.[4-11] Despite their dependence on and slavery to western thoughts, ideas, diagnostic classifications and treatment options, medicine and psychiatry in India, continue to be reluctant to emphatically support these norms for the country, due to local religious prejudice and social orthodoxy.

Indian social and religious conservatives argue that legalizing same-sex orientation, behaviour, lifestyles and relationships will lead to the breakdown of the family. Nevertheless, the threat today to marriage and family in India is from heterosexual men with their high rates of alcohol abuse, physical and sexual violence, harassment for dowry, unprotected extramarital sex and the abandonment of the wife and children.

Despite an increase in awareness and annual Gay Pride parades in

Indian cities, data from India on same-sex orientation, behaviour and lifestyle is sparse. There is a dearth of good data on the subject using large and representative samples of the population. Research into the issues in India is crucial for increasing our understanding of the local and regional context.

The Supreme Court's conservative ruling on Section 377[16] is in contradiction to its stand on enlightened and liberal stand on transgender rights[19] reveal conflicts and confusion of thought within the Indian judiciary. Its shows clear inconsistency in the application of fundamental rights to specific contexts. The legal status of same-sex orientation, behaviour and life style are currently under review by India's Supreme Court. It calls for a clearer understanding of the relationship between science, medicine and psychiatry on one hand and society and religion on the other.

Homosexuality and the Church

The Old Testament describes a conservative and patriarchal society, which privileges men over women.[9] It also highlighted heterosexist norms. Such interpretation was in keeping with the culture of the region at the time. In fact, the Old Testament has many rules, which allowed for genocide, racial and ethnic discrimination, polygamy, slavery, selling daughters into slavery, strict dietary laws, exacting agricultural practices, stringent rules about facial hair for men, ostracising people with leprosy and stoning people to death. It also prohibited cooking on the Sabbath and asking for and receiving interest on money lent or borrowed.

Nevertheless, the Church and many Christians today have rejected many of these Biblical standards including slavery, apartheid values and racial discrimination and have also whole-heartedly embraced capitalism, with its lack of equity and quest for quick profits.[9] And yet, many conservative Christian and churches continue to focus on people's sexuality rather than highlighting their humanity.

There are interpretations within Christianity, which support alternative sexual lifestyles.[20-22] They argue that there is no need for guilt, shame or condemnation for those with a different sexuality. They interpret the passage in Genesis (18:20-19:29) about Sodom as censure against homosexual rape rather than denunciation of consensual adult same-sex intercourse. The Leviticus code (18:22) is seen in the context of prevention of ethnic contamination. The passages in the New Testament mention same sex relationships in the context of forsaking God (1 Corinthians 9:6), idolatry (Romans 1:24-27), prostitution and paedophilia (1 Timothy 1:10) and not within loving and, faithful relationships. There is also much debate about the meaning, contextual use and translation of the words used in the original Biblical texts.

The former Archbishop of Canterbury, Rowan Williams, and Pope Francis have publicly argued that we should not be judgemental about people's sexuality. Texts describing ancient social customs should not be used to spread prejudice and discrimination in today's context.[9] After all, Jesus did not condemn the LGBTIQs life-style. Today's religious leaders seem to define their religion by whom they exclude rather than by what they embrace and those they include.

Societal challenge

Stereotyping LGBTIQ life-styles and emphasising heterosexual norms result in a toxic mix. Behaviours of the past, which openly discriminated against human beings, based on sex, gender, caste, race, ethnicity, language, religion, are not now openly advocated. However, prejudice is now cloaked in subtle language and sophisticated arguments, but still employing old justifications and norms.[7,9] Such practices ensure the persistence of discrimination. Bigotry related to sexual orientation is now rarely manifested in its crude form (i.e., capital punishment or putting people in prison) but is still widely prevalent within social and religious conservatism. It not only prevents equalities of opportunity but also of outcomes for LGBTIQ people. We need to be aware of and debate sophisticated forms of prejudice in today's world.

The secularization of societies has resulted in the withdrawal of religion from public spaces. The separation of religion from the state is widely accepted in many countries. However, religious leaders who interpret ancient texts literally have viewed such liberal ideas with suspicion. Prejudice against different lifestyles and against the minorities is a part of many cultures, incorporated into most religions and is a source of conflict in several societies. In fact, the separation of church from the state has resulted in unfair practices within religions resulting in legal challenges. Religious institutions have used their right to continue their religious practices with its consequent patriarchal bias and discrimination of women and marginalized groups.

In addition to the challenges of living in a predominantly heterosexual world, the diversity within people with homosexual orientation results in many different kinds of issues. Sex, gender, age, ethnicity and religion add to the complexity of the issues faced. The stages of the life cycle (childhood, adolescence, middle and old age), family and relationships present diverse concerns.[7,9]

Religious ideas, cultural perceptions, social positions and medical opinions on many topics are often inter-related. However, their movement may not be in lock step and they may take time for converge. Nevertheless, each of these positions are strongly influenced by prevailing social standards and currently acceptable norms. Many religious tenets, which appear to be chiselled in stone, have given way to more enlightened reading over time suggesting the impact of social and cultural changes on their interpretation.[9] Religions, even those with revealed text, have softened their interpretations to keep up with the times. While complete convergence with current social standards will take time, most societies are slowly but steadily marching towards the goal of equality for all humanity.

The way forward

The society needs to acknowledge that social stigma and consequent discrimination of people with same-sex orientation cause much harm. It should respect the dignity and human rights of all people, irrespective of their sexuality.[4-11]There is a need to accept the normalcy and universality of same-sex orientation, behaviour and life style. Religious leaders and the Church should support the need to de-criminalise same–sex orientation and behaviour and to recognise LGBT rights to include human, civil, religious and political rights. The recognition of people's humanity also advocates the legal recognition of same-sex relationships, anti-bullying legislation, anti-discrimination laws in employment and housing, immigration equality, law for equal age of consent and laws against hate crimes, thus providing enhanced criminal penalties for prejudice-motivated behaviour and violence against LGBTIQ people.

The secular society, professional associations, religious congregations and community leaders should lead in showing the way to justice, equality, freedom and dignity.[4-11] It is the everyday heterosexist attitudes in society, which encourage prejudice and bigotry. We need to emphasize people's humanity rather than focus on their sexuality. Just as women's rights in the patriarchal Christian culture are slowly but surely gaining ground, so will the LGBTIQ people achieve equality and their rightful place in society.[9]

We should measure our own goodness and humanity, not by the people we exclude, but rather by the attitudes we embrace and those we include.

The views expressed are personal and do not reflect those of any institution or organisation.

Endnotes

[1] American Psychiatric Association. *Diagnostic and Statistical Manual of Mental Disorders*. IIIrd edition. Washington, DC: APA 1980.

[2] World Health Organization. *International Classification of Disease 10: Classification of Behavioural and Mental Disorders*. Geneva: WHO. 1992.

[3] United Nations Human Rights Office of the High Commissioner. *Born Free and Equal: Sexual Orientation and Gender identity in International Human Rights Law*. New York and Geneva: Office of the High Commissioner United Nations Human Rights; 2012. Available from: *http://www.ohchr.org/Documents/.....EqualLowRes.pdf*. [Last accessed on 2013 Dec 31]

[4] Jacob KS. Homosexuality, medicine and psychiatry. The Hindu. 25. 07. 2009 *http://www.hindu.com/2009/07/25/stories/2009072555940800.htm* (accessed 5.10.2014)

[5] Rao TSS, Jacob KS. Homosexuality and India. *Indian Journal of Psychiatry*, 2012; 54:1-3.

[6] Rao TSS, Jacob KS. The reversal of Gay Rights in India. *Indian Journal of Psychiatry* 2014: 56:1-2.

[7] Jacob KS.Gay rights and bigotry. *National Medical Journal of India*. 2015; 28: 241-242.

[8] Rao TSS, Rao GP, Raju MSVK, Saha G, Jagiwala M, Jacob KS. Gay rights, psychiatric fraternity and India. *Indian Journal of Psychiatry*, 2016; 58: 241-243.

[9] Jacob KS. Gay Rights and Bigotry: Reflection on the relationship between science, medicine, psychiatry, society, religion and the Church. In: *Church and Homophobia: Re-imagining Church as Rainbow Community*Editor George Zachariah Publisher: CISRS and ISPCK, 2014.

[10] Sadock VA. Normal Human Sexuality and Sexual Dysfunctions. Kaplan and Sadock's Comprehensive Textbook of Psychiatry 9th ed. (In: Sadock BJ, Sadock VA, Ruiz P, Editors) Philadelphia: Lippincott Williams & Wilkins; 2009. p. 2027-59.

[11] Drescher J, Byne WM. Homosexuality, Gay and Lesbian Identities and Homosexual Behaviour. Kaplan and Sadock's Comprehensive Textbook of Psychiatry 9th ed. (In: Sadock BJ, Sadock VA, Ruiz P, Editors) Philadelphia: Lippincott Williams & Wilkins; 2009. p. 2060-89.

[12] Miettenen O. The modern scientific physician: 2.Medical science versus scientific medicine. *CMAJ* 2001; 165: 591-592.

[13] O'Farrell C. *Michel Foucault*, London: SAGE. 2005.

[14] Forstein M. The pseudoscience of sexual orientation change therapy. BMJ 2004;328:E287-8.

[15] Naz Foundation vs Government of National Capital Territory New Delhi. Delhi High Court WP(C) No.7455/2001; Date of decision : 2nd July, 2009 available at *http://www.lawyerscollective.org/files/Naz%20Foundation%20Judgement.pdf*

[16] Koushal SK and another versus NAZ Foundation and others. Civil Appeal NO.10972 of 2013.*http://www.judis.nic.in/supremecourt/imgs1.aspx?filename=41070* .

[17] Iyer M. Homosexuality not a disease, psychiatrists say. Times of India 7 February 2014. *http://timesofindia.indiatimes.com/india/Homosexuality-is-not-a-disease-psychiatrists-say/articleshow/29965430.cms*.

[18] Verghese A. A fresh look at homosexuality. Indian J Psychiatry 2014; 56: 209-10.

[19] National Legal Services Authority versus Union of India and others. Writ Petition (Civil) 400 of 2012 with Writ Petition (Civil) 604 of 2013. *http://judis.nic.in/supremecourt/imgs1.aspx?filename=41411* (accessed on 25.4.2014)

[20] Davis R. Justified through Christ. Gaychurch.org *http://www.gaychurch.org/homosexuality-and-the-bible/justified-through-christ/*

[21] Cannon J. The Bible Christianity and Homosexuality. Gaychurch.org. *http://www.gaychurch.org/homosexuality-and-the-bible/the-bible-christianity-and-homosexuality/*

[22] Lowe B. A letter to Louise. Gaychurch.org. *http://www.gaychurch.org/homosexuality-and-the-bible/a-letter-to-louise/*

Bibliography

Publications on Human Sexuality, revealing Churches' Perspectives

Anglican World Communion, Conversations on Human Sexuality, London 2005 (*http://www.anglicancommunion.org/media/189015/conversations_on_human_sexuality.pdf*)

Amanze J, Demythologizing human sexuality in Africa, University of Botswana (*http://inerela.org/2010/07/demythologizing-african-conceptions-of-human-sexuality-a-gateway-to-prevention-and-eradication-of-hiv-and-aids-in-africa-prof-james-n-amanze/*)

Balka C, and Rose A (eds), Twice Blessed: On Being Lesbian, gay and Jewish edited by, Beacon Press, 1989;

Berner-Rodoreda. A, Neuenroth. C, The Burden of Breadwinning: Transformative Masculinities in the Context of HIV, Violence against Women and Gender Inequality, Dialogue 17, Practise, Brot für die Welt, Stuttgart, (2016), *http://sidebysidegender.org/wp-content/uploads/2016/11/Burden-of-Breadwinning-transf-mascs-HIV-GBV.pdf*

Cannon JR (ed.), *Homosexuality in the Orthodox Church*. Self-published, Createspace: 2011.

Cherniak M, Gerassimenko O, Brinkchröder M (eds.), "For I am Wonderfully Made": Texts on Eastern Orthodoxy and LGBT Inclusion, European Forum of Lesbian, Gay, Bisexual and Transgender Christian Groups, 2016

Chitando E, Klinken A (eds), Christianity and Controversies Over Homosexuality in Contemporary Africa, Routledge 2016;

Chitando E, Chirongoma S (eds), Redemptive Masculinity: Men, HIV, and Religion, WCC, 2012

Chitando E, Njoroge N, Contextual Bible Study Manual on Transformative masculinity, WCC, 2013 *http://sidebysidegender.org/wp-content/uploads/2016/02/Contextual-Bible-Study-Manual-on-Transformative-Masculinity-English.pdf*

Childs K, Harris J, and Cisneros A (eds), Anglicans and Human Sexuality. A Way Forward?, London 2016 (*http://www.lse.ac.uk/website-archive/IPA/ResearchAndEngagement/AnglicansAndSexuality/AnglicansAndSexuality AWayForward.pdf*)

Church of England, House of Bishops: Report on the Working Group of Human Sexuality, November 2013, Church Publishing House (*https://www.churchofengland.org/media/1891063/pilling_report_gs_1929_web.pdf*)

EKD Head Office, Homosexuality in contemporary discussion, Hannover 1996 (*https://www.ekd.de/english/1730-tensions_1997_homo1.html*)

General Synod of the Anglican Church of Canada, A Resource Guide for Discussions on Human Sexuality, Ontario 2007, (the *http://www.anglican.ca/wp-content/uploads/2010/10/resources1.pdf*)

General Conference Mennonite Church, Human Sexuality in the Christian Life, Mennonite Publishing House, Pennsylvania 1985 (*https://mennoharmony.files.wordpress.com/2011/01/human-sexuality-in-the-christian-life-1985.pdf*

Gennrich. D , Created in God's Image A Gender Transformation Toolkit For Women And Men In Churches, Norwegian Church AID, Oslo/ Pretoria, 2008, 2013 *https://www.kirkensnodhjelp.no/contentassets/c2cd7731ab1b472789 7258c5d49246c8/nca-createdingodsimage-completebook-jun2015-open2.pdf*

Gregorios P, Human Presence: An Orthodox View of Nature, Geneva, WCC, 1978

Germond P, de Gruchy S (Editors), Aliens in the Household of God: Homosexuality and Christian Faith in South Africa – David Philip Publishers, Claremont, South Africa, 1997

Gomes P J, The *Good Book: Reading the Bible with Mind and Heart,* San Francisco: William Morrow and Company Inc., 1996.

Gunda M R (ed), Report on Methodology, Challenges & Opportunities in the work of Inclusive & Affirming Ministries (IAM) 2009-2014, Harare Zimbabwe 2016.   (*https://www.hivos.org/sites/default/files/publications/stepping_stones_and_stumbling_blocks.iam_.pdf*)

Heyward C, Our Passion for Justice: Images of Power, Sexuality, and Liberation, The Pilgrim Press, 1984;

Helminiak D A, What the Bible Really Says About Homosexuality, Alamo Square Press, 1994;

Jung PB and Smith R F, *Heterosexism: An Ethical Challenge,* Albany: State University of New York Press, 1994.

Kenmogne J B, Homosexualite, Eglise et Droits de l'homme. Ouvrons le Debat, Edition CEROS , Yaounde 2012 (*http://www.cipcre.org/index.php?option=com_content&view=article&id=57:homosexualite-eglise-et-droits-de-lhomme&catid=63&Itemid=62&lang=fr*)

Kireopoulos A, Mecera J, *Ecumenical Directions in the United States Today: Churches on a Theological Journey*, Paulist Press, 2012.

Klinken A, Sexual Orientation, (Anti-) Discrimination and Human Rights in a "Christian Nation": The Politicisation of Homosexuality in Zambia, University of Leeds, 2017 (*http://eprints.whiterose.ac.uk/86909/3/Sexual_Orientation%2C_Anti-discrimination_and_Human_Rights_in_a_Christian_ Nation.pdf*)

Klinken A, Chitado E (eds), Public Religion and The Politics of Homosexuality in Africa, London and New York 2016;

KlinkenA, Transforming Masculinities in African Christianity: Gender Controversies in Times of AIDS, Routledge 2015

Knutson, Lebethe et al 2004. Called Gathered Sent: A Bible Study Guide on the Role of Men and Women in Church and Society. Cape Town: Evangelical Lutheran Church in Southern Africa (ELCSA)

Koulagna J B, Quelques réflexions bibliques et contextuelles sur l'homosexualité, Lulu Edition, Yaounde 2014

Kolodny D R (ed), Blessed Bi Spirit: Bisexual People of Faith, Continuum, 2000

Kurian M. 'An Ecumenical Framework for a Liberative Human Sexuality: Toward a Culture of Justice and Peace', Ecumenical Review, Volume 64, Number 3, October 2012, Pages 338- 345

Larsson B "A Quest for Clarity", The Ecumenical Review, Vol. 50/1, WCC Publications, Geneva. 1998

Lewin E, Recognizing Ourselves: Ceremonies of Lesbian and Gay Commitment, Columbia University Press, 1998;

LWF, A Chronological Compilation Of Key Official LWF Discussions And Decisions on Family, Marriage and Sexuality 1995-2013, (*https://www.lutheranworld.org/sites/default/files/LWF-Emmaus_chronological_compilation1995-2013.pdf*)

LWF Guidelines on respectful dialogue on family, marriage and human sexuality (*https://www.lutheranworld.org/family-marriage-and-sexuality*) and:(*http://www.luthersem.edu/library/doc_37bs8ll1q/ST2420Hansen/LWFTask_Force_Report-EN.pdf*)

McNeill JJ, *The Church and the Homosexual*, Boston: Beacon Press, 1993.

McNeill J J, Freedom, Glorious Freedom: The Spiritual Journey to the Fullness of Life for Gays, Lesbians, and Everybody Else, Beacon Press, 1995);

Nalunnakkal G M, Reflections on Church Statements on Human Sexuality- presentation at the WCC Central Committee Hearing on Human Sexuality, February, 2005, Geneva

National Conference of Catholic Bishops, *Always Our Children: A Pastoral Message to Parents of Homosexual Children and Suggestions for Pastoral Ministers*. A Statement of the [U.S. Roman Catholic] Bishops' Committee on Marriage and Family. Washington, D.C., 1997.

Nelson J B, *Embodiment*, Minneapolis: Augsburg Publishing House, 1978.

Nelson J B and Longfellow S P, Sexuality and the Sacred: Sources for Theological Reflection, Louisville: Westminster John Knox Press, 1994.

National Council of Churches in India, **Asian Consultation on Church Responses to Human Sexuality and Gender Minorities Bengaluru, 2017,** (*http://queerala.org/asian-consultation-on-church-responses-to-human-sexuality-and-gender-minorities/*)

Nordic-FOCCISA Church Cooperation, One Body, Human Dignity - Inherent in every Human Being: Towards gender equality, including young people and overcoming abuse. The Nordic-Foccisa Church Cooperation:(2014) *http://www.norgeskristnerad.no/doc/One%20Body/2014/onebody.pdf*

Okondo H, Racherla SJ, Lukale NH, RECLAIMING & REDEFINING RIGHTS ICPD +20: STATUS OF SEXUAL AND REPRODUCTIVE HEALTH AND RIGHTS IN AFRICA , World YWCA 2013 *http://arrow.org.my/wp-content/uploads/2015/04/ICPD-20-Africa_Monitoring-Report_2013.pdf*

Plume M W, Stranger At The Gate: To Be Gay and Christian in America, 1994;

Paterson G and Long C (eds), DIGNITY, FREEDOM AND GRACE, Christian Perspectives on HIV, AIDS, and Human Rights, 2016 WCC Publications, Geneva

Rajkumar C (ed), *Studying Scripture: Publically and Sensually*, NCCI, 2012.

Rajkumar C,(ed*), An Ecumenical Document on Human Sexuality*, NCCI, 2012.

Roman Catholic Church, The Truth and Meaning of Human Sexuality. Guidelines for Education in the Family, Vatican 1995 *(http://www.vatican.va/roman_curia/pontifical_councils/family/documents/rc_pc_family_doc_08121995_human-sexuality_en.html)*

SAVE Toolkit , INERELA (2012). *http://inerela.org/wp/wpcontent/downloads/INERELA%20SAVE%20Toolkit%20Full.pdf*

Scanzoni K, Mollenkott VR, Is The Homosexual My Neighbor?: Another Christian View (Revised)Harper & Row Publishers, 1996;

Scroggs R, The New Testament and Homosexuality: Contextual Background and Contemporary Debate, Fortress Press, 1983;

Stückelberger C, Familienethik. Familien stärken aus christlicher Perspektive, Genf 2015   *(http://www.globethics.net/documents/4289936/13403252/GE_Focus_23_web.pdf/40b4bc02-b869-4227-9688-50774293daa3)*

Smith R, Living in covenant with God and one another: A guide to the study of sexuality and human relations using statements from member churches of the World Council of Churches Paperback, Geneva, Switzerland : World Council of Churches, Family Education Office, WCC 1990

Tulleken L, Mokgethi-Heath JP (eds), Behold, I Make All Things New – What do the sacred texts of Judaism, Christianity and Islam really say in regard to human sexuality?, Eco-labelled publication, 2016

United Church of Christ in the Philippines 2014, 'Let Grace be Total. UCCP Statement on Lesbian, Gay, Bisexual, Transgender (LGBT) Concerns; *http:/ /www.peaceucc.org/ let-grace-be-total-the-ucc-philippiness-initial-statement-on-lgbt-concerns/*

UNAIDS, More than a prayer: Faith communities' response to sexual violence- A dialogue between Archbishop Rowan Williams and Michel Sidibé of UNAIDS for World AIDS Day. 30 November 2012

http:/ /www.newstatesman.com/ lifestyle/ 2012/ 11/ more-prayer-faith-communities-response-sexual-violence

WARC, Created in God's Image: From Hierarchy to Partnership. A Manual for Gender Awareness and Leadership Development. World Alliance of ReformedChurches, 2003 Geneva: Imprimerie Corbaz SA.

WCC, AIDE MEMOIRE: WORLD COUNCIL OF CHURCHES AND HUMAN SEXUALITY, World Council of Churches, CENTRAL COMMITTEE Document No. GEN 14, Geneva, Switzerland, February 2005

https:/ /www.oikoumene.org/ en/ resources/ documents/ central-committee/ 2005/ reports-and-documents/ gen-14-aide-memoire-world-council-of-churches-and-human-sexuality

WCC (2009), Letter of the WCC General Secretary to the Uganda President Yoweri Kaguta Museveni, "Raising concerns regarding The Anti Homosexuality Bill, 2009"; *http:/ /www.oikoumene.org/ en/ resources/ documents/ general-secretary/ messages-and-letters/ letter-to-the-uganda-president.html*

WCC, MORAL DISCERNMENT IN THE CHURCHES: A Study Document, Faith and Order Paper No. 215, WCC, Geneva, 2013 *https:/ /www.oikoumene.org/ en/ resources/ documents/ commissions/ faith-and-order/ i-unity-the-church-and-its-mission/ moral-discernment-in-the-churches-a-study-document*

WCC 1997 Facing AIDS - The Challenge, the Churches' Response. A WCC Study Document, Geneva, first ed. 1997— reprinted in 2000, 2001, 2002 and 2004. *http:/ /wcc-coe.org/ wcc/ what/ mission/ ehaia-pdf/ facing-aids-eng.pdf*

WCC 1997 'Facing Aids – Education in the context of Vulnerability' - Study Guide accompanying the World Council of Churches' Study Document on HIV/ AIDS, "Facing Aids – The Challenge the Churches Response", containing a structured framework for group learning sessions, designed to equip resource group leaders to undertake HIV /AIDS awareness building. *http:// hivhealthclearinghouse.unesco.org/ sites/ default/ files/ resources/ bie_world_council_ churches_facing_aids_en.pdf*

WCC, Churches Recommit to Accelerate HIV Response- Pastoral Letter from the Central Committee of the World Council of Churches, Trondheim 28 June, 2016- *https://www.oikoumene.org/en/resources/documents/central-committee/2016/churches-recommit-to-accelerate-hiv-response*

West. G, Zondi-Mabezela. P, The bible story that became a Campaign: Tamar Campaign in South Africa (and Beyond), Ministerial Formation, 103 July 2004, WCC *http://ujamaa.ukzn.ac.za/Files/the bible story.pdf*

Wiesner-Hanks M E, Christianity and Sexuality in the Early Modern World, Regulating Desire, Reforming Practise, London and Ney York 2000, *(http://www.thedivineconspiracy.org/Z5220H.pdf)*

Zachariah. G, Rajkumar.V, (eds.), Disruptive faith, inclusive communities: church and homophobia, ISPCK, Bangalore, 2015.

Contributors

Anshi Zachariah is a theologically trained activist, working as Programme Officer at ANEKA, a Bangalore based human rights organization working among the LGBTIQ communities and sex workers.

Aruna Gnanadason, directed the programme on Women in Church and Society and the Justice, Peace and Creation work of the World Council of Churches, Geneva. She now lives in Chennai, India and resources the churches and the ecumenical movement in India and globally reflecting on the role, the challenge and the alternatives offered by the gospel in addressing the impact of patriarchy, caste and global capitalism on the people and the earth.

Arvind Theodore is an Adjunct Faculty in the Department of Theology and Ethics at the United Theological College, Bangalore.

Dr Bandangtemjen is a Faculty of History of Christianity and Missions at the Leonard Theological College, Jabalpur. He also serves as the Registrar at the college.

Dr Bendanglemla Longkumer is a Faculty of Theology at the Leonard Theological College, Jabalpur.

Debjyoti Ghosh is a Human Rights lawyer from Kolkata, India. Currently, he is pursuing his Doctoral studies in Juridical Science from Central European University in Budapest, Hungary in Comparative Constitutional Law. His research is on the right to health for transgender people and focuses on India, Brazil and South Africa.

Metropolitan Dr Geevarghese Mor Coorilos is the Bishop of Malankara Jacobite Syrian Church (Syrian Orthodox Church) in India and an esteemed Theologian who is a visiting Faculty to various theological colleges across the globe.

Dr Gladson Jathanna is an Assistant Professor at Karnataka Theological College, Mangalore and teaches History of Christianity and Missions.

Gopi Shankar is an Intersex & Genderqueer person from Madurai, having done his studies in Philosophy and Sociology from the Department of Religion, the American College, Madurai. He is a recipient of the Commonwealth Youth Worker Asia Regional Finalist Award & Her Majesty The Queen's HCRY Leader, London, Student of "Leading Change QYL Program" University of Cambridge, U.K.

Gowthaman Ranganathan is a lawyer pursuing his Post Graduate studies in Law.

J. M. John Marshal is the Director of *Srishti Madurai,* a space for Psychoanalysis, Gender & Sexuality and cultural studies, an NGO engaged in the advocacy of LGBTIQ rights.

Fr Dr Jacob Mathew is a Professor of Old Testament at Orthodox Theological Seminary, Kottayam. He takes keen interest in engaging with issues related to Human Sexuality and Gender Diversities, both in Kerala and at a National level.

Fr Dr Jogy C George is a Faculty of New Testament at the St Thomas Orthodox Theological Seminary in Nagpur.

Dr K.S. Jacob is a Professor of Psychiatry at Christian Medical College, Vellore.

Rev Dr L Jayachitra who till recently served as the Faculty of New Testament at Tamilnadu Theological Seminary, Madurai is presently the Director of Education at the Church of South India Synod, Chennai.

Lai-shan Yip is a PhD student at the Graduate Theological Union at Berkeley, Californai in Interdisciplinary Studies (Christian Sexual Ethics, Confucianism, Critical Theories) and Cultural Studies.

Dr Lalnghakthuami is a Faculty of Theology at the Aizawl Theological College, Mizoram.

Dr Manoj Kurian is the Coordinator of Ecumenical Advocacy Alliance initiative on Food Security and HIV and AIDS, working along with the World Council of Churches, Geneva. As a Public Health Expert, his long standing ecumenical experience in the field of HIV and AIDS at a global level has immensely helped church initiatives across the world.

Rev Miak Siew has been serving in Singapore as Free Community Church's full time pastor since he was ordained by the Metropolitan Community Churches in 2011 after completing his Masters in Divinity at Pacific School of Religion in Berkeley, California.

Rev Dr Mothy Varkey is an ordained Minister of the Malankara Mar Thoma Church. Dr Mothy is an honorary Research Associate of the Murdoch University, Western Australia. He also serves as an adjunct professor of the NT studies both at the UTC, Bangalore, and at the Mar Thoma Theological Seminary, Kottayam.

Rev Pauline Ong serves as an executive pastor at Free Community Church in Singapore. She has a Masters in Intercultural Studies from Singapore Bible College and a Master in Counselling from Monash University, Australia.

Pawan Dhall has been engaged in queer activism, human rights campaigns, writing and research on gender, sexuality and HIV issues since the early 1990s. He is the Founding Trustee of Varta Trust, a gender and sexuality publishing and advocacy non-profit organization (www.vartagensex.org).

Rev Phanenmo Kath is the Asstt Prof. Pastoral Counselling & Psychology at Eastern Theological College, Jorhat, Assam.

Rev Philip Vinod Peacock is the Associate Professor of Social Analysis at Bishop's College, Kolkata.

Rev Fr Philip Kuruvilla is an ordained minister with the Indian Orthodox Church, who was till recently the General Coordinator of the ESHA Program of the National Council of Churches in India. He now serves as its Consultant.

Fr Dr Reji Mathew is a Professor of New Testament at the Orthodox Theological Seminary, Kottayam. Besides being the Former Principal of the St Thomas Orthodox Theological Seminary, Nagpur, he is presently the Dean of Studies at the OTS and the Registrar of the Federated Faculty for Research on Religion and Culture (FFRRC), Kottayam. On the social front, he serves as the Secretary of the Kerala Council of Churches, an ecumenical body in Kerala, actively engaging the churches at an ecumenical level in addressing various social issues, particularly those relating to Human Sexuality and Gender Diversities.

Rev. Dr. Rohan Gideon is Assistant Professor of Christian Theology at the Tamilnadu Theological Seminary in Madurai (South India).

Rosy Zoramthangi Ralte is a Faculty of Aizawl Theological College, Mizoram and is presently a Doctoral student in Old Testament at the United Theological College, Bangalore.

Rev. Dr. S. D. Deva Jothi Kumar teaches History of Christianity at Indian Theological Seminary, Chennai since 1999.

Sandhya Raju is a lawyer who till recently worked as the Director of the Human Rights Law Network (HRLN) in Kochi, which is legal network advocating for LGBTIQ rights in India.

Santosh Koshy Joy is a freelance journalist from Delhi. His interest in Human Sexuality and Gender Diversities lead him to interview Ms Selin Laxmi, a leader of the Transgender community in one of the *Dera* in Delhi to come up with an article of her life story in this book.

Rev. Dr. Wati Longchar is a Baptist Minister from Nagaland. Currently, he teaches at Yushan Theological College & Seminary, Taiwan.